SONGS

in the

DRIFT

KEN GAGNE

To my sisters,
Cheryl and Linda.

This novel is a product of the author's imagination. The cast of characters within these pages—their stories, actions, and personalities—are fictional and exist solely within the confines of this narrative. Any resemblance to real persons, living or deceased, is purely coincidental.

It is important to note that this novel explores themes of mental illness and suicide. While the story addresses these topics with care, it is crucial to prioritize your mental health and well-being. If you or someone you know is struggling with similar issues, please seek help from a qualified mental health professional or support service.

Music, at its essence, is what gives us memories.

—Stevie Wonder

*We shall not cease from exploration, and the end
of all our exploring will be to arrive where we
started and know the place for the first time.*

—T. S. Eliot

Where is she? Remember. Find her. She's out there? Picture her. Where? I need to… I'm sorry. You saw her? Not sure… murky. Help! I need her! Someone… please help!

"It's all right, you're okay, just breathe. That's it. Now close your eyes and say your name."

"My name is… Hollyann McIntyre."

"Good, real good. And where are you?"

"My name is Hollyann."

"Yes, it is. Can you tell me who's with you?"

"My name is Holly."

"It's okay, Holly. Let's start our countdown.

"My name is…"

"Here we go. Begin with thirty."

"My name…"

:30

The Journey

WHENEVER SHE DECIDES I need some rest, Rose asks me to count down from thirty. I don't always reach the end, and it frustrates me, but the rhythmic sound of descending numbers serves its purpose and wipes me out. While we count, my eyes get heavier and heavier. Do you know what I call the time it takes for my lids to close? I call those strange moments "the drift." The word has a smell to it, wouldn't you say? An aura of magic and mystery; like birds in flight, visible one second, out of sight the next. Or frost on the windows, beautiful and changing, always changing. Don't worry though, I'm not drifting away just yet. You and I have plenty of time to visit.

Thirty is an interesting number, don't you think? Your opinion on a song becomes clear within the first thirty seconds. And stories, too. Some say that within half a minute, a story should hook the reader. If it doesn't, it's not worth the time. Same thing with songs—they have to hook you.

I was a singer once. I wrote some songs. None of them any good, though. Here's the thing, songwriting is about leaving a mark that lasts longer than we do, to keep us from disappearing. The goal is to make something timeless, like this story. It's not really *my* story, though. No, not really.

See, I know my son better than any mother knows her child. His given name is Carlton, but we've always called him Race. And Race, well, he tells me the most fascinating anecdotes, with so much detail and color. So much enthusiasm, such gusto. I always liked that word: *gusto*. Anyway, Race visits me all the time, every week. Sundays, sometimes Saturdays, too.

My snug one-room apartment is comfy and well-equipped. I have a bed, a couch, a dresser, and a leather recliner that Race bought for me the week I moved in. He knows I despise sleeping in the bed. That's why he purchased the chair. Usually, I drape my robe over the recliner since I can't always find it in the closet.

I switch on my television set once in a purple moon. Someone misplaced the remote control months ago, but I never understood that wretched gizmo anyways. Same with the cellular phone that Race's wife, I mean *ex*-wife, Jessica, gave me last year. For Christmas, I believe. The telephone and I are not on the friendliest of terms. That lady was really sweet to give me a gift, though. Maybe it was for my birthday. Her heart was, I mean *is*, in the right place. Why did she and Race split up? Probably because they couldn't have children. Or maybe one of my son's old girlfriends came back into the picture. Oh yes, that's a definite possibility. You see, once upon a time during his professional baseball career, Race had more lady friends than you could shake a Louisville Slugger at. I didn't know about those women then, but my boy tells me everything now. Everyone does.

I'm afraid for him; I don't want him to be by himself. I wish he'd settle down with someone nice, open himself up some, you know? But Race likes to be alone, prefers it that way. I have no idea why. I don't like to be alone…

Hold on… It's happening again. Lines crossing, circuits misfiring. It'll pass, always does. Quick, watch and wait… *This world is not yesterday or tomorrow… It is always today.* They make no sense, these odd interruptions, thoughts or voices, images too, arriving, retreating, from somewhere else, rushing to the front of my mind. Tiny zaps of lightning, flashes in the darkness, lighting up my brain for a fraction of a second. Don't know who, or what, the flashes are, or when or where they come from. Don't know why, or how, they go. Just the way I'm wired, I guess. Just the way we're wired.

Wait, what am I doing here? Oh, yes…

When my wits go missing, I see myself as plain unlucky, like a poor woman who's lost a penny. She flips on a flashlight and searches her entire house until she finds her coin, totally committed. When I lose myself and my words wither, I need Race or Rose to search for me and make sure I don't slip away. Who knows what else I'll lose, or what else I can get back? Others might have to look high and low for me, tip over the place until they find me. I'll play the searching woman while I can, but maybe soon I'll be the penny.

Allow me to explain. Sometimes I say things that are

real to me, but not factual. The weird thing is, I'm not fibbing, even if the information is false. It's no use arguing with me; it never solves anything. Better to let sleeping horses lie, or is it don't look a gift dog in the mouth? Sorry, even the most used-up clichés elude my cranium.

When Race visits my cozy apartment, he brings the energy of Sea Point, stories of the people he meets, and the steady rhythm of life in our quaint Oregon town. He and I don't just chat about the weather, though, like most people around here. The rain might be a constant in our lives, but my son's visits are a special kind of companionship, breaking through the solitude and boredom I often find myself in.

My memory may get fuzzy, but when Race enters the room, his words become my lifeline. Amid the haze of my recollections, his stories offer clarity, pulling me out of my old world and into the new one I now know. My son is an open book, like my husband, Colin, was before he stopped visiting. Race is honest, kind, and patient. He's different. I love the man he has become, but I also loved the boy he once was. He's been through a lot, and he's shared all the details with me. I worry my son will soon find more productive things to do than come see me, his own mother who might forget him the second he walks out the door. Some days it's like I'm already gone, and he probably wishes I were.

Yes, I'm scared for him, and for me. My songs keep me calm though, especially the one that plays from my music box. I bought the mahogany box a while back to remind me of the ballads I loved, the kinds I wished Colin would write for me, the songs I longed to sing. When you lift the lid of the box—covered in painted-on daisies and loaded with unmet promises—a slow, chiming rendition of my favorite tune plays. It's a beautiful song, by a Joni or Jodi somebody-or-other. Before I lay down each night, I open the box and play my music… *Something's lost, but something's gained in living every day.*

When Race leaves me after our weekly visits, and I'm alone in my room, I replay my son's lovely voice in my head. I retell, or rethink, his stories again and again because I never want to forget them. And I never want to forget *him.* The memories he shares with me are like a collection of beloved songs, their lyrics etched onto my soul but fading with time. I may not recall every word anymore, but I hum the tunes to myself until the last notes vanish into silence. Then I wait for those songs to play again.

Can you tell me the time? Is it morning or night? On most days I do something now, don't I? My father taught literature. Have I mentioned that? Greek mythology, all the classics. Before bedtime, when I was a child, he'd read those stories to me. The resilient Persephone, the curious Pandora, the lovelorn Psyche. But I always liked the one about Sisyphus best. Do you know that one? Sometimes, I see myself as poor Sisyphus, the tyrant punished by the gods. Like him, I'm forever pushing my rock up a hill, only to witness it tumble back down again. I'm always in pursuit of something, trying to catch it before it slips away. But despite my efforts, it slides right through my fingers, leaving me stuck in an endless loop. It's a painstaking thing, not being able to keep what's important to you.

The words I sing now, the stories I tell myself, are the ones my son and husband have shared with me, the truth as they claimed it happened. We sang some of these songs together once, not necessarily in the correct key, not always in perfect harmony. But we sang at the top of our lungs. Now, in the quiet corners of my mind, I sing our songs again.

❧

On a fateful April morning in 1915, there was a scene in Armenia that—when I imagine it—still rips at my heart. Turkish soldiers, mercenaries, and ex-convicts conducted a raid on the town of Hrazdan, near Lake Sevan. They bound a group of four hundred women and children and ordered them to march south over difficult terrain, toward the Syrian desert. Among the Armenian prisoners, a young mother, her eyes sharpened by dread, clasped her thirteen-year-old daughter, Akabe, keeping her close.

Later that day, when the caravan arrived at a concealed valley, a violent mob assaulted the group of innocents, using axes, hatchets, shovels, and pitchforks. The attackers inflicted severe injuries, hacking off noses, ears, fingers, and limbs. The Turks threw children against rocks in front of their mothers. The victims' screams reverberated through the canyon, traveling over the surrounding hills and into the caves. While the indifferent mob continued to pull apart the bodies, even the stones cried out for mercy.

After four hours of carnage, night's black blanket covered the bloody land, and half-naked corpses were strewn across the valley floor. When the mob fled and returned to town, the hyenas, wolves, and jackals came to finish the job. Akabe and her mother huddled in the night, among the raspy drone of death and the moans of the wounded. Only by some miracle did anyone survive.

The next day, the mob returned and the group of battered women and children, now fewer than two hundred, continued their march toward the desert. In small villages along the way, Turkish townspeople butchered, burned, and violated the Armenians using whatever tools they had—hatchets, saws, spades, hoes, clubs. They threw them into wells, buried them alive, tortured and killed them, all in the name of ethnic cleansing. The terrified children—the unaware little ones—cried and begged for protection, latching onto the legs of their mothers.

The caravan moved forward, accompanied now by Turkish police and military officers, some of them riding horses, others on donkeys, still others on foot. Heading for the Euphrates River, they left a trail of anguish, wailing, grief, tears, and an eternal curse. Akabe and her mother trudged past decomposed human skeletons, littering the fields on both sides of the road. The skulls clearly belonged to women, as their long hair remained intact. The mother picked up the skulls and kissed them, prayed for them, knowing the same fate awaited her and her daughter.

Young Akabe, whose name spoke of ocean jewels, found herself thrust into a gruesome reality she couldn't comprehend. With each deafening beat of her hammering heart, despair consumed her soul. To ease her daughter's agony, the mother hummed a shaky melody, a fruitless balm. Deep within Akabe's dark eyes—which held horrors too heavy for the fragile child to bear—embers of surrender danced with flares of determination.

As she and her mother approached the rocky banks high above the Euphrates, marveling over the silver waters below, an evil figure crushed their hopes of finding solace in nature's beauty. Emerging from the shadows, a hulking

Turkish soldier loomed, his eyes revealing cruel intentions. "I will have the girl," he said, his voice dripping with hate.

As he got closer, mother and daughter backed up, nearing the edge of the cliff. The woman's heart splintered, her instincts overriding all reason. Standing like a wall between the soldier and Akabe, she took a red silk scarf from her shoulders and offered it to him.

"No, that is not what I want." His sinister grin said the rest.

Forcing back tears, the woman moved behind her daughter and embraced her. She pulled back Akabe's long hair and whispered something into her ear. Then the girl placed her quivering hands behind her back while her mother tied the scarf around her wrists. Tighter and tighter.

The soldier crept toward them. "Yes, now give her to me."

At that agonizing instant, the mother had one choice. With indescribable pain in her bones, she pulled Akabe away from the soldier and pushed her off the cliff.

The three seconds of her falling felt like three years to Akabe. Upon impact with the water, the icy river enveloped the young girl. As the current grabbed her, Akabe's mind raced, memories of her family and the love they shared flooding her thoughts. But the laughter and joy she had known faded, disappearing like morning mist. She kicked to stay afloat, fought to break free from the binding on her wrists, desperate, clinging to life. Then, a sudden calm washed over her, a peculiar tranquility. Her struggles ceased, and she embraced her destiny…

It's happening again. It'll pass, always does. Quick, watch and wait… *I'm not a monster… I'm hiding from monsters.* Don't know who, or what, the flashes are. Just the way I'm wired, I guess. Just the way we're wired.

As the river claimed Akabe, a comforting presence surrounded her like a shroud. Graceful arms encircled her, warmth replacing the cold. Squinting through the blurry water, the girl beheld a vision of ethereal beauty. A radiant being in the shape of a woman held her, guided her to the surface, and carried her to the riverbank with effortless strength. Surrounding Akabe on the shore, the corpses of mothers and children who had leaped to their deaths lay scattered in the mud. Their bodies, swollen and blue. Tongues, black and half-eaten. Hair like old grass.

Gasping for breath, Akabe turned to her savior and asked, "Who are you?"

"I am Tsovinar," the woman said. "Goddess of fire, daughter of the seas. You are safe now, child. But one day, you will repay me."

Akabe's eyes widened, and she shivered. "How?"

Tsovinar smiled. "With a sacrifice," she said. "You will have a granddaughter one day, and when she reaches her twentieth year, I will call her to the water."

:29

A Man I'll Never Be

Now, LET ME tell you about Sea Point, our bucolic little lumber town on the northern coast of Oregon, as remote as you can get. Where the steady rain taps on our windows, like an old friend saying hello. We're right where the Columbia River meets the Pacific, and it feels special, you know? The streets are cute, with old houses and shops that make you wonder if you're lost in a bygone era. Trapped between the vast ocean and the untamed wilderness, Sea Point is a perfect protective prison.

I love the morning breeze coming in off the water. It brings the calls of seagulls and that fishy smell from the docks. You can see colorful boats bobbing in the harbor, telling stories of journeys far away from shore. And there's this big bridge, the Pointbreak Bridge, I believe it's called, stretching across the water like it's watching over us. The hills are green and pretty, providing lovely views of the town and the ocean. But sometimes, the fog creeps in from the

Pacific, hiding secrets from Sea Point's past. There's more to this place than meets the eye.

I will recall the details of my story, to the best of my knowledge, but forgive me if I lose my place, or my way. Like a passing shower, my memory comes and goes, and it gets harder every day to hide behind this dream.

In late October, on a Friday afternoon, my son, Race, sat in his shrimpy office, muddy boots propped up on his desk. He stared out a tiny window at the drizzle outside, while the giant bridge connecting the states of Oregon and Washington loomed in the distance. Oh, that steel cantilever bridge is quite a marvel, spanning four miles, the longest continuous truss bridge in North America. As the river flows beneath, the bridge defies time, linking the past and future, stretching into the unknown. The river never stops, and the bridge keeps going, like it's inviting us to explore what lies beyond.

When Race was young, he hated that bridge, cried every time we crossed over it. Well, ever since my husband told him the story of an unfortunate man, a coworker of Colin's at the cannery, who threw himself off the Pointbreak. A "lucky bastard," Colin called him while recalling the gory details of the leap. But I always thought that bridge was beautiful—almost as beautiful as my son. Yes, Race was the most adorable little boy, and he became such a handsome young man. But women don't say he's gorgeous; they say he's "drop-dead-and-come-back-to-life gorgeous." The Lord blessed that boy with a smile to end all smiles, perfect teeth, sturdy lips, and darling dimples that could disarm the most prudent of prudes. His silky, shoulder-length hair, emerald eyes, and that gleaming smile team up well to mask the hurt in his heart.

Race's cramped office at the city's Parks and Recreation Department smelled of sweaty socks and a half-eaten egg sandwich in the trash can. On the wall opposite the window was a framed number 71 Boston Red Sox jersey that the team's equipment manager had sent as a gift years ago.

Race popped a stick of gum into his mouth and whipped the tiny balled-up tinfoil wrapper across the room, hitting his buddy, Glenn Dedmon, smack in the nose. "With accuracy like that," Glenn said without so much as a blink, "you'd make a decent outfielder."

"With jokes like that," Race shot back, "you'd make a shitty comedian."

Glenn leaned against the wall and crossed his arms. "So, Coach Buck is retiring."

"Finally tired of winning, huh?" Race reclined in his chair, gripping a scuffed baseball.

"Yeah," Glenn said, "and he can thank me and you for eighty of those five hundred victories." Race and Glenn had played for Rupert "Buck" Charles at Sea Point High School, starred in center field and at shortstop, respectively, and won three straight state championships back in the early '90s.

"You mean Coach can thank *me*." Race never shied away from taking credit. "You were just along for the ride, G-Dog."

"Yo, seriously, Mac, you can step in right now and take over the program."

"I'm happy with this job, thanks." Race had convinced himself that mowing grass and emptying trash was gratifying work—all he could handle and more than he deserved.

"This isn't happiness, Mac." Glenn moved closer and plopped his palms on the desk. "Happiness is waking up in the morning surrounded by ten puppies wanting to play with you. Except the puppies are all supermodels."

"I'm good."

"The whole city wants you to take the job."

"The whole city, or just you?"

"When I'm mayor in a month, I will *be* the city." Glenn's teeth gleamed like the grillwork of a fancy automobile, and he spoke like a guy who breezes through the Sunday crossword using permanent marker.

"So, you're obviously running on a platform of humility?" Race grinned. "I can see the campaign posters now: *Vote for Glenn Dedmon: The Only Thing Bigger Than His Ego Is His Commitment to Modesty*."

"I'm serious, bro," Glenn said. "You were meant to be a coach. But yeah, if I convince you to take the gig, it might win me a few votes."

"Only one problem, G-Dog." Race flipped the baseball into the air and caught it without looking. "I hate kids."

"Then why'd you want to be a dad?"

"Same reason you want to be mayor," my son said. "So I could pretend people loved me." He tossed the ball at Glenn and laughed.

As icy rain fell in the parking lot of the rec center, Race's untamed shoulder-length brown hair stuck to his face, while his brilliant green eyes held the mysteries of our hometown. Across from him, Glenn's dark, narrow eyes were robust, like the fir trees lining our streets. With his handsome bald head, Glenn kept you guessing whether he was practical or vain. Made folks wonder if he shopped for TV dinners or employed a personal chef. The two friends were tall and lean, but only remnants of the accomplished athletes they once were.

"Please, take the coaching gig, dude." Glenn's determined voice flowed, an unstoppable current. "You and me, man, we built this town's reputation. We can own this place for the next twenty years."

Race nodded in the way he always does—a sort of casual disagreement mixed with deeper contemplation. "It's not gonna happen."

"Yo, you gotta do this," Glenn said as the rain picked up. "Think of how proud your pops would've been. He might even come back from the grave and give you a hug."

"This conversation is over."

"Why?"

"You know why." My boy strutted through the lot and stopped at a black Mercedes coup. "I gotta go."

Glenn followed and took a set of shiny keys out of his pocket. "Lemme give you a ride."

"No thanks, got my bike." A recent DUI charge had robbed Race of his driver's license for ninety days. A costly mistake; a night that slipped out of control. Like raindrops on a windowpane, unforeseen and unceasing.

"You know," Glenn said, "I can clear your record after the election."

Race unlocked his bicycle from a metal rack, leaped onto it, and said, "See ya at the funeral." Then he peddled away into the rain, a solitary figure against the blank backdrop of his lonesome world.

The wind whipped him as he rode down Main Street, but Race was colder than the wind and didn't feel the chill. His hasty departure and snippy exchange with Glenn revealed a rich history between the friends. It went beyond words, even beyond the squishy fact that Glenn was now engaged to Race's ex-wife, Jess. Glenn had broken the news to my son over beers at a Fourth of July barbeque—another dastardly curveball life had thrown, one Race never saw coming, buckling his knees, leaving him wishing the pitch had been a fastball in his ear instead.

In his forty-one years, Race had seen his share of upheavals, but none as powerful or as welcomed as his father's death one week earlier. At this point, I should tell you about my husband. His name was Colin, and he was no ordinary man, not by a long shot. He buried secrets, layers of them, hidden beneath the surface. That complexity, well, he wove it far down into the fabric of his being. When we were both younger, Colin's gaze was so captivating, his green eyes so distant, I couldn't tell if they reflected an entire forest or a single leaf. We had quite a life, him and me. Now, as I sit here alone in my little world, memories drift in and out like wayward dreams—dreams within dreams—slipping through my fingers.

The closing of his years with Colin was an iron door slamming in my son's face. He navigated through the baffling days that followed, trying to ignore the aftershocks of his father's absence—different than the absence that haunted Race while my husband was alive. Now, on this late afternoon in October, the dark skies matched my boy's wounded soul.

It was just another day for me by the seaside, listening to a snippet of Race's life during one of his visits. I don't know what I'd do if he didn't come see me at Blue Horizons. His words bridge the old and the new for me, creating an out-of-tune medley of family, relationships, and a boy who had become a man before my eyes.

In my life, here and now, the days turn to night and back to day in quick succession, and the seasons change without permission. The hours my son and I spend together will remain in my memory. They weave together into a patchwork of stories, becoming a constant presence that lights up my world like stars in the sky.

If my son had owned a dog, he would've kicked it that day.

Instead of pedaling back to his empty apartment after work, Race grabbed a sandwich and headed toward his childhood home. It was a modest two-story ranch that he and I once shared with Colin. But that was before we all went away, one by one. Following a downpour, the rain had stopped, but the skies weren't clear. My son's goal that day was to clean out his father's house—an intolerable task necessary to get the place on the market as soon as possible. To be honest, Race needed to sell the house, as his finances had seen better days. After thirteen years playing professional baseball, mostly in the minor leagues, what little he earned had dwindled away because of two failed investments and one ill-fated relationship.

Approaching the house, Race paused and straightened up, let out a long breath, and braced for a deluge of memories to sweep him away. Instead, a strange emptiness jabbed him in the gut when he walked through the door—the start of a fresh chapter. Within the previous week, he'd already sold some furniture and donated all of Colin's clothes. What remained in the house? Piles of doodads, stacks of thingamabobs, and the remnants of his father's withdrawn love. The rooms uttered stories about the past, undertones of the moments that defined us. As Race moved through the house, chomping on his meatball sub, a fusion of nostalgia and uncertainty overwhelmed him. Like trying to play catch with a ball he didn't remember how to throw.

Our home, once a bastion of hope and promise, now stood as my son's own personal Waterloo. When our family was new, Race would bounce through the door after a game or practice, greeted by the rustic scents of cedar wood and my homemade marionberry pie. He'd flick on the TV in the living room while sunrays streamed in, casting warm patterns on the scratched wooden floor. Family photos were everywhere, capturing periods of bliss and love that I thought would last forever. The couch and chairs, inexpensive and worn, exuded familiarity and comfort, inviting him to sink into the plump cushions. Colin always had a fire crackling in the stone hearth, its glowing flames spreading a gentle light throughout the room. In the corner, a vintage record player spun soothing melodies, transporting me back to simpler times. Despite its modest size, the raised ranch radiated warmth and contentment, a haven from the bustle of the outside world. Oh, what a wonderful house.

Now, Race waited at the top of the basement stairs. The dingy cellar—or "the cave" as we called it—was my husband's private sanctuary, off-limits to both me and my son. Like the cave, Colin's love was dark, and often hidden. His outward expressions were stoic; grins and laughs were reserved for the rare special occasion.

My son chucked his sandwich wrapper onto the floor and descended the basement steps. The concrete walls and tile flooring giggled while he filed through cardboard boxes jammed with old bank statements and copies of tax documents, reams of articles about Sea Point's relevance in our country's history, maps of Oregon's trails and waterways, and biographies on the early explorers of the American West. Colin loved researching the past, a skill his managerial job at the Lewis and Clark National Historical Park required, but he never discussed his work at home. My husband's fortyish-year career at the park added layers to a life that had remained an enigma, even to his own family.

"Of course, nothing here about me," my son said to nobody as he rooted through the boxes. That Colin hadn't hung on to *any* keepsakes from his boy's playing days was of no surprise. Race expected nothing of his dad, and that's exactly what he got. My husband's absentee fathering taught our son to disbelieve the fallacy of unconditional care, and Race learned the lesson perfectly. During their eighteen years together, the man and boy spent few meaningful days with one another. Like quicksand, Colin's work and his music sucked his attention away from what should've mattered more. Even when my husband was home, he wasn't present. As a child, Race would beg his father to play ball with him, but Colin had no time for games, left our boy to entertain himself, offered him a quarter for every hour he played outside alone. Most nights, Race fell asleep with an extra two dollars in his piggy bank.

To offset my husband's apathy, I attended every one of Race's baseball games, tattooing my unwavering support onto my boy's heart. From T-ball to American Legion to the pros, from the thrill of victory to the sting of defeat, I was there for it all, a witness to his journey. I cheered during the MVP presentations, tournaments, and championship games. I was there for the records he set in high school and most of the ones in Triple-A. But I was more than my son's number one fan; I was the woman who made him.

I raised Race to be accountable and selfless. Growing up, he obeyed my two simple rules. First rule: He got three chances to do his chores. If I needed to ask him a third time to clean his room or set the table for dinner or whatever, I took away his Game Boy for a week. Second rule: He had to do at least one nice thing for someone each day. We all make one conscious decision every fifteen minutes, I told him. Once a day, he had to think of someone else when making his decisions. Accountable and selfless—that was the man I hoped to make. Where did I go wrong?

In the dank basement, as Race tripped and stumbled down Memory Lane, his father's mangled acoustic guitar leaned alone in an otherwise empty corner, its neck cracked and bent. The guitar had been in one piece minutes before Race last spoke to my husband. Now, my boy could almost hear the plunks of Colin's guitar notes parading in the air. He imagined himself as a child, sitting at the top of the basement stairs, trying to decode his dad through the music. Flickers of those episodes danced before Race's eyes, flashes of the songs that were such an intimate part of Colin. The cave, swathed in darkness, was a place of unlawful exploration, a part of his father's world that Race had rarely glimpsed, a trail he couldn't follow.

The cellar was flush with a musty, mildewy odor, accompanied by the creaks of nostalgia and knocks of longing.

Race latched his eyes on to a gray canvas curtain near his father's outdated stereo equipment, pulled back the cloak, and discovered a half dozen plastic storage crates. When he opened the biggest box, it was empty, but a potpourri of scents sprung out. Every smell that ever existed in our house emerged from that container: herbs on the windowsill, wet carpeting, drab drapes, wood furniture, hard well water, Palm Olive dish soap, and mold dust, powdery and floating in the streaming light. Last out of the box: the memorable aroma of lazy summer days in our cool, dark den, where I'd read enchanting stories to my son. "One more, Mommy," he'd say. "Please, just one more."

Opening crate after crate, Race discovered hundreds of perfectly preserved classic rock albums from the '70s, '80s, and '90s in their unblemished sleeves. The names of legendary bands greeted my son's eyes—Led Zeppelin, the Rolling Stones, Pink Floyd, and AC/DC, among a slew of lesser-known others.

Screaming for his attention was the smallest box, with *Special* written in black marker on the lid. He unlatched the plastic clips and found six albums, along with a dozen forty-fives, all from the rock band Boston. Race flipped through the records and noticed the futuristic artwork on the covers, featuring a guitar-shaped spaceship. He tossed his head back and cackled after he read the following two album titles in succession: *Walk On* and *Don't Look Back*. Seemed like good advice, the best his father ever gave.

Why was that man so obsessed with Boston? The question puzzled Race, but before he could delve deeper into it, his curiosity drew him to an object at the bottom of the box: a dusty brown leather-bound notebook. The thing was no larger than your average run-of-the-mill Bible, but it weighed a ton. On the cover: a strip of white duct tape with *Seven Songs* written in sweeping, slanted letters—Colin's distinguishable style. If the book could talk, it would've yelled, "No trespassing!"

Hesitating only for a millisecond, my son opened the notebook and thumbed through the pages, finding a treasure trove of love songs, far more than seven, each dripping with youthful sentimentality. Every tune had a title and date marked on it; the first from November 1975; the last from September 2018, only a month prior. Race assumed his father had written the songs for me, Hollyann, his wife. It was a fair guess, but I knew better as soon as my son told me this story. During our marriage, my husband had often sailed to a distant shore, a place beyond my touch, and he was emotionally unavailable for days or weeks at a time.

For Race, the lush ballads painted an unfamiliar picture of Colin—a favorable image of a man consumed by passion, a romantic poet. Someone who, it seemed, had lost the love of his life. Someone who believed, or hoped, that love might've been waiting for him somewhere else. My son turned to the middle of the book and stopped.

> **"Start Again"**
> *April 1989*
>
> *What would it take for a boy like me,*
> *To be everything you want me to be?*
> *I love you with all of my heart,*
> *Say we can start again*

What would it take for a girl like you,
To realize that, in me, you found a love so true?
You're a dream,
I still can't believe you're gone

If only I gave you a little more,
We still would be together
If only we had tried to reach the shore,
We wouldn't have sailed forever

I guess somehow we just ran out of room,
Beginning too quickly and ending much too soon
God, I hate how it feels to be so alone

What did "start again" and "you're gone" and "so alone" mean? Colin had written the song almost thirty years ago, but it didn't sound like it was about me, so who was it meant for?

While Race flipped through the book, the questions left him pondering. Until he spotted an inscription nestled within the pages: *Willow Spelman, Seven Mt. Auburn, Cambridge, end of time.* He grabbed his phone and tapped out the name and address into a search engine, intrigued at the prospect of unraveling the puzzle his father had left behind. As he waited for a result, my son's batting order of emotions was as lethal as Murderers' Row, with the lineup featuring anger, resentment, and purpose at the top of the order.

Sitting hunched on the floor, his back against the box of records, Race stared at his phone. The internet had unearthed close to thirty cities called Cambridge in the United States, but the one in Massachusetts, outside of Boston, was the only Cambridge with a Mt. Auburn Street. Race struck out on finding Willow Spelman, though. There was no one by that name, not from Massachusetts, not from anywhere. Continuing the investigation, he located the address: 7 Mt. Auburn Street in Cambridge, near Harvard Square. The satellite image showed a nondescript concrete apartment building on a busy double-yellow lane road.

There you are!

The thought of this faceless woman, this muse, someone who had captivated Colin more than his own family could, lit a fire in Race. He had to track down the tramp who stole his dad and my husband, the Jezebel he believed wrecked our lives. The songbook's pages came alive, fluttering in Race's twittering fingers. With a grunt, he closed it shut, like a relief pitcher sealing the last out in a tight game. Oh, the paths that spite ushers us down. If only I could've spared my boy the ache.

Race swam in speculation, head barely above water, drowning in suspicions. His chest knotted up, but that wasn't abnormal. He always felt a tangle of love, hate, and disappointment when he regarded Colin. Our home, once a sanctuary of happy memories, was now a trap of secrets and lies. The house collapsed upon Race, each toppling brick a reminder of his father's absence and the unspoken truths that tore our family apart.

:28

Hollyann

The next morning, a gloomy Saturday, Race slouched in the front row of a listless church sanctuary, the scent of Pine-Sol and lilies blending with a whiff of stress and sympathy. My son squirmed in his ill-fitting suit, the itchy fabric foreign on his skin. Our family had never been very religious; that kind of belief wasn't our calling. As Race's mother, I used to fret that his talent, looks, and charm would hinder his spiritual growth. Yes, I admit, I worried his substantial *gifts* would limit his inner, personal development. I didn't care if my boy believed in God, I just hoped he'd mature someday.

Jess and Glenn sat beside him, the closest thing to family my son had left. They were also two of the only people in Sea Point who knew my husband well enough to call him by his first name. Jess rubbed Race's back, and he tried to smile but failed; his ex-wife's low-cut blouse was inappropriate for the occasion, as if she'd never been to a funeral and didn't know the dress code, or she'd been to several and just didn't give a darn.

As Race glanced around the church, the lack of anyone who had known or cared much for his father was obvious, a void created by Colin's inability to form genuine friendships. Admittedly, I added to that void, unable to attend the funeral due to what my doctor had called an "unpredictable condition." Not being there pierced my heart, and I yearned for the closure my affliction had stolen. But pardon my nonsense, I shouldn't be so melodramatic.

While visiting me at Blue Horizons afterward, Race relayed the events of my husband's farewell ceremony. I could almost hear Pastor Kinsley's voice droning in my son's narrative. I envisioned the handsome pastor in his long white robe, pretending to know Colin well, his acting skills on full display. The reverend's convincing interpretation of a close family friend might've rivaled Richard Chamberlain's gripping portrayal of Father Ralph in *The Thorn Birds*.

According to Race, the minister's kind words and dutiful tribute to my husband did little to mellow my boy's hardened disposition toward his father. But memories of my love for Colin and his unreturned affection cascaded through my brain like an endless chorus line of frigid waves. With detachment and strife, Race rehashed the clergyman's eulogy for me. Like most in Sea Point, Pastor Mark Kinsley, or was it Mike, didn't know my husband well. Therefore, the good reverend recounted Colin's life journey with vague reverence, a hodgepodge of highs and lows.

The eulogy at the lectern triggered another at the pulpit, and I imagined Race standing there, delivering his father's story. My son's voice was steady and composed, in contrast to the turmoil churning in his belly. He began the tribute by recounting what little he knew of Colin's exodus from the

Midwest to the Pacific Northwest. Race could only briefly touch on Colin's itinerant childhood, marked by loss and longing. From what Race had been told, Colin's parents had died young, leaving the teenager adrift, a boy in search of his place in the world. Race spoke of Colin's move to Oregon in 1979, when a cousin arranged a job for him at a tuna cannery in Sea Point. Then, a fateful encounter with me soon after, of which Race had no specific details, followed by marriage and my son's arrival into our lives.

The half-hearted eulogy wove through Colin's short years at the cannery and, later, his lengthy career at the Lewis and Clark National Historical Park. Standing before the funeral goers, Race grappled with Colin's sphinxlike nature, my son omitting his complex relationship with his father. But without spelling it out, the story Race told the congregants, the story he later relayed to me, resonated with questions left unanswered, conflicts unresolved.

The service ended, and the mourners dispersed. On the concrete steps in front of the church, Race stood amid the mousy crowd. His heart was made of molasses, his father's lifelong detachment thick and sticky on his mind.

A stranger in an oversized, wrinkled gray suit limped over to my son and introduced himself. "I'm your dad's cousin Billy, the guy you mentioned in your little speech." The whiskey in his breath whacked Race in the face.

"So, you're why he moved to Sea Point?" my son asked. "He never told me your name."

"Probably didn't tell you lots of shit."

Race shook the man's bony hand. "Well, nice meeting you. Thanks for coming."

Billy was a peculiar character—homely, some might

say. He had the most misshapen cheekbones ever, an undersized upper lip, teeth that shouldn't be mentioned, and beady, watery eyes. His skin, hair, and mouth were all a pale shade of yellow, and his portly dome sat atop a thin and unsteady body. He had a bulbous nose and a shifty disposition, reminding Race of a fairy-tale goblin who lived in a hollowed-out tree trunk and stole shiny objects from unsuspecting travelers.

"There was more to your daddy than you know," Billy said, a drunken grin on his lips.

Race's instincts told him to ignore the words, but he couldn't tear his eyes away from Billy's untamed gaze. "Yeah?" my son said. "Like what?"

Billy pulled Race to the side, away from prying ears. "Colin had another life," he muttered. "One he hid from you and everyone else."

"You got the wrong guy," Race said, shaking his head. "My dad was as simple as they come."

"That's what he *wanted* you to think," Billy said, "cuz your old man was trying to forget who he was back in Boston, all that crazy shit that happened."

"Boston? My dad told me he was from Ohio."

"Christ, you're even way more stupider than you look." With a jiggly hand, Billy slid a flask out of his jacket pocket, lowered his chin, and brought the liquor to his lips. The container slipped from his fingers and fell onto the ground, tumbling down three steps, clanging against the cement.

Race tensed and turned away from the crowd. After Billy picked up the flask, my son stared into the old man's glazed eyes. "Get outta here, dude."

Billy limped off, muttering and giggling.

Jess and Glenn approached, asking in unison, "Who the hell was that?"

"Nobody," my boy said.

"Really?" Jess smirked. "Looked like you two were best buds."

"Just some bum," Race replied. "Must've ducked into the church to get out of the cold."

Glenn slapped his friend on the back. "Hey, nice tribute to your pops, by the way."

"Yeah, my work here is done." Race nodded and beamed. "Now I can finally bury the son of a bitch."

When my boy relayed that story to me, I sensed his thirst for closure, for answers about his father that he hoped I'd have. But I recognized another part of Race that didn't want to know anything more about Colin. I hoped he might find the peace he sought, even as I grappled with my own messy recollections. After he left me that day, I couldn't wait until his next visit. The hours pass by like months when he's not here, and the story in my brain keeps changing.

Several days later, when Race stepped into the lobby of Blue Horizons, an antiseptic funk whiffled through the air and garbled conversations packed the cavernous room. He sat next to me, sinking into a comfy leather chair that told its own tall tales. Race has always enjoyed his visits here, described them once as an emulsion of dear friends and, um… that thing… oh, never mind. Be what it may, the lobby is a pretty space, with pastel colors adorning the walls and cheerful artwork that brings a grin to his face.

"So, I spoke with Rose," my son said to me, loud

enough to wake poor old Gretta Stinson snoozing in her rolling chair near the reception desk.

Gosh, lower your voice, I may have told him. *You're acting like I'm in another room.*

"Rose says you're not eating a lot. Why don't I hit Papa Murphy's and smuggle you in one of those chicken and garlic calzones you used to love?"

That would be wonderful, dear. Bring one for Rose, too, will you?

As I listened to him chatter away, the image of my friend, a familiar face with a sparkle in her eye, came into my mind. My Rose—from a family of indigenous Alaskans, Inuit, I think—has firm red cheeks and a patient demeanor. Her hardiness, resilience, and ability to bloom day after day speaks true of her namesake. She looks out for me, keeps me safe, brings warmth and comfort to a place where hope often runs cold.

The weekend days Race spends with me seem to be a sour potion of pain and duty for him. I'm not the vibrant woman I once was, a distant memory of that person now, and I can't quite calculate how it all shifted. It stirs up something inside me, you know, like building a puzzle with missing pieces that refuse to fit together.

"I'm cleaning out the house, Mom. Putting it on the market soon."

The house? Why on Earth would you sell our house?

"Your husband left it like a rat's nest. But I'll take care of it, don't worry. Gonna order a dumpster and get rid of everything."

No, not everything! I exclaimed. *Please don't throw away everything.*

"Yep, in a few weeks, no one will ever know the McIntyres ever lived under that roof."

Thinking about our lives together on Bellwether Terrace, I imagined myself and Colin from our son's perspective, like a faded photo in a brand-new frame. Race brought up the fact that I had missed my husband's funeral—only because my crabby doctor cocooned me from the world—and I felt horrible about it. But that was nothing compared to the pain Race dragged around about Colin's absence in his own life, an old scar that still ached. It flattened me to see my son lugging that yoke around for so many years. While I sniveled, the stink of hand sanitizer, the muted colors on the walls, and the irritating buzz of a hallway light formed a third-rate jazz trio, complete with bad timing and broken instruments.

My heart performed back handsprings at the sight of Rose entering the lobby. "Hi there, Ritz," she said to Race, calling him by the nickname only *she* uses. It's a play off his real name, Carlton, she explained to me a ways back, but I still don't understand the reference. Plus, my son already has a nickname. How many people can he be at once?

Race eased out of his chair, placing a firm hand on his cranky lower back, and kissed my friend on the cheek. "Hey Rosie, how was your week?"

"Peachy," she said and put a finger to her plump chin. "Actually, more like oniony." She laughed her earnest laugh, which always makes me chuckle inside. "How's your mom feeling this afternoon?"

"You tell me," Race said.

"Not to be negative, but I think she's getting worse." Rose stared straight into my eyes. "I can tell by the way she looks at me."

What? I interjected. *How do I look at you, Rose?*

"Like she knows, but she doesn't know. You get me?"

"Yeah," Race said.

No, I said.

Rose and Race, they chatted away like old pals. Their voices pirouetted between the little things, like my adult diapers, and the bigger worries, like my pain medication. It was as if I wasn't even there as they discussed my recent days at Blue Horizons. In this community, folks love to share their stories and struggles, creating the perception of family. But like in any family, not everyone listens.

Rose took my hand. "But Miss Holly sure lights up when you're here, Ritz."

The weird way my son eyeballed me across the table, the agita in his gaze, tugged at my soul-strings. "You were so full of life, Mom," he said. "I hate how you've changed."

Changed?

Arnold Percival grunted at a table next to us, and his wife, Joan, shushed him while wiping cottage cheese off his mouth with a linen napkin.

Race glanced at the couple and laughed. "Could be worse, I guess."

It was like he was scribbling a picture with his words, showing me the differences between then and now, between me, Hollyann, and the other folks here.

My son picked up his chair and moved it next to mine. He leaned in and whispered, "Hey. Remember when you knew every detail of my baseball career, like you had it etched in stone? The stats, the seasons, the teams? Remember that, Mom?"

Race's question rattled something inside me, and I nodded. *Yes, I remember.*

"Okay, think for me now," my son said. "Was Dad from Ohio, or was he from Boston?"

I smiled. *Well, that's a silly question.*

"Blink once if he was from Boston."

Oh, don't be ridiculous, Race, I said. *You know the answer.*

"What about a woman named Willow? Do you know who she is?" Race's voice grew louder now, becoming testier, as if I was annoying him.

Quiet down, son.

"Or a notebook Dad kept in the basement, with 'Seven Songs' written on the cover? You know what I'm talking about? Just nod, yes or no."

Race, please.

He leaned back and covered his face with his enormous hands, which had about a hundred callouses on them. "Jesus Christ," he muttered, running his long fingers through his thick hair. He puckered his lips and exhaled so deeply he could've blown out all the candles on my birthday cake.

"I'm sorry, Mom," he said.

No, I was the one who should've been sorry. I didn't have any answers for Race, could only muster a few mumbles about my favorite rock band, a pretty tree with long weepy branches, and Colin's lucky number. Memory is a complex thing, isn't it? It comes with beauty and ugliness, all tangled up.

"I won't be visiting next weekend, okay?" my son said. "I'm taking a trip."

Where are you going?

"I'm going to fix this," he said.

Oh, our visit that day was bittersweet, stretching our ties to each other beyond the fuzzy boundaries we'd drawn, stretching so far that it hurt. When Race hugged and kissed me, my heart overflowed with fondness and pride. There was frustration, yes, at the way things slip away, like how my vocal range decreased as I aged, and there was nothing this old starlet could do about it. But there was also love, strong and enduring, and the comfort of the time my son and I had shared.

"Okay, Mom. See you in a couple of weeks." My son's lovely emerald eyes were mere inches from my face.

Believe I still love you, Race, even if I'm having trouble showing it.

After he left the dining room, I replayed the hour we spent together over and over in my head. The memory of him stayed with me for a tick, like how shadows linger at the close of day. It was a reminder, you see, that nothing can erase our bond. Then I recalled what he said before he left, and I wondered what he might "fix," and how he might fix it.

The Launch

WHERE'S MY SISTER? She was right here! Here, beside me. Memories… a shout, a train… What happened? Worried, so worried. Piece it together… I'm trying, I promise, I'm trying!

Throughout my wayward journey, I've been a chameleon, adapting to the colors of my surroundings. In times of struggle, I morphed, becoming different versions of myself to brave the storms. We all do the same thing, don't we? My fellow residents at Blue Horizons are perfect examples of such transformations. I know, because they've told me.

Take Helga Morgenson, for instance. Years ago, at her law firm, she was assertive and cold, tackling court cases head-on to excel in her career. But at home, she thawed, becoming nurturing and patient to tend to her disabled daughter. Then there's Stanley Wellbright, who, as a child with dyslexia, learned to be the class clown, using humor as a shield to deflect bullying. As he matured, that persona evolved, with Stanley mastering the art of wit and charm to navigate social situations and gain acceptance. And let's not forget Maria Epstein-Herrero, who, growing up with alcoholic parents, adopted the role of referee, burying her own needs to keep the peace. Over time, that pattern of prioritizing her family's happiness became ingrained, shaping Maria into a selfless caregiver, always putting others before herself.

We shape-shift to meet the demands of our environment, I think, driven by our innate desire for love and connection. In the end, none of us truly knows who we are, as the circumstances of our lives and the relationships we cherish constantly mold our identities. Now, if I don't even know myself, how on Earth could I recognize my son on his own wayward journey?

The day after Race interrogated me about my husband, he woke up early in his lonely apartment, satisfied with his decision to go on a road trip to Boston in search of the formless woman his father had loved. Colin's passing and their complicated relationship had ignited a seven-alarm fire under our boy. His focus was as clear as mud on a sunny afternoon.

Race was determined, with his belongings packed and bus tickets saved on his phone, though he wouldn't leave for another twenty-four hours. You know, he would've flown if he wasn't so scared of planes, plus money was tight, so the bus it was. But before leaving, my son needed one more thing.

Fifteen minutes later, he was in his childhood home again, the place that had introduced him to the maddening puzzle he was so eager to cobble together. As he stomped down the basement staircase, his footsteps bellowing through the house, his target was obvious: that old leather-bound book of songs.

"I blame you, goddamn Willow Spelman," Race grumbled, slaloming around a gauntlet of cardboard boxes, his stern words laced with frustration. Like he was arguing with a one-eyed ump who couldn't tell a strike from an orangutan. "You're why our lives went to hell, and I'm going to fuckin' find you." My son's fury must have been out of control, since he never curses, but Colin's well-guarded secret was a ponderous load Race couldn't haul without venting.

Holding the book of songs, his mind buzzed with questions, and he offered every one of them up to the god of unknown answers. "Who are you, and what kind of hippie name is *Willow*? Did you know about me? Or my mom? Or the crap you left in your wake?"

My son, a chip off the old apple tree, lost himself, trying to snatch answers that kept slipping away. He wondered aloud if I'd been privy to his father's infidelity. The discovery of Colin's back-alley actions, his sneaky second life, infuriated Race. I could imagine my son's furrowed brow, gritted teeth, and the demonstrative way he would lower his head when something peeved him.

Amid all that drama, his ex-wife sent him a text. He checked his phone and saw that the message was the third Jess had sent in the past half hour; he had missed the other two. Race and Jess weren't the best communicators, didn't converse much anymore, and, when they did, all either of them heard was a never-ending, grating static.

Jess: got ur voicemail. WTF!
Jess: boston tmrw?
Jess: where r u now?
Race: yep, dads place, meet here in next 15 if
u can

As he hit Send on his text, repeated knocks and rings rippled through the house like a woodpecker was going to town on the wind chimes outside.

Race flung open the door. "Wow, that new hot rod Glenn bought you must be fast."

Jess rolled her devilish eyes. "Faster wheels than you ever had."

"How'd you know I was here?"

"You're not a complicated man," Jess said. "Actually, let me rephrase that. You're not a complicated *person*. I'll leave out the part about being a man."

"Charming, as always." Race pivoted and walked toward the kitchen.

Jess followed. "Why the fuck are you going to Boston?"

Race held up the old leather-bound book and wagged it in front of his face. "This."

"Hmm. Wait, let me guess, you wrote your autobiography, and the Red Sox are selling copies as commemorative doorstops?"

"Good one," Race said. "You're getting funnier in your old age." He licked his lips and backed up against the oven. "This is a book of love songs, proof that my dirtbag father was having an affair."

"Oh, really?" Jess took a scrunchie from her wrist and tied back her wavy brown hair. "That's hilarious."

"Hilarious? You know what's hilarious? People who cheat and lie and ruin lives and have the balls to act like they did nothing wrong. Well, let me tell you, Jessica, those assholes deserve every ounce of blame, every bit of pain they've caused. They should feel it in their fuckin' bones, like the rest of us have to." Race waved the book again, this time in his ex-wife's face, and laughed like one of those sinister villains in an old-timey suspense flick. "There's zero excuse for betraying someone's trust, for tearing apart families, for obliterating fuckin' dreams. And if this woman thinks she can screw my loser of a father with no consequences, she's wrong."

"You're crazy, Race," Jess said, her tone stocked with exasperation. "Yeah, the guy was a shitty dad, but you can't do this. Do you have any trace of this woman, any evidence she even exists? It's pointless."

My son stood his ground, teeth gnashing. "I need to find Willow Spelman," Race said, "confront her, make her face the provisional music."

"Proverbial, dumbass."

"What?"

"The word is proverbial, not provisional. Unless the music is temporary."

"Fuck you." Race walked toward the living room.

"You're chasing a ghost!" Jess yelled.

Race wheeled around and stormed back into the kitchen. "I'm tracking down the truth."

"You really want to do this to your mother?"

"My mother has no idea what I'm doing."

"You're unbelievable, you know that? You never listen to reason," Jess shot back through clenched teeth. "That's why we fell apart."

"Oh, *that's* why? I was wondering when you'd come up with a new theory."

"Look, I'm tired of your shit. We've all got baggage, but you can't keep holding on to the past like this. It's dragging you down, and it's dragging me and Glenn down with you. You need to stop obsessing over what went wrong and focus on what's ahead."

"Okay, just so I'm clear, you and Mr. Mayor want me to give up?"

"Not give up," Jess said, "move on." She took a step closer to Race, then stopped and continued speaking, her voice quiet yet firm. "Quitting means you've lost, but letting go means you're finally taking control."

"Sounds like you bought another self-help book."

"Stop it with the third-grade pity party," Jess said, sneering, "and start living for something else besides your offended inner child."

The dregs of their argument spasmed in the air as Jess rumbled out of the house, leaving Race alone, clutching the old leather notebook. Tension tugged at his tendons, and the thin walls of our home pressed in on him. He stared at the book, his heart rife with vengeance, while the ache of the past clung to him like a frightened toddler at a busy intersection.

On a picturesque Monday, Race fidgeted at the Portland bus station, scanning the surroundings, hands clenching and unclenching at his sides. He had left Sea Point at sunrise, two hours earlier, and now would embark on a weeklong trip from Oregon to Massachusetts. Stops along the way: Idaho, Wyoming, Iowa, Illinois, and New York.

The depot buzzed with lunatic footsteps and hushed chitchat. Body odor, brewing coffee, and bus exhaust created a curious smorgasbord of scents. Wooden benches lined the walls, their surfaces polished by years of use, offering weary travelers a smooth spot to plunk their fannies. Colorful posters adorned the walls, advertising local attractions and events, adding a touch of vibrancy to the otherwise ho-hum space. The fluorescent lights above provided a pleasant glow, lighting up the ticket counters and departure boards. Even with people coming and going, the station felt like a holy place, a temporary home for voyagers starting or ending their journeys.

As Race sat and stewed, a slew of nerves ping-ponged in his belly. Things would've been different if he hadn't failed that breath test. He wouldn't have served eighty hours of community service, and he would've been driving to Boston alone right now, as he preferred, along the familiar New England roads he'd traveled countless times during his baseball days. But fate had intervened; he'd had one too many IPAs, and the judge suspended his license. Now he'd be stuck among fifty strangers on a bus, facing the first leg of a cross-country trip he never expected.

"All aboard for Boise, track nine. Boise, track nine."

Race's aversion to aviation was a well-known fact. The fear of flying began when his father introduced his own mistrust of planes to his son. "Listen, kid," Colin had grumbled back then, "planes are just metal birds waiting to fall out of the sky. Trusting those contraptions is like believing in fairy tales. And don't get me started on the incompetence of pilots. You know how many crashes happen every year? It's a death trap up there. Stick to solid ground, where at least you have some control. Remember, life's too short to take risks."

Since then, Race only flew when necessary. Whenever his minor league teams traveled by air, his performance on the field took a nosedive. Years ago, during his tenure with the Pawtucket Red Sox, after a turbulent flight to Reading, Pennsylvania, he struck out five times and committed two errors in a crucial game. Once his career ended, my son embraced the superstition, following the one shred of good advice his father ever gave him, and kept his feet on solid ground.

After he found a seat in the middle section of the bus, away from the others, Race's thoughts shifted to his argument with Jess the day before. Despite her concern, her words only made him more determined and convinced him he was doing the right thing. Looking back on their relationship, he couldn't believe they'd ever been in love, their differences now crystal clear and impossible to resolve. But what if Jess was right? What if his journey had no actual destination?

Race checked his phone: 9:55 AM, twelve hours till the Greyhound would reach Idaho. As the bus pulled away, a chubby teenage boy approached my son. He had kind eyes and held a plastic baggie of apple slices. "Can I sit here, sir?"

"Any other seats open?"

"Yeah, a couple, I think."

"Okay," Race said, "then no, you can't sit here."

The teenager shrugged and moved on.

A woeful weariness cramped the stale air, while the incessant hum of scuttlebutt, the cushioned clamor of music escaping from headphones, and the rustle of newspapers created a disconcerting background melody. From the back of the bus, the fumes of a greasy Sausage McMuffin and hash browns coasted past Race's nose, seeping into the stained upholstery of the seat in front of him.

As the trip began, the scenery outside the window transformed, the cityscape giving way to rolling hills and vast open fields, each passing mile coloring a new picture. At a rest stop, Race grabbed a quick ham sandwich, but it didn't hit the spot.

Time sped up, and darkness fell as the day pressed on. My son dug into his backpack and pulled out his father's notebook. The heaviness of the book in his hands was an all-too-real reminder of the mission that had propelled him on this adventure. He flipped through its pages, his eyes tracing the lines of every song. Each lyric held a fragment of the past, a link to the indecipherable man who had remained elusive even in death.

Rage overcame Race as he scanned the pages, the words imprinting on his brain. He squeezed his fists and closed his eyes, trying to calm the turmoil inside. He couldn't help but imagine the horrid face of Willow Spelman, the woman who had disrupted the course of his life. Questions ruffled in his gut about what I might have known, or if I'd known anything at all. His jaw tight and knuckles pale, my son clutched the book like he might tear it in half, his scowl locking onto the pages. Years of silent grievances had etched long lines on his forehead, all digging farther into his skin. He saw himself confronting Willow in Cambridge, asking long-buried questions and venting pent-up accusations. The bus rumbled along the highway, the miles stretching out ahead like an uncharted path leading to an uncertain venue.

More Than a Feeling

COLIN HAD BEEN a man of few words; he locked away his thoughts, buried beneath folds of silence and stoicism. But during his last month on Earth, he shared with me the secrets he kept guarded for so long. I often found it strange that he revealed so much only weeks before he died. One story he told me, just days before he passed, was about how he met the love of his life.

If I remember correctly, he first bumped into the girl in the summer of 1973. Colin was just fifteen years old, standing in a record store called Spin Central in the middle of Watertown, Massachusetts, a humble suburban haven a hop or two away from Boston. The city's streets, shaded by ancient trees, snaked through friendly neighborhoods. An active community of Armenians had thrived in the town for decades, infusing the place with a vibrant culture, delicious food, and lively music. Despite the chaos surrounding the

Vietnam War in the early '70s, the people of Watertown stayed close and dealt with change as best they could.

Spin Central was sheer heaven for music lovers, with all the best albums and singles from that time period. Colin's eyes lit up as he browsed through the vinyl records, recognizing the names of his favorite folk singers and bands—Bob Dylan, the Carpenters, and Crosby, Stills, Nash & Young.

He wore bell-bottom jeans, a tie-dye shirt, and a gray woven bracelet on his pipe cleaner wrist. My husband never drank or did drugs, but in the store that day, the vinyl scent and record player hum intoxicated him. When I think of Colin, his bright green eyes come to mind. They resembled a magical blend of mint leaves, sliced limes, and gemstones, a color found only in storybooks. They were the kind of eyes reserved for dreamers.

Colin had Spin Central all to himself and took his time perusing the albums. The manager, Cat, was laid-back and sometimes let him in outside of business hours. Cat was short for Catherine, an appropriate nickname for the twenty-five-year-old who admired the singer Cat Stevens. Her oversize square spectacles and pink sequined jean vest were appropriate, too, announcing that she wasn't afraid to make a loud statement. She had frizzy, shoulder-length orange hair and a face smothered in freckles—even had one on her upper lip. When Colin told me the story, he described Cat's personality as "spunky-meets-spiritual."

In the back of the store, as Colin scanned the inventory, the brand-new releases drew his attention. "Hey, Cat," he said, "Mother's Milk put out a demo recently. Have you seen it?"

"Yeah, their head guy, Tom, gave me a copy last week," Cat yelled from the counter up front. "Got it right here."

Colin hustled over to her. "Outta sight! Can I take it home for the night?"

"No can do, kid," Cat said, a freckled smirk propping up perky cheeks. "I promised it to someone."

"Who?"

"Some girl who comes in here a lot, your age. Don't remember her name. Supposed to be here soon, though. Maybe you can fight her for it." Cat squeezed one of Colin's twiggy biceps and scoffed. "Hmm, my money's on the chick."

Curious about the stranger who shared his quirky taste in music, Colin scratched at his chin, as if feeling for his first whisker. "Shoot, I'm dying to check out those tunes."

"What about *your* demo, kid?" Cat asked. "You showed me the songs you've written. When will you take my advice and record them?"

"They aren't any good," Colin said. "Unless you're into angsty tunes about pets dying, wars ending, and parents fighting."

Cat nodded and tried to smile. "What you need," she said, "is a muse."

The bell above the door jingled. Colin swiveled, and his eyes met those of a slim girl with a dusky complexion, quite unlike his Irish fairness, and a deep tone that lured him in. Her simple beauty captivated the boy, whose plain appearance and awkwardness demanded no such attention. She had tied her wicked waves of dark hair in a ponytail. Her red lips portrayed boldness, while her ebony eyes reflected doubt, the color of a shifting storm. Three months shy of her fifteenth birthday, she wore a certain gumption, a clear depth of insight far beyond her years. Everything about her was unusual, made no sense, like a shipwreck in a swimming pool.

As the girl nodded at Cat, Colin's gape overstayed its welcome, rapt by the unearthly aura surrounding her. It was her smile he remembered most vividly, an expression that left a permanent scar on his memory, a smile that didn't quite reach her eyes.

"Hi, Cat," the girl said. "Got that demo?"

"Sure do." Cat retrieved the cassette tape from behind the counter.

Colin took a half step toward the girl, feeling a thrumming behind his sternum. "Hey, um, how much do you know about Mother's Milk?"

"Enough," the girl replied, a different smile gracing her lips now, one that hinted at warmth and playfulness.

Colin's zest got the best of his shyness. "I haven't seen you around," he said, trying hard not to stammer. "What's your name?"

"Sevan," she replied, and the unique sound of the word widened his eyes, perhaps only because it came from her lips.

"Spelled like the number?" he asked.

"No," she said, rolling her gorgeous eyes and doling out the letters. "*S-e-v-a-n.*"

"But you pronounce it like the number, right?"

"No, not really."

"But you just did."

She tilted her head. "But people never ask how it's spelled."

"So, how should I pronounce it?"

"Why do you care?"

Colin swallowed hard and shuffled his feet, forming an apology in his mind. He wanted the girl to forgive his forwardness before he left the store. But he didn't apologize, and he didn't leave. Maybe, if he had walked away from Sevan that day, none of us would be here now, sharing in this story.

"I'm sorry," the girl said before Colin could unleash his own apology. "That was rude of me." She grabbed a thin marker and scribbled on the back of an obscure album cover lying on the counter.

Cat threw her slender arms out wide, mouth open just as wide. "Hey, what are you doing, kid? You out to lunch?" The manager slid her square glasses to the tip of her pointed nose and glowered over the top of the frame. "Your signature won't increase that album's value, you know."

"Mellow out, Cat," Sevan said, examining the front of the cover. "No one's ever heard of this Bruce Springsteen guy, anyway."

"Let me see what you wrote," Colin said.

Sevan handed the record to him, and he inspected the inscription:

Not SAY-vin like haven, not SEV-en like heaven, sev-ON like Sevan.

Colin ran a finger over the words. "I get it now," he said. "I have a cousin named Siobhan. It's pronounced the same as Sevan, but everyone gets it wrong."

Sevan spun and flipped through some T-shirts held hostage on a rack. "I hate my name. No one says it right. When they read it, half the time they don't know if I'm a boy or a girl. I got teased about it a lot. So, I started spelling and pronouncing it in school like the number seven. My friends think that's way cooler, so things are better now. But I don't know. My family calls me one thing, my friends another. I feel like I'm two different people." She turned back to Colin and looked through him, like she was fading into a dream. "I always wished my name was different, that my mother had named me Khloe. Isn't that a pretty name, the perfect name? Khloe. It means 'orchid' in Armenian."

Colin grinned. "I like Sevan."

The corners of Sevan's mouth twitched, but the rest of her face remained still as she stared into Colin's eyes—those striking green eyes. She stood there, inanimate, body limp, head to the side, ponytail dangling in front of her short-sleeved white blouse embroidered with blue and purple flowers. Just stood and stared, for what seemed like forever. Then, as if zapped by a bolt of lightning, Sevan came to life again. She grabbed the Mother's Milk cassette from the counter and said, "Did you know this band is from Watertown?"

"Um, yeah," Colin said, still dazed from the power of Sevan's stare. "They used to be called Middle Earth. I love their stuff. Might try to see them at a club in Boston this summer."

"Good luck getting in," Sevan said. "You look like you're ten years old."

Colin stood on his tiptoes and puffed out his bony chest. "What about now?"

"Nine."

"Hey, maybe we can listen to that demo together," Colin said, and immediately wished he hadn't. He'd never done anything or gone anywhere with a girl, not alone. *Holy shit*, he thought. *Did I just ask her out?*

Sevan raised her eyebrows and peeked at Cat behind the counter. The manager shrugged, whipped around, and unfurled a rolled-up Jefferson Airplane poster. "What do you think, Cat? Should I let him listen with me?" Sevan asked.

Cat glanced over her shoulder and smirked. "Up to you." Then she snapped her fingers, rotated in place, and rolled up the poster again.

"We don't have to," Colin said. "I don't know why I asked."

"Tell you what," Sevan said. "I'll listen to it by myself tonight, but I'll meet you back here tomorrow and give a full review of every song."

Colin's spirit soared, and his green eyes clashed with his red cheeks. "I'll be here."

In the sentimental way Colin recounted that story to me, I felt the thrill of that young boy's first brush with Cupid's arrow. Each word conveyed a yearning and vulnerability he'd kept concealed for an eternity till then. He talked about what he experienced that day—falling in love for the first time—how his heart had surrendered to Sevan, and it cut deeper than I cared to admit.

I couldn't unriddle why my husband cared more about a young girl he barely knew than he did about me. But that was before I knew the entire story. I can't explain what roiled in my belly—sadness, resentment, and a desperate desire to understand the man I had spent almost forty years with. Colin's revelation unveiled a side of him I'd never known. In his final days, he allowed me to glimpse a world he had kept hidden.

Sometimes, even now, when I think about him and Sevan, I wish she'd never existed.

❦

Have I mentioned Colin became an avid storyteller a few months back?

Whenever he visited me, he'd talk all about his past life, years before we met. He'd go on and on, but I didn't look forward to those stories very much. They made me feel insecure and sad, like an outsider in his world. But even though it hurt, I'd listen with all my might as he remembered loving someone else. I'd lose myself in his songs about Sevan, close my eyes, and slip away.

One story he shared was about her home life. He spoke of her strict Armenian household in East Watertown, where age-old customs ruled. Sevan was an only child who lived with her parents, Petrak and Yeva, and her grandmother, Akabe. They owned a white duplex on Porter Street, right behind the St. James apostolic church, where her family attended services. As my husband described the details, I visualized the exterior of Sevan's house—a trite, "very American" abode in the shadow of a grand Armenian cathedral—and I felt the sweeping impact of their religion and traditions.

Colin said he and Sevan spent a lot of time together in the summer of '73. They'd meet up at Spin Central, or at a burger joint, or at the park. Sometimes they'd hang out at her house, but never at his. Although I didn't ask, Colin painted a vivid picture of the Zakarians' home interior for me. He described the chaotic clutter and delicate decor, along with the many crucifixes, old photographs, and abundance of religious artifacts on the walls. What did my husband remember most about that place? Him and

Sevan being alone, talking about everything and anything, surrounded by the smell of lamb stew filtering in from the kitchen and the indistinct sounds of Armenian folk music playing in the background.

But there were times during those innocent days together when Colin wondered if Sevan had wished she were somewhere else. Spells of perverse confusion, extended minutes when she'd forget what she was saying mid-conversation. Like the exterior and interior of her home, Sevan was a contradiction. What she was on the outside differed from what she was on the inside. For that, my husband blamed her family.

Colin got along well enough with them, especially her father—though Petrak Zakarian had a gothic and intimidating presence about him. In line with their culture, Petrak wore a long, thick beard that obscured his neck, revealing all you needed to know about him. He was strong and caring, ethical and moral, committed to ideals, and never wavered from his intentions. A man who, if he believed in ghosts, would've welcomed one haunting his house.

Petrak's tough demeanor stood in stark contrast to Yeva's gentle presence, with her homemade knitted shawl wrapped around her shoulders and her satiny auburn hair tucked into a bun. Yeva wore many handcrafted rings, made of gold and silver, on each of her slender fingers—as if she were arming her dainty hands for battle. But thick coats of purple polish couldn't protect her nails, which she picked at nonstop, like a hell-bent raccoon clawing on an oak, hankering for beetles behind the bark.

Like typical parents, Sevan's folks worried about their teenage daughter. The girl was dead tired every day, lost track of time often, suffered long lapses in memory, and spoke to imaginary friends. Natural for a young woman? Perhaps. The product of hormonal swings? Maybe. But in this case, Petrak and Yeva attributed Sevan's inappropriate behavior to rebellion, a phase they would not tolerate.

As my husband described the Zakarians, I could almost hear the clan bickering. Their words were a concoction of worry and stress that defined their unusual familial bond. Colin shared one specific incident where Sevan and her parents engaged in an intense and passionate argument about church. Sevan's parents, steeped in Armenian tradition, cleaved to their beliefs, while their only child longed for the freedom that was always beyond her grasp.

"I can't live like this anymore!" Sevan screamed. "It's not fair! You're suffocating me with your stupid rules!"

Her mother's face reddened. "How dare you speak to us like that! We're protecting you from corrupting influences!"

"Protecting me? More like controlling me! I'm a prisoner in my own house!"

Petrak rose from his chair. "Watch your tongue," he said. "We are your parents, and we know what's best for you."

"Yeah, right," the girl scoffed. "You can't shove your religion and traditions down my throat!"

Yeva grabbed Sevan's wrist. "You will respect our heritage and our faith. It's what keeps this family strong and united."

Sevan pulled away. "Strong? United? More like close-minded and backward. I'll live my own life and make my own choices."

"Sevan, please," Yeva said, taking a cleansing breath.

"This is about Colin, isn't it?" Sevan put her hands

on her hips and stiffened her upper lip. "You disapprove because he's not Armenian, is that it?"

"It's not about him, specifically," her mother said. "It's about you, never wanting to go to school, pretending to be sick, how much you've been straying lately."

"Do you hear yourself?" Sevan laughed. "You're talking about me like I'm a barn animal."

"Why have you been acting like this?" Yeva continued. "Breaking curfew, missing church, skipping family meals, all of it!"

"Because I hate it here!"

Petrak raised his hand. "Enough! You will not dishonor us with this behavior! You will obey our rules or suffer the consequences!"

Sevan stormed off to her room, slamming the door behind her.

Her bedroom was a clash of Fleetwood Mac posters, geometric-patterned sheets, Armenian ceramics, and religious statuettes. Alone in her world, Sevan often struggled to find her true self. Her frequent blackouts, or "shifts," as she called them, added to her helplessness. Those odd occurrences, which she'd known since she was little, brought with them a partial loss of memory. Like waking up from a daydream. Like time had sped up and disappeared. Afterward, when she came back, she remembered only the basic details of what happened.

I can imagine Sevan, curled on her bed, head in her hands, unsure if she should follow her heritage or go her own way. It was in one of these blinks of conflict several years earlier that she had taken control and reshaped her identity. But she did more than spell her name differently—from Sevan to Seven—an alteration that carried a new pronunciation. She redefined herself and changed the person *behind* the name.

Despite this small semblance of control, she couldn't shirk the influence of her *tatik*, her grandmother. A diminutive crone, Akabe had thin lips that spoke of strange stories, blurring the line between reality and the phantasmal. A survivor of the Armenian genocide, she bore the burden of a traumatic past. Akabe's eyes, once wide and dark, now squinty and gray, had witnessed more horrors than the eyes of a thousand victims of a thousand crimes. The woman had the ragged, weary face of an old clock, tired of telling the time.

On the night Sevan fought with her parents, Akabe knocked on her granddaughter's bedroom door. Upon entering, her very presence transformed the atmosphere of the room, overloading the air with a mystical energy. That night, like a hundred nights before, Akabe told Sevan a passionate story about a pagan goddess named Tsovinar who had rescued her from drowning.

"My dear child, the heart of my life, there was a time long ago when dread filled the world, a time of unspeakable horror. I was just a girl then, and my mother, my blessed *mayrig*, did all she could to protect me."

Sevan listened, as always, honoring her grandmother with respect and attention.

"As we were forced to march to the Euphrates River, a soldier approached, his eyes swollen with evil desire. He wanted to take me, but my mother, with a strength I never knew she had, tied my hands and pushed me into the water. As I struggled, the teeth of death clamped down. Pulled under by the current, I could not breathe. I used my feet to lift myself up, but the water continued to cover my head. Screaming for my mother, I swallowed water and gagged. Then, as I abandoned hope, a miracle occurred. The goddess Tsovinar, in all her divine glory, embraced me and pulled me up from the depths."

Sevan remained attentive.

"In shock on the riverbank, I trembled and could not move, compelled by the surrounding corpses to stay until morning. With the rising sun, three Turkish cowherds, no older than you, saw me moving as they crossed a nearby bridge. They approached me, took pity on me, and brought me home to their father's care. The family forced me to work as a slave and made me renounce my Christian religion."

That family raised Akabe, but she hated her existence, childhood, and humanity. She was only happy when she got lost in her imagination while wandering in the courtyard—pretending she was somewhere else, someone else, trying to disappear. When she was eighteen, she fled to Greece, then to the United States, hoping for a better life. Though her status improved in some ways, she experienced a severe sadness, an emptiness, a death march of grieving. She couldn't leave her sorrow behind, couldn't start over without her guilt. The pain had followed her to America, never left her, tracked her everywhere, lived inside her.

Sevan braced for the end of the tale, the worst part.

"Tsovinar saved my life, but at a cost," Akabe said, lowering her eyes. "She demanded a sacrifice, a summons I carry with me. I am so sorry, my dear grandchild, but I cannot spare you from her will."

In Colin's retelling of the story, the way he characterized

it, Sevan's attitude toward her grandmother was an emulsion of reverence and skepticism. Sevan thought Akabe's mind had been impacted by her experiences, distorting her perceptions. The tale of Tsovinar saving Akabe during the genocide was a constant presence in the Zakarian household, a myth too unbelievable to be true. However, that story, even if her grandmother had invented it, became embedded in Sevan's core.

On stormy nights, the old woman would retrieve an ancient document, go to Sevan's room, and sit with her granddaughter on the bed. Akabe would unroll the document, hold the brittle paper up close, and force the girl to read the calligraphy along with her. The two would chant an invocation together, the sound of which Sevan likened to hailstones slamming against her window…

We invoke thee, Nar, thou goddess of the wind and storm. Hear us, Nar. We greet you. We know you. We love you, Nar. For thy gift is the air that is alive with your lightning. Blessed be the wind and the water and the storm, which is sacred to thee, and blessed be the miracle of fresh growth from thy water. Hail to Nar, our beloved goddess.

And they chanted…

We invoke thee, Nar, for you have taught us the way of wind travel. Hear us, Nar, and let us ride once again into the winds beyond the Earth, into the infinite stars, that we might experience the waters of the universe.

Akabe's concern for Sevan's future seemed awfully real. She warned her granddaughter about the threat that would arise once Sevan reached the age of twenty, when Tsovinar would come to claim her. The way Colin recounted Akabe's words, I could smell the old woman's anxiety, taste the depth of her conviction. She believed that the goddess who had saved her life would call Sevan "home to the water." The conflict within the young girl, caught between her grandmother's passionate beliefs and her own desires, created a tension that mirrored the larger struggle of her life. Late at night, alone in her room, Sevan would write in her journal…

After the genocide, the Ottoman Empire left behind a shameful graveyard, a scrap heap of malice. For what? Nationalism? Scapegoating? Religion? God doesn't distinguish between the dead, insecurity makes liars of everyone, and setting others apart is the great oppressor. There is no them. There is only us.

And she'd write…

My grandmother has seen humanity descend to a level of hatred where it hunted and killed people. There is no way to explain how primitive that fear must've felt, the fear of being hunted. Now, Tati is forever wounded. My parents are wounded. My family is not well. We're broken and stuck. We're dead inside, even if we're still alive. We'll never have closure until we have justice, but how can we possibly achieve that?

As my husband told this tale, I marveled at Sevan's complex youth. Her quest to find her identity, battles against tradition, and the prophecy from Tsovinar all meshed into a disturbing and incredibly human story. One that revolved around a young woman trying to decode her disconcerting life. Colin, in the twilight of his own life, shared many stories with me, narratives of love, loss, and longing. Stories my husband turned into songs.

"The Orchid"
December 1991

*Day after day, he traveled the path but never took
notice of much
His mind was consumed with dilemmas and
doubts, not with things he could actually touch
He'd stare straight ahead as he hurried along while
flowery fields passed him by
Till a late summer's day when his heart took a
turn, and a wonderful sight caught his eye*

*He stepped off the path and walked through the
field, but somehow did not feel alone
Then a smile crossed his lips when he knelt at the
spot where a beautiful Orchid had grown
Her petals were silk, her colors unique, and her
fragrance had called out his name
There were hundreds of thousands of flowers about,
though none, he was sure, quite the same*

*So, day after day, he ran through the field, admir-
ing the Orchid in bloom*

*He laughed with her leaves, trusted her stem, and
her scent was his favorite perfume
Then suddenly, somehow, the season had changed,
before he could possibly know
His world had turned white, and the field lay deep
under an ocean of untimely snow*

*He did not understand, and couldn't believe, that
what he had witnessed was true
So he prayed on that day as he knelt at the spot
where the beautiful Orchid once grew
He prayed for the sun to return with the spring,
bringing winter's cruel reign to an end
For though he respected what nature had done, he
felt he was losing a friend*

*Now someday, he knows, his heart will recover the
love that he wished could've been
When days become brighter, and hope becomes
new, the Orchid will bloom once again*

:25

Turn It Off

Race leaned against the cold window of the bus as it journeyed eastward from Boise to Cheyenne. He caught glimpses of boundless cities, paltry towns, and sprawling farmlands through the foggy glass. The changing landscape outside reflected the tumultuous thoughts in his head—a never-ending cycle of disbelief, remorse, and curiosity. As he studied the scenery passing by, every hill, every patch of green, every distant horizon held secrets waiting to be uncovered. Would this trip bring him closure or trouble?

A young woman had taken the seat beside him after the last rest stop. Her hair was straight and blonde, falling around her shoulders. Her features were unremarkable, and she wore bold eyeshadow. She sported a rhinestone-studded T-shirt and extravagant jewelry, much too fancy for a bus ride. To my son, she seemed like a woman who'd wear a ball gown to a desk job. As the kids say, she was "trying too hard." She would've made Pete Rose—Charlie Hustle himself—look like an absolute slouch.

Her crystal blue eyes were intense but empty, and Race coughed when inhaling her floral perfume. According to him, she was "semi-attractive," but she wasn't the sort of woman he usually dated. What *was* his type? I couldn't tell you, and neither could he. But regardless, Race couldn't help but ogle this woman. No matter how hard he pretended to fight it, he always entertained the urge for attention and conquest. He wouldn't—no, couldn't ignore her for the entire five-hour ride.

After they traded sideways glances, Race gave in. "What's in Cheyenne?"

The woman giggled, twirling her yellow hair. "Lots of things, I guess," she said with a Texas twang.

Race couldn't tell if she was being coy or profound, or if she was just being herself. "I mean, why are you going there?"

Her words rushed out all at once. "Oh, I'm so sorry," she said, neck bent, smile slanted. "I misunderstood. I'm normally not this ditzy." The girl was smitten by my son, and she was at least twenty years younger than him.

Race flashed one of his apathetic smirks, a careless look that still makes women swoon. "Don't sweat it," he said and turned toward the window.

"Oh, I won't."

"Great." Race focused on the passing landscape.

The woman then engaged in a one-way confab, making small talk about the weather, the bus ride, and even the elderly couple holding hands across the aisle. "Aren't they the cutest?" she said to the back of Race's head. "Hope I find a man who's that devoted to me when I'm shriveled and decrepit."

Five intolerable minutes later, Race took the bait and faced the girl. "What's your name?"

She picked at a rhinestone on her shirt and batted her empty eyes. "Daisy."

"Interesting." Race thought back to ten years earlier, to a three-game road trip to Pennsylvania where he'd spent a calamitous night with an exotic dancer called Buttercup. He hoped this flower's odor wouldn't stick to him like the memory of that icky encounter.

Daisy held out her pasty hand. "It's a pleasure meeting you."

"You, too." Race smirked again, this time less apathetically.

Daisy flicked his shoulder with a playful finger and swooned. "Aren't you going to tell me your name, silly?"

"It's Race."

"Mmm, I like it. So, what do you do for work, Mr. Race?"

"I'm the manager of a rec department." He let his vanity do the rest of the talking. "But before that, I was a pro baseball player."

Daisy lit up at the mention of his past profession, and she angled her body to face him. "Really? That's super sexy."

In that tiny instant, Race understood her. She hadn't met many famous people, and his past life intrigued her. She was interested in the confident athlete he used to be, rather than the person he had become. Daisy's interest shuttled him back to the days when he was unstoppable, at the peak of his powers.

As their jabbering continued, Race found himself caught up in a cyclone of words, bragging about his minor league achievements—his record number of stolen bases, triples, walks, and runs scored. I never liked it when he boasted; it wasn't becoming of him. But what's that old idiom? Can't teach an old goose new tricks? To be fair, though, my son had only eaten a granola bar that day, and he never made brilliant decisions on an empty stomach.

Daisy swished her hair away from her face. "Wish I'd seen you play."

He shared stories about the women he'd met during his pro career, proud and nostalgic about it all. This unbecoming version of Race was the one I'd call "morally casual."

"When I was playing ball," he told the young girl, "I got tons of fan mail, you know? Some women got pretty creative, sent panties and bras, even sex toys sometimes."

"Wow."

"As for staying in shape, I've kept myself together. Not hitting the gym like I used to anymore, but still got a decent bench press—two hundred ninety pounds ain't too shabby. Gotta keep up with things, stay sharp, you know? My agent could call any day. You never know, some lucky team might wanna sign me."

"Really? That's incredible."

"Yeah, I was one of the fastest guys in the sport. When I played in Sarasota, the promotions department had me race a thoroughbred before a game to draw in more fans."

"Amazing."

"I was a switch hitter, too. Righty, lefty, a killer from either side of the plate. Those line-drive home runs I used to smack? The announcers called them 'Race tracers.' Kinda cute, huh?"

He didn't tell Daisy about the most significant statistic

of his career—his lone plate appearance in the majors. The memory of that fleeting, thrilling moment bubbled up. His September call-up to Boston, followed by the terrifying flight from Dulles to Logan, and the strikeout looking that stained his major league debut, ending his big league career. He would never forget that one at bat. It had been haunting him for years, a scathing memento of his wasted potential.

As the bus rolled on and the hours ticked away, Race lost track of time and reality. He found himself immersed in a haze of half-true memories, embellishing his past to occupy the void of his present. Daisy's voice became a distant hum, her words fading into the background as my son grappled with insecurity and regret.

When the bus arrived in Cheyenne, Race got off without looking back. He left behind the fawning young lady who had caught his eye and stroked his ego, just like the countless women before her. He walked into the station carrying an emptiness, his attempt to find validation through past accomplishments deepening his disappointment, his stiff back and creaky knees only deepening his fear of aging.

My son's voice shivered when he shared that story with me, and tears welled up in his baby blues—I mean greens. He had once been a star athlete, only accustomed to winning. But now he appeared defeated, through his own eyes, not mine. His journey had been—and would be—a constant struggle to find himself and scramble around life's curves and veers. I, too, felt the pressure of his unmet dreams and the freight of expectations pressing down on his shoulders, but I always gave my best motherly advice. Whenever he faced adversity in his playing career or failing marriage, I reminded him that success is not always straightforward.

It takes time to understand ourselves and what life has in store for us.

⋘

According to Race, the bus ride from Cheyenne to Des Moines was nothing less than surreal. He was drowning in pain and guilt, and the cloudy sky threatened to increase the flooding. It was four in the afternoon, three days into a planned six-day trip. Race occupied a seat by the window on a half-full bus while the other passengers were lost in their own stories.

Before the Greyhound left the terminal, my son's thoughts reverted to his father, my beloved Colin. Their relationship had frayed over the years, snapping entirely after the Red Sox drafted Race at age eighteen. Colin had wanted our son to attend college—Oregon State had offered a full scholarship, like they had with Glenn. The two boys could've been standout teammates again. But Race wanted to get away, far away, and knew for certain he was ready for the majors. "Why do you care about me all of a sudden?" he asked his dad back then. Like it was only yesterday, I remember how Colin shook his head and turned away. After that, while Race immersed himself in the beauty of baseball, he shrugged off the ugly relationship with his father. Amazing, how long they dragged around their rift.

The engine revved.

A husky Native American man wearing a suede jacket decorated with colorful beads lumbered onto the bus and squeezed into the aisle seat next to Race. The man was large, both in stature and presence, with a blue bandana wrapped around his forehead. His long, braided ponytail fell halfway down his back, and he smelled like a forest of pines. Race figured the man was in his early thirties, but his godlike physique suggested he was ageless.

When his seatmate cracked his gnarled knuckles, my son squirmed and thought, *What's up with this guy?*

Sharp grooves around the stranger's pensive eyes and down his cheeks hinted at a life marked by hardship.

Race stared out the window. *Just my luck.*

The bus rolled along while the strapping man groaned in rhythm, engaging in a quiet chant. "Ermm. Ermm. Ermm." The solemn sound reverberated throughout the bus.

My son, at six foot three and well over two hundred pounds, felt like a gnome compared to the giant. Even when Race leaned away from the armrest between them, he couldn't seem to find more room. *No way will the two of us survive sixteen hours to Iowa like this.*

The man turned his head, fixed his grimace on Race, and extended a beefy hand. "Nathan Lone Bear," he said in a low, resounding tone.

My son gripped Nathan's hand and met his gaze. "Race McIntyre."

"Hope I'm not taking up too much space."

"You're good," Race lied. "Funny, I'm usually the one taking up space."

"I'll move if you're uncomfortable."

"It's fine," my son said, but didn't know why.

With his thick fingers, Nathan fiddled with a necklace around his powerful neck. Seemed like a cherished talisman with a wooden pendant shaped like a bear's claw. It was a beautiful piece of art, secured to a brown leather string. The detailed lines on the claw showcased precise and skillful craftsmanship.

With his sneaker, my son nudged his backpack farther under the seat in front of him and turned to Nathan. "You going all the way to Des Moines or getting off in Denver?" Race asked.

"Probably Des Moines," the man mumbled.

"A man without a plan," my son joked. "I like that."

"My father and brother live here in Wyoming. My home is in Iowa."

"Married?"

"I am," Nathan said, then paused, breathing in deep. "Um, I was."

"Hey, man, I get it." This unfamiliar urge to sympathize stunned Race. "Not all marriages work out."

"My wife and I loved each other very much." Nathan's almond-shaped eyes were hazy with hurt, and he stared hard at my son. "She died two days ago, giving birth to our daughter."

Race was stunned silent.

"I should've been there," Nathan said.

Still, my son found no words.

Nathan pulled out a photograph from his jacket pocket. The image depicted a beautiful young woman in a white dress, laughing in a hayfield, with sunlight dancing in her long dark hair. He handed the picture to Race. "Her name was Desiree."

My son pressed his fingers against the sharp corners of the photo. "I'm so sorry," he said and gave the picture back to Nathan. "If you don't mind my asking, what's the baby's name?"

"It would've been Jane." Nathan's thumb traced the contours of the bear claw pendant, as if seeking comfort in its form. In my imagination, the wooden icon represented the overflowing contents of the sad man's soul: resilience, survival, impermanence, connection to nature, renewal, healing, and hope. But Nathan Lone Bear didn't wear the necklace; the necklace wore him.

"I should shut up," Race said.

"No, it's okay. Life is a sacred gift. When we share our words and strengthen our connections, we honor that gift."

"Sharing words and strengthening connections aren't exactly in my wheelhouse."

Nathan smiled. "As kids, my brother and I disagreed with our father all the time, and he'd tell us over and over, we're all different wolves running in the same pack."

"Don't get me started on fathers," Race said.

The extensive dialogue that followed flowed like opposing currents in a river of sorrow, Nathan's honesty and agony cutting across Race's stubbornness and spite. As the hours went by, their stories became entwined. Without revealing his complete self, my son bonded with Nathan over their shared personal pain. Just before Race fell asleep, Nathan said, "Life tricks us, deceives us, makes sinners like me seem like saints. But my sin isn't what I did wrong, it's that I want to know why."

At nine in the evening, the vehicle stopped in Denver. Race woke in time to stretch his legs and find some dinner. He invited Nathan, but the man declined. When my son returned twenty minutes later, Nathan was gone. Race's heart sank for the man whose story had struck a chord my son didn't know how to play. Why did the big man stay behind? Perhaps he postponed his trip home, or he realized there was nothing left for him there.

As the Greyhound departed, Race surveyed the Mile High City's lights vanishing into nothingness. The bus cruised along the highway while my son fidgeted in his seat. He stared out the window at the endless stretch of farmland and towns, but his thoughts were elsewhere. He remembered Jess's laughter, her warmth by his side, and their dreams of starting a family. But those memories turned bitter as he recalled the hormone testing and semen analysis, their struggles with infertility, and the emptiness that followed—a painful song playing on repeat in his brain. As the night grew darker, Race remained wide awake, mental images of *what could have been* digging up the anguish he had buried deep inside. While the bus rolled east, the passing scenery mirrored his own life, full of desolate dreams and squandered opportunities.

:24

Amanda

My sister? My daughter? Where? Who are they? Mixing them up. Faces in mirrors… She left? The girl… slipping. Gaps, my mind… Holes, my sweater. The moths! The holes, the moths!

When the Greyhound pulled into the packed Des Moines terminal, an angry October chill burst in through the opening door—a rude wake-up call for the groggy passengers. The second Race stepped outside, a severe urgency tore at him like a ruptured Achilles tendon. Finding Willow Spelman was all he could think about. He checked his watch, struggling for a second to remember the day. *Right, it's Thursday.* With only thirty minutes before his next bus departure, he navigated through the sea of commuters, each face lost in their own world.

My son's steps hastened as he entered the station and located the men's room. The chipped tiles on the floor and walls had seen better days, but the disinfectant smell and flushing toilets were oddly refreshing. After splashing icy water on his face, he flinched at his reflection in the mirror. The lines on his forehead and cheeks cracked up at the sight of themselves. He would've liked to blame the rugged bus ride for his appearance, but the inevitable signs of mortality had crept in, a reality he couldn't escape. The invincibility that had once accompanied his youth had now given way to pains and aches that accompanied his every step. He placed a hand on his lower back and winced.

Tracing the creases on his face, he smirked and muttered, "You old-ass motherfucker." The glass showed his inner chaos, torn between the nostalgic past and the unknown future. Race was the same person in the mirror as he had been on the field, but that person wasn't him. There was a time when he believed he'd remain forever young, running as though the wind itself had conceived him. Floating. Flying. But now, whenever my son made even the slightest movement, his knees and back sent painful pinches to his nervous system, an SOS to his cortex. Time was an unstoppable force, an unbeatable opponent.

He sighed as he exited the restroom, trudging toward the Greyhound bound for Chicago. Once on board in the back of the bus, he tossed his bag under the seat and braced himself for the seven-hour journey ahead. Seven: a number that had struck at his heart like a rattler, poisoning his thoughts since the day he found his father's songbook. As he leaned his head against the window, Race second-guessed himself. *What the hell am I doing?* He was losing sight of his mission, the whole reason he embarked on this trip. *Is it worth the aggravation?* The words *Seven Songs* ricocheted in his brain, fixated on the temptress he sought in Cambridge and the secrets he hoped to dig up.

My son took my husband's notebook from his backpack and flipped through the worn pages that bore traces of Colin's soul. At first, Race hadn't noticed the woman sitting across the aisle from him, but the sound of sniffling compelled him to glance in her direction. Her messy, short blonde hair appeared white under the harsh fluorescent lighting. The snappy hairstyle seemed to symbolize her rebellious nature and a need to hide her true self. She wore jeans, a blue sweater, and a tan tweed jacket. She was holding some type of stuffed animal—a bright purple elephant or rabbit—Race couldn't make out which.

Something told my son to get closer, and he slid from the window seat to the aisle. As tears welled in the woman's pale gray eyes, she brought her hands to her face, taking lengthy breaths to steady herself. Like he had experienced with Nathan, Race sensed another smidge of sympathy, a foreign agent reintroducing itself. "You okay?" he offered.

"Fine," she replied, her voice strained yet genuine as she straightened up. "Sorry, I almost never break down in front of strangers on buses." A haggard smile graced her lips, a feeble effort to hide the sadness behind her eyes.

"Race," my son said, a simple gesture of comfort masked as an introduction.

The woman wiped a tear off her cheek and smirked. "Race?"

"Yeah."

"You might want to rethink that," she said. "I was conference champ in the four-by-four hundred meter relay at Cleveland State in 2004."

"No, that's my name."

"I know. It was a joke. But a bad one."

"So, you weren't really a track star?"

"Oh, that part was true," she said and tried to laugh. "I'm Amanda."

While her name levitated in the air, she exhaled, as if the six letters had teamed up to hoist a weight off her shoulders. She turned away, wiped her eyes again, and went back to fondling the purple stuffed animal in her hands, which Race now determined was a floppy-eared beanbag dog. He didn't ask about the toy, or the silver bracelet with the letter *M* charm dangling on her wrist.

The bus roared to life, its engine propelling them toward Chicago. Race leafed through his dad's leather notebook once more, revealing pages bursting with ballads and poems that Colin had once intended for another love, not me. My son's mind wandered as he considered the complicated string of sentiments that had tangled my husband's heart.

Amanda had closed her eyes, her hands resting on the toy dog, keeping it safe on her lap. She was gorgeous while sleeping, Race thought. There was an allure in her stillness, and my boy couldn't take his eyes off her. In that tick of time, with her head tilted back and short haircut leaving her neck exposed, he imagined Amanda as a horror film heroine rousing a vampire's thirst. Was she an unaware victim? A knowing and willing sacrifice? Or a steely seductress with a wooden stake hidden under her coat?

The vulnerability of her resting form touched something within Race, urging him to make a move. He shifted in his seat and coughed, stirring her from her nap. When their gazes met, he saw surprise and gratitude in her eyes. Like I always told him, if you scrabble around in the right place, you can find anything.

"So, um, I guess you're a dog person," Race said, hoping to reignite the spark he presumed they had both felt a few minutes earlier.

"Oh, this?" Amanda scratched the back of her neck and smiled at the beanbag toy cupped in her hands. "Yeah, I take this little guy with me when I'm traveling. He's the perfect companion. I've had him since I was a kid."

"You can't be serious. I mean, I'm not questioning your age, but he looks brand-new."

"I'm thirty-five," she said. "I take care of my stuff."

My son waited for Amanda to continue, but she stayed quiet. He assumed the lead again and said, "Your bracelet's pretty. What's the *M* stand for?"

"Thanks," she said, fidgeting with the charm. "But, uh, it's actually a *W*."

"Meaning?"

"It means, well, it was a gift from my college track coach. When my teammates and I graduated, she gave us these bracelets. The *W* is for Warriors. That was our school's nickname, the Cleveland State Warriors."

Race nodded. "Got it." He flashed a broad smile, buying himself time before following up, wondering if he should call out Amanda for lying. When he and Glenn were kids, they had memorized the nicknames for every Division I college and university—because that's the sort of thing sports-crazed boys do. My son knew Cleveland State's nickname was the Vikings, not the Warriors.

"Where are you headed?" Amanda asked.

Race forgot all about college nicknames and said, "Boston."

"For?"

"Tracking down an old friend," Race said, with no intention of elaborating. "And you?"

"Me? Oh, uh, Chicago, to see my sister."

As the bus cruised onward, Race and Amanda chatted across the aisle, their smooth discourse flowing like a soulful duet. They shared stories and laughed, enjoying their sudden camaraderie without getting too personal. It was a unique experience for Race, with the open accord and Amanda's challenging nature chipping away at his walls of self-righteousness and hardheaded assurance.

"Can I get your opinion on something?" Race said, opening Colin's notebook and handing it to Amanda. "What would you say this song is about?"

"Did you write this?" She examined the page and glared at Race. "Wait, this is from, like, forty years ago."

"My buddy's father wrote it," Race said. "What's your interpretation?"

"Write You a Song"
June 1978

If I write you a song of how lonely I feel and how hard it has been to get by,
It'd be selfish of me because deep down inside I'd be writing to make myself cry

If I write you a song of how sometimes I don't understand what you do or you say,

*It wouldn't be fair that I'm questioning you just
because things aren't going my way*

*If I write you a song of my hopes and my dreams,
thinking that you will always be here,
How silly it'd seem to be writing of dreams when
my hopes fall along with each tear*

*If I write you a song of the laughter we shared and
the moments I keep in my heart,
It wouldn't make sense as those memories are only
reminders that we're far apart*

*If I write you a song of how lovely you are and how
I think the world of you,
The lines wouldn't end, and the song would go on
for as long as the sky remains blue*

*So I'll write you a song simply saying goodbye, hop-
ing someday I'll see you again
Though my head will be taking the easy way out,
my heart will be losing a friend*

"Wow," Amanda said and closed the book. "That guy was *all* in his feelings, huh?"

"Yeah, which is weird," Race laughed, "because my buddy always jokes that his dad was born without a heart."

"Seems like your friend didn't really know his father."

"He says no one did."

"Except maybe the girl in that song." Amanda crinkled her pretty forehead and twisted the charm on her bracelet. "Was your friend even alive in June of seventy-eight?"

"Probably like a year old," my son said, hoping to camouflage the quick answer with his blasé tone. "Sounds like the guy was leaving his wife, right?"

"But unless they had just separated, it can't be about his wife," Amanda said, opening the book and scanning the song once more. "Look, he wrote they were far apart." She pointed to the lyric. "Then he added he hopes to see her again."

Race reached across the aisle, took the book back, thumbed to the page with Willow Spelman's address, then held it up for Amanda. "Check it out," he said. "That's not my buddy's mom, so this must be who he wrote it for, don't you think?"

"I guess so, yeah."

"So it's all her fault, then," Race said, almost under his breath.

"Hmm, that seems like a stretch. I wouldn't blame her for anything."

"Really?" Race scowled and threw his head to the side, his long hair teasing his cheeks. "I don't see a better explanation."

"Listen, I don't know what happened to your friend's family. But maybe it wasn't anyone's fault." Amanda leaned in, her gray eyes appearing bluer in the new light. "Think about it, most relationships end. Friendships, romances, marriages. They break, they die. People move on and let go."

At four in the afternoon, the bus arrived in Chicago. The hours had passed in a blur of conversation, and neither Race nor Amanda could believe their journey was over. "Well, I've been on worse bus trips," my son said, the awkward joke landing with a thud. "Thanks for sitting in for my therapist."

"I wouldn't qualify for that job."

"You probably wouldn't apply for it either."

"It was nice talking with you," Amanda said and buttoned her jacket.

"You, too." He tried, and failed, to think of something more to say.

She stood, gathered her things, and stuffed the purple dog into her bag. "Well, Race, I guess this is goodbye."

He detected a note of reluctance in her voice, but it wasn't enough to keep her from weaving into a band of hurried passengers and disappearing down the aisle. "Guess so," my son whispered, wishing that goodbye didn't always mean forever.

⁌

Then he went, um, so, after the bus… It was there, on the streets of that place, the city with the wind… No, wait, I know what I'm trying to say, but the words aren't available to me at the moment. I'll get it right…

My son strolled through the busy streets of Chicago, submerged in a kind of congenial gloom. He replayed his time with Amanda in his mind, wishing he had said more, wishing she hadn't left him. But for now, he needed to focus on finding the Marriott where he had a room for the night before his early morning bus to Buffalo.

The Windy City was alive with the chaos of rush hour—honking car horns, chatter from pedestrians, and meaty smells kebabbing through the crowd. As my son navigated the sea of humanity, he repelled the surrounding energy. The swift pace of commuters, lively street performers, and tourists clicking cameras vied to capture his attention. But despite the vibrancy all around, a growing listlessness ached in Race's bones.

He bumped shoulders with a millennial in a sports coat, grunting into a cell phone. "C'mon, dude," the guy growled, stopping in his tracks and holding his arms out wide. My son zipped past a crew of sidewalk musicians, four teenage boys thumping on upside-down plastic buckets, adding their own melodies to the urban concerto. Amid it all, Race seemed to be searching for something other than a hotel, something missing, something he'd lost, something important scattered in the flurry.

Then, in the distance, a half block away on the Magnificent Mile, he spotted her. She stood alone on a corner, a lone figure adrift in an ocean of passing faces. Her short silver hair snatched the sun's attention, shimmering like a beacon, for him alone to see. His heartbeat escalated, his steps matching the rhythm of his quickening thoughts. He increased his pace, his voice breaking through the rhapsody of the city as he called out, "Hey! Amanda!"

He couldn't understand why he was acting against his easygoing nature. *Hey, man, be cool.* He had never been the type to chase after strange women, to engage out of desperation. He always let the strange women chase him.

Amanda turned, like a chipmunk wary of a nearby hawk, her eyes darting around. But she didn't notice Race and strolled away like he wasn't even there.

A storm of grit and pluck soaked my son. He needed to catch up to her and address the unusual affinity he felt for her. No time to waste, he took off running, maneuvering through the crowd. His creaky knees creaked while he kept his eyes fixed on Amanda. With each stride, his lower back screamed in agony.

"Hey, wait!" my son called out again, dodging a woman pushing a stroller, his voice more urgent now. Amanda stopped, frozen in time, while Race closed in on her. He slowed down, trying to catch his breath, trying to regain composure, his ticker pounding at hyper speed, beating like a bongo drum. He stumbled to her side and bent over at the waist, sweaty and exhilarated on that busy Chicago street. "Whew!"

Amanda laughed.

My son brushed his hair away from his face, panted, and clutched his chest. "Hey," he said, huffing, beaming, and placing shaky hands on quaky knees. "It's me, Race." Emerald eyes met gray eyes. The clamor of the city faded away, leaving only the two of them—strangers united by a twist of fate.

"I know," she said, "we just spent three hours talking, remember?"

Race cringed at his awkwardness, reverting to a teenager trapped in a strange, surreal dream. "Yeah, well, I'm kinda hard to forget."

Their comical reintroduction erased the self-imposed boundaries of their initial meeting. Talking away, they strutted through the city, as if they'd known each other for years.

As dusk fell and the wind picked up, Amanda tugged on the collar of her jacket. "First time in Chicago?"

"No," Race replied. "But it feels that way."

"You know what?" She skipped a few feet ahead, then whirled and faced him, walking backward. "If I didn't know better, I'd swear you were someone famous. You got that look, you know, like a young John Stamos."

"Me, famous? Impossible."

"Days like this make everything seem possible." She stared up at the towering buildings and grinned, arms out wide. "God, there's so much to love about this town."

He glanced at her. "Definitely."

Their banter brimmed like a bubbling brook, one topic after another. The interaction was effortless and intoxicating. Amanda's spirit, authenticity, and openness drew him in—and Race felt more than a spark between them. He didn't want to let her go, needed her to remain with him somehow, had to say something to make her stay. *It's now or never*, he thought, *and tomorrow may be too late.*

As they walked, the streetlights casting a warm glow, my son grew bolder, his words taking on a gutsy tone. "How about dinner? On me."

Amanda's lips curved into a smile, her nose crinkling, her eyes meeting his in a playful challenge. "You sure you're not tired of me yet?"

Race chuckled, the energy between them palpable as pecan pie. "Pretty sure."

"Then all right," she said. "Carpe diem, right?"

"Honestly, I'm more of a get-through-the-diem kind of guy."

Amanda's smile grew wide, and they stood there, two people thrown together by destiny, their souls tangled up in the possibility of something greater. My son admired the silver bracelet shining on her wrist and decided the *M* should stand for *Magic.*

Didn't Mean to Fall in Love

MEMORY IS A jigsaw puzzle, with a million pieces shifting and changing with time. That's the way I see it. What we remember, what we forget, it's like choosing which corner to turn on a busy street, which direction to travel. Each step, each choice is a ripple, spreading out, touching everything around us. And like the roads we decide to take, each memory shapes our lives and the lives of everyone we touch.

Race and Amanda ambled through the crowded Chicago sidewalks in search of a restaurant. Her high-pitched laughter kissed the buildings, injecting the air with comfort. Her animated gestures and genuine smile enamored Race, and she made him feel at ease. As they traded silly one-liners, their voices meshed and created a cozy cocoon amid the busyness. It seemed as if their connection had always been there, lying dormant, waiting for them to find each other, a switch ready to be flipped. Like a tidal wave, once you're in its path, you're swept away.

"So, who's in Boston?" Amanda asked.

"Just a buddy from high school," Race said, not wanting to reveal the true reason for his trip, an admittance he assumed Amanda would find either suspicious or ridiculous. "Haven't seen the guy in a while."

"Where're you from?"

"Oregon, close to the Washington border, a city on the edge of nowhere." My son had never been proud of his hometown. "What about you?"

"Ohio, suburbs outside of Dayton," she said. "Not as idyllic as it sounds."

"What's wrong with it?"

"The place is fine. I mean, it's more than fine. It's very nice." She hesitated, slowed her pace, and let out a sigh. "I don't know."

"Don't know what?"

"This might sound weird, but my friends say I'm too satisfied with everything. Too accepting, you know?" Her tone grew weak, as if she were apologizing for a crime she didn't commit. "They say I deserve more out of life, that I should demand more."

"And what do *you* think?"

"I think we're all hopelessly helpless." She bobbled her head and walked faster. "We pretend to be in control of our lives, but we're just along for the ride. But that doesn't have to be a bad thing. The whole point of life might be to enjoy the ride."

As they made their way through streets awash with honking cars and chattering pedestrians, Race couldn't resist

Amanda's presence. Her face showed a hint of exhaustion, and smoky shadows underscored her eyes. It was clear she had seen some tough times, but when Amanda smiled at my son, when her nose crinkled, her energy infected him.

A cool breeze blew through the city, and Amanda wrapped her coat tighter around herself, while an Italian eatery called Vito's aroused Race's curiosity. The aroma of garlic and tomatoes wafted out, and his stomach rumbled. It reminded him of his boyhood, when he devoured mounds of my homemade lasagna, hoping to grow big and strong enough to play in the major leagues someday. As they stepped inside the restaurant, Amanda removed her coat, revealing her full figure. She chose a table for two in the corner, but Race's regard was elsewhere. He was so preoccupied with Amanda, so oblivious to their surroundings, he could've been dining on Mars. Her appearance wasn't all that blew him away; her confident yet vulnerable spirit attracted him as well. This was more than a physical magnetism—my son wanted to feel this woman on a deeper level, to unravel the mystery underneath the exterior.

"What are you thinking?" Amanda asked as they checked out the specials written in chalk on the wall. "Anything calling your name?"

Race snapped out of his trance. "Eggplant parmesan, all day every day."

"You've got to be kidding," Amanda said. "Eggplant parm is the stepchild of Italian food. It doesn't deserve to share a menu with the classic entrées."

"Classic?" Race buttered half of a round roll. "That's just another word for *boring*."

Bursts of laughter punctuated their playful back-and-forth, and my son enjoyed the peppy exchange. He used to laugh all the time when he was young. Long ago, that sound kept me sane, and as Colin became more distant, my little boy's laugh was all I had. But then Race's laugh went away, disappearing years before he was drafted and left Sea Point.

With their orders placed and drinks in hand, the handsome couple's communion deepened, sparked by a playful game. "It's called five questions," Amanda said, smiling. "Have you ever played?"

"You mean, have I ever asked anyone five questions?" Race replied. "Yes, I have."

"Bravo," Amanda said, rolling her gorgeous gray eyes. "I'm talking about heavy questions, stuff that's at your core." She placed her elbows on the table and rested her chin on her fists. "Here, I'll start. Okay, what's your most irrational fear?"

"Honestly?"

"Yes."

"Flying," he said. "But there's nothing irrational about that."

"You don't think?"

"Absolutely not," Race said. "Exactly one hundred twenty-three people died in plane crashes last year, worldwide."

"Wow," Amanda said. "But weren't there, like, thirty thousand motor vehicle fatalities in the U.S. alone?"

"That's beside the point." He buttered the other half of his roll. "What's your irrational fear?"

Amanda raised her glass of water. "This."

"Fancy tableware?"

"H2O," she said. "I'm terrified of it, even hate taking baths. I haven't been in a pool, lake, or ocean since I was seven years old."

"Bad experience?"

"Kind of." Amanda's answer was cut short when a server arrived with their orders. She licked her lips at the sight of her osso buco while scrunching her brow at Race's eggplant parm. When the server left, she tapped her fork on the table and said, "So, what's your biggest regret?"

"Can we eat first?"

"Last question, promise," she said. "Biggest regret?"

Race put his fork down and took a long sip of his merlot. "I played minor league baseball a million years ago," he said.

"Ah, so I was right. You *are* a celebrity."

"Hardly."

"What's the regret?"

"So, in the offseason we'd play winter ball somewhere warm. When I was nineteen, the organization sent me to Venezuela for a few months." Race lowered his wineglass and stared over Amanda's shoulder, as if he were speaking to the wall. "I thought I was the shit back then, tried to impress the scouts every chance I got. One game, we were going against the best player in Venezuela, Edgar Dominguez. They called him El Toro, the greatest hitter anyone had seen in decades. Incredible catcher, too. Anyway, I'm on first base when the guy at bat lines a single to center. I was stealing on the pitch and figured I'd make third base easy. I was pretty fast back then. So, as I'm cruising into third, I peek over my shoulder and see the center fielder glove the ball and lob it back toward the infield. I still don't know what I was thinking, but I took off for home. The throw from the shortstop beat me by a mile. Edgar was waiting at the plate for me, ready to make the easiest tag in the history of baseball. I should've stopped and gone back to third, but

I kept running. Dominguez braced himself for contact, and I went low, threw my shoulder at his knees, and took him down."

As my son went to sip his merlot, Amanda put her hand to her cheek and said, "You hurt him, didn't you?"

Race swirled the wine in his glass, watched the red liquid spiral. "Ended his career."

"That's sports, though, isn't it?" She leaned back. "That stuff happens all the time."

"Edgar moved his family to New York, and he died in an accident ten years ago. I went to the funeral, talked to his eleven-year-old daughter, Izzy, wanted to apologize but couldn't. She plays softball for Northwestern now. Pretty close to here."

"And you want to see her?"

My son shook his head and tucked his hair back behind his ears. "I want to, but I can't," he said. "Got a bus to catch tomorrow."

When dinner ended, they stepped out into the chilly night. The wind howled through the streets, and Amanda shivered. My son rubbed her back as they walked, and she swayed into him. Her hand found its way around his waist, and her finger hooked onto his belt loop, a simple gesture that gave Race an unexpected rush. He straightened up and swung his arm around her, his muscles loosening. Then he smiled and squeezed her shoulder, thinking about her in a way he hadn't thought about anyone in ages. She mattered to him, already. In the past, he had treated scores of women like objects, consumed by selfish, hormonal desires. But this was different. Amanda deserved more than a forgettable encounter. But why?

Their bodies on autopilot, they talked about nothing and everything while making their way to Race's hotel. At the Marriott bar, they downed a few drinks and chatted away. Around midnight, my son paid the bill and handed Amanda her jacket. Without a word, they walked together to the elevator, the tension between them pulling, pushing. The anxious door opened, after the chime begged for the couple to enter. My son pressed the button for the seventh floor, and his hand found Amanda's. Their hot fingers teased and caressed one another, remaining interlocked until they reached Race's room.

Once inside, Amanda stood with her back against the wall, her voice tame but firm. "I don't think it's a good idea for us to spend the night together."

Race covered his shock and disappointment with a sly smirk. "I agree." He'd never been in a hotel room alone with a woman who shot him down before he even made a move. "That was the last thing on my mind."

Running her hand through her shock of short silver hair, Amanda raised a well-manicured eyebrow. "The last thing on your mind? Why does that sound like an insult?"

"It wasn't an insult," Race said. "It was a lie."

She kicked off her shoes, sucked on her lips and moved closer to him.

My son stepped aside, opened the minibar door and said, "Now, is there any way you wouldn't agree to not having another drink with me?"

"Yes. I mean, no. I mean, what?" Amanda threw her jacket on the back of a chair, and they laughed hard while she plugged her phone charger into an outlet by the desk.

As the couple relaxed on the love seat, side by side, sharing a beer, Race admitted his recent DUI. "It was a fluky traffic stop, cop said he saw me swerving. I don't know, maybe I should quit drinking for a while, but I don't *really* have a problem." He leaned back, handed Amanda the beer can, and chuckled. "Wow, I sound like such a cliché."

She pulled off her socks and dropped them onto the floor. "Why not get some help?"

"I will," he said, "when I get back from Boston."

Amanda set the can on the end table. "Hey, remember at dinner, about my fear of water?" Her voice was steady as she leaned into Race, glancing up to catch his eyes. "You asked me why I was afraid, but I never got the chance to answer."

"Did you almost drown or something?"

"When I was a little girl, I had a neighbor, Nellie O'Bryant. We were in first grade together, and she had an in-ground pool in her backyard." Amanda leaned forward, propping her elbows on her knees and averting Race's eyes. "The day before my seventh birthday, Nellie invited me over to swim. Her parents weren't home, and she had one of those big black rubber inner tubes… and… we were playing this game in the shallow end where we'd hold hands and stand on the tube, trying to keep our balance. I just, I remember laughing so hard I could barely breathe. We kept doing it over and over again, for ten, fifteen minutes, I don't know, but it was so fun. Nellie was so… I can see her smiling, climbing back up onto the tube and… 'One more time,' she said, but it sounded like one long giggle. I got on, and we got to our knees, wobbling on the water, and we slowly stood up, holding hands. But then… I don't know why but… we were drifting close to the edge and I… I let go of her and fell backward, and the last thing I saw was her trying to keep her balance but falling back, too. She looked so… She was so scared. Then I heard a thud underwater, like a hammer hitting the side of the pool, echoing, ringing in my ears. When I came to the surface, Nellie was… She was floating on her stomach with… with blood in the water, all around her head. I didn't know what to do, just froze. But it was too late to help, and I was… Oh, God…"

My son moved closer to Amanda, placed a calm hand on her back, and let the silence breathe. She turned to him, and he ran his fingers along her forehead, quelling the ghost hidden in her brow, the specter haunting her memory. When she closed her eyes, a tear escaped and clung to her lashes, waiting for permission to drop. She fell into him, sliding down and curling up, then rested her head on his thigh.

"It's okay," Race whispered, moving his hand onto the small of her back, pressing his palm against her spine. "You're okay. I'm here."

"Thank you." She opened her eyes. "I don't know… It's just crazy, everything is too unpredictable. Water, wind, cars, animals, people… they're all killers. We live with them every day, but they can all turn on us in a second."

Race wouldn't turn on her—he'd be predictable and harmless—and hoped to be someone Amanda would always open up to, would want by her side. He leaned back on the love seat, his forearm alert and standing guard on her hip. "Hey, remember what you told me on the bus," he said, "about relationships ending?"

"Yeah."

"Why do you think it happens?"

Amanda sighed. "Who knows? I just feel like, no matter

how much they shine at the start, over time, all our connections lose their luster. Misunderstandings, hurt feelings, unmet expectations… they pull us apart. It's human nature. We evolve, our needs and priorities change. Emotional baggage, grudges… all of it conspires against us."

"What about relationships that *do* last? What's the secret?"

"I'm no expert," Amanda said with a slight smile, "and I don't think it's a miracle when people stay together. They just beat the odds."

As they talked, her words grew fainter, her breathing now steady and rhythmic. My son's spirit warmed the moment she fell asleep, her pretty head resting on his stomach now, her quiet hands folded. He'd met no one quite like her—someone who was unapologetically herself, who seemed to face life's challenges straight on, who accepted her fate with grace. But he had to admit, he didn't really know this person. Not in the way he wanted to.

Twenty minutes passed, maybe an hour, and their bodies settled in together. Joining. Molding. Her interlocked arms formed a pillow on his lap, and Race closed his eyes. As he focused on Amanda's breathing, a vision of her lulled him onto a cloud of pleasure. Then, he, too, fell asleep, while her aura played games with his thoughts, a dream of wanting to be a better man taking root.

It was five o'clock. The early morning light filtered through the windows of Race's hotel room, casting a guiltless glow across the space. His cell phone alarm caromed off the walls, and he stirred on the love seat with a blanket from the bed covering him. The distant sounds of traffic outside told my son that the city had already opened its eyes, while a whiff of fresh coffee whisking through the air added that Amanda was awake.

He scanned the room, called out her name, but no one responded. An uneasiness creeping into him, he sprung to his feet, the events of the previous night playing back on high speed in his brain. He dipped into the bathroom, found nothing. Searched every corner of the room, no note, no sign of her socks, shoes, or phone charger. Race's heart drove off a cliff when he noticed her bag was missing. Why would she vanish without saying a word? She must've left just minutes earlier, covering him with the blanket and brewing the coffee before sneaking out the door. But why didn't he hear her milling around? And why didn't they trade phone numbers?

His bus to Boston would depart in one hour, making stops in Buffalo and New York City. He showered and dressed, hoping he'd find Amanda waiting for him in the hotel lobby. But when he got downstairs, his hopes went up in smoke as quickly as she had. With a dramatic sigh worthy of a soap opera, he called an Uber to take him to the station.

On the way there, with the din of desertion thumping in his chest, Race reflected on the people who had come and gone in his life. From Amanda's sudden disappearance to his father's gradual detachment, at some point, everyone left him behind. The only constant had been me, his mother, who had always comforted and supported him. But now I was fading away, too, and like all the others, I would eventually abandon him.

Arriving at the bus depot, he bounced from gate to

gate, searching for evidence of the woman he hadn't slept with but had slept beside. Pacing that busy building, forth and back, he was a madman looking for a silver lining in a haystack. Frustration and disappointment stewed in his belly, like the time in Double-A when he dropped an easy fly ball in center that would've ended the game. Amanda had left him without a trace, exactly how he used to leave women behind without saying goodbye. But no, this was different; he had shared a genuine closeness with Amanda, something magical and worth exploring. Something he'd felt only one other time.

He let his mind wander back to his glory days, when he and Jessica were in high school. Since freshman year, they had been on-again, off-again, navigating the complexities of immature love. After graduation in 1995, when the Red Sox drafted Race and labeled him as their "next star center fielder," his journey through the minors tested the couple's relationship. He got promoted each year—from rookie ball with the Gulf Coast Red Sox, to Single-A with Sarasota, to Double-A with the Trenton Thunder. Through all the travel and uncertainty, somehow his bond with Jess remained strong. On the night the organization elevated him to Triple-A Pawtucket, Race called Jess from a pay phone at a Pennsylvania diner, got down on a knee and proposed, believing that marriage would narrow his focus and expedite his path to the majors.

But my son's love for America's pastime, and the trappings that accompanied it, trumped his love for his spouse. As Race McIntyre's popularity soared in Pawtucket, he identified as an athlete only, not a husband, and others recognized him as such. This measured persona had been years in the making. When he was young, baseball had defined him, shaped him. He was muscular and strong, agile and aware, fast as lightning. The part of himself he respected the most was the ball-playing part. The sport allowed him to impress fans who had never met him, to earn their praise without saying a word. My son struggled to articulate what baseball meant to him, couldn't explain why putting on a pair of spikes and sliding his hand into his glove offered him a glimpse of the star he aspired to become. But as he roamed center field, moving like the wind across the grass, or sprinted around the bases with the grace of a gazelle, or connected with a perfectly placed pitch and the ball exploded off his bat, he was the happiest boy who ever lived.

At twenty-three, Race and Jess tied the knot, their young hearts full of hope for the future. They faced the difficulties of trying to start a family, all the while waiting for Race's call-up to Boston. When the promotion finally came, seven plodding years later, it was a dream come true. But the euphoria evaporated in a flash as the Red Sox sent him back down to Triple-A after just one game, leaving him defeated and uncertain about his future. He hung up his spikes the following spring, claiming that after multiple surgeries, his damaged knees and aching back couldn't take the pounding anymore. But it was his ego that couldn't withstand the beating.

According to Race, his marriage with Jess ultimately fell apart because she hadn't believed in his dream of making it to the major leagues. *She never trusted me*, he thought on the gray afternoon when he spied the divorce papers on the kitchen counter under a coffee mug he'd bought for her birthday. It was a pretty ceramic mug, orange and yellow, with *Trust Me* written on the side. As time went on, his frustration toward her only intensified, and he saw her as the cause of his unhappy life in Sea Point. She didn't offer any support or encouragement, just hurt him more with her snarky comments, leaving him fed up and bitter about their relationship. No one could save what they once had, and their love began its long journey of rotting.

As the sun rose behind the Chicago terminal, passengers on the bus to Buffalo settled in around Race. They were a weird and weary goulash of travelers, jabbering and laughing, creating an aggravating backdrop of off-white noise. The Greyhound departed, and Race watched the streets pass by outside his window—final flitters of the city where he'd spent a memorable night with an unforgettable woman.

He glanced at the empty seat beside him, while his union with Amanda lingered in his brain—a beautiful conundrum wrapped in a bothersome enigma. It was a sweet-smelling spoilage, a fragrant corpse. Race stewed over her departure. *How could she not leave her number?* His mind swayed and swished, his sentiments scattering like dandelion seeds in a hurricane. *Did I misread her?* At that possibility, a fistful of frustration smacked him in the kisser. *Did I come on too strong or not strong enough?*

The raindrops of uncertainty dotted Race's road ahead. He'd seen this movie before; my son had missed another opportunity, one that might've changed the course of his life in unexpected ways. Maybe for the better.

We're Ready

THE MIDDLE OF the night always frightens me. For lots of reasons.

No matter what kind of day the previous day was, it's over and done with, and a new day will begin in a few hours. But how will I handle it? Probably no better than I did the day before. But also, maybe soon, a day will arrive when I'll remember even less than the ones that have gone by. That last day of my life, I'll be as irrecoverable as the days that have passed. Yes, one day my eyes will no longer look out at the world. They will miss morning roll call. The sun will rise for others, but not for me.

Sometimes, in the middle of the night, I reconcile all of my pain, apologies, and mistakes. Alone in the dark, I wonder, since life will end one day, why not forgive myself and live again, one more time? Why not try to recall what's worth living for? If there is a God, I hope she grants me the courage to continue my journey and face the end with the same bravery I've always admired in others.

Now, what am I looking for? Something that's just out of sight.

They say only love can outlast death. But who's *they?* I'm not sure, but in the middle of the night, when love is a world away and my childhood wounds throb, death appears as a solitary light on a dark mountain road, where I have lost my way forever.

Daddy once told me that all lives intertwine with other lives, and when I'm gone, much more than my life will go along with me. When Race connected with Amanda, they became intertwined as well. Then after she left, a part of him went with her, too.

During my son's day-and-a-half journey from Chicago to Boston, he rode a Tilt-A-Whirl of moods that changed as often as the scenery. He spent most of the trip with his headphones on, listening to music, staring out the window, and sleeping. He didn't even remember stopping in Buffalo. Now, it was Saturday, October 27. When he stepped off the bus that afternoon, into the bosom of Boston, he felt like he was home for some strange reason—probably because it was raining.

My boy hurried to a taxi stand, juddering like a jackhammer with every anxious step. He shifted his focus from the woman he'd lost in the Windy City to the one he hoped to find in Cambridge. Willow Spelman was the riddle he was here to solve.

Aside from scuffling with thoughts of Amanda and Willow, my son wrestled with memories of his glorious failure in Beantown. Like falling into a recurring nightmare, he recalled the haunting at bat during his one and only game with the Red Sox. The cheers, the pressure, the unexpected fastball, the sting of the strikeout, and the jeers that followed. An everlasting moment of humiliation, the sour start *and* end to his big league career.

Race grabbed a cab to his hotel. The cheery driver whistled "Sweet Caroline" as they drove by Fenway Park. Happiness personified behind the wheel, the elderly cabbie wore a yellow fedora atop a gray fluff of cotton-candy hair. He stopped whistling and said, "Welcome to Boston, buddy boy." The man spoke like a national news anchor, without a speck of an accent and no trace of an ornery attitude. The way my son described him, he was to Boston cabbies what librarians are to Black Sabbath groupies: the anti-stereotype.

Race grunted.

The driver flashed a grateful grin. "When do you think this rain'll stop?"

"Dunno."

"What's that?" The cabbie swiveled and glanced at my son. "Sorry, my darn hearing hasn't been the same since the war."

"I said, I don't know." Race enunciated the five syllables as if he were a worried parent admonishing a rambunctious three-year-old on a crowded sidewalk.

"Chance of snow? Maybe." The cabbie laughed. "Where are we, the Swiss Alps?"

My son threw his head back. "Yep."

"How 'bout our Sox up two games to one?"

"Mm."

"This place'll go bonkers if we win the next two in Los Angeles."

"Haven't been paying attention." It had been a while since Race caught a ball game on TV, and he especially avoided watching the Red Sox. Through the rain-streaked window, he stared at the famous CITGO sign looming beyond Fenway's outfield walls.

"Well, you won't believe it, buddy boy." The driver pushed up the brim of his fedora and got an eyeful of Race in the rearview mirror. "We won the first two at home, but yesterday, the Dodgers got a walk-off dinger in the eighteenth inning."

"You don't say." Race figured the cabbie might recognize him and bring up the infamous record my son held as the player with the second longest minor league career before appearing in a major league game. Thirteen years of tempered glory, and for what?

"Tonight's the big one," the cabbie said. "If we can win Game Four, we'll be one victory away from another title. Mookie's gotta do more than he did yesterday though, went hitless in seven at bats. He's our leader. We go as he goes."

Boston's center fielder, twenty-six-year-old Mookie Betts, one of the best players in the majors, had started his career four years earlier, in 2014. In an ideal scenario where my son's career had gone according to plan, Betts would have succeeded Race in center, a graceful passing of the torch, as smooth and poetic as a serene river carried by the whispers of the wind.

"Mookie won't come through," Race said. "The guy's overrated."

"Underrated? I agree," the driver said, nodding. "I got faith in that kid."

"He'll tighten up." My son's glance met the old man's eyes in the mirror. "Just watch."

The cabbie smiled and whistled another Neil Diamond tune, singing out the lyrics when he reached the chorus. "'And I'll be what I am, a solitary man.'" The taxi pulled up in front of Race's hotel. "Enjoy your stay," the driver said. "And go Sox!"

Like an exhausted zombie, my son handed the old man the fare without breathing a word of thanks, then walked inside and checked in at the front desk. Brow crumpled, Race shuffled into the elevator, feeling like a success and a failure at the same time. In his dull hotel room, he hung up his wet coat and put the old brown notebook of songs on the nightstand. The room smelled like mildew and despair. Outside, the bangs and beeps of construction and delivery trucks cramped the air, clattering in Race's skull. He flopped onto the bed and opened the songbook.

> ### *"Brightest Colors"*
> *July 1981*
>
> *I can dream about tomorrow and look back*
> *at yesterday*
> *But it will not erase the sorrow that I'm feel-*
> *ing today*
>
> *When you were with me all the brightest colors*
> *colored my world*
> *Now all I have are faded memories of when you*
> *were my girl*

*So, the days I spent beside you, they may
never return
But the flame in my heart for you will continue
to burn*

*And if you ever asked me back again, you know I'd
be there
For though we cannot be together, I still can't help
but care*

My son lay on the hotel room bed and sighed, his warped perspective clouded with doubt. He once again questioned his motives for embarking on this journey. Would the pursuit of this shadowy woman be worth the effort? Why should he care? He was positive his dad never cared about *him*, and now the man was dead. The irritating memory of his father and their strained relationship added fuel to the psychological bench-clearing brawl going on inside Race's head. He flashed back to the last conversation he had with Colin, the yelling that erupted, the wrath it unleashed. But he shoved the image out of his mind.

He sprang out of bed, grabbed his coat and the songbook. He had to act; he couldn't wait any longer for some amount of closure or a trifle of understanding. He believed that the book in his hand held the key to unraveling his father's secrets, and he was intent on finding out more. As he scuttled toward the door, his brain twitched with questions and an insatiable desire to uncover the truth that had remained hidden for far too long.

Race squirmed in the back seat of a black Ford Fusion, while his Uber driver sucked on a cigarette and navigated the rainy streets of Boston.

Gagging on the smoke, my son fixed his gaze on the scribbles in his father's old notebook: *Seven Mt. Auburn, Cambridge, Willow Spelman, end of time.* The words held an otherworldly allure, a trail of breadcrumbs he hoped would lead him to the answers he sought. Sour nerves swirled along with the coffee in Race's stomach. He mouthed the name, trying to surmise its significance. *Willow Spelman*—why was she important to his father? But also, how could my son be completely sure this was the woman Colin had written the songs for?

"Aren't you sick of this fucking place?" The driver's smoky voice broke through Race's thoughts as the car sped toward Cambridge, home of the prestigious Harvard University.

"I'm not from here," Race said.

"You're lucky." The driver's chiseled arms protruded from the sleeves of his tight blue T-shirt, while his chest bulged and the veins in his neck rippled. Even his mustache had muscles.

My son checked his phone—just past four o'clock. "How much farther?"

"Ten minutes," the guy said. "Gotta get through this shithole town first."

"This isn't Cambridge?"

"No, even worse." The driver rolled down his window and spat into the wind. "Watertown."

"What's the difference?"

"Rich assholes in Cambridge and like ten million fucking Armenians in Watertown. I swear it makes me puke, illegals pouring over the border every day, infesting our country like fucking maggots. We're taking it back, though. You can count on that."

As the car crossed the Watertown border and entered the slick streets of Cambridge, Race squinted at the buildings and the pedestrians passing by. The architecture seemed to tell a story of history and progress, a blend of old and new that mirrored his own journey to uncover the past. The raindrops on the window blurred the scene, as if nature itself was conspiring to keep the city's secrets hidden.

My son drummed his fingers on the seat, his eyes flicking between the road ahead and the driver's face in the mirror. Tension lined Race's square jaw, his foot tapping an impatient rhythm against the floorboard. He was an outsider in a strange new world, a world that held potential connections to his father's unreadable biography. In my son's hands, the notebook felt both comforting and daunting. Like how Race felt when trotting out to center in the top of the ninth during his appearance with the Sox, after manager Terry Francona inserted him into the game as a defensive replacement for the oft-injured Jacoby Ellsbury. That one inning against the Yankees marked the end of a journey, but the book in his hand was the beginning of another, the key to understanding Colin's inexplicable life.

As the smoke-filled Uber approached the address on Mt. Auburn Street, Race's heartbeat put the pedal to the metal. On the brink of something significant, my boy was ready to face the woman who, according to his father's saccharine songs, had driven a wedge between him and Colin—and between Colin and me. My son wanted answers, a resolution, and the opportunity to vanquish the ghosts that had haunted him for so long. He seethed at the very idea of Willow Spelman, and his father's betrayal churned in his gut, fueling his animosity. His mouth watered, his pent-up frustration banging at destiny's door. Race craved revenge like a retired ballplayer craves a second chance and planned on repaying that hussy for the pain she caused.

The car slowed to a stop.

"This is it?" Race asked, staring out the window at a bland five-story concrete building in Harvard Square, gloomy and unwelcoming in the rain.

"Must be," the driver grunted. "No number on the door, but GPS says it's your spot."

"Who'd want to live here?" my son whispered to himself, assuming there might be apartment units inside.

He stepped into the rain, his body temperature jumping through the clouds, his pulse playing double Dutch with trepidation and determination. "Thanks," he said to the driver before slamming the door shut.

The car sped off.

Ahead of Race, Mt. Auburn Street stretched out past the limits of his sight, an unknown path leading to an unknown place. People rushed about on sidewalks, holding umbrellas tight. The trees alongside the road, with their leaves turning red and yellow, stood out against the dull sky. The air smelled like wet grass.

With the songbook stashed inside his backpack, Race stomped toward the lifeless building, each step bringing him closer to the truth. The rain continued to fall, washing away any last remnants of indecision. His only questions now:

What does Willow Spelman look like and how will she react when I introduce myself?

Race sloshed over the slick pavement, searching for a sign of familiarity in this part of town he had never visited. He couldn't believe he was doing this—about to confront the stranger who had destroyed his family. As much as he wanted revenge, a part of him wondered if his brave attempt would bring closure or just open up old wounds. But he couldn't stop now, not after years of unanswered questions and broken trust. He had to see this woman, even if it meant facing the painful truth.

:21

Used to Bad News

You! You saw her? My sister? She's gone... where? How? Thoughts scrambled... pieces missing. My hand, take it! This weight, my chest. Chasing me, chasing! Find her... the girl. Hold on!

⤳

Race stood in front of the building at 7 Mt. Auburn Street and waited several moments before approaching the entrance. The door was locked, and a sign declared that the space was available for lease. His trail had gone cold.

"Motherfucker," he said.

He explored further, rounding the corner of the building. On the other side, several abandoned storefronts lined the street. Only one shop seemed to be open—a custom framing store. With a smidgeon of hope, Race entered, fixated on finding information about Willow Spelman or any link to the address in the notebook.

Inside the store, a college-age woman behind the counter chewed on the end of a red pen. When she saw Race, she slid the pen behind her ear and said, "Hi there."

"Hey, do you work with someone named Willow?"

"How do you know I'm not her?" The young woman's appearance hadn't stirred Race at first, but when she smiled, he saw her in a different light.

"I don't know," he said. "You just don't look like a Willow."

"What do Willows look like?"

Humored and annoyed, he asked, "What's your name?"

"Imani." The young woman was short and busty, with a collection of small silver rings piercing her lips and eyebrows. An indecipherable neck tattoo seeped into her dark, glossy skin. She sported torn jeans, an untucked white blouse, and a cleanly shaved head.

"You go to school here?"

"Grad student at MIT."

"Got it," Race said.

"Massachusetts Institute of Technology," Imani added, her tone pen-point sharp.

"I know what it stands for."

"My bad." The woman ran a palm over her bald dome and pushed out another smart smile. "Usually, hot guys don't have the brains to match their looks."

"Consider me an exception." Race opened his backpack and showed Imani the name and address on a faded page in his father's songbook. "Seven Mt. Auburn. Isn't that this place?"

The woman grabbed the book and examined the note. "Yes, but other than this store, the building is empty."

"Who else works here?"

"My boss, Carol."

"Can you call her?" Race reached out to take the notebook back from Imani. "Hopefully, she knows more than you."

"Wait." Imani chewed on her pen, stared at the front cover, then flipped through the pages. "There are tons of songs in this notebook, more than just seven. Why would someone write 'Seven Songs' on the front?"

"Maybe he originally planned to write seven of them," Race said, "but then he kept going."

"Or maybe, in this case, 'Seven' isn't a number, it's a name."

"That's a stretch. I've never heard of anyone named Seven."

"Stands within reason though," Imani said. "You can't deny the logic."

"MIT must be *so* proud of you."

"Listen, there's another Mt. Auburn around here—Mount Auburn Cemetery, about a mile away. It's an enormous place, over a hundred acres, mostly in Watertown, but with a Cambridge entrance." Imani pointed to the address written on the page. "Maybe the 'Mt. Auburn' scribbled here refers to the cemetery."

Race's muscles twerked. Could this quirky young woman's calculated idea lead him somewhere useful? "Worth a shot, I guess," he said.

She stuck the red pen back behind her ear. "It's a simple case of computational complexity theory and the concept of NP-hardness."

Race's face scrunched up. "Sounds like a case of erectile dysfunction," he said. "Can I get a translation?"

"It's a mathematical theory that classifies problems into different complexity classes based on their difficulty and the resources needed to solve them. NP-hard problems include those for which no known polynomial-time algorithm exists."

Race blinked twice.

"The odds of solving these problems," Imani continued, "can be challenging because experts believe that solving them with existing algorithms would take exponential time. Meaning, as the problem size increases, the time to solve it grows exponentially, rendering it impractical to solve within a reasonable time limit."

"I have no idea what you're talking about," Race said. "But I appreciate the help." Before leaving the store, he considered asking Imani for her phone number but thought better of it. Usually his libido called all the shots, but now his throbbing noggin needed to focus on the newfound lead.

As an ambitious drizzle persisted, he carved his way through Harvard Square, following the GPS on his phone to the cemetery. An uneasiness hovered around, as if the rain had a message for him but was too bashful to cough it up. The scent of damp pavement mingled with the odor of car exhaust and pastries, creating a curious conglomerate of comfort and disquiet. Tall buildings loomed overhead, their facades shimmering with a wet sheen, casting long, hulking shadows in the ashen light. Despite the rain's soothing touch, an unspoken tension loomed in the air, suspended like a ghost in the fog.

The sprinkle tapped an offbeat rhythm on Race's shoulders. His backpack, loaded with zeal, was so heavy that every step demanded immense effort. Despite the gray skies, the energy of the square enveloped him, pulling him into its hectic embrace, while pangs of determination and hesitation poked at him. His mind swam with opinions about his father's indefinable past and the journey ahead. Yet, amid the inner turmoil, there was a sniff of hope. He was on the scent, and it was getting stronger.

Darkness would soon cloak the city. When Race arrived at the entrance to Mount Auburn Cemetery, he found a stoic groundskeeper standing with a shovel behind a black iron gate. The man looked a lot like former Boston pitcher Oil Can Boyd, one of Race's childhood heroes, with a thin gray mustache and a Red Sox cap perched on his head. He gripped the wooden handle of his rusty shovel as one might hold a newborn, gentle yet firm. The groundskeeper's loose black sweatshirt and baggy blue overalls hung off his slender frame like an outfit designed for a scarecrow. The glint in his eye suggested he'd rob you blind in a game of poker without even knowing how to play.

When Race approached the gate, the tarnished old man swung around. "Can I help you, sonny?"

"Just here for a quick visit," my boy said.

The groundskeeper regarded the watch hanging loose around his wrist, the dark semicircles under his eyes blending in with his dusty, wrinkled face. "Afraid you're too late."

"The sign says you're open till eight."

"True, but we shut down at five after daylight savings time."

"That's still a week away," Race said.

"True again, but in late October, we lock these gates tight right around dusk." The old man appeared to smile. "Nothing good happens here after dark."

"Give me ten minutes."

"Can't do it."

The drizzle had morphed into mist, and my son removed the hood of his sweatshirt from his head, raking the hair away from his eyes. "I didn't get your name," Race said to the stoic groundskeeper.

"I didn't give it to you." The old man adjusted his Red Sox cap.

"Fair enough," my son said. "I'm Race McIntyre." He hoped his borderline celebrity status might gain him entry to the graveyard.

The groundskeeper squinted through the iron bars. "Hmm, you seem familiar. Do I know you?"

"Probably. I used to play baseball in the Red Sox organization."

"Oh, yes, Race McIntyre." The old man's eyes sparkled. "Five-tool outfielder, built like a Mack Truck, faster than a Maserati. It's really you, huh?"

"In the flesh."

"Holy Moses, I sure thought you'd become a superstar someday." The groundskeeper wielded his shovel like a baseball bat. His smile was grim, a wry, gap-toothed grin, the space between his teeth wide enough to ride a lawn mower through. "I was really pulling for you, kid."

The comment reaggravated archaic wounds within Race—yet another knifelike reminder of his unfulfilled potential and missed opportunities. Shifting the topic, my son said, "Hey, do you know if a Willow Spelman works here, or if she's buried here?"

"Can't say I'm friendly with many folks within these gates, least not the ones with a pulse. But after thirty years trimming hedges, pruning trees, and cutting every blade of grass around these gravestones once a week, I'm on a first-name basis with the deceased."

"Is Willow Spelman one of them?"

The groundskeeper shook his head and stroked his mustache. "Don't know her." Then his brow perked up. "But there's a Willow Pond on the grounds *and* a Spelman Road. Might have something to do with what you're looking for."

Race's green eyes glowed. "How about letting me in?"

"Sorry, sonny." The lanky man stuck his shovel into the stubborn earth and pulled a jangling chain of keys from his overalls. "Told you already, shutting the place down for the night."

"I just need a few minutes."

With rigid fingers, the groundskeeper counted the keys on the chain until he found the one he needed. "Hey, I don't make the rules," he said without looking up.

"But can't you bend them for a former superstar ballplayer?"

"Nope," the man chuckled, inspecting a long brass skeleton key. "Can't bend them for you either."

"Thanks for nothing," Race said. "You open tomorrow?"

"Seven days a week," the old man replied. "Dearly departed don't request time off."

My son nodded and pivoted, about to walk away.

"Hey, superstar!" the man called out.

Race wheeled around.

"It's Jeb, by the way."

"What?"

"My name, it's Jeb, short for Jebediah." He locked the gate, removed the key, and rattled the bars to double-check his handiwork, an angry clanging sound reverberating down the street. "My wife says it means 'friend of God' in Hebrew."

Race laughed and shouted, "No wonder you're holding the keys!"

⁘

I never blamed Colin for his rocky relationship with our son, but I couldn't explain to Race why his father was the way he was. My husband, by placing grief above people, broke our son's heart early, and drove him away.

After everything that happened with Sevan, Colin fell into a bizarre reality, or rather, an addiction to unreality. At a tender age, Colin had lost his perception of self. How could he love Race if he didn't know himself? How could Race grow up, confident and self-assured, if no one loved him? According to my daddy, a child can go without money, security, safety, and possessions, but if there isn't a loving example to follow, the child becomes lost.

Colin never gave Race limits, never took time to show him what to do, what *not* to do, how to act, or how to behave. If I hadn't done those things for him, Race would've spent his life trying to discover them. Maybe I didn't do a good enough job, didn't teach our son where his limits were, or prepare him well for his journey. But I can't blame Colin—before we met, he had become an ageless boy, determined to remain young, writing songs for a ghost, living in the past. No, I don't blame my husband. It's not his fault we are where we are.

During Colin's weekday visits to Blue Horizons, I tried to tell him I forgave him for not loving our son as fully as a father should. I tried to say I understood. One day I will explain the total story to Race, too, and I look forward to the weekends when he stops by and sees me. He shows up each Saturday, or maybe Sunday—and someday, I promise I'll tell him the truth. Why haven't I told him yet? I fear his judgment.

Now I'm lost and disconnected. Losing myself. Falling apart. Why? I can't find a reason for sure. I keep drawing and redrawing my son's face in my mind, searching for him and getting to know him again. But that weekend in late October when Race didn't visit plopped a peach pit in my stomach, left me plum queasy. Where was he? What happened to him? Why hadn't he come to see me? My psyche spun with worst-case scenarios, and I couldn't help but worry that something horrible had occurred. I sat like a statue in my recliner and couldn't move, weighty as a grand piano, my hands too tense to tremble.

"It's okay, Miss Holly," Rose said, spreading a blanket over my lap. "You just relax." My friend knew I wasn't feeling hunky-dory. She measured my days by the accuracy of my lipstick application: the more the color strayed from my mouth, the more anxious I was.

Where is Race? I struggled to say. *Where is my boy?*

Rose, my constant support in times of turmoil, leaned over and wrapped me in her arms. It was almost like she could read my thoughts. "Your son will be back next weekend."

Why? Where?

But even as she reassured me of Race's safety and that he had informed her of his absence, a discomfort clawed at my chest. Why hadn't he contacted me? Was he avoiding me? Every word from Rose's mouth only fueled the torrid questions in my mind.

Sinking into my chair, cocooned in the warmth of Rose's handmade blanket, I struggled to calm the storm raging inside me. Each stitch of that familiar blanket only amplified the pain in my soul. Was this all a facade to hide something sinister? I surmised there was more to Race's disappearance than what I could or couldn't remember.

Despite Rose's soothing words, my nerves refused to relent. I pointed to the phone, as if suggesting I'd call Race myself, desperate for any sign of his well-being. As Rose dialed his number, my heart thudded against my ribs. When Race responded and Rose began speaking to him, relief rushed through me like white-water rapids. But along with it came a mistrust that gripped at my throat.

Rose and Race conversed in hushed tones, their words colorless, private. I couldn't help but notice Rose's caution with what she was saying, like there were things she didn't want me to overhear. After a brief exchange, Rose handed the phone to me, her eyes voicing her quiet concerns.

Race! I wanted to say. *Where have you been? What's going on?*

My son's patient voice on the other end of the line reassured me. He explained he was in Boston, searching for an old friend. His words left me with a bit of déjà vu, as if we'd had the same conversation just a week earlier, or maybe a decade ago.

Your father loved Boston, I recalled, a touch of nostalgia seeping into my brain, *and he knew every song by heart.* The memory of Colin's fondness for the band tickled my thoughts with a bittersweet touch.

"Now, Mom, I know you might be thinking of Boston the band," Race said with a laugh, "but I'm talking about Boston, the city."

As my son questioned me about his father's visits to New England and my knowledge of someone named Willow and Colin's "Seven Songs" notebook, the inquiries confused me. It was like the time when, after I'd nailed a set at a lounge in Columbus, half the crowd gave me a standing ovation, while the other half chucked rotten fruit at me. My belly ached at the miles between us; I couldn't understand why my son had embarked on his cross-country journey.

"I'll be back next week," he said.

I wanted to make him promise not to leave me like that again, to keep me in the loop about his whereabouts and his intentions. I couldn't bear the idea of him disappearing from my life without a trace. The pain of Colin's absence was still fresh in my heart, and I didn't want to lose my son, too.

I should've asked Race if Colin was in Boston with him, and if they were together exploring the city. *I haven't seen your father in a few days*, I tried to say.

The phone call left me with more questions than answers. My son reminded me that Colin wouldn't be visiting me anymore, wouldn't be sharing his stories with me, but he didn't explain why. This new information about my husband deepened the mystery, bamboozling me more than ever.

Before we hung up, I wanted to say goodbye. *I love you, Race. Tell me you know that.*

"I love you, Mom," he said.

After I handed Rose the phone, I lifted the lid to my music box. The beautiful tune played, taking me back in time. I reached into the box and pulled out my son's first baseball card from his rookie year in the minors, still glossy after all these years. How handsome he was, and so very proud to be playing the game that he loved. We were all proud, even Colin, I suspect. From the mahogany box, the song continued to play, and I sang to myself: *If you care, don't let them know. Don't give yourself away.*

In my room that late afternoon, the light was out of balance with the dark. The shadows on the wood floor got longer and longer, but it didn't seem like night would arrive soon. I sat in my recliner, in the stillness, and felt a twinkle of joy. The gentle sounds, the extended patches of quiet, and the golden hour itself made it less painful to say goodbye to the day. Little birds sang in the trees outside my window. A car passed in the far distance, and the cedars swayed in the breeze. Someday, I hope, that kind of peace will consume all of us and we'll disappear forever.

Let Me Take You Home Tonight

To MY SON, Watertown was like every other middle-class suburban neighborhood he had visited during his baseball days, a mundane collection of garden-variety office buildings and stores along ordinary streets. If you removed the New England accents, he could've been in any random Small Town, U.S.A. However, the red, blue, and orange flags flying above the gas stations and the aroma of baba ghanoush in the air might convince anyone that a group of Armenian food enthusiasts had established the town of thirty-three thousand, rather than seventeenth-century English settlers.

Standing outside the gates of Mount Auburn Cemetery, Race pocketed his phone. The mist in the air had morphed back into a steady drizzle, reflecting the discouragement in my son's bones. He stared at the iron gate while raindrops raced down the shiny black bars, faster than his plummeting thoughts. He pulled his sweatshirt hood over his head.

Then the skies opened up. Before ordering an Uber

back to his hotel, Race sought refuge from the relentless downpour. He dashed across the street, finding shelter in a nearby grocery store. In his haste, he hadn't noticed the sign outside, but as he stepped inside, his eyes landed on the words above the door: *Armenian Jewel Specialty Market.*

A pretty woman, no older than thirty, stood behind the counter, her long, dark hair draped over her shoulders. She wore a moving smile, with eyes as sensuous and playful as grape jelly beans. Race's chuckle caught her attention, and she asked, "Something funny?"

"Not really, just never heard of a grocery store described as a jewel," he replied, brushing off the cold and wiping the moisture off his jacket.

Before the woman spoke again, her nose crinkled, and she came out from behind the counter. "There's a famous lake in our country, Lake Sevan. It's known as the Jewel of Armenia. My mother named this store for her friend with the same name."

"Her friend's name is Jewel?"

"No, Sevan."

Beside an array of cans and boxes stacked on wire shelving, the full-figured woman entranced my son, her silky midnight locks framing a face that conveyed a quiet confidence. Clad in a black skirt that hugged her hips and a cotton sweater the color of storm clouds, she upgraded the yawnsome atmosphere of the shop.

"It's nasty out there," Race said.

"Did you come in for food or shelter," she said, sizing up my son, "or something else?"

"All the above." He took off his hood and brushed a wet strand of hair off his cheek.

"Then you're in the right place."

The curvy woman, with her polite demeanor, emitted a starlit aura, but one that seemed to dim by the minute. She looked like someone who'd awoken from an amazing dream when she was a child and had devoted her life to trying to get back into it.

As he had done countless times before in the company of pretty girls, Race put on a performance, his charisma strutting to the forefront. He beamed and leaned against the counter. "What's your name?"

"Khloe," she said with a grin. "It means 'orchid' in Armenian."

"Wow, yet another voluptuous Armenian named Khloe." Race glanced at a dull wedding ring on the woman's finger. "Sorry, but the extent of my Armenian knowledge starts and ends with *Keeping Up with the Kardashians*."

"That's okay." Khloe twirled a lock of hair resting on her shoulder. "If you're willing, I could teach you a few things."

"Sounds great," my son said, gladly taking the bait. "But I have to warn you, I'm a slow learner."

As the innuendos swelled, an older woman appeared from the back of the store, her eyes piercing and dark, her short brown hair flecked with gray. She wore a mask of suspicion draped over her face, and ruby earrings shaped like halved pomegranates dangled from her lobes. Striding down the aisle, the woman threw a sideways look at Race and blurted, "Can we help you with your selection, sir?"

My son leered at Khloe. "Thanks, but I'm still deciding," he said. "It all looks delicious."

"This is my mother, Sonia," Khloe said, taking the older

woman's hand. "Mom, what would you suggest to someone who's never tasted Armenian food?"

Sonia stared at Race and said, "It all depends on his receptiveness to new discoveries."

Judging by her dubious behavior and ornate earrings, Khloe's mother could've been a thief with blood on her hands, or a gypsy with magic in her eyes.

"I'm not picky," my boy said.

With Race following behind, Sonia weaved in and out of the store's four short aisles, guiding him to a substantial buffet of prepared foods in shiny tins. "We offer many traditional dishes here. You may enjoy our dolma, carefully prepared with rice and spices, or perhaps our kebabs, grilled to perfection. Our salads are fresh and flavorful, with tomatoes, cucumbers, and other vegetables. Our lavash bread is homemade and pairs well with hummus or tzatziki. For dessert, we have baklava and other delicacies."

"It all looks great," Race said, "and smells even better."

"Please take your time and let us know if you need any help."

"Will do," my son said, perusing his options.

Across the aisle, Sonia rearranged several cans of lentils on the shelf, studying him, and asked, "Are you from here?"

"No, just visiting," Race replied. "So, how long have you owned this place?"

"It's been in the family for decades," Sonia said. "But our store is just one of many Armenian businesses in Watertown; our community is deeply connected to our roots."

"Cool," my son said. "If it ever stops raining, I'll check out the area."

Sonia beamed. "If you get the chance, visit the Armenian

Museum of America. It's a wonderful place, a true testament to our heritage."

"I'd love to," he said, "but I might not have time."

"If you explore our city, you will feel the culture, warmth, and hospitality that has thrived here for generations."

"I apologize for my mother," Khloe said, stepping between Sonia and Race. "She gets a little excited when visitors stop in from out of town."

"It's fine." My son dove into Khloe's big brown eyes. "This is all really interesting."

Khloe gazed back. "What's your name, anyway?"

"It's Race."

Khloe turned to her mother. "So, let's get Race something to eat?"

Sonia's face went ashen, as if she'd stumbled upon a ghost. "Sorry, what was that?"

"Race's food." Khloe tilted her head and gawked at her mom, who was picking at her fingernails while staring at the floor. "What should he get?"

The silence lasted a lifetime. "Are you okay, ma'am?" my son said, placing a hand on Sonia's arm.

"Excuse me, I forgot to call in a delivery order." The old woman scratched her cheek and retreated toward the back room.

"I'm sorry," Khloe said once her mother was out of earshot. "I don't know what that was about." Her full lips remained parted, as if wanting to add to the story.

"I should go." The skies had cleared, and something about Sonia's urgent departure told Race it was time to return to downtown Boston.

"Here, take this." Khloe handed him what appeared to

be a slice of pizza. "It's on the house, payback for all the weirdness."

My son laughed. "Maybe you should rename your store the Italian Jewel Specialty Market. Seems like a multicultural situation here."

"It's Armenian pizza, called lahmajoun," Khloe said while scribbling on the back of a pink Post-it note. "Let me know if it's too spicy."

"Thanks," Race said. "I'm sure it's perfect."

As my son took a bite, Khloe handed him the slip of paper. "If you get the urge while you're in town," she said with a warm smile, "text me, and I'll show you around."

Later that evening, excited Red Sox fans packed the sports bar across the way from Race's hotel, ready to witness Game 4 of the World Series. A cacophony of frenzied chants swarmed the air, along with the aroma of greasy bar food, the clinking of glasses, and the occasional burst of laughter. The energy was soupy, every cheer and jeer fueled by a potent cocktail of passion and loyalty.

Race, in black jeans and a gray sweatshirt, sat alone at a high-top table near the window, his blue baseball cap pulled low over his emerald eyes. He nursed a pint of Guinness, savoring its rich, roasted flavor. He knew he shouldn't have ordered the beer and probably needed to quit alcohol altogether, but he'd already had a couple of drinks in Chicago. No harm in one more. He wondered where Amanda was at that very instant; wondered why she left him that unfair morning, after all they'd shared.

My son scrolled through the unread texts on his phone.

Jess had sent two messages inquiring about the belongings in his father's house and where to donate them. Glenn had sent one text regarding a realtor search for the McIntyre home, and another updating about the Dedmon mayoral campaign. *You're about to be the big man on campus again, G-Dog,* Race thought. My friend Rose had also messaged my boy, apologizing for her abrupt call earlier that day, explaining that she should've warned him about my deteriorating condition before reaching out. I think that's when Race started worrying about me. Though he's never said so.

From his pocket, he retrieved the slip of paper bearing Khloe's phone number. Teasing the note with his fingers, my son couldn't help but smirk at the cute heart Khloe had drawn around her name. For a minute, he wished it were Amanda's number he held, longing for another opening to explore their connection and what might've been. Why had Amanda vanished? Was the universe playing a cruel joke on him, retaliating for all the times he'd ditched women after one-night stands? Like always, temptation got the best of Race, and he texted Khloe.

The next half hour zipped by in half a second.

When the ravishing woman arrived at the bar, she ushered in an air of intrigue and her presence lit up the room. Khloe was no longer wearing the skirt Race had seen her in earlier. Instead, she had changed into tight jeans and a violet button-down blouse, leaving two buttons unbuttoned. Her pitch-black hair, now pulled into a ponytail, swished over her shoulders and captured the glow of the overhead lamps. With each step, she oozed poise, attitude, and what Race described to me as "reckless femininity," mesmerizing everyone in the room—both men *and* women.

My son stood as Khloe approached. "Hey," he said with a calm smile.

Even in six-inch clogs, the beauty was half a foot shorter than him, and she swanned her neck to catch his eyes. "Hi, stranger," she said.

"You didn't reply to my text." Race pulled a stool out for her. "I wasn't sure you'd come."

She plopped her purse onto the table as they sat next to one another. "I'm not always like this," she said. "I'm really kinda shy."

"Oh yeah? Then I need to meet more shy women." My son laughed, motioned for a server's attention, and swiveled back to Khloe. "You look…"

She placed a finger on Race's lips and said, "Spectacular, I know."

He latched on to her wrist and, with surgical care, moved her hand down to his chest, their gazes fixed on each other. "That's one way of putting it," he said, releasing his grip.

"But not the only way." She spread her fingers wide and pressed them against his heart. Sliding her hand down over his abdomen, she scraped his sweatshirt with her long burgundy nails. Then she stopped and raised a dark eyebrow. He raised one of his own, and they broke into kindred grins.

Two hours flew by while they chatted and drank, their playful teasing launching Race into another world. The whole time, he never once corkscrewed his neck around to glimpse the TV on the wall, never clocked the score of the World Series game as the innings slogged by. He only focused on the sultry Khloe, and the gold wedding band strangling her finger—but not necessarily in that order.

After downing another satisfying gulp of Guinness, my son said, "So, you're married?"

"Kind of." She drew her first sip of her third glass of chardonnay.

Race leaned back. "And you're good with what's happening between us?"

Cheers erupted and the entire bar quaked as my boy glanced at the TV; the Red Sox had surged ahead by three runs in the last inning.

"I can't wait to see this place go berserk when the Sox win," Khloe said amid the commotion.

"That makes one of us." Race wanted to leave the premises before Boston's impending victory; he didn't need another reminder of the team's success in the wake of his own failure.

There was a time, long ago, when my son didn't know the meaning of the word *failure*. Often, I reminisce about his childhood. He was a talented athlete, labeled a "phenom" at an early age, with a unique charisma that everyone in Sea Point loved—except for his competitors, who called him cocky. During his formative years, Race spent more time at his best friend Glenn's house than at our own, slept over several nights per week. Glenn's father, Joe—or maybe it was Jim—coached the two boys on their travel baseball teams. My husband, Colin, well, he didn't give a hoot about sports. To him, Race's dreams meant nothing. I still recall how Joe-Jim Dedmon molded my son into a skilled player, practicing with him daily and providing him with support and guidance, while Colin remained detached. Now, as the broken memories of those days clog my thoughts, I'd kill to hear Race's bashful laughter, watch him compete on Sea

Point's puddle-pocked ball fields, and relive the irretrievable summers of his youth.

Everyone in the sports bar went gaga when the Sox held on for the win, 9–6. Shielding Race's view of the TV, a plump woman in a snug David Ortiz jersey boogied in wide circles and yelled in a thick-as-chowdah accent, "Friggin' awesome, baby! One more *W* and we get another ring!"

My son chugged the last of his beer, slammed the mug on the bar, and turned to Khloe. "Let's get out of here," he said.

Along with the dropping sun, the temperature outdoors had plummeted. The wind, erratic and ticked off, swept through the Boston streets, leaving heaps of dead leaves strewn in the gutters. Neither Race nor Khloe said a peep on the short walk to his hotel, but as soon as they entered his room, Race tasted the tension between them. They both wanted the same thing, he was sure. Khloe untied her ponytail, releasing her hair from bondage, glancing at Race while he made drinks. He filled their glasses with purpose and nonchalance, and the atmosphere buzzed with unspoken desire. The quiet room, charged with anticipation, smoldered with the intimacy about to unfold—the intensity of their seduction, the raw desire that drove them.

No two ways about it, I can understand what Khloe was expecting, plotting, and sensing. Remember, I'd been a young woman once, too; felt that same burning passion before. Knew the explosive gray area between wanting someone and being wanted.

I recall the sweltering summer of 1979, the night that changed everything. Late that July evening, I was singing at a dive bar in Sea Point, my voice weaving its magic over the enthralled audience. Known as Holly "Purple" Hayes onstage back then, I had a way of captivating listeners with my smoky vocals. But offstage, I was more reserved and guarded.

In the middle of "Killing Me Softly," I saw Colin for the first time. Not yet twenty-one years old, he was a very different man from the one who, for four decades, I tried to know and love. He had a sunken shyness about him, but his excessive drinking brought out his sociable nature and helped him cast away his painful past. There was an eleven-year age difference between us and a certain resignation in his eyes, as if he were always leaving something unsaid. And yet, we couldn't resist our chemical connection, a spark that set us both on fire.

That first night, we couldn't keep our hands off each other. Back at my apartment, our heated desire whisked us into the early hours of the morning. Colin's intense eyes consumed me with their combustible combination of longing and danger. Our dialogue was effortless, but there was something foreboding around every subject, like we were hurtling toward a future danger. I still can't shake what he told me the morning after we met. Should've taken it as a warning sign, but his words seemed sweet in the moment: "You're exactly what we need, Hollyann."

That following week, we clung to each other, but it felt more suffocating than loving. We spent all our time at his house, the one that became our family home. Our passion was uncontrollable, devouring everything in its path, and on some nights, I found it hard to keep my voice down. It was all fine that first week—more than fine. But after that, the jitters crept into my vulnerable heart. Was our intensity too good to be true? Or too *true* to be good?

You know, they always say you should fall in love for the right reasons, but no one ever spells out what those reasons are. Colin and I, well, we had our reasons, that's for sure. But were they the right ones? Hard to say. We were young and full of dreams, maybe too full. But we had each other, and that counted for something, I suppose. Maybe it's less about having the right reasons, and more about making the reasons you have right.

Our second week together, Colin said, "You should keep some clothes at my place."

Okay.

The third week, he said, "You should have a key."

Sure.

The fourth week, he said, "Why don't you sell your apartment?"

Back in those early days together, we had our routine: Each morning, he'd jump into his airbrushed van with a moon-shaped side window and head off to the cannery, leaving me to tend to things around the house. Those quiet days imbued us with contentment as we found comfort in the familiar. After Colin came back from work, when the sun dipped low and the shadows lengthened, I'd slip out into the night, making my way downtown to sing in the clubs. Oh, but when I returned home, tired and exhilarated, Colin and I would share a passion that defied time itself. Those nights held a magic all their own, a heat that burned hotter than the rising sun. Then, after he left for work again, I found solace in the rhythm of everyday life—and the companionship of a curious little soul.

Within two months of our whirlwind romance, Colin had proposed, and we became a family of three. Admittedly,

I had never yearned for a child, my dreams tied instead to chasing fame as a singer. Life, though, had its own plans and pulled me into a different story, interlaced with motherhood and love, with no hint of stardom. Something harsh fell away in me then, while something milder emerged, and I became not a better Holly or a worse Holly, but merely a different Holly.

Heaven on Earth

LOVE, TO ME, isn't always the stuff of grand romance or tales of soulmates destined to be together. Sometimes, it's more about duty and purpose, about standing by someone through thin and thick, offering staunch support. But then, there are instances when love is just a matter of the heart—a coupling so acute that it thumbs its nose at logic and explanation. No cry or plea or song or shriek can untangle itself from the roar of love. I wish Colin had reserved some of his love for me, but he had already spent it all elsewhere, long before we ever crossed paths.

My husband once shared another story about Sevan Zakarian that transported him to a memorable October night in 1975. It was Game 6 of the World Series between the Boston Red Sox and the Cincinnati Reds, held at Fenway Park, a forty-minute train ride from Watertown. In two short years of friendship since their chance meeting at the record store, Sevan and Colin shared the biggest parts of their insignificant lives, growing closer despite the stark differences between them—this Irish boy and this Armenian girl.

Before the game at historic Fenway that brisk night, with the Red Sox on the brink of elimination, Sevan followed Colin to their seats in the right field bleachers. "I can't believe you got these tickets," she said, staring at the paper stub in her hand like she'd won the lottery.

Colin loved doing nice things for his friend, he had told me. She'd get down on herself a lot; no matter how happy she seemed on the outside, there was a sadness, a foreboding, behind her dark eyes. "Gimme a break," he said as they squeezed into their seats. "I had to do *something* special for your birthday."

"But you're eighteen days late."

"Not true, I'm forty-nine-and-a-half weeks early." He tugged on his Red Sox cap, smiling sideways. "Did you tell your parents we were going to the game?"

"As far as they know, I'm with Sonia at *The Rocky Horror Picture Show.*"

"You're still ashamed of me, aren't you?"

"Don't be a dunce," Sevan said. "We both know Yeva and Petrak like you way better than they like me."

"Then why lie?"

"Because, to my family, baseball is *way* more American than the movies."

"Got it," Colin said. "Then this stays between us. I can't risk being on their bad side."

With his awkward teenage charm and devil-may-care attitude, Colin had a talent for engaging with people, whereas Sevan projected an air of composed aloofness. They complemented each other in ways that no one could have foreseen. Since meeting, they had laughed, shared secrets, and explored every inch of Watertown together, their bond a bridge between two worlds.

"Have you been to Fenway a lot?"

"Yeah," Colin said, "my dad took me and my brothers a bunch of times."

"How come you never told me that?"

"We just haven't been in a while." He bit his lip and scratched his neck. "You know, not since what happened with Liam."

When the game began, Fenway Park was a spirited symphony—the smell of grilled hot dogs, the fizzy taste of soda, and the roar of the crowd all overloading Colin's senses. Excitement cut through the air, the atmosphere electric.

Between cheers, Sevan leaned into Colin and said, "Did you hear Mother's Milk changed their name?"

"What? They didn't break up, did they?" Colin stiffened, shocked by the news, his jaw hanging open. "Is Tom Scholz still part of the group?"

"Chill out" Sevan said. "They kept most of the same guys. They've even recorded a few new songs, coming out with an album sometime next year."

"What's the name of the band now?"

"Boston."

As the contest unfolded, the tension in the park ratcheted up. Every swing of the bat and every pitch thrown held the promise of victory or defeat. Colin and Sevan had been standing and cheering since the early innings, their feet now sore, their voices hoarse. When Red Sox pinch hitter Bernie Carbo smacked a game-tying three-run homer late in the eighth, the two pals lost their minds, forgetting all about their aching feet and strained voices.

Carbo's teammates mobbed him at home plate, while Sevan cupped her hands and shouted for the entire planet to hear. "Woo-hoo! Way to go, Bernie!"

As the cheering died down, the corners of her mouth curled up a bit, but a full smile never formed. She stared off into the distance, her gorgeous eyes searching for something far beyond the bleachers, for what seemed to Colin like a full minute.

"Hey, you okay?" he asked.

"I feel like running somewhere," she said, or something like that. Her voice was too low for him to pick up her exact words.

He leaned in closer. "What?"

She raked a hand through her long, dark hair and said, "What were we talking about?"

Neither team scored for the next three innings, but then it happened. In the twelfth inning, with the game tied 6–6, Red Sox catcher Carlton "Pudge" Fisk faced Reds reliever Pat Darcy and hit a high drive down the left field line. The three seconds that followed lasted a lifetime.

Colin grabbed Sevan's hand, squeezed her fingers, and yelled, "There it is!"

The crowd craned their collective necks, eyeballing the enormous thirty-seven-foot outfield wall called the Green Monster, while Fisk flailed his arms, attempting to use his body language to keep the ball fair.

Sevan jumped and screamed, "Go, go! Come on! Get out!"

The ball collided with the yellow foul pole for a miraculous game-winning home run, and the stadium erupted in a deafening roar. Colin and Sevan, caught up in the collective insanity, spun and hopped and slapped hands with strangers. During the next sixty ticks of unbridled elation, that never-ending swath of time, they drew closer together, laughing and yelling. Then, with a simple, knowing glance, they embraced. It was as if the universe had conspired to create the perfect moment.

Years later, my husband would tell me his pulse had stopped as he held his friend in the Fenway stands that night. The fresh-flower fumes of her hair filling his heated face. His arms locked around her body, unable and unwilling to let go. "I love you," he whispered to her then.

He couldn't hear her muffled response. Didn't need to.

With the world cheering around them, Colin and Sevan shared their first kiss that magical evening, a kiss drenched in all the hope, excitement, and promise of youth. When their lips met, Colin felt an explosion behind his rib cage, an eruption of unreal belonging—a connection that transcended words and left an indelible mark on his soul.

During our fortyish years of marriage, Colin had been tight-lipped about his childhood. It wasn't until the last year, during our many visits, that he started opening up. I couldn't understand why he shared his stories after all this time, but I welcomed his honesty.

He told me about the tumultuous household he grew up in. Their home on Beechwood Street, near Watertown Square, across from the Perkins School for the Blind, was far from serene. Danny and Orla, Colin's parents, were first-generation Irish immigrants, devout Catholics with a penchant for alcohol and quarreling. In the McIntyre household, arguments were the norm—a relentless and grating soundtrack to Colin's youth. My husband was one of three boys, the middle child, with an older brother, Liam, who had died in Vietnam in 1970. His younger brother, Kyle, six years his junior, leaned on Colin for protection from the crossfire of their parents' battles.

When tensions in the house grew too stifling, Colin would walk with Kyle to the end of Beechwood, where the Charles River flowed. There, they'd spend hours fishing, throwing rocks at lily pads, and watching college crew teams glide by in aerodynamic boats. The Charles, oh, it was a sight to behold for those young boys as they wandered its banks, daydreaming and exploring. Often, Colin told his little brother stories about the river's history, of long-ago Viking voyages and urban legends about mutated sharks.

"You're such a liar," freckle-faced Kyle would say.

"I never told a lie in my life," Colin would reply.

"Really, then why are your pants on fire?" Their laughter helped wash away their troubles, but not completely.

The Charles River drifted along, lazy and unaware—like time itself had slowed down just for the brothers. Slithering through Boston, the waterway traced easy curves that mumbled clues about their futures. But beneath the tranquil surface, a darkness, an unseen depth, hinted at secrets lurking below. Though only fifteen feet at its deepest point, the river held mysteries untold, stirring Colin's imagination as he dreamed along its shores.

One day, while skimming stones, seven-year-old Kyle turned to Colin and said, "Promise you'll never leave me."

"I'm not going anywhere," Colin answered, sure of his thirteen-year-old self.

"Scout's honor?"

"Scout's honor," Colin said. "And I'll even add a pinky promise." The boys locked fingers and saluted one another before shattering the glassy water with more stones.

But years later, after his climactic first kiss with Sevan, Colin's world tilted on its axis. His broken family mattered less to him now, and warm thoughts of his new girlfriend and their shared future took center stage. At only seventeen, Colin gained a mature understanding of responsibility and a fierce desire to grow up, move out, pursue his music, and build a life with Sevan. Love has a knack for infusing ambition into even the most fragile hearts, I suppose.

It was Thanksgiving of 1975, one month after that cataclysmic kiss, when Colin revealed his intentions to his parents. The day was a clamoring blend of familial chaos, with the tantalizing scent of turkey and all the traditional fixings jousting each other for airspace. Drunken relatives bustled about the house, their screechy voices ricocheting off the walls as tensions simmered beneath the noise like hot gravy bubbling under its rubbery film.

Around the dinner table, amid the clinking of cutlery and clatter of dishes, the topic of Colin's love life arose. His aunt Sheila fired the first shot. She was thin and wispy, like she was built with toothpicks and pigeon feathers. "Tell me, Collie," she said between sloppy slurps of whiskey, "who's the apple of your eye these days?"

"More importantly," his uncle Patty butted in after letting loose a booming belch, "does she have a nice set of apples?"

"Come on, don't embarrass the poor sap!" Older cousin PJ was a picked scab of a guy, shoveling a forkful of mashed potatoes into his mouth as he continued talking. "Little Collie's probably got a boyfriend, anyway."

The dining room exploded with cackles, and Colin hesitated to speak up at first, reluctant to divulge the truth about Sevan. However, his family's prodding coaxed him into a confession. "Fine, I have a girlfriend," he said, so loud that young Kyle spit out his milk. "She's prettier than anyone I've ever met and smarter, too. She's funny and good to people, and she comes from a normal family, not like this one. Okay, everyone happy now?"

"Oh, really?" PJ's smirk stank of sarcasm. "What does this *girl* look like?"

"She has, um, long hair," Colin said, his noggin on a swivel.

"Great, so she's not bald," PJ said. "What else?"

"She, um, has a nice, um, nose." Colin snatched up his napkin and wiped a pretend smudge of food off his cheek. "Ears, too. She has nice ears." He was cautious about revealing Sevan's dark features, aware of his mother's prejudices and expecting the potential backlash if he mentioned his girlfriend's heritage.

"So, let me get this straight," Uncle Patty said, scratching at his double chin, "she has hair, ears, and a nose."

"Maybe she's a sheep." Aunt Sheila raised her whiskey glass, snickered, and snorted. "Oops, sorry. That sounded like a pig, not a sheep."

PJ laughed and pointed at Colin. "What's her name, loverboy?"

"It's Seven," he said under his breath, pronouncing the name like the number.

His mother slammed down her glass of wine, rattling the table. "She's Armenian, isn't she?" Her angry, melodramatic reaction played out exactly as her son had feared. "You can't fool me with that name!"

Orla McIntyre's brown hair, greasy and coarse like a crop of wet hay, sprouted out of her scalp. Her pug nose, tiny ears, and long fingers mismatched with her chunky face and stubby legs. Behind Colin's back, and sometimes even in front of him, the boy's friends called his mother Mrs. Potato Head.

"I forbid you to date an *Armo*." Orla's slur slid off her tongue, and she sat up tall in her chair. "Don't even think about bringing that dirty girl into our house."

Colin's father, Danny, banged his fist on the table. "Orla, please," he said, attempting to quell the brewing storm.

"Do not interrupt me!" Orla shifted her glare from son to father. "One of us needs to honor the family name. Lord knows you haven't."

Danny's flushed cheeks—reddened by the dual culprits of vodka and a life on the sea—accented his full head of gray hair, and the white scruff coloring his jawline told the timeworn tale of an unhappy man aging at warp speed. In his eyes, a collage of kindness and dismay suggested he wanted to both save the world *and* disappear from it. "Let the boy be with whoever he chooses," Danny said, his voice growing gruff.

Orla recoiled. "I will not sit here and watch him throw his future away by allowing him to sleep with some sinful creature."

"We're not sleeping together!" Colin's words jumped out of his mouth before he could reclaim them. "And if you say one more bad thing about her, I'm leaving, for good this time."

Sitting back in her chair and sucking in her thin lips, Orla reloaded and aimed her ire this time at Colin's musical aspirations. "Well, then I hope you enjoy your misguided life, your ridiculous dream of being somebody, and your sick infatuation with that dime-a-dozen basement band you always blab about."

"That band will be famous someday," Colin said, breathing in deep, "and I will be, too."

Kyle let out a little cough. "Hey, can we watch football?" He pushed back in his chair and threw his napkin onto his plate. "Are the Patriots playing today?"

One by one, all combatants evacuated the war zone and retreated from the kitchen. That night, in the darkness of his room, Colin lay sprawled across the bed, his resolve ablaze, casting a red-hot glow over his desires. His mother's words had stung, but they had also kindled a fire within him. He burned like mad, hungry to prove her wrong, defy her expectations, and build something sustainable with Sevan. The world was his stage, and he was ready to take the spotlight.

From the nightstand, he grabbed a glossy brown leather notebook that his father had given him for his birthday in July. "This is for your music," Danny McIntyre had said to his son then. But now, when Colin picked up a pen and opened that book, he set in motion an unstoppable chain of events. Putting ink on paper that night, my husband started writing his very first song for Sevan—a song that would take him over forty years to finish.

"The Story"
November 1975

The story, they say, is the story of hope
For young people in love in this world
Though the moral is simple, few may understand
This tale of a boy and a girl

The boy was just that, just a boy without cares
But with dreams that flew far and beyond
And he prayed for a beautiful girl he could share
All his dreams with before they were gone

"I will find her," he thought. "Someday soon." He
was sure
But his search just grew longer in years
For he felt like a man, yet he loved like a boy
And his hopes fell along with his tears

Then the day finally came like a shower in spring
Upon which the flower relies
Yes, the day that the boy truly did find the girl
As his dreams found a home in her eyes

The girl was the sun, shining bright with a smile
Warming all she could reach with her love
And she lifted the boy more than words
can describe
Bringing peace to his heart like a dove

Oh, they laughed, and they cried, and took walks
in the rain

And did all the things young lovers do
Then there were times when they spoke of
their dreams
But those times were too short and too few

They were perfect together, their friends all agreed
"What's their secret?" they frequently hissed
But their secret was really no secret at all
Just a friendship that grew with each kiss

(to be cont'd...)

We Can Make It

MY SISTER, DAUGHTER... her name? Come back? Laughter, dreams... years gone. She's in the car. Stop the car! Please, no! Lost, grasping. Time, go back. Alive... So real!

On Sunday, Race woke up in his hotel room next to Khloe. Both of them lay on their backs, her foot rubbing against his calf, his hand resting on her thigh. A whiff of last night's passion mingled with the undeniable stink of remorse. The city sounds outside, though muffled by the hotel walls, told my son Boston was coming alive.

In the tender morning light, Khloe's dark hair spilled across the pillow, framing her face like a broken halo. The sheets hugged her body, accentuating her breasts and hips, and as she stirred from sleep, a frisky yawn stretched her full lips. She turned her head, revealing a beauty mark on her cheek Race hadn't noticed before. She opened her eyes and beamed, her gaze warm and inviting. "Hey, you," she said.

"Hey," he said, suspecting their intense night together meant more to her than it had to him. This situation was nothing new—a humdrum pattern that had repeated itself time after time during his baseball career: passionate interludes in random hotels, fulfilling his carnal needs but leaving him empty. The room itself, similar to countless others Race had slept in, was functional but devoid of character. The generic furnishings, bland color scheme, and a large window offering a view of the skyline were all elements he'd encountered before. And Khloe, with her attractive features and magnetic charm, resembled so many of the women he had shared one-night romps with, their names vanishing into the depths of his memory.

She rolled onto her side, leaned in, and kissed him, slow and wet. "I'm off today," she said. "All yours if you want me." Her breath carried a sweetness, an unexpected treat for the early hour.

"That's quite a proposition, but there's something you're not telling me," Race said with a smirk. "I can feel it." He reached over and touched her face, his fingers traveling across her olive skin, down to her chin. "Wait, I know. You totally smoked Kate Moss in the World's Best Cheekbones competition, didn't you?"

"You nailed it," she said. "That's just one of my many award-winning body parts." She grabbed his hand and pressed it against her lips, breathing into his warm palm, staring into his green eyes.

"I'll be the judge of that," he said and readjusted his pillow.

Khloe let go of his hand and asked, "How does brunch sound? Or a walk through Boston Common." She lay her head on his chest. "Or we could stay right here."

"Sorry, I can't." He slid out from under her, rolled off the mattress, and stepped into his boxers. "I need to meet up with someone today."

Sitting now with her back against the tufted headboard, Khloe wrapped the sheet around her torso. "Dare I ask who?"

"Just an old friend of my father's," he said, pulling on his jeans. "But first I gotta find her, and my only lead might be a dead end."

Khloe twisted the gold ring on her finger. "Sometimes, dead ends are just new beginnings in disguise," she said, staring over Race's shoulder. "Beginnings and endings… they're not so different. Both promise something fresh, something unknown, but it's what we do between the two that matters."

"Speaking from experience?"

She sighed and turned away. "I've been trying to get out of Watertown for a long time. Don't know where I'd go, but I'm tired of being held captive. The place itself is fine. It's because of me, my fault. I've put myself in this situation."

Race draped his T-shirt over his shoulder, sat on the side of the bed, and stroked Khloe's blanketed leg. "Wanna tell me about it?"

"I'm thirty years old and stuck in a loveless relationship," she said. "All because I caved to people's expectations." She shook her head and laughed, clearly out of disgust rather than amusement. "There was only one guy I ever really loved, but he was American. My mother insisted I marry within our community, and so I broke it off and ended up with Abraham."

"Where's your husband now?"

"He went back to Yerevan to settle a real estate matter," Khloe said, looking at Race with eyes that weren't her own. "That was two years ago."

"When is he coming back?"

She paused and said, "Why is finding your father's friend so important?"

"Because she ruined my family."

"Sounds a bit dramatic."

He grabbed the songbook off the nightstand and opened it for Khloe, pointing out the scribbled reference to Willow Spelman—the invisible lover his father had written about. "I need to locate this woman, tell her about the damage she caused, how her affair with my dad destroyed me and my mother."

"And she's in Cambridge?"

"I'm not sure, but I'll track her down," Race said. "Although my biggest clue might be in the cemetery across from your store."

"Mount Auburn?"

"Yep."

A glint of curiosity sparkled in Khloe's dark eyes. "Besides those songs, do you have any evidence of an affair?"

She reached for the book, but he quickly tossed it onto the floor. "Whatever."

She bit her lip, then said, "Are you sure *this* is how you want to remember your dad?"

"My father deserves to be forgotten," my son said. "He never cared about anyone but himself."

"Did he grow up in Boston?"

"No," Race said. "Midwest, I think. It's debatable."

"Did he spend a lot of time here?"

"Who knows? I don't think so." The conversation grow-ing heavier, Race used Khloe's undeniable allure to end the inquisition. "God, you're the sexiest thing I've ever seen." He yanked on the sheet wrapped around her, revealing her naked body.

She gripped his arm and hauled him back into bed. Straddling him, she threw her head back to get the hair away from her face and began tugging off his jeans. He was no match for her playful moans and gentle caresses, the irresist-ible pull of a beautiful woman.

Colin and I had shared chemical moments like this, once upon a time—as if we'd discovered something lost and refused to let go, our urgent, lustful kisses cementing our connection. When his heart thundered against my chest, apprehension slipping from his face. When my every nerve sang in response to his touch, emptying my brain of all thoughts, only to replenish as his skilled hands swept over my body. When he fastened me into his arms and took me to bed. When we became one, our movements slow, like the hush of a lullaby. When the world dissolved around us, taking with it all doubt, burying the painful ghosts of our haunted memories.

Race turned to Khloe, probing her warm brown eyes, hoping to find something that would diffuse their affair and ease the desire within him. While they lingered, tangled in the sheets, his subconscious strayed, sneaking off with an image of Amanda, the woman he had lost. But he couldn't explain how, or why, she had planted a flag in his mind and in his soul. There was just something about her, a presence he couldn't outrun.

❦

As Khloe piloted her Jeep through Boston with Race by her side, the cityscape gave way to the familiar roads of Watertown, and the early afternoon weather couldn't decide what to do. Gray clouds covered the town and the sun struggled to shine through, creating sporadic patches of subdued light that languished on the street.

In my current condition, that's how my son must see me: languishing in a subdued light, succumbing to the darkness. But why must there be a bias against darkness? Why is light always right? Some may argue that my "darkness" makes me invisible, but by excluding darkness and embracing only light, we become unbalanced. My struggle, my fight to remember, is like peering into a dark mirror. I can't see the complete picture, don't know it all. I need others, now more than ever. But I never bemoan the dim glass. To me, obscurity is necessary for growth; darkness is integral to my journey. It's not a malevolent force to be exorcised. It's liberating, a symbol of freedom, sending my soul to play beyond the stars. For me, now, the darkness is enough, and through it, I recall Race's story.

The atmosphere in Watertown buzzed with passing cars, the occasional cranky horn, and snippets of chitter-chatter riding on the wind. Delectable aromas from nearby Armenian restaurants and cafés skittered through the Jeep's open windows, mingling with the fragrance of fresh rain on the pavement. While cruising along Mt. Auburn Street, swerving around potholes, Khloe eyeballed Race and said, "What exactly are you looking for in the cemetery?"

"I told you, Willow Spelman, though she may not exist." The breeze whipped through the windows and tousled his long hair, obscuring his vision as he spoke. "But yesterday, a groundskeeper there mentioned a Willow Pond and a Spelman Road."

"Did you check it out?"

"He wouldn't let me in." Race took the blue cap out of his backpack and pulled it onto his head, imprisoning his lawless hair. "They were closing up when I got there."

"Might've been a sign." Khloe squinted ahead. "Maybe someone, or something, doesn't want you there."

"Listen, I don't know what I'm looking for anymore, but this lead is all I have, and I'm not turning back." He checked the GPS directions on his phone—still a few more miles until they reached the cemetery. He rubbed Khloe's shoulder and said, "So, is it just me, or does Watertown feel like the center of the Armenian universe?"

"Well, besides L.A. and Fresno, we've got the largest population of Armenians in the U.S." She smiled and peeked at him. "The first immigrants settled here in the early nineteen hundreds," she said, "fleeing persecution and seeking a better life. Many of them found jobs at the Hood Rubber Company and worked hard to make ends meet." As Khloe spoke, Race saw Watertown through her eyes. "The community was close-knit back then, centered on churches and neighborhoods, which helped them overcome the language barrier and discrimination."

When the Jeep passed a restaurant called Ararat Spice Kitchen, my son grinned. "No problem finding authentic food here, huh?"

"It's a taste of home, a reminder of our heritage and the past." She put her hand on his thigh. "That's one thing Armenians don't forget—the past."

"It's amazing," he said, "having such strong ties to your homeland."

"That grip on the past comes with a price, though. As time goes by and our culture erodes, the older generation fears that our traditions will fade away. But the tighter they hold on, the more the younger generation resists."

"Can't blame old folks for not letting go of history, can you? It's all they have."

"Listen, I get the whole culture preservation thing, but it's not smart to cut off the next generation from the American way of life. If we embrace our heritage and the opportunities we have here, we'll build a stronger community for the future."

Race saw a different side of Khloe then, no longer just an attractive woman, but someone with a rich background and the need to share it. "I have to be honest," he said, "there's a lot more to you than I thought."

"There's always more beneath the surface," she said as the sun snuck out from behind a cloud, splashing silken light onto the windshield. "But not everyone bothers to look."

As they approached the cemetery on Mt. Auburn Street, Race grabbed his backpack resting at his feet. "This is the entrance," he said, unbuckling his seat belt. "Thanks so much."

The Jeep picked up speed.

"Wait. What are you doing?" He buckled up again, concluding that she wouldn't be stopping anytime soon.

Khloe drove on, her silence stretching across another quarter mile.

"Can you please tell me where we're going? You know,

if you really wanted to have brunch, all you had to do was ask."

A minute later, Khloe veered onto Porter Street and pulled up in front of a modest, two-story home. "You can go to the cemetery after," she said, "but you need to visit this place first."

Race stared at the house. "Who lives here?"

"His name is Petrak Zakarian. My mom told me about him. She was best friends with Petrak's daughter. She said he might have some answers for you."

"I don't get it," my son said. "What does that guy know?"

"Sorry to ambush you like this."

"You can apologize by taking us back to the cemetery."

She kissed him on the cheek. "Call me later, okay?"

Race stepped out of the Jeep as uncertainty billowed in the air. Thick and heavy as waterlogged blankets, the clouds threw faint shadows onto the street. As Khloe drove away, my son wondered what mysteries lay inside the unassuming bone-white house, and what secrets the brawny brick church looming in the background might be keeping. Standing stiff on the sidewalk, he sensed the puzzle pieces of his father's past coming apart and together all at once.

When Race told me this, it seemed like a pivotal juncture in his story, when everything took a sudden, life-altering turn for him. But how could I be sure? In my life now, everything *seems* to be something or another. It's never all the way this or all the way that. All good or bad. All useful or useless. All holy or unholy. Before, people were sick or well, asleep or awake, confused or lucid. For a while, I was sure about so many things, but that's not my world anymore. Now and then, though, the air clears and the clouds lift, and I'm certain that my life is much more than it seems.

:17

Cryin'

RACE STEPPED ONTO the front porch of the plain house on Porter Street and tapped on the large wooden door. With a loud creak, the portal opened, revealing an old man's face, etched with wrinkles and anchored by a long, gray beard. His egg-shaped head featured sunken eyes, and he wore a stately wool hat, one meant for a snow squall or frigid temperatures, not for mild fall days. But this was the sort of man who let piety make his wardrobe decisions, a man prepared for the elements, a man who'd stand strong against a blizzard. The dusky half-moons under his eyes, however, were proof that he couldn't weather *every* storm.

"Sorry to bug you," Race said, fidgeting with his backpack. "Are you Mr. Zakarian?"

"Yes, but please call me Petrak," the man said, his voice creakier than the door. "It's a pleasure to meet you, Race McIntyre."

My son recoiled and locked in on the old man, their eyes level. "How do you know me?"

"From your baseball days," Petrak said, propped up tall in the doorway. "I'm thrilled to see you in person." But the look on his weathered face expressed something far darker than happiness.

"Well, don't ask me why I'm here," Race said, forcing a chuckle. "A friend of mine, Khloe, dropped me off and told me I should speak to you."

"Forgive my manners. Please, come in." With a wave of his arm, Petrak stepped aside, allowing Race to enter. "We'll sit in the living room."

Walking past the elderly gentleman and into the house, my son tried to cut the awkwardness with a joke. "Beauty before age, right?"

Petrak didn't laugh. "Armenian pride roots itself in gratitude for our ancestors," he said as he closed the door behind Race. "Our honor is based on respect for our elders and all that is sacred, in this life and beyond."

The interior of the house showcased a rich history and tradition, decorated with religious artifacts and a variety of trinkets. The living room smelled of old furniture and an underlying isolation. Worn yet resilient antiques, statuettes, and tchotchkes occupied every corner and nook, all of which had surely witnessed countless stories and memories over the years.

A sleek white cat, its fur matted and its disposition surly, roamed the room, hissing at Race and baring its fangs. There was a brown circle of hair around one of its ears, and its tail had a brown tip. "I don't think your pet appreciates washed-up minor leaguers as much as you do."

Petrak's words clawed their way out from behind his beard. "Arpi is an Armenian Van cat," the old man said, "a rare and regal species, known for their independence and intelligence. Despite her irritated demeanor at the moment, she is quite playful."

"Me, too," Race replied under his breath.

"Please, sit." Petrak gestured toward the couch while he settled into a floral-patterned upholstered chair with a high wooden back. "Tell me, how do you know Ms. Torosian?"

Race cocked his head. "Who?"

"Khloe."

"Oh, I just met her and her mother, Sonia, yesterday." In several sporadic stages, Race lowered himself onto the couch, wincing in pain from his aching knees, and plopped his elbow on the armrest. "I'm only in town for a quick visit."

"When did you stop playing baseball?" The old man's stare drilled into Race.

"Retired ten years ago. Enough was enough." My son shifted on the couch, failing to mention the 520 weeks of endless denial following his last game.

Dozens of old photographs adorned the walls and fireplace mantle, telling tales of better days in the Zakarians' past. Among the images: a pretty teenage girl, an elderly, oracle-like woman, and a younger Petrak with his wife, most likely, both wearing traditional Armenian clothing, possibly on their wedding day.

"Nice family." Race pointed to the mantle. "You all look happy."

Petrak got up and walked to the fireplace, tall and proud. "Sadly," he said, stopping next to the wedding picture, "my wife, Yeva, is no longer with us. She passed away shortly after…" His words faded into the photo.

"I'm sorry," Race said, leaning forward and placing his clammy hands on his knees. "Hey, can I ask you something? How do you know about my career? I wasn't exactly a superstar."

"I attended the one game you played in Boston." Petrak stroked his beard with long, knowing fingers. "Also," he said, "I saw a few of your minor league games in Rhode Island years ago."

"So, you're a baseball fanatic?"

"Never much of a fan of the game itself."

An undercurrent of unspoken sentiments swept beneath Petrak's comment, reminding my son of the way his father, Colin, used to hold back. When Arpi the cat hissed again, Race wanted to leave, convinced this visit was a mistake. He got up off the couch, walked over to Petrak, and extended his hand. "Well, thanks," he said. "I'd better get going."

Petrak reached out, but instead of shaking my son's hand, his strong, wrinkled grip settled on Race's shoulder. "Wait," the old man said, the creak gone from his voice.

Race avoided eye contact with Petrak, his pulse quickening. "Listen, it was nice meeting you," my son said, "but why waste any more of each other's time?"

Petrak lowered his gaze, his hold on Race's shoulder tightening and loosening all at once. "Why waste more time?" The man inhaled and raised his head, his tired eyes alive now. "Because I'd like to get to know my grandson."

Race squinted and laughed, pulling away from Petrak. "Grandson?" He sucked in his lips and tossed his backpack over his shoulder. "Sorry, sir, but you're the least Irish-looking person I've ever seen. Put a bottle of Jameson in your hand and you'd fool me for maybe a second."

The old man adjusted his wool hat and took a half step toward Race. "I am your mother's father," he mumbled.

My son's amusement teamed up with his hostility before he subbed both of them out for bewilderment and disbelief. "My mother's parents were Scandinavians from Toledo," he said, "and last I checked, they were dead."

Petrak slouched, drained and worn. "Perhaps."

Race headed for the door. "You've got the wrong guy, pal."

"I am talking about your *actual* mother," Petrak said, gesturing to a picture on the wall. "Her name was Sevan."

My son froze.

Do you think time moves fast or slow? I think it only *seems* to pass quickly. You see, I believe time stands perfectly still, and we move around in it, sometimes lazily, and sometimes at a furious pace. I'll do something, and the day races onward, and I forget about time. Then, in a jiffy, it surrounds me again. I can't see it, smell it, or hear it. But it surrounds me on all sides; I'm used to it by now. Our most memorable moments get frozen in time, I believe, like if you ever kicked a beehive during a snowstorm. That'd be something you'd never forget. I don't believe I've ever done anything that silly, not that I know of, but I can recall one of my most memorable moments.

When the Red Sox drafted Race in 1995, kicking off his journey into the world of professional baseball, my excitement knew no bounds. Despite receiving endless offers for college scholarships, Race eschewed his education. I supported his choice, albeit with a mixed bag of feelings. The idea of the Sox sending him wherever, separating us by so many miles, unsettled my nerves. It was beyond what I considered comfortable. Despite everything, I appreciated his desire to test himself in the pros, but I questioned his motivation. Did he want to spite his father? Become a star and prove Colin wrong? Or maybe he wanted to make his dad proud? The way I saw it, the boy and the man had different minds with the same old dreams.

The night of the draft, Race and I had shared a heartfelt discussion, one that ambled into both baseball and life. During his childhood, I'd taught him the values I held most dear: honesty, loyalty, and kindness. I encouraged him to carry these principles with him on his journey. Before he left Sea Point, I urged him to embrace whatever life had in store for him. But I couldn't force him to take my advice.

As my head swirled with the story of Petrak's claim—that I wasn't Race's biological mother—I couldn't help but wonder what my son must've thought of me. If Petrak spoke the truth, then I had abandoned my three key principles—I had been dishonest, loyal to a lie, and I neglected kindness. In short, I had failed my son.

The Zakarians' living room captured Race in a web of memory-triggering smells and familiar sounds. He wanted to leave, run away as fast as he could, but strands of the past created a sticky barrier blocking his exit. He pointed at Petrak, miffed by the man's accusation. "You're delusional. My mother is Hollyann McIntyre."

Petrak took a full step forward. "Son, listen to me, please."

Race backed away. "Do *not* call me that."

The old man turned and glared out the window, as if memorizing the bewitching shapes of the dark clouds gathering above Watertown. "Life can be like a savage storm," he said before facing Race again.

My son held his breath.

"Your mother, Sevan, was only a girl when you came into this world, and she confronted a crisis far beyond her years. Some souls rise to meet their trials, growing stronger with each challenge. But others, they lose their way in the tempest. Your mother, she was a child, thrust into a situation she could not fathom. Very often, I wonder if I could have done more for her. But the trial was hers to face, not my own. Life's path is winding, fraught with shadows and light, and sometimes, even the strongest among us falter in the dark."

Like the spinning laces on a deceptive forkball, the Zakarians' living room whirled around my son, leaving him in a dizzying state of shock and revulsion.

The elderly man repeated his claim. "I swear on my dear Yeva's grave, this is true. You were born here to Sevan and Colin, both of whom were just teenagers."

"Then what happened to her, huh? Where is she?" Race demanded, his voice quivering. "Tell me now!"

"Please, there is no reason to shout. I can explain."

Race stood there, locked in place, struggling to assemble the fragments of this new information and align them with his cherished memories of me, of him. Doubt chewed at his infamous self-assurance, threatening to whittle down his identity. Who was he, if not the person he believed himself to be?

His glower fell upon the photograph of teenage Sevan on the wall. Her eyes, frozen in time, seemed to convey a message—mirroring the way I've tried to communicate with my boy recently, through our shared gaze. It was as if Sevan's dark eyes were pleading with Race, imploring him to discover the truth.

"Come with me," Petrak said, breaking the silence and moving toward the living room staircase. "I will show you, and then you will understand."

"No thanks." Race didn't want to know what was upstairs. He had come to Boston to expose his father's infidelity and berate Colin's mistress. He had come to avenge me, not forsake me.

Petrak stopped on the second step. "Please, come," he said as the weak wood moaned beneath his shoes.

The pull was too much, and Race followed the old man, their footsteps clomping up the stairs. In the second-floor hallway, cobwebs swayed from the ceiling, like forgotten memories drifting in the currents of time. My son peeped into an open door, spying a dusty time capsule of a room cluttered with relics of the 1970s—an era of shag carpeting, vinyl records, Pop Art, and psychedelic patterns.

The two men passed through a click-clacking hanging veil of colorful beads leading into a tiny bedroom. Red Sox banners and felt paintings of unicorns adorned the walls, alongside a framed album cover of the band Boston and a poster of its long-haired, mustachioed members. Race's heart pumped slower, the gap between beats lengthening, the growing quietude as unexpected as the curveballs the day had thrown him.

Crammed in one corner of the room, a meek double

bed lay lonely, its blankets and sheets crumpled and worn. On the opposite wall, a crib cooed a silent song. Stepping on a matted purple rug, Race struggled to reconcile the room's contents in the wake of recent earth-shattering revelations.

Petrak watched my son's movements, his expression reflecting a lifetime of profound grieving. The density of unspoken history thickened, infusing the syrupy air with both sweet and bitter remembrances.

Race broke the silence, a rattle in his voice. "Was this her room?"

Petrak nodded. "Yes, it was hers," he said. "She shared it with her husband, your father." The old man removed his wool hat and held it to his chest, setting his gaze upon the crib. "They lived here with us for a short time, and you were here, too."

Race moved toward a white wooden desk near the door. Its rickety legs bore the marks of time, scratched and worn. Photographs, books of poetry, and a diary littered the surface, each with their own stories to tell. The Polaroids strewn on the desk revealed fleeting glimpses of a life Race couldn't fathom. There were baby pictures of him, perhaps; the little boy peeking back at him could've been anyone.

Petrak studied my son's frown, as if deciphering each muscle movement on his face. He joined Race by the desk and picked up a tar-black book, faded by time. "This is your mother's diary," he explained, tapping a tepid finger on the journal's gold latch, his voice laced with reverence and sorrow. "After she was gone, I found it in the desk drawer, along with this." Petrak offered Race a small envelope.

My son accepted it, hand trembling. "What is it?"

The old man's eyes held the weight of decades. "It is

an apology, an excuse, a goodbye letter," he said. "It has been many things over the years." He tugged at his long, gray beard and bowed his head, as if the recollections had crushed his tired spirit. "But one thing I know for certain, she did not intend it for me."

With wary hands, Race opened the envelope and pulled out a creased piece of yellowed paper. His eyes welled with tears as he glanced at the words penned by his apparent birth mother, Sevan. Each sentence steered his imagination in a separate direction, animating a puppet show of emotions that had lain dormant within him, buried beneath layers of dismay.

My dear son, I'm leaving you because I love you.

This is the hardest thing I've ever done, but I want you to have a chance at a better life, a quiet life, a full life. I'm so sorry, Race, but that life can't be with me. Someday, I hope you'll understand my decision. I pray your father can explain all of this to you, in his own time.

For all my days, time has carried me, but today I carry time. In the past, I longed for tomorrow, for whatever was next, though I should've rejected it. I lived in the future, making plans, looking ahead, hoping for more. I knew my place on the timeline. Like everyone, I stood there and waited, determined to get to the end. But destiny won't allow me to see the end. That's not my fate. Yesterday, I was bound by time, but today I'm overwhelmed by dread, knowing my greatest enemy is the future.

Race, you are my blood and my soul, but I couldn't have imagined the living nightmare that haunts me. I can't wake up, can't escape this real-life horror.

As you grow, I hope you find strength in the suffering of our people. Find meaning in the suffering. It will make you see things you wouldn't have seen otherwise. Be proud of your ethnicity. It means you're a survivor. That's who you are.

Please forgive me… and know how much I love you. I will never stop loving you.

Race folded the paper, as if preserving the sentiments held within the creases. He placed the letter back into the envelope, fingers throbbing. He wasn't sure if Sevan had ended her life, or if she had run away from it; her note didn't make that clear. Tears blurring his vision, Race reached out and offered the letter to Petrak.

The old man shook his head, his eyes overrun with a sad insistence. "Keep it, and the diary, too," Petrak said. "They belong to you now."

Race nodded, his throat clogged with unformed words. He wiped his eyes with the back of his hand, gratitude and turmoil heaving within him.

"You must have many questions," Petrak said. "I will tell you what I can."

Flipping through the pages of the old diary, Race peered into a forgotten world, which held the secrets of his origins and the untold stories of his birth mother's heart. Page after page after page, he glanced at the words but understood none of them. A tsunami of confusion engulfed him, casting him off into a sea of memories and distrust. He didn't know what to think, what to ask, what to feel.

"This is crazy," Race said, holding up the diary, face

flushed. "I knew nothing about this person five minutes ago, and now this? What am I supposed to do with this?"

"Do what you will."

My son closed the book. "I need to go."

:16

With You

My daddy was so silly. You know what he'd tell me? He'd say, "Holly, everyone in the world is one of three things: a potato, an egg, or a coffee bean. And we all get into hot water sometimes, don't we? Now, you can be the potato, appearing strong but becoming soft under pressure. Or the egg, hardening your heart when faced with troubles. But try your best to be the coffee bean. When life's boiling point comes, spin adversity into opportunity and change the situation for the better. You have that power, my little girl."

Forgive me, I'm having another dizzy spell. Scared and tipsy as a squirrel on a rocking chair. Here I go… Falling into you, with you, with me. Oh, dear. Okay, that's better…

⤌

After walking in a daze for twenty minutes, Race stood at the open iron gate outside Mount Auburn Cemetery.

His phone read four o'clock, and the overcast sky seemed to press down on the world, its weight intensifying with every passing second. He reflected on his visit with Petrak, the peculiar old man who claimed to be my son's grandfather. Part of Race didn't trust a word of what he'd heard. The shocking information had been much more than he'd expected, and his cross-country journey for answers only led to more questions.

The meager contents of his backpack yanked down on his shoulder—Sevan's diary, her haunting farewell letter, and his father's book of songs. It was as though he were hauling a lifetime's worth of deceptions. He hadn't yet digested all the journal's pages, at least a hundred of them in total. Most of the entries he'd glossed over told only of Sevan's love for Colin, along with many references to the name Tsovinar. But none of the entries contained dates, or any mention of him or me.

As Race stepped through the open gates of the cemetery, he pondered the questions simmering within him. Why hadn't he asked Petrak more about Sevan? If she ended her own life, how did she do it? If she ran away, why did she leave? He knew next to nothing about his so-called *real* mother, save for the inscrutable words in her letter and what he might decipher from her diary.

But before my boy metaphorically wandered down the strange path ahead of him, he wanted to follow one that felt more familiar. He stormed through the cemetery gates and made his way to the main office building. The lobby of the visitors center was warm and inviting, with historical photos and maps adorning the walls. Gauzelike lighting illuminated the open space, while the shady scent of soil and snapdragons sauntered in the air.

Race plucked a map of the grounds from a rack, startling a stout woman in an indigo pantsuit sitting behind a desk, her blueish-gray hair set in a bun. "Oh, hello, I'm Robin," she said. "Can I help you?"

"I hope so."

"Well, look no further." Robin put down a thick Russian novel, stood, and smiled. "I always say that when someone offers us help, we should take it. It's their way of stopping us from being our worst selves."

Race chuckled, thinking the dense novel should be in the hands of an Ivy League literature professor, not the adult version of the gum-chewing girl who turned into a giant blueberry after disobeying Willy Wonka. "I need to find someone," he said, "and I need help getting somewhere."

"Okey doke, fire away."

"I'm looking for Jeb," Race said. "He's an old grounds-keeper here, sarcastic and lanky. I met him yesterday as you guys were closing."

"Jeb, you say?" Robin couldn't hide her puzzled expression. "I'm not familiar with anyone by that name, but I haven't worked here long."

"Never mind," my son said with a smirk. "Can you tell me how to get to Willow Pond?"

Robin flattened a map on her desk and highlighted the directions. "Just follow Spelman Road until you see Thyme Path, which is a narrow walkway that branches off into Azalea Path." She looked up and pointed the yellow highlighter at my son. "But listen, don't go down Azalea, stay on Thyme till the end, then you'll reach the pond."

Her instructions echoed in his head—"stay on Thyme till the end"—a statement he might also interpret as: follow to the *end of time*. The words mimicked the cryptic message he had found in Colin's songbook. My son laughed, thanked the woman, and began his trek toward Willow Pond.

Serenity covered the cemetery's vast landscape, casting a soothing spell on Race. The historic graveyard, a national landmark known for its natural beauty, served as the eternal resting place of many notable activists, poets, educators, and politicians. Spectacular flowers, shrubs, and trees were everywhere. It was like walking through a botanical garden in heaven, with colors and smells from another world.

As Race strolled along the paved roadway, following Robin's highlighted instructions on the map, he absorbed his surroundings—the faint fragrance of damp earth, the distant mutterings of the past. Each stride he made was a voyage into history. Chickadees flitted from tree to tree, chirping and singing beautiful songs, nothing like the repulsive noise he'd gotten used to since leaving Sea Point: the figurative sound of vomiting up his own anguish and gagging on it.

Then, a rustle in the quiet. "Hey, Race."

My son stopped and glanced over his shoulder. "Jeb? That you?"

No response—only a lethargic breeze breaking the haunting silence that settled over him like an executioner's hood. Race strained his ears, convinced he'd heard someone say, "This way" in a familiar voice, but no one was there. Stumped at an intersection, scratching his lip, my son looked up and saw a sign for Spelman Road.

Goose bumps prickling his flesh, Race took a gander from side to side and meandered onto the road. *Okay, Jeb, how much farther?*

Soon, my son found Thyme Path and followed it to the

end, until he reached Willow Pond. Prodigious trees and vibrant flowers framed the water's edge, painting a tranquil picture, and a canopy of peace fell upon Race. Buzzing insects and croaking frogs were all too antsy to tell of the wonder.

Fixing his gaze across the water, he discerned the broken outline of a figure behind the elegant branches of a willow tree, and he called out, "Hello?"

The figure strolled alongside the pond, its shadowy form obscured by the bushes, headstones, and concrete statues that dotted the path. Race's heart pattering, he could tell now that this person was a woman, and with each step, she came closer into view. It was Sonia, Khloe's mother.

Dressed in a long black cotton sweater and a gray scarf over her shoulders, the woman moved with equal amounts of grace and solemnity. Except for her shorter hair and thirty extra years, she could've been her daughter's twin. "Hello, Race," Sonia said, taking shape from behind a wall of hydrangeas.

"What are you doing here?"

"These are special grounds," she said, scanning the peaks of the trees around the pond. "I like to come here sometimes to think. It's rejuvenating."

"It's really beautiful… simple." Race canvassed the scene and scratched his nose. "But rejuvenating? Seems ironic that a graveyard could add years to your life."

"Our people find joy in simplicity." Sonia smiled. "In our culture, we wish everyone health, happiness, and a long life. Material wealth is secondary to what truly matters. We learn from an early age that all life is equal and that, above all else, nature is sacred."

"I've seen lots of Armenian names on these headstones," he said. "Seems like we're surrounded by your people."

Sonia moved closer to Race, only a cool breeze between them now. "Many Armenians have been buried in this cemetery, but the most famous of them no longer rests here."

"Tired of being dead?"

Her bracelets jangled as she wrapped her scarf around her neck. "Drastamat Kanayan, known to us as General Dro, was a military leader who helped end the genocide, a brave man whose legacy we honor and respect. He would say that the perfect hero is a humble hero. General Dro held no grudge against any nation but promised to rain thunder down on anyone who attacked Armenia."

"Why isn't he here anymore?"

"In the midfifties, they buried his remains not far from this pond, but then transferred them to the old country, as was his wish. I suppose we are all drawn to our homes, called back to that place where our hearts have always been."

Race shuddered at the thought, or perhaps it was the breeze that chilled his bones. "I met Petrak Zakarian earlier today, as I'm sure you know."

The birds chirped a melodic response as Sonia tilted her head and glanced up, her dark eyes apologizing. She breathed deep and placed her hands inside the pockets of her long sweater.

"Petrak told me about my real mother," Race said, furrowing his brow, grappling with this surreal conversation.

"Sevan was my closest friend," Sonia said. "For a long time, my only friend." Her stare dampened. "She was a young girl, a beautiful girl, haunted by depression and yet deeply devoted to her husband and to you, her son."

With both hands, Race raked his fingers through his hair. He sighed, depleted, and lowered his chin. "You knew me then?"

"You were the cutest little boy," she said. "So rambunctious, so much energy. I would babysit when Sevan needed time to herself or when Colin had to work late." Sonia smiled, and Race recognized that smile. "We had fun together, you and me." Her eyes glazed over in that blink of time, as if she were calculating the price of loss. "I tracked your achievements over the years, read about you, followed your success."

"Yeah, right," Race said, staring to the side. "My *success*."

"I wish Sevan could see you now." Sonia tried to smile again but failed. "She would be so proud."

The birds quieted. The breeze died.

"I need to know," Race said and swallowed hard, "is she buried here, too?"

Sonia's eyes clouded over. "There is no grave, and there was no body," she said, almost humming the words. "Someone called the authorities in November of seventy-eight, reported seeing a woman matching Sevan's description on a bridge over the Charles River. But when the call came, your mother had already been missing for three weeks. Sadly, the Armenian church refused to bless her spirit and conduct a burial because of the assumed nature of her passing. Instead, there is only a bench, a humble tribute to her memory, donated by an anonymous benefactor in honor of Sevan and the Zakarian family."

"A bench?"

"This may not make sense to you, but in our religion, suicide is an unforgivable sin, the result of a weak faith. The clergy say that when faith is lacking, hope is lacking, and if a person has strong faith, she does not lose hope." Sonia hung her head. "They claimed Sevan was selfish and weak-willed; said if she had a strong will she would've fought to survive."

Sonia led Race to a clearing near the end of the path, beneath the sheltering branches of a spruce tree. There, nestled among the peaceful surroundings, stood a modest concrete bench, smooth to the touch, adorned with a copper plaque. "I called your father years ago, only once," Sonia said. "I told him about this place, gave him directions, exactly how he could find her."

"It was you."

"What?"

"Nothing," Race said. "It's just that, I don't know, something makes more sense now."

The copper plaque bore Sevan's name, her date of birth, and the date she went missing. Beneath those simple facts, the poignant words: *Loving Daughter, Wife, and Mother.*

"This epitaph captures the essence of her existence," Sonia said, running a hand along the speckled concrete, "and her significance in the lives of those who knew her." But the engraving captured nothing of the trusted friend, or the troubled girl Sevan had been.

Leaning over, Race traced his finger along the engraved letters, and a monsoon of love and unasked questions swept him away. A wellspring of belonging arose inside him, yet the realization that he'd never truly known his birth mother, or his own past, tore at his soul.

Sonia laid her hand on his shoulder. "I'll leave you to your thoughts, Race," she whispered. "You must have many."

Race nodded.

"It is wonderful to see you again," Sonia said. "I'm

sorry it's under such unusual circumstances." Her solemn demeanor perked up. "Perhaps you could join me and Khloe for dinner during your stay. I'll prepare my famous sarma, or my khashlama."

"We'll see," my son said, "but thank you."

"My daughter speaks highly of you." As she raised an eyebrow, the corners of Sonia's mouth curled up. "I named Khloe for your mother, you know. Sevan always loved that name; never liked her own name."

Race waved goodbye as Sonia walked away, blending into the peaceful surroundings of Willow Pond. He settled on the concrete bench and lowered his head into his hands, imprisoned by phantoms of the past behind a stockade of newfound truths.

In the cemetery's quiet, he spoke aloud, addressing both Sevan and me. His murmured voice lugged the weight of longing and misgivings, battling the complexities of his identity and the unknown journey that awaited him.

"Why all the secrecy?" My boy gaped into the clouds, his tone rife with frustration. He stood and raised his arms to the heavens. "Why keep me in the dark for so long? I deserved to know my story."

High in the trees, the chickadees whistled a sad tune.

Race's gaze shifted to the plaque bearing his mother's name. "Did you care about me at all? Was I something you wanted to forget?"

The breeze picked up once again.

He pondered his relationship with me, his adoptive mother, and began to ask things of me I could never answer. "And you, Mom," he mumbled, "were you protecting me, or were you part of the lie? Can I still call you my mother after all of this?"

A frog hopped into the pond.

"Who am I now?" His question dangled in the air.

When he told me that story, I wondered if Race had had the courage to travel down this indistinguishable path. Would he replace what he knew to be true and embrace the wild revelations of his untold past?

I'm not sure what I would've done if I were him, but that's what's special about my Race—he's as predictable as the daily Oregon rainfall. I knew what he'd decide, but that mattered little to me. I only cared that he wouldn't leave me behind with the discarded remnants of his previous life. Looking back now, I shouldn't have doubted him. But when I learned he had discovered his birth mother, I feared my son would let me slip from his memory, just as he was slipping from mine.

Race emerged from the calm depths of Mount Auburn Cemetery, his backpack slung over his shoulder. When he approached the front gate, ready to leave, a familiar face materialized from behind a thorny rosebush. It was Jeb, clutching a metal rake and sporting a friendly gap-toothed grin.

As the late-afternoon sun avoided a low-hanging cloud, Race nodded to the groundskeeper. "Must be closing time soon," he called out with a muffled laugh. "Surprised you haven't locked me in already."

Today, Jeb appeared slightly younger with fewer wrinkles and no dark circles under his brown eyes. Maybe it was the lack of shadows over the grounds or the lighter set of overalls he wore that made him appear livelier.

"Hey there, superstar." Jeb moved closer, his wise eyes crinkling at the corners. "Find what you were fishing for down by Willow Pond?"

"Not quite." Race paused for a moment. "But only because I didn't really know what I was looking for."

Jeb's eyes caught fire. "Gonna watch Game Five of the Series tonight? The Red Sox are one win away from clinching the title."

"I haven't cared about baseball since I retired," my son said. "But I root against Boston every season, no matter if they're good or bad."

"Understood." Jeb tugged on his Sox cap and nodded. "Good and bad can seem an awful lot alike from a distance. Not always easy to tell one from the other."

Race contemplated Jeb's words for a second before saying, "Yeah, what's the difference? Good, bad, success, failure. I chased success my whole life, but now I'm running from failure, and it all feels the same. Nothing's changed."

"Mm," Jeb said and shrugged.

The weather had pulled a fast one, clouds of steel wool quickly trapping the sun, casting a drab twilight over the cemetery. The dying day added an eerie quality to the solemn atmosphere, and the noise of the city beyond the gates faded.

Race surveyed the well-maintained grounds. "This place is kind of amazing," he said. "I've been thinking of all the stories etched into these stones."

Jeb brushed a rose petal with his blistered hand and studied its delicate structure. "Funny how this cemetery can make you feel alive again."

"It makes me *feel* again," Race said. "Maybe that's enough."

Jeb grinned, the wide gap in his front teeth acting as a doorway to his soul.

Race took a minute to honor the surrounding headstones, each one representing someone who had dreams, made choices, and had their own questions in life. "You know what I see when I look at these graves?" My son turned his back to Jeb. "I see people who wanted to leave something behind, but all they left was a two-hundred-pound slab of granite."

Jeb's gravelly voice was as firm and reassuring as a concrete bench. "We all want to prove our greatness and leave something behind. We all want to be heroes, superstars. We need that illusion. Because we don't want to believe we're going to die. So, what do you do? You hang your name among all the other names and hope it survives beyond you."

"No way I could enjoy life while thinking about dying." Race spun around and faced the wise groundskeeper.

"You're like most folks," Jeb said. "Which is why they buy fancy things, avoid honest emotions, build pretend identities on their phones, tranquilize themselves with trivial matters. All as protection against the fact that we're just mortal animals. We attach ourselves to our jobs, our careers, our status, our ego. It's easier that way; detaches us from the truth."

"So, if I worry about being a shitty ballplayer, or whether women will want me after I lose my sex appeal, that makes me a selfish prick who doesn't live in reality?"

"Your words, not mine, superstar," Jeb said with a pitiless cackle. "The world doesn't care what we did or what we'll do. It's only focused on the right now."

"Appreciate that, Yoda."

"But what do I know about life? I work in a graveyard."

Race laughed and scanned the area. "You ever see one?"

"What?"

"You know, a ghost."

"Sure, lots of times."

"Yeah? Ever wonder what they want?"

"When the dead come to visit, they want one of three things." Jeb smiled and rested the rake on his shoulder. "They either want to see you, want to tell you something, or they want to take you with them."

Again, Race turned his back to his new friend, taking in the tranquility, the understanding, and the anguish fluttering in the air. My boy knew some spirits were watching him there; he could smell their presence. But was Sevan watching? And if she was, what did she think of her son now?

"Hey, I lied to you before," Race said. "I did find something at Willow Pond, something important." My son turned to address Jeb, but the old man was gone, replaced by a curious crow pecking at fresh grass seed under the rosebush. *Really? You leave me just like that?* Race dropped his head and passed through the cemetery gates.

Clouds thickened. The racket of the city pummeled his ears as he stared across the street at the Armenian Jewel Specialty Market. The chance of another passionate night with Khloe deflected his attention away from the sandstorm of questions spinning in his skull regarding his family and identity. Part of him wanted to forget everything he'd unearthed to this point, while the other part needed to find out more. What's that saying about falling off a horse? Or is it a bike?

Race unzipped his backpack, glancing at the pink Post-it note with Khloe's phone number and grinning at her hand-drawn heart. He moved the paper aside and plucked out Sevan's diary, his fingers wavering between wonder and reluctance. He dropped his bag and flipped through the book's worn pages, fighting the fear of what else he might discover. Deciding to read only one entry, he turned to the middle of the book:

Our condition keeps us company every hour of the day. The disease, once named, is a noose around our necks. Pain matters. The hurt sticks with us. Are we the same person? Not precisely, but in a way, yes. Doubting is easier than believing. We wanted to be something else, anything, except what we were. This body, our home and battlefield, is a constant source of conflict. Half-asleep and half-awake, the merging, questioning what's real all the time.

At the bottom of the page, Sevan had jotted down a phone number with Boston's 617 area code next to the initials "D.M." *Perfect*, Race thought, but only the ghosts of Mount Auburn picked up on his invisible sarcasm. The number and initials were hazy hints, another path leading to somewhere else, like a finger pointing at the moon. *Who are you, D.M.?* My son scratched at the stubble on his chin. *And why did she write your number here?*

"What the hell, why not?" Race said aloud, pulling his cell from his pocket and dialing the mystery number.

One ring, then another, followed by a third. As he was about to bail on his effort, a gruff voice on the other end snapped, "Yeah? Who's this?"

Race gulped and stammered, "Oh hey, yeah… My name is Race… Race McIntyre."

The man on the other end of the line grunted. "And?"

Race hesitated, then muttered, "Ah, nothing… Sorry, dialed the wrong number."

The other guy's tone livened up. "Hold on a sec. McIntyre? Any relation to Danny?"

"Um… I…" Thrown off-balance, Race didn't know whether to answer the question or hang up. Danny was his grandfather's name, that much he knew. He remembered Colin talking about him a few times, but that seemed like forever ago.

"Hey, you there?"

Fighting the urge to abandon the sputtering exchange, Race said, "Yeah, I think Danny and I were related. I mean, he might've been my grandfather. Who am I talking to?"

"Joe Hart, worked with Danny as a lobsterman forty years back. This is the marina where he kept his boat."

"A marina? Where?"

"Watertown, on the Charles." The gruff voice mellowed. "Whenever anyone wanted to get ahold of Mac, they knew where to find him. The guy was always here, especially after he left that wife of his."

For years, from what Colin had told him, my son believed his grandfather had no interest in him and that Danny had abandoned his family. Yet here was a stranger named Joe painting a different picture—one of a man who may have distanced himself from his loved ones but had remained present in other ways. Race gathered his guts and asked, "You don't know if he's alive, do you?"

"Alive?" Joe laughed so loud, my son had to take the phone away from his ear. "Nothing can kill that old pitbull."

"Really?" Race wanted to know more but couldn't bring himself to ask. Part of him longed to contact his grandfather, to associate with his past, and to ask Danny what he knew about Sevan's disappearance.

Joe broke the silence. "So, you don't know Mac?"

"Never met him," Race said. "Probably better that way."

"Mm, well if you care, he's up in New Hampshire now. Want his cell?"

Race bought himself a few valuable seconds while weighing his options. "Um…" Contacting Danny would be a concrete step into the unknown. But my son needed closure, to assemble the missing pieces of his family's history, and to gain some understanding. "Yeah, I'll take the number. Maybe it's time me and Mac got to know each other."

Joe obliged, sharing Danny's cell phone info with Race, who saved it in his contacts. When they ended the call, my son questioned what might happen when, or if, he reached out to his paternal grandfather. Was he prepared to find out the truth about his family and himself? While he weighed his choices, the honks and beeps on Mt. Auburn Street multiplied, and the overcast day got gloomier.

"I've come this far," he said to nobody while staring at Danny's number. "I should do this." He hit the call button, and the phone rang… and rang… and with each passing ring, my son's heart pumped faster, the moment pressing upon him. He shook his head, disbelieving he might talk to both his grandfathers, for the first time ever, in the same day. With tension ripping at his ribs and a buzz growing in his brain, Race writhed alone in a timeless space. Stuck in a state of anticipation and discontent, he winced as the world around him blurred.

Finally, the call went to voicemail, and a message played, featuring an old voice with an indifferent tone. "This is Danny. Leave a message… if you want."

Race stalled, his thoughts twirling like the leaves around his feet on the sidewalk. He swallowed hard, his voice quivering as he spoke. "Um, yeah, Danny," he began, "this is Race, um… I mean, Carlton McIntyre. This might sound crazy, but I think you're my grandfather. I don't know why I'm calling you… but I'm pretty sure we should talk."

My son's words hung in midair, as if waiting for a response.

"Thanks," Race said. "Call me back at this number… if you want."

"Find the Words"
June 2004

Why do I remember the first time I ever saw her?
The way she walked into the place, I knew she
wasn't shy
And why do I remember our first words to
one another?
How I couldn't help but lose myself within her
deep, dark eyes

And why do I remember the way we used to dance?
How I held her oh so close and prayed the songs
would never end
And why do I remember the way I held her hand?
How the feeling deep inside me said that we were
more than friends

*I know why I remember, and I know now why
it hurts,
But because I'm still in love with her, it's hard to
find the words*

*She never told me what was wrong, she never said
a thing
We never looked beyond ourselves to ease love's
painful sting
I never thought I'd lose her, and I never thought
we'd part
Now all I have are memories locked away inside
my heart*

*But why don't I remember how I used to say I
loved her?
Could it be that she was gone before I had
the chance?
And why don't I remember how I stayed with
her forever?
Maybe 'cause the time had come for us to end
the dance*

*I really don't remember, and I don't know why
it hurts
But sometimes I pretend I do when I can't find
the words*

To Be a Man

No! No! Don't let go! Not my sister. My daughter. Yes… remember. My girl… missing. They took her… a boat, a car. Who? Why? I wish… I'm sorry. What happened? Tell me! I won't let go.

My daddy was a teacher, and he loved Greek mythology—just as much as he loved his little girl. He read all the legends to me, explained every allegory, but I have trouble recalling most of them now. I remember Sisyphus, though, the tyrant who cheated death and angered the gods. As punishment, they forced him to push a rock up a hill over and over, for all eternity. Like Sisyphus, again at the foot of the mountain, I always find my burden. But why should we obey the gods? Why not defy them? Why keep pushing our rocks? I don't think a universe without a master would be empty or pointless. In my imagination, someday far off in the future, Sisyphus and I are both happy.

I always wished my son could drop his burden and be happy, too. He had defined himself by the losses in his life, but he was so much more than that part of his story.

After returning from his trip to the cemetery, Race sat on the same stool at the same sports bar as the night before. The sizzle of chicken wings hobnobbed with a chorus of cheers and jeers riffling through the air. He was glad that night's World Series game was being played in Los Angeles. The city of Boston plagued him with enough terrible memories, new and old. The last thing my son needed was the Red Sox celebrating their championship right under his nose, rubbing his face in his failure.

He stared at his phone, its screen displaying Khloe's number. She hadn't called or texted him since she dropped him at the Zakarians' house earlier that day, and he hadn't reached out to her either. Now, he couldn't decide if he regretted that or not.

Race took a sip of his beer, and the icy bitterness washed over his tongue. A disquiet settled onto the stool next to him as he questioned why he'd left that message for Danny McIntyre. Why would he crack open a door to his past? What was waiting on the other side? He'd give the old man till tomorrow afternoon to call back. If he didn't, then Race would skip town and go back to Oregon, sell the house, get rid of everything, and forget Colin and the baggage he left behind. Besides, Boston had nothing more to offer my son, and he was so eager to leave, he had decided to *fly* back to Sea Point. With his entire life upended over the past six hours, he might not even care if the plane crashed. He would've done anything to escape; would've faced his most barbaric demons.

But flying wasn't what frightened him most. Fear itself was the ghost that haunted Race's shadows, purring uncertainties into the corners of his consciousness. Yet, for him, in that moment, his desperation screamed louder than his fear, and he conjured the courage to confront the darkness within.

At the sports bar, activity buzzed all around. Whoops and hoots of fans cheering for the Red Sox overloaded the room, punctuated by occasional outbursts of "Fuck yeah!" and "Fuck you!" My son tuned out the noise, and why wouldn't he? The baseball world and the game he once loved had moved on without him.

As Race slumped at his table, picking at a chicken wing, a raucous group of men standing behind him let out a roar and began laughing. Their drunken enthusiasm propelled one of them backward, knocking into my son. The stumbling man flailed his arms, braced himself against the wobbly table, and sent Race's phone toppling to the ground.

My boy glared at the drunk and stooped down to pick up the cell. When his fingers grazed the cold, sticky floor, his short fuse reached its end, and he reacted like he'd lost a close game because of a blown call. "Asshole," he grumbled, looking up at the guy.

Another louse by the window said, "Yo, Bobby, you hear that?"

"Yeah, I heard it." The thin, thirtysomething-year-old man who caused the mishap wore a faded Bruins cap and a ragged Curt Schilling jersey. He stood over Race, frothing at the mouth, with one hand on his hip and the other gripping a bottle of Sam Adams. "Hey, jerkoff, what'd you call me?"

"Oh, sorry." My son stood, rising higher and higher like

a deliberate elevator, fierce emerald eyes never losing contact with Bobby's reddened face. "I called you an asshole."

Twitchy and short, with a wispy mustache, Bobby turned his cap backward and stared up at Race. Puffing out his bony chest, the drunk ran his tongue over his yellow teeth and said, "How 'bout I make you *lick* my asshole?"

Four of Bobby's rowdy friends surrounded Race, joining in on the fray. "Yeah, fuckface," one of them shouted. "Lick it!"

Race recognized the type—boisterous Bostonians with anger management issues and low self-esteem, who frequented bars hunting for trouble after ten too many beers. Only men who'd once been stuffed into high school lockers showed such a reckless brand of cockiness. My son scanned the group, ready to swing. "You boys don't want to do this," he said. "Trust me."

Bobby's bloodshot eyes grew wide. "Holy shit, no way," he blurted, pointing a skinny finger at Race, a sly grin plastered across his face. "Look who it is! Carlton McIntyre, worst fuckin' draft pick in Red Sox history, the Pawtucket legend who blew his load in the minors and couldn't even take a fuckin' crap in Boston."

My son's pulse quickened, his hands curling into fists. His revved-up mind flashed to the image of Bobby lying in a pool of blood, but then to Khloe lying naked in bed. This night had two probable outcomes, and he could blow off steam in either scenario. But a good brawl would satisfy him more than a sexual sparring match. "You should stop talking now," Race said, leering down at Bobby.

"Yeah? And you should go fuck your mother."

Race cocked his arm, but before he could thrust his

fist forward, someone grabbed him from behind and ripped him away from the fray. My son whipped around and locked eyes with an older man, a familiar face—clarity in the chaos.

"Settle down, Rook." The man's gritty voice was calm, yet forceful.

"Dobie?" Race said.

"How about stepping outside with me?"

With glacial urgency, Race followed the man to the door, while sneering over his shoulder at the boys by the bar.

Bobby took a small step toward them and shouted, "You're a fuckin' failure, McIntyre!"

Race stopped in his tracks and threw up his arms. "I'm right here, tough guy."

"Let it go, Rook," Dobie said, placing a loose hand on my son's stiff shoulder.

Out in the cool evening air, the two men walked half a block before pulling up at a busy corner. "I'm good now," my boy said.

"You sure?"

"I don't believe it." Race's surprised smile seconded the sentiment. "Friggin' Dobie Salazar, you're the last person I expected to see."

After laughing long and hard, Dobie said, "Ditto." He had a crooked nose and an affable grin that ran the length of his broad shoulders. The age spots on his forehead, wrinkles around his eyes, and stubbly gray beard belied his youthful build. Dobie's weathered face might've spelled out AARP, but his muscular physique spelled out MMA.

Neon signs illuminated the crowded sidewalk as people in Red Sox gear hurried past, their peppy footsteps pelting the asphalt. Laughter and chatter stuffed the air, along with the aroma of hot strombolis, while cars and trucks rolled by, their headlights slicing through the darkness.

The blood that had flushed Race's angry cheeks had since receded, leaving behind his natural complexion, the color of composure. "Sorry about that little dispute at the bar," he said. "You spared those dudes from some expensive-ass dental bills."

Dobie eyed Race, compassion written on the old man's face. "Hey, don't sweat it," he said. "No matter what we do, some stuff follows us around. Our shadows, man, they stick to us, till the blackest clouds roll in."

Dobie Salazar, a former assistant equipment manager for the Red Sox, had already been with the organization for forty years when my son first met him in 2008. On the day of Race's major league debut, Dobie presented him with his uniform, number 71, a forgettable number for a forgettable career.

"It's been a minute," Dobie said as they leaned against the smudgy window of a Dunkin' Donuts. "Crazy how much has happened in ten years."

Race nodded, a spout of empty memories gushing back. "Speak for yourself."

Dobie's eyes twinkled. "I remember your call-up like it was yesterday. You had the world at your feet, and then that at bat, well, you know." His voice trailed off, his nostalgia hitting the showers.

"Thanks for the reminder." Race wagged his head. "I still have nightmares about it, striking out looking in front of Red Sox Nation, everyone expecting me to do something with my chance."

"Hard to know when to swing sometimes, Rook."

Dobie poked Race's shoulder. "Life can break off some wicked curveballs when we least expect 'em."

"Those are wise words, but Pettitte threw me three fastballs." Race sighed, appreciating his bond with the man who'd seen my son flop that dreadful day from the dugout steps. "Fuck, I'm a mess right now, Dobie."

"More than just that whiff eating at you, I'm guessing?"

"You're right. Found out some shit about my family today," Race said, staring at the passing traffic, wondering how much it might hurt if he threw himself in front of a bus. "Got me questioning everything."

Dobie nodded. "I think it's time."

"For what?"

"That conversation you've been meaning to have."

"With who?"

"I'm looking at him." Dobie smirked. "Lemme make a call."

No one values me much anymore. Despite Race's invitations, my friends stopped visiting after I moved into Blue Horizons. They were nice people, and I enjoyed our wine tastings, weekend trips, book clubs, and luncheons, but eventually they abandoned me. Just shook their heads and said I'd changed. Seems I had become a fake version of my former self, and they no longer saw Holly as *Holly*.

Trust me, it's lonely when no one knows you, when people no longer recognize who you used to be. Luckily for Race, one person in Boston knew the *real* him.

The streets surrounding historic Fenway Park erupted into a frenzy of mayhem and madness, the stench of impending triumph growing more pungent. Fans spilled out of bars, their slurring voices raised in jolly chants of "Let's go Red Sox!" boomeranging in the air. Race and Dobie navigated through the throng of blitzed hooligans, which was thick and oozy as a tub of baked beans in the crisp night. The energy of expected victory electrified the city as the Sox—who, until 2004, had gone eighty-six years without a World Series title—made up for lost time, on the cusp of winning their fourth ring in the past fourteen seasons.

While Race and Dobie walked toward Jersey Street, formerly Yawkey Way, the undigested chicken wings in my boy's stomach fluttered. Outside Fenway, Boston's holiest cathedral, police set up barricades to prevent rabble-rousers from storming the park if the Sox won the series that evening.

Race's heart shifted into third gear, his palms sweaty. "What are we doing here, Dobie?" My son couldn't sidestep, or bypass, or evade a sense of déjà vu.

Dobie reassured him with a jagged smile. "Follow me."

The intrepid presence of Fenway loomed ahead, casting a familiar shadow over Race. Memories of his past failures as a player resurfaced, causing a lump to form in his throat. He coughed to clear the airway but couldn't ease the discomfort. As he and Dobie approached the stadium, a large police officer halted their progress. "This area is closed, fellas."

Staring the cop dead in the eye, Dobie said, "Captain Sullivan gave us clearance. Feel free to call him."

The officer used his walkie-talkie to call the captain, and Sullivan confirmed Dobie's story over the radio. "All right, you're good to go," the officer said, moving a sawhorse aside.

My son followed Dobie to the players' entrance on

the opposite side of the park, where an attendant opened the door for them. Race's anxiety continued to mount, the weight of his past mistakes pressing down on him. He was walking on air, but not in the pleasant sense of the expression. Rather, he felt disconnected from the world around him.

In the underbelly of Fenway, memories of his days as a skilled but unfulfilled player saddled Race's thoughts. Being in that place again was like waking up in a dreamworld, or a netherworld. With one numb step after another, my son moved through the dimly lit corridor, passing by the clubhouse and ascending toward the home team's dugout. The once-revered surroundings were unnerving in their emptiness, the deafening roar of a frenzied crowd replaced by an unsettling silence.

Race and Dobie reached the top of the dugout steps, and the field stretched out before them, asleep in the darkened stadium. For a nanosecond, my son was like a spry kid again, full of life, running roughshod on the wind. He peeked at his phone—one hour till he'd turn back into a middle-aged pumpkin. The vast and sterile outfield, with the iconic Green Monster in left field, mocked Race in its slumber—not to be awakened until the *real* players came home.

Dobie nodded toward home plate. "Go ahead, Rook." He gave Race a gentle pat on the back before moving aside.

Race's steps were short and slow as he rambled out of the dugout, pretending to swing an invisible bat. The grass beneath his sneakers felt fleshy and vaguely familiar, the night air around him drawn-out and heavy, like a seventh-inning stretch on a sweltering summer day.

Dobie craned his sturdy neck and yelled into the darkness, "Okay, Fitzy, we're ready!" In an instant, the park lights burst into brilliance, illuminating the entire field.

His throat constricting, my son glared out over the shimmering stadium. Then he laughed and squinted back at Dobie in the dugout. "Unbelievable, man. You got more connections than the Green Line to Kenmore Square."

Dobie grinned and peeled back, disappearing into the dugout tunnel.

Race entered the batter's box, the weight of his past descending upon him once again, more crushing than ever. He leaned over and scooped up a handful of dirt, rubbed it into his palms, let it sift through his fingers, and he swore the clay cried to him as it fell. Standing at home plate on that cool October night, wielding an imaginary Louisville Slugger, he couldn't resist deriding himself. *Swing the fucking stick!* For the billionth time, he replayed the fateful incident in his mind, reliving the situation, the score, the heated rivalry, and all three pitches. Last week of the season, bottom of the ninth inning. The hated Yanks winning 4–3 with two outs, runners on second and third. It all happened so fast. Four-seamer inside corner. Strike one. Four-seamer outside corner. Strike two. Four-seamer right down Main Street. Strike three. The harsh recollections swamped Race's consciousness, and he bowed his head.

Then, an explosion devastated the stillness, a cacophony of cheering and celebration from outside the park. As if someone had cut out his knees, Race crumbled into a crouch. The Red Sox had clinched the Series, won another title without him, without even the memory of him. The jarring realization made a monkey of my son, adding to the jungle of what-ifs that had aped him for years.

He cast his eyes over the illuminated stadium, while glaring reminders of his missed opportunity swooped around him like ghosts. "My whole life would've been different," he said to nobody. "None of this shit would have happened if I took the bat off my goddamn shoulder."

The deafening cheers surrounding the hallowed park overwhelmed Race. He wrestled with a paradox—the uncertainty of what might've been. He considered an alternate reality where he had succeeded in the majors, where a hit in his first at bat catapulted him into a life of fame and fortune. Presumptions and judgments swirled in his psyche like the whirling October wind.

I remember traveling alone from Oregon to Boston for my boy's major league debut. Oh, I was so excited for him, but also apprehensive. The Red Sox had kindly paid for my ticket, and they even gave me a seat behind home plate. When Race stepped into the batter's box in the last inning of that tight game, I couldn't watch; I shielded my eyes. Gosh, it feels like only a week or two ago. Well, maybe not that recent. Sometimes, I like to change the result of that at bat in my mind. Do I imagine he got a hit, maybe a line drive double in the gap or a go-ahead home run? No, I'm not that aspirational. When I visualize that game, I imagine my son still struck out, but he struck out swinging.

Maybe Race would be better off if he had seized that moment, if he managed a bloop single or a seeing-eye grounder that snuck through the infield. But maybe his life would've been worse. It's impossible to determine, and my son can't alter the past.

Beyond the confines of Fenway, the crowd noise hit a deafening crescendo. Car horns blasted and music blared.

The Red Sox had won the Series again, like they'd done five years earlier in 2013, and back in 2007, the season before Race's debut. *So close, yet so fuckin' far*, he thought. But amid the city's dreadful euphoria and the hapless ghosts from his past, a trickle of hope dripped into his brain. Was his life really that bad? Was he a lost cause going nowhere? Or was he right where he belonged? So close, yet so *flippin'* far.

Someday

THE NEXT MORNING, as Race gazed out of his hotel window, the littered streets of Boston appeared to have weathered a typhoon. It was reminiscent of the post–Mardi Gras parade route in New Orleans, strewn with a chaotic aftermath of celebration. Broken bottles, discarded banners, and trashy debris from the all-night revelry dirtied the pavement, a shameless testament to the insane festivities that had followed yet another Red Sox World Series triumph.

Race flumped onto the edge of the bed, his stomach in knots. His priority that morning: securing a nonstop flight from Logan Airport to Portland, Oregon. It was a three-hundred-dollar expense that would put a huge dent in his wallet; he never made more than $25,000 per year in the minors, and his job at the Sea Point Parks and Rec Department was just enough to pay the bills. But he had to escape the jubilation in Boston and so he gladly forked over the money. In that moment, his long-standing fear of flying felt like a distant concern, overshadowed by the turbulence of the past day.

With sixty minutes left until checkout, and seven hours before he'd be on the plane, Race took a quick shower and packed his belongings. After he stuffed clothes and toiletries into his backpack, his eyes landed on Sevan's diary. Since receiving the book from Petrak, curiosity had gnawed at my boy, but he'd only mustered the mettle to read one page. That uninterpretable passage spoke of a "disease" and "pain" and "doubt" and "reality." Part of him didn't want to look at the other entries, figuring they'd only fluster him more. Finding closure in her words was a hopeless task, like fitting a round peg into a square hole.

He picked up the journal, hesitated for what felt like weeks, then cracked it open. The pages he perused played a sad, haunting symphony of Sevan's confounding life. He hadn't noticed before, but she'd used several styles of writing throughout the book—some passages in pen, some in marker, a few in crayon. Some entries written sideways, printed in large block lettering, some scribbled upside down, some thoughts squeezed onto the pages in perfect script.

Sudden changes alter me without my approval. I'm not who I was. I'm not the girl you think I am. I can never know her again. Even her name is unfamiliar. Our fantastic, terrifying journey is dependent entirely on things unseen.

Many pages contained indecipherable gibberish, but Sevan's clearest writings covered a wide-ranging swath of shadowy topics.

The horror repeats in my mind. Growing up with flashbacks, triggers, and anxiety. I can't speak of what I don't understand. I internalize the violence my people have survived. I don't talk about it. I live with it.

In her writing, she depicted the intensity of her love for Colin, capturing the vivacity of their early encounters, the exhilaration of their budding romance, and her eventual descent into lasting sadness. She included details about Orla McIntyre's animosity toward Armenians, the derogatory language used by Colin's mother, feeling unwelcome in their house, and Colin's unsuccessful efforts to change Orla's perspective. Her diary also revealed truths about the Zakarian family, their strict adherence to religion, and unbreakable bonds to their culture.

To my parents, I'm too American. To my friends, I'm not American enough. Balancing both, being two people at once, is impossible.

Then there were the many passages written in red ink, describing the influential role of her grandmother. Page after page detailing Akabe's tale of survival in the currents of the Euphrates River and the chilling prophecy that followed regarding Sevan's ominous fate.

My grandmother praises a myth, not God. She believes God betrayed her long ago. As a girl, she did not sense God, just violence, hate, and despair. How can she ever believe in something that was absent during her greatest suffering and pain? She feared the people

*trying to kill her more than she feared any God. Now,
I live with her fear.*

Race let the journal drop to the floor. The pages hesitated, then stood at attention, pleading for him to reenter their world. He paused, fighting the urge to kick the book across the room, while longing for more. He snatched it up and turned to the last entry. Though he'd glanced over this one before, the words had called him back, every syllable another dart in his heart. The journal slippery in his hands, my son read his mother's words silently—for only himself and the dead to hear.

Within these pages, I struggle with a legend. My grandmother tells the story of how Tsovinar, the Armenian water goddess, saved her from death. But distrust tugs at me, like the currents of the Euphrates. What is true? What is reality? Did my grandmother imagine this tale? Was it her only choice, the only way to survive the darkest days of her life? And now, the only way to survive her memories? If I can't escape her past, how will I survive my own darkness?

Race absorbed the density of Sevan's terror as he read. The legend of the goddess and the prophecy had invaded the girl's thoughts like a tenacious ghost. History bore down on her, and she questioned whether her grandmother's account held a kernel of truth—wondered if, and when, her own death was approaching. The ancient tale of Tsovinar loomed over Sevan's young life, embodying both hope and distress in a world scarred by untellable horrors.

Though Race sympathized with his presumed birth mother, he was determined to hold on to the bond we had always shared. After all, I'm the one who raised him. Before closing the diary, my boy spied a page marked with sloppy etchings about *ending things*, along with an address on Beechwood Street in Watertown, under which Sevan had written *McIntyres*.

And then, and then… Oh, I seem to have lost myself. Who was I talking about? Sometimes, in this dreamish world, you wonder if no one's real. It's interesting, though—each time I have a lapse of memory, I think of the anguish that must afflict those poor souls who *know* they no longer remember anything. I imagine that, in their forgetting, a hidden joy must overtake them, and I doubt they'd exchange that joy for any of their memories, no matter how beautiful they may be. Oh, yes… I've found my place again.

Next thing he knew, Race was stepping out of a taxicab in a quiet Watertown neighborhood, near the banks of the Charles River. He stood before his father's childhood home, as shattered recollections orbited within him at the speed of light, fractured images desperate to assemble and escape. The uninspiring two-story brick home boasted a modest patch of grass in front and three frail brick pillars on the porch that seemed incapable of supporting the structure. For sure, the old McIntyre house, still standing, held untold stories within its walls.

Across the street, students at the Perkins School for the Blind played and sang on an expansive, fenced-in green lawn. Race marveled at their world, living in perfect darkness, untouched by sights no child deserves to see. For a beat, my son saw himself in this place, in a previous life. He shut his eyes, while haunting sounds pierced his mind—arguing, screaming, a woman crying, wailing so loud he smelled her tears.

Here's my theory: We choose which memories we keep and which ones we throw away. Our recollections are not random. They are a choice, a constant choice. Like verses to our favorite songs, lyrics we know verbatim, lines burned into our brains. We recall those words because of how they make us feel, because they mean something to us. We remember because we *want* to remember.

Observing the house where his dad once lived, Race envisioned Colin's life in various stages—from his days as an innocent child, to the time he fell deeply in love, and finally to the moment he took a daring leap, escaping Watertown and embarking on a one-way, cross-country expedition with his son. Race's takeaway: his father had mastered the art of leaving the past behind him. But what about Sevan? Why would she leave *everything* behind?

My boy pulled out his phone and used the thing that people use to search for things, the Giggle button, or something like that, and typed out "Armenian Jewel Specialty Market." Upon discovering the number, Race paused, his finger hovering over the screen before placing the call.

"Hi, it's Race," he said when Sonia answered, his voice reflecting the sincere side of him most people didn't get to see or hear. "I just wanted to say… I've been reading Sevan's diary, and I have a million questions."

Sonia paused before speaking. "You have her diary?"

"I didn't tell you before, but Petrak gave it to me."

"Mm, I thought he might." Sonia's empathy reached through the phone. "I gather that book has stirred up a lot inside you."

"It led me to my father's house. I'm here now." Race let out a sigh, releasing fumes of relief and apprehension. "Feels like I've stumbled onto something important, something that's been hidden for a long time."

"Sevan didn't spend much time at that house," Sonia said. "Your father's mother, Orla, didn't approve of our kind. But Mr. McIntyre, I think his name was Danny, he was always nice to us. Sevan got along with him well. She told me he was like another father to her."

"Wait, my grandmother didn't approve of what?"

"Our kind, Armenians." Sonia's unarmed tone sharpened. "Discrimination against us was not so bad back then, at least not for me—just a crude comment or a suspicious leer here and there. It's much worse today, but of course, there were ignorant people then, and Orla was one of them."

"Tell me more about Sevan," Race said. "I need to know."

Sonia's voice reclaimed its reassuring tone. "Race, I can only say so much. The person who can help you the most is Petrak."

"I've been there," he said. "You had your daughter deliver me to him, remember?"

"Yes, but please, see him again. He has the deepest connection to your mother's past. You shouldn't leave until you find what you need to know."

"I'm not sure what I need to know," he said. "Or if I *want* to know?"

"Promise me you'll go."

Joyful cries of the kids playing behind the gates of the Perkins School floated across Beechwood Street, distracting Race for a stretch.

"Hello? Race, are you still there?"

My son snapped back to the present, back to the phone call, twisting around the idea of confronting Petrak again. "Yes, I'm here." If he paid the man another visit, the conversation wouldn't be easy. But worthwhile? Necessary?

Sonia's voice waned. "Your mother's journal is a precious keepsake, a symbol of her complicated life, and I am glad it's in your hands. But a book can only say so much, Race. On paper, words are just letters assembled in a meaningful manner. However, when words leave a person's lips, propelled by the heart, they carry the full weight of truth, revealing the essence of the soul. Speak with your grandfather again. Please."

"I'll think about it," he said. "Thank you." While not fully divulging his mother's past, Sevan's diary had unlocked an entrance into his own personal history. Would he step through that passageway if it meant confronting the truth?

"Good luck, Race."

Sonia's casual farewell surprised him. "Yeah, I'll need it."

"I'm sorry," she said. "I didn't mean to sound crass." Her warm laugh begged for forgiveness. "In Armenian, the word for 'good luck' and 'goodbye' is the same: *hajoghutyun*."

"Okay, then good luck it is," he said.

Slipping the phone into his pocket, Race stared at the place where his father grew up, as if it held the key to all his questions. Alongside his fascination, however, a creeping paranoia slithered into his bones. Shouldn't some secrets remain buried? Perhaps, but his talk with Sonia, awash with shared understanding, had reassured my son that he wasn't alone on this journey. Facing Petrak again might lead to more answers, and Sonia's suggestion had set him on that path. But as he stood on the sidewalk, the cloud cover cast a shadow over his quest.

Stepping onto the lawn and moving closer to the house, Race peered into a large picture window, intensifying his focus as he discerned what lay hidden within. But the more he tried, the less he could see. He walked closer, cupped his hands, and placed them on the cold glass. Darkness still. He backed away, a couple of steps at first, then a few more, all the while looking into the window. When he reached the sidewalk, he stopped, back where he started, and a distant reflection glared at him, but it wasn't his own. It was Colin, his face younger and handsome, sad and lonely. His mouth didn't move, but his lifeless green eyes shouted at the person on the other side of the glass. Silent words, begging to be heard.

In a cozy kitchen on Porter Street, two very different men sat facing each other, reunited over steaming cups of Armenian tea. Petrak, with his grizzled gray beard and haggard face, wore a pressed shirt, a testament to his unshakable dignity. And my Race, well, he was nothing more than a clenched jaw in faded jeans. The room had a simple charm to it, with the comforting scents of lemon, cinnamon, and ginger wafting in the air. Sentimental whatnots and knick-knacks occupied shelves and sills, with each item telling a long-ago story of a family's life. On the wall, a clunky old clock kept unsteady time, providing an out-of-step back-drop to the silence.

As Race considered how to crack the ice, a nagging noise bedeviled his mind, a ticking time bomb of yearning.

His frustrating visit with Petrak the previous day still irked him, like the way he felt after going hitless in a double-header. "I'm sorry about yesterday," he said to the old man. "I shouldn't have rushed out."

"This is a difficult time," Petrak said, nodding. "I am glad to see you again, no matter the circumstances."

With a shaky sip of hot tea, Race steadied himself. "I'm leaving today, going back to Oregon, but I wanted to ask you some questions first." His eyes met Petrak's, searching for answers.

The old man placed his cup on a saucer. "Ask what you need," he said and sat back in his chair. "I will do my best to help."

Race took a breath. "Why didn't you ever call me or write to me?"

"I tried several times when you were young. Sent cards and letters, called now and then. But your father warned me that if I continued, he would tell you terrible things about me. I preferred your heart knowing the quiet truth over your ears hearing uproarious lies."

"I never got any cards or letters."

"Your father did his best to hide from the past." Petrak sighed and lowered his head. "At that time, many of us tried to disappear… in our own ways."

"Can you tell me about my mother's childhood? Was she happy?"

Petrak's stormy eyes appeared to turn inward, as if searching the corridors of memory. "Sevan was a dynamic and brilliant child," he said, his voice streaked with equal traces of pride and melancholy. "At an early age, she possessed an unquenchable thirst for knowledge and deep-rooted ties to our Armenian traditions. But her path was a dark one. She may not have seemed like it at the end, but she was a fighter, determined to navigate life's labyrinth. Still, like many before her, she lost her way."

"What do you mean?"

"Your mother was a radiant spirit. In her youth, she danced with lightness, sang with joy. She cherished her heritage, her family, and her church, weaving the threads of our culture into her very being. Yet, like all young souls, she could not resist the allure of the new, the foreign. American music, American boys—these were her siren songs, leading her away from the familiar shores of our traditions. Yeva and I, we watched and waited, hoping she would find her way back to us, to the songs of her ancestors. But the currents of youth are strong, and sometimes they carry us far from home."

Listening to the tales of her childhood, Race pictured a young Sevan, full of life and promise, and it brought a bittersweet ache to his chest. "And my father?"

Petrak's eyes deadened. "Yes, my daughter loved Colin. Their journey together was tumultuous, as is any journey worth taking, marked by highs and lows. But through it all, their hearts remained entwined, bound by a love that transcended life's tribulations."

A lump formed in Race's throat. "Hard to see my dad being capable of that kind of commitment," he said, his voice barely audible.

"Your father was a good man," Petrak said. "But I understand how he might have changed once Sevan was gone."

"I need to know…" Race's voice wavered as he ventured

into uncharted territory. "Why did she decide… to end things?"

Petrak nodded, his eyes teeming with affinity. "I appreciate your courage in asking, Race. It is a difficult subject, but one we should explore together. Sevan was a complex person. Yes, she held a fierce love for her heritage, but she also bore an affliction few knew of. Her past, her grandmother's prophecy, these were the specters that plagued her when she gazed into the water that day. Specters she left behind on that bridge."

The temperature dropped in the kitchen as Race delved into the darkest corner of his mother's story. "The prophecy…" he said, recalling Sevan's diary entries. "How much did it affect her?"

Petrak's stoic expression conveyed the gravity of the past. "That prophecy cast a long, unyielding shadow. It spoke doubt into her being, while confirming her destiny. She carried its burden with her throughout her days. I believe it played a significant role in her battles, in the depths of her depression."

"How could believing in a legend convince her to leave her family?"

"My daughter was a troubled girl." Petrak glared through Race, into the floral wallpaper. "Her decisions were her own, but I cannot say they were unaffected by outside sources."

The room held its breath as the conversation unfolded, each word carving a deeper understanding of Sevan's intricate, problematic life. There was a bleakness to the remarks, a shared pain and a yearning to unlock the secrets of a woman's anguish, piece by agonizing piece.

"What outside sources?"

"Our past, our history." Petrak's voice was low and gruff. "The Armenian genocide, it's a wound that cuts deep, a wound that we carry within us, generation after generation. Our people, they braved horrors beyond imagination."

Race leaned forward, his spirit sinking. "I've heard of it," he whispered, "but I know nothing about it."

"The stories…" Petrak began, his voice cracking. "Families torn apart, lives shattered, dreams extinguished. Innocent children lost to senseless brutality. As many as a million souls slaughtered." He paused, taking in a frail breath, history pushing down on his shoulders, his eyes pleading for understanding. "The world has turned a blind eye to our suffering, to the truth. The denial, the refusal to call it what it was… a genocide. It is a wound that festers as the years pass."

The walls converged on Race, and a dagger pierced his heart. But he refused to yank it out or do anything to ease the pain. He couldn't fathom the agony his people had tolerated.

"Yet, despite the torment, we have survived, dragging the millstone within us." Petrak's voice gained strength. "To worsen the matter, still, the United States refuses to use the word 'genocide,' refuses to admit the facts."

The room rumbled with screams from generations past, while Race bonded with his heritage, a history of suffering and resilience—now ingrained within him, though it had always been a part of him. "I want to understand," he said, helpless to expound on the comment, like trying to grab a handful of water.

Petrak's eyes held a glimmer of hope. "Then before you

leave Watertown, there is somewhere else you need to go. There you will see and feel the truth of our history, and you must never forget."

:13

Don't Be Afraid

In THE MARROW of Watertown, Race fidgeted on the side-walk outside the Armenian Museum of America, a place that promised to fill in his narrative. The revelation that his birth mother was Armenian had ignited an ember of intrigue within him. As he approached the entrance, his steps were tentative, but his heart swarmed with readiness. When he hesitated, a brisk morning breeze urged him inside.

The second he passed through the doorway, the air around him transformed, embracing him with a solemn and comforting aura. He bathed in the tranquility of the spacious lobby, with polished marble floors that gleamed and greeted him, accompanied by downy, diffused sunlight streaming through large windows. Powerful and evocative exhibits adorned the entire space, each one designed to convey the history and culture of the Armenian community.

In one corner, a striking display highlighted traditional costumes, their vibrant fabric and intricate embroidery telling stories of ages past. In another corner, a long glass case held musical instruments, children's toys, and household items. Nearby, a series of notes, poems, and drawings captured both joy and trepidation, depicting the indomitable spirit of the Armenian people and the hardships they withstood.

After climbing a set of winding stairs to the second floor, Race encountered a wall exhibit regarding the genocide—a series of haunting photographs, all of which joined to call out his name. The black-and-white hues of the pictures inside the frames contrasted with the lustrous colors of the world outside. Race fixed his gaze on the images, the grief-stricken faces, each photo a testament to strength amid incomprehensible suffering, evidence of the Armenians' will to survive after the Turks dismantled hell and reconstructed it on Earth. The pictures captured the victims' hollow stares, the weary bodies, the devastation etched into every line on their foreheads and cheeks.

A faded photo of an Armenian family drew my boy's attention, their forced grins a defiant protest against the darkness that had cloaked their world. A young girl's eyes met his through the picture's sepia-tinted lens, and for a flashing moment, Race sensed an inexplicable connection. It was as if her gaze had reached across time, touching his soul and singing songs of his ancestors. His breath hitched in his throat as he dwelled on the genocide's magnitude. It was a history he hadn't been conscious of, a legacy of pain he had never felt.

Next to the photographs were artifacts that spoke of perseverance and resistance. Faded letters and diaries penned by survivors uttered tales of hope walking alongside despair. There were shreds of clothing, remnants of lives once lived, now preserved in honor of the lives lost. Another display case protected delicate handcrafted objects, reflecting the eternal fortitude of a people determined to reclaim their identity. Intricate Armenian rugs, handwoven with care, symbolized the threads of resilience knitted through bloodlines. Each piece seemed to pulse with the heartbeats of those who had crafted them, a bridge between then and now.

As Race moved through the museum, absorbing the stories of survival and perseverance, the gravity of his heritage settled onto his shoulders. A furious scramble of morbidity, fury, and pride collided in his mind as he contemplated the lives extinguished, the injustice endured, and the vitality that had prevailed.

He peered through a round window, and the sunlight painted the streets anew, revealing the world he'd always known, yet now viewed through a different lens. He had been unfamiliar with Armenian culture and history, but a legacy lived within him, a heritage buried until now. With every shallow breath, my boy embraced a newfound kinship to something greater than himself. The photos, the artifacts, the stories—they etched themselves into his bones, reshaping his identity. He wasn't just Race anymore, but a courier for his descendants, whose history deserved to be remembered, revered, and shared.

A young attendant with warm eyes and a welcoming smile approached Race. "Hello," the man said, his voice trimmed with genuine interest. "You must be Mr. McIntyre."

"Yes, how do you…"

"Your grandfather called ahead," he said. "The museum is typically closed on Mondays, but when Mr. Zakarian asks for a favor, we're happy to oblige. My name is Elias."

"That was nice of him, but I don't mean to bother you if you're busy."

"Not busy at all," Elias said. "Is there something specific you're hoping to find?" Bookish, thin, and maybe just out of college, Elias wore tan slacks and a stylish brown sports coat while modeling a cultured etiquette. With a long and deliberate finger, he pushed his wire-framed glasses up on the bridge of his nose, like a sophisticated wealth of knowledge in a ten-dollar haircut.

Beside an elegant rug hanging royally on the wall, Race shoved his hands in his pockets. "I'm curious about the myths of Armenia," he said. "Have you heard of Tsovinar?"

Elias's eyes lit up, like my boy's inquiry had unlocked a treasure chest of stories. "Ah, Tsovinar," the attendant said in a reverent tone. "She is not just a legend, but an essence of nature, a symbol of bounty and destruction, quilted into the fabric of our culture. The Armenian people also call her Nar."

He guided Race to the opposite wall, where they viewed an elaborate drawing of Tsovinar in a magnificent golden frame. The image portrayed a serene yet powerful woman, her hair cascading like liquid silver, her eyes boundless and luminous. "She was the goddess of water," Elias said, "the guardian of rivers, lakes, and springs, the protector who sustained our land."

My son studied the drawing, his face inches from the frame. "She's incredible," he said.

Elias described a time when Armenians revered the elements that nurtured them. "Folklore tells us that people would gather by Nar's sacred waters, seeking her blessing for rain to quench their thirst and sustain their crops. But she was more than a benevolent spirit; she held dominion over the wild forces of nature."

With each word, Elias painted an evocative picture of a deity who could tame tempestuous storms with a mere whisper. "Tsovinar's waters held both life and power. To stand by her side was to stand on the threshold of the divine and the uncontrollable."

Race's eyes gleamed with the light of an ancestral past he had never known. The lifeblood of ancient Armenia flowed through him, connecting him to a legacy that time had buried. "It's amazing," my son said, his voice choked with deference.

Elias nodded, lingering on the image of Tsovinar. "Indeed, it is. Our culture embraces stories that reflect our steadfast connection to the land and its elements. Nar reminds us of the delicate balance between humanity and the forces of nature."

As Race consumed Elias's words, his thoughts shifted to his mother Sevan and his grandmother Akabe—who had honored a haunting prophecy, murmured through decades. It spoke of Tsovinar's claim on Sevan's soul as payment for saving Akabe's life during the genocide. Even now, the mere notion of such a sacrifice sends shivers into the seams of my spine.

"Please, forgive me for being blunt," Elias said, a savvy gleam in his eyes, "but your curiosity on this topic goes beyond the ordinary."

"Yeah, well, my next question might sound nuts." Race hesitated, his voice dripping with suspicion. "But tell me, are there stories of anyone actually encountering Nar? I mean, have they seen her, or has she ever spoken with them?"

Elias's smile held a drop of mystery. "There are hushed tales, told by elders around hearths, of those who have felt her presence. Some say she communicates through dreams, offering guidance to those who seek it. But remember, my friend, legends are like water—they take on the shape of the vessel that carries them."

Upon leaving the museum, Race had not only gained new knowledge about Tsovinar but also developed a profound admiration for his ancestors—those with lives shaped by a formidable goddess capable of both blessing and challenging them. Out on the street, as he walked away, the air hissed secrets of a world waiting to be unraveled. For Race, that world was three thousand miles away. My son was coming home.

At Logan Airport, Race squirmed in a cramped seat at his gate. His heart was ready to get on the flight to Portland, but the rest of his agitated body showed signs of refusal. His fingers, slick with sweat, twirled his phone in his palm, and he kicked at the backpack resting by his feet. Only two other people shared the gate area, while the clock above moved at a glacial pace.

To his left, a teenage girl wearing headphones immersed herself in a well-worn novel, oblivious to the world around her. Across from her, an older gentleman, absorbed in a newspaper, bore the weary face of somebody who'd seen many of life's difficulties.

The airport buzzed with busyness. Hectic. Hurried. Yammering and yattering all around, punctuated by crackling intercom announcements. The smell of Auntie Anne's pretzels twisted in the air, melding with the sterile smack of industrial-grade disinfectants.

Race's mind was a mess, trading punches with the anxiety that challenged him before every flight. The magnitude of the horrific photos he'd seen and what he'd learned at the Armenian museum crashed down on him, adding a layer of lament to his unease. On top of everything, there was the jarring revelation of his heritage, a new chapter in his story that he had yet to fully comprehend.

Amid this turbulence, the faces of two women manifested in his brain: Khloe and Amanda. One he had drifted away from; the other had disappeared into thin air. He took their memories with him, as well as the haunting question of what might've happened had he pursued either woman.

With a wag of his handsome head, Race reached out to Khloe. In his text, he apologized for not saying goodbye in person and revealed that he was returning to Oregon. He invited her to come visit someday, grateful for her help in uncovering his family's secrets. During one of his talks with me, my boy shared the precise words of that text, but all I recall is that the message ended with a dab of sadness, a skosh of nostalgia, and no reference to Khloe's unhappy marriage.

Race sent the text and stared out the window, watching planes take off and land, a picture of constant motion. The roar of jets and the sight of folks rushing around in the airport both excited and unnerved my boy. He moved to another seat, his back now to the window, distancing himself from the outside commotion and the persistent reminder of his imminent flight. With a giant-sized breath, he called Glenn. The phone rang a few times before his friend answered. "Mac, my man! Where are you?" Glenn's voice was a double-play combination of scrutiny and warmth.

"Logan Airport," Race replied, his words oozing with discomfort. "Heading back home tonight."

"Hold up. You're flying?" Glenn's response was swift and earnest. "Yo, I'll come pick you up when you land in Portland."

Race deliberated on that statement, mulling over Glenn's offer. "Don't worry about it, G. That's a two-hour drive from Sea Point. I'll manage without you, like always."

"Mac, I need to talk to you, it's important." Glenn's tone grew more insistent. "I'll make the drive, no problem."

Race sighed, knowing his buddy well enough to realize this debate wouldn't dry up soon. Glenn wanted to vent about the drama of his mayoral campaign, my son figured. "Okay, man, if you're sure," Race said. "But you don't have to."

"Come on, bro. You know I got your back."

"Like junior year, when you told Coach Buck I broke curfew?"

"Yo, that wasn't my fault, and you know it," Glenn said. "The man figured it out on his own. I swear he's the love child of Casey Stengel and Sherlock Holmes, or some shit."

"Right."

"Hey, why haven't you called or texted? Jess has been worried sick."

"Probably her indigestion," Race said. "She always had a weak stomach."

"Don't be that way, dude."

There was a pause, and then Glenn brought up a subject that had been weighing on both their minds. "Hey," he said, "did you ever track down your dad's mystery lady, Willow, or whatever the hell her name was?"

Race's voice grew somber. "It's a long story," he said, "and it'll take way more than a two-hour car ride to tell it."

"Got it," Glenn said. "I'm officially intrigued. We'll catch up later."

"Cool. See you in Portland."

"Oh, hold on," Glenn blurted before Race hung up. "Forgot to tell you, I pulled some strings and got your license reinstated."

"You're shitting me."

"You owe me one, brother."

Once the call was over, Race's thoughts shifted back to his newfound heritage and the hidden truths that were now ingrained in him. He wondered if he should share the story with me; he wasn't sure I'd understand. Should he tell me about his actual mother, of her Armenian roots, and the silence that had wallpapered her existence? What could it hurt? The truth, he knew, was no longer a weapon capable of harming me.

As Race sat at the gate, contemplating his return to Sea Point and what waited for him there, the airport's overhead speakers crackled with two announcements: a flight to Phoenix canceled, another to Tampa delayed. His anxiety swelled as a frazzled family of seven zoomed past him, scrambling about like chickens with their heads in the clouds. Oh, that's not right, is it? Either way, their panic reminded Race why he hated flying—the lack of control, the need to rely on strangers, and the dread of missing a connection.

Race got up, settled at a nearby bar, and asked for a bourbon on the rocks. The drink was seductive, an invitation, an escape, and he admired the amber liquid. Despite the promise he'd made to himself, Race hadn't come close to staying sober after his DUI. It was a losing battle, but at that instant, he granted himself forgiveness, convinced that he deserved this window of reprieve, considering the weight of his discoveries. *No harm in one more*, he reasoned with himself, the way he always did. He took a sip, and it burned his lips.

My boy recollected his trip, the mystery he'd solved, and the characters who helped him along the way. Khloe, Sonia, and Petrak had been the key actors, but several others played semi-significant roles. There was Daisy, the flirty chatterbox who pried Race out of his shell on the bus to Cheyenne, the plain blonde enamored with the *successful* portion of his baseball career. There was Nathan, the stoic Native American who befriended my son on the Greyhound to Des Moines, the grief-stricken soul who lost his wife and daughter and blamed himself. In Cambridge, Imani the clever store clerk had cracked the code on the address in Colin's songbook, pointing Race toward Mount Auburn Cemetery, his destination all along. Then, of course, there was Jeb, the strict old groundskeeper who guided Race to Willow Pond, the man who taught my boy that the iron bars encircling the graveyard represented more than a barricade between the living and the dead; they served as a decree to honor life itself.

While he swirled his drink to the muted clinking of ice cubes, his phone rang. An unknown number flashed on the screen, the possibility of yet another twist in his journey. He was reluctant to answer, but then he remembered Danny—the other grandfather who'd resurfaced from his past. He gulped down the bourbon and stepped into an exchange.

"Hello."

"Race?" Danny's tentative voice reflected their uncertain past.

"Danny?" There was a touch of surprise in my son's tone, the old man's name swaying in the air for what seemed like forever.

Danny coughed, clearing his throat as an obvious stalling tactic. "Um… there's a lot to say." An understatement after four decades of silence.

"Then let's talk," Race said. "I've got some time before boarding my flight."

"Where are you off to?"

"Oregon, back home."

"We can't do this over the phone," Danny said. "It needs to be in person."

"All right, I can fly back tomorrow instead." Race surprised himself with the quick decision, almost as if something else had decided for him. "When do you want to meet?"

"Soon as you can."

Race leaned forward as the ice melted in his glass. "Where?"

"I left Boston behind long ago, living on Star Island now, off the coast of New Hampshire." The old man's cadence shook like a timid tambourine. "Please, come."

"How do I find you?"

"There's a dock in Portsmouth, across from the Sheraton. Tomorrow morning, at eight o'clock, a boat will be waiting. Sam Heatherton, a good man—he'll take you to Star."

"I'll be there." Race hung up, wondering what the next day would bring. The unknown lay before him, the promise of an allegiance he never saw coming, yet one deep down he had always craved.

:12

I Need Your Love

My brain... a puzzle. My baby, my girl! Where are you? The angels... angels, so pretty. Ice cream, remember. Your hand... Dark, so dark. Don't leave... stay close. Wait! Don't go!

Love is strange, wouldn't you say? It swoops in, spins you around, and suddenly, you're not sure where you're headed. It's tricky, that thing called love, dancing its own steps, never following a straight path. No one knows how long it'll stick around, no matter how bright it shines. Sometimes, when I'm lost in my memories, I hear my husband's voice calling from the past, saying something about love.

One day, recently, I think, Colin dropped by and told me a story from his youth, a sweeping tale about a passionate love that had sparked and spread like a wildfire. His relationship with Sevan had begun in 1973, and a few years later, they committed themselves to each other forever. He was only eighteen years old, as was Sevan, on that sunny October afternoon when they traded vows at the local courthouse. Colin had simple and beautiful dreams—buying a home in a year or two, starting a family when the time was right—but they'd both have to work hard and sacrifice to achieve those dreams. While the couple lived with Sevan's parents on Porter Street, sharing her cell-like childhood bedroom, the young wife juggled working at her father's garment shop during the day and studying for a teaching certificate at night. For his part, Colin had secured a job as a maintenance man at the historic Watertown Arsenal, an entrenched presence in the town for a century, dedicated to crafting supplies for the United States military.

In his spare minutes, Colin poured his soul into songwriting, his biggest dream of all. He was a gifted guitarist, but his lyrical prowess set him apart from other young musicians. A timeless idealist, he believed with every molecule of his person that he'd find fame as a songwriter and performer. No matter how long the road, he was going to become a rock and roll star. No ifs, ands, or whatchamacallits about it.

Every week, he stuffed envelopes with copies of his demo tape and mailed them to record companies across the country. But the replies never came back. Undaunted, he hand-delivered his lyrics and demo to local music studios in the area, except Foxglove Studios on School Street in Watertown. Tom Scholz, the visionary behind the burgeoning band called Boston, lived in the studio's basement apartment. Though Colin walked past the location weekly, he never found the courage to drop his music into Scholz's mailbox. Because of this inaction, my husband missed the chance for his music to reach his idol's ears.

"I don't get why you don't do it," Sevan said, forty-eight hours after their wedding, while she and Colin waited in line at an ice cream parlor. "It's all you talk about."

"If I'm going to play him my demo, it has to be in person." Colin fished out sixty cents from the pockets of his jean shorts. "I just need to knock on his door."

"Your songs are fantastic. Have a little faith in yourself."

"I have the faith," Colin said. "But I'm waiting on the guts."

"You were brave enough to propose to me. Can't be tougher than that."

"That's different," he said. "There's no way you would've rejected me. The regret would've killed you." He might've worded that joke differently if he'd been aware that Sevan already knew how she was going to die.

Boston, the band, had scheduled tour dates that summer to promote their debut album, which included the hit single "More Than a Feeling." On multiple occasions, after news of the tour came out, Colin expressed his desire to attend a show with his young wife, believing he'd have a chance to meet Tom Scholz or lead singer Brad Delp. In his mind, they'd listen to his music on the spot, fall in love with every chord, and help catapult him to stardom.

"We have to go when they play here later this month," Colin said between licks of his chocolate-vanilla-swirl soft-serve cone. "Tickets are sixteen bucks each, but I've been saving up."

"Now I get it." With her thumb, Sevan wiped a smudge of ice cream off her husband's chin. "That's why you've been working extra shifts at the arsenal."

"I wanted to surprise you," he said.

"You're terrible at surprises, unlike me." Sevan elbowed Colin in the ribs, dug into the back pocket of her cutoff shorts—which folks would call "Daisy Dukes" a few years later—and flashed two concert tickets in front of his face. "I'm an absolute expert."

"No way!" Colin snatched the tickets and inspected them with the hyper-disbelief of a lottery winner. "Are you kidding me? How the heck?"

Sevan smiled, like she always did when she made someone happy. "I've been doing some saving of my own," she said, flipping her long, dark hair back over her shoulders. "But I can neither confirm nor deny whether or not your dad chipped in ten dollars."

"Insane!" Colin kissed the tickets and held them up to the sky. "Good ol' Danny boy, coming to the rescue."

When he told me this story, my husband said the two weeks leading up to the concert crawled by at a terrapin's pace, so slow, in fact, he thought the big day might never arrive. But, sure enough, it did. New days always arrive, until they don't.

Time, it's odd, isn't it? Often, when you're waiting for something, it feels like the world just stops. Oh, I remember waiting for my record deal, or my daughter being born, and it felt like centuries. But time doesn't stop, does it? No, it keeps going, even when we think it's standing still. And then, when something bad is coming, time seems to go so fast. Days that used to be long, they just fly by. It's like the more you dread something, the quicker it gets here. I've seen that, yes, I have. Living through so many things, good and bad, I've learned that, well, time doesn't actually change; it just feels different because of what's happening inside us.

So, it's better to focus on the now, on the moments we have, because those moments are what really matter in the end. In a way, that was at the core of Colin and Sevan's relationship, that one question we all struggle with: What really matters in the end?

On a warm autumn night in Beantown, the couple attended the Boston concert at an open-air venue. Some say the show was indoors, at the famed Music Hall, but I think they held it outside. Why? Because I remember my husband telling me how excited he and Sevan were when Tom Scholz and the other guys took the stage. To my face, Colin recalled his new wife's beauty to me, the wind in her long hair blowing as they stood for the band. Now, explain to me, if they were indoors, how could her hair blow in the wind?

My husband also told me Sevan had been acting "different" that entire day, complaining of headaches and dizziness. Also, though she usually had a healthy appetite, she'd eaten only a fish taco at dinner—which Colin found curious since Sevan hated seafood.

"What's wrong?" he recalled asking her. "You're not yourself today."

She laughed, more timid than joyful. "So, why are you telling *me*?"

He brushed off her odd behavior, chalking it up to excitement. Good heavens, he could certainly relate, since he had major jitters of his own that night, with his idols fifty yards away from him, performing in the flesh. While the band played, Colin clutched a large envelope stuffed with his demo tape and the songs he'd written. His plan: get backstage after the show and present his songs to the band. His heart thrummed, and he sang along to every tune, losing himself in the music. He and his wife danced and kissed and hugged, the harmonies of their love flying high in the beautiful, noisy, marijuana-infused air.

Then, in a moment that would forever change their lives, when the song "Something About You" ended, Sevan dropped a bombshell. "Colin," she said, grabbing his hand before he could clap, "I'm pregnant."

The crowd erupted, screaming and applauding, everyone on their feet. The energy surreal, the reverberating guitar chords charging the atmosphere. Pulsating. Billowing.

In Colin's conflicted soul, an army of emotions waged a fierce battle for control. Sure, he had assumed Sevan wanted kids, but he hadn't expected this, not so soon. He had hoped to buy a house of their own, dreamed of getting a better job before establishing his music career, and now that dream had taken an unexpected detour. He looked at Sevan and let go of her hand, his mind racing. "This changes everything." His voice was five parts trepidation, two parts awe.

As she gazed at him, her eyes reflected a strobe light shooting out from the stage. "I know, but it's a new beginning, a new life. It's what we wanted."

"But we never talked about it," he said. "Not really."

"It's amazing though, isn't it?

He nodded, suppressing the grin tugging at his lips. "It *is* amazing. But it's also crazy. Are we ready for this?"

Sevan took his hand again and placed it on her belly. "We'll figure it out together," she said. "We're a team, remember?"

"But the world's a shitty place," he said.

"We'll leave the world behind," she said, completely sure of herself.

Again, the strobe light flickered in her eyes, and it was the only light in Colin's world. He knew he'd always be able to trust it and find it in her eyes, because it was always waiting to be found. He had discovered the light in the darkness—after all, that's what the darkness is for—but going forward, everything would depend on how he took care of that light. Yes, he trusted Sevan, because he loved her. If she wanted to be a mother, he wanted that, too.

Another song began, and the crowd roared. The young lovers ignored the scene, continuing to talk about the new baby, even throwing around a few names. Their nervous words melded together as Colin grappled with, and appreciated, the magnitude of the unexpected news. They sat down holding hands while the dynamic, uplifting rock-and-roll music dissolved into the background, eclipsed by the rebirth of his dreams and the enticing call of the future.

But then, something changed in the night air. Sevan's enthusiasm for the miracle growing inside of her waned, ripped away like a drastic tide, and she got quiet. After a full minute of silence, she jumped up, scanned the arena, and said, "What's this?"

"It's one of their new songs," Colin said. "We haven't heard it before."

She picked at her nails and stared at him. "Why are we here?"

Right then, Colin forgot about his desire to meet the members of the band, forgot about sharing his songs with the world. His music, for the first time, was no longer the focal point of his life. He'd have to be strong for her, prepare his new family for the unknown, and brace for the unexpected. It was the love between him and Sevan and their life together, the one they'd soon embark upon, that took center stage.

Here, at this part of my story, I'm at the point of no return; I have finally crossed the line. I need to keep moving; don't want to stop and watch the bridges burn. For my husband and his first wife, that kind of destruction seemed inevitable, a predictable fire with invisible flames. But I could've never guessed who lit the match.

In May of '77, when Carlton Ernest McIntyre was born, life transformed for Sevan and Colin. The grateful parents had picked the child's name together, inspired by the Red Sox catcher Carlton Ernest Fisk, who sparked their first kiss with an iconic home run less than two years prior. For all of his wishy-washy feelings early on, Colin loved being a dad. He wanted to teach his son the fundamentals of life, from playing baseball to riding a bike, from talking to girls to being a man. A father imparts these cherished lessons to his boy, instilling in him the values that will guide his path in life. That's what my husband thought back then.

Colin's devotion to his infant son was undeniable. He embraced parenthood with fervor, lavishing little Carlton with the care and attention only a doting father could provide. He changed poopy diapers, learned how to swaddle, and wore out a track around the living room while the baby cried himself to sleep each night. When Carlton outgrew his cradle, Colin searched flea markets until he found a secondhand crib. He refurbished it by sanding it down and re-staining it to perfection. Then, he positioned it in a corner of their modest bedroom at the Zakarian residence and hung a mobile overhead, with seven strings attached to seven objects: a glove, a ball, a cap, a bat, a jersey, and two yellow stars.

During the day, Colin worked twelve-hour shifts at the arsenal. Afterward, he'd speed home to spend precious time with his son, often keeping the infant awake well past midnight, whenever the Red Sox played on the West Coast and the televised games ran late. Little Carlton threw his first ball, a fuzzy green cat toy, when he was just eight months old, twice as soon as most advanced babies. He was walking at nine months, primarily because of his dad's encouragement, and the boy was soon racing nonstop around the house. It was in the middle of one of those mini track meets when Sevan's exhausted mother, Yeva, dubbed her lively grandson "Race."

Colin was so very proud of that boy. I've heard, over and over, that Race was a striking sight with his toddler's charm. He had a full head of dark hair and an olive complexion, inherited from his mother, and the vibrant green eyes of his father. He was a *lavash leprechaun* of a kid, a beautiful blend of his Armenian and Irish heritage.

Yet, for all the love and devotion Colin showered upon Race, Sevan couldn't bear to look at her own son. From the very beginning, motherhood proved to be a daunting challenge for her. She struggled with the basics, starting with breastfeeding, and even the simplest of tasks became insurmountable hurdles. The infant refused to latch on to her breast, causing endless sleepless nights laden with willful attempts to nourish her child, only to be rewarded with his colicky cries. During one dark evening, as Carlton wailed in his crib, Sevan tore the baseball mobile from the ceiling and stuffed it into the trash.

Each morning, to help cover the droopy bags under her eyes, Sevan spent thirty minutes applying heavy makeup. While putting on concealer in the cramped bathroom, the new mom would recall her own mother's scolding. It was long before Sevan met Colin that she first started wearing eye shadow, rouge, and lipstick. Before middle school one day, Yeva banged on the bathroom door, demanding that her rebellious daughter come out. In the slender hallway, with Sevan backed up against the wood paneling, her mother's stern lecture had begun.

Metal bracelets clinked down her thin arms as Yeva gestured with desperate hands, her purple nails bitten ragged. "With or without makeup," Yeva had said, waving a thin finger, "you reflect the survival of the Armenian people. Embrace your nose and eyes, your cheekbones, forehead, and chin. Your forefathers were killed because of those features. Be proud of your face; let it remind you of your true self. Accept who you are and love that person."

"Accept who I am?" Sevan's shout clanged off the walls, like a bell's toll, and she stormed off into her bedroom. How could she tell her mother the truth? She couldn't even begin to figure out who she truly was, let alone accept that person.

Following several steps behind, Yeva entered the room and closed the door. Sitting beside Sevan on the bed, she traced the veins in her daughter's hand. "Never forget, your ancestors live in your blood."

Years earlier, Yeva had explained to the girl that Armenians used to have fair skin and light eyes, but throughout history, including in 1915, rape had been a nefarious tool of genocide. Before ever hearing that story, the youngster had felt it, known it. Every summer when she was little, as she played in the sun, her hair and skin got darker, invoking a sinister past. Back then, to Sevan, darkness and evil were the same.

Now that she was a mother, that comparison had come back in spades. While standing on the banks of the Charles River one warm winter's day, in a quiet hour of confidence with her best friend, Sevan asked, "Do you ever want to disappear? Just walk away and go?"

"I'm here for you, always," Sonia said, putting her arm around Sevan's shoulder. "You know that, right?"

"No… I mean, yes." The new mom grabbed her scalp with both hands and tugged at her thinning hair. "God… I think stuff, Sonia. Bad stuff."

Sonia sighed. "Why don't I take Race for a few days, let you get some rest?"

Sevan narrowed her focus and concentrated on the rolling current. "Something's calling me, and I have to follow," she said, sounding as flat as a pawnshop guitar. "This isn't who I am anymore. I don't belong here. This is just someplace the wind blew me."

At the time, Race was less than a year old, yet the torment of raising him was an anchor yanking on Sevan's heart. She was a remarkable failure in a role she had envisioned herself thriving in. Her initial idea of motherhood had painted an extraordinary picture—dreams of ease, fulfillment, and a natural maternal instinct. Instead, she encountered overwhelming distress and utter disappointment. Every day she lost more ground until it reduced her to nothing.

Desperate and breaking, Sevan engaged her hopeful husband in lengthy, exhausting conversations. But she struggled to convey the depth of her shame, the vipers of helplessness nesting within her. They ripped her in two, as she said to him, expressing that she "wasn't meant to have children" and that she felt inadequate for the role—"cursed," as she put it.

"I hate my baby," she claimed one thunderous night. "What's wrong with me?"

"You're exaggerating," Colin said, grabbing her by the shoulders, unable to stop her from shaking. "You're tired, frustrated. It'll be okay."

He kept telling her to never give up, saying that being a mom would make their bond stronger. It was an uphill war, with Sevan clinging to her husband's belief that her exasperation would subside. All the while, as she grappled with panic attacks, dizzy spells, and the unending trials of motherhood, another unsettling presence loomed—her grandmother.

At seventy-three, Akabe was only six decades removed from the heinous events of the Armenian genocide, a living repository of history's darkest memories. The old woman never ceased muttering about the ominous prophecy once shared by Tsovinar. According to the divine goddess, Sevan would be called "home to the water" when she turned twenty. After marrying Colin, Sevan had stashed her grandmother's omen into the far reaches of her mind. Until Race was born, she hadn't given her tenuous destiny much attention, even daring to look forward to enjoying a long life.

But now, whenever the nineteen-year-old looked at her grandmother, or at her son, the relentless march of time drew closer, a foreboding presence haunting her every thought. Closer, and closer, and closer. During that living nightmare, to ground herself as she foraged for hope, she opened the desk drawer in her bedroom, took out Colin's notebook, and read a song he had written for her.

"Only You and I"
August 1977

They said we wouldn't last, time wasn't on our side
The odds were all against us, despite how hard
we tried
We could've given up and thrown it all away
But if we did, we'd never know the love we
share today

Only you and I will ever understand
No one else could ever feel the way I feel for you
And if while I'm asleep, you gently touch my hand
I'll know that at that moment, my dreams will all
come true

Each day we spend together is like a fantasy
And in this storybook, the tale ends happily
I'll never let you go, and if the world should end
We'll always be together. You'll always have a friend

Please know that in your eyes, I see a special world
Where only I can live, 'cause you're my special girl
My heart has found a home, and forever we will be
You'll never walk alone. I'll love you endlessly

Cool the Engines

AFTER CANCELING HIS flight home, Race waited in line at a rental car office at Logan Airport. Despite his recent DUI, he hoped to secure a vehicle, relying on Glenn's claim of having reinstated his license. Traveling by bus had become exhausting, and my son needed a different option. Besides, the last Greyhound to Portsmouth would depart from South Station in just thirty minutes. With Boston's infamous construction and traffic, a cab would never get him there in time.

The rental office was crackling with a symphony of chatter, clinking keys, and the phantasmal hum of an overhead vent. All of this combatted the scent of stale coffee and recycled air. As Race shuffled toward the front of the line, he second-guessed his decision to contact his estranged paternal grandfather. He hadn't even told Danny about Colin's death during their quick phone call. Did Danny know his son's aorta had ruptured three weeks earlier, killing him in the kitchen as he fixed himself a tuna sandwich at midnight on a rainy Tuesday? Did he care? Or did apathy run in the family genes?

Because the Sea Point police had seized and kept Race's license when he failed their breath test, my son retrieved his passport from his backpack and examined the photo, taken eight years earlier. Oh, the changes that had swept over him in that time. His face, his body, everything seemed different now that he had crossed the threshold into his forties. The unshakable belief that he'd remain the agile and robust athlete of his youth had crumbled overnight. Now, his knees ached constantly, his back cringed in agony, and his eyesight had deteriorated—though he refused to wear his prescription glasses. Refused to admit Father Time had scratched his name from the starting lineup, benching him for good. If he wore glasses, if he couldn't move a muscle without wincing, then why even be on the roster?

"Next in line," someone screeched, snapping Race out of his misery. He stepped forward and stood before the counter. A woman in her late thirties, with curly red hair pulled back in a ponytail, focused on her computer screen, pounding the keyboard like a possessed Keith Moon in a frenetic drum solo. Without looking up, she said, "Name?" Her shrill voice reverberated throughout the room.

"McIntyre."

The well-endowed woman wore a badge on her chest reading *Sheri.* When she met Race's gaze, the corners of her mouth shimmied upward, as if her lips had finally remembered how to smile.

"I don't have a reservation," my son said, handing over his passport, "but I was wondering if you had anything available."

"Holy crap," Sheri exclaimed.

Race glanced to the side. "What?"

Leaning over the counter, she tapped Race's elbow. "It's me, silly."

Race raised a thick eyebrow, then his eyes widened in fake recognition. "Oh, hey you!"

"You're such an asshole," the woman whispered, bending forward, revealing her substantial cleavage. "Ringing any bells now? Duh… Sheri from Cranston."

Race's mind, and several other body parts, flashed back to a summer from a former lifetime. He snapped his fingers and said, "Wait, I know. Fourth of July weekend somewhere, um… gimme a second."

"Newport, 1999." Sheri laughed and licked her lips. "Does *that* stroke your memory?"

Race couldn't hold back a smirk. "It certainly does."

"C'mon, you seriously didn't recognize me?" She laughed again, her eyes sparkling with nostalgia. "Hey, I'm sorry we lost touch."

Race nodded, genuinely pleased to see her again. "You're still as beautiful," he remarked. "Your laugh hasn't changed. And those lips…"

Sheri blushed and ran a finger down her cheek. "I'm married now, four kids," she said. "It's a lot, you know, but not too bad."

Race offered a reassuring smile. "Sounds like you're doing great."

"So, where's your license, Romeo?"

"Left it at home. Stupid move. Figured a passport might work."

"Sure," she said. "Don't sweat it."

As Sheri entered his information into the computer, her demeanor shifted, hazel eyes narrowing. "Did you know your license is suspended?"

A gush of surprise arose in Race. "What? That can't be right." Either Glenn had lied, or my son's best buddy didn't have the political pull he bragged about.

Sheri glimpsed around, making sure her manager wasn't within earshot. "You know what, Race, it's fine," she whispered. "I've let worse things slide for creepier guys."

"Thanks, I owe you."

"No need to make me any more promises." Sheri sighed and tried to smile. "Where are you off to?"

"New Hampshire," he said, wishing he hadn't made that last comment. "Probably for a day or two."

She giggled, swanned her neck, and pulled her curly red ponytail from back to front. "You got it, and I'll give you my discount."

"You're the best, Sheri."

"Yeah, I know." She leaned in closer and handed him his paperwork, a forgiving grin on her face. "Spot thirty-six-D, handsome."

"Thirty-six-D, huh?" Race chuckled. "Oh, now I remember you."

"Good one." Sheri blushed once more, smoothing out the wrinkles in her shirt. "Don't get lost now, I remember you always had trouble finding a spot."

✍

The moon hid behind a thick veil of clouds, clothing the night in obscurity. In the rental car parking lot, Race settled into a gold Ford Fiesta. It had been two months since he had driven a car, a sensation now both familiar and foreign. He pondered his luck, grateful that Sheri had done him this favor, reminding him of the "favors" she had performed for him that holiday weekend nineteen summers ago. A wistful frown crossed his face, and he pushed the lewd memories away. Why should he remember their fleeting fling? After all, he was only a twenty-two-year-old kid back then. And Sheri? Just another face in an endless series of weekend romps. Another soul he *took* from, without giving much back.

Race opened the GPS app on his phone and retrieved directions to Portsmouth. After taking a focused, decompressing breath, he pulled out of the parking space. The trip would take a little over an hour, edging him closer to unraveling the enigma that was Danny McIntyre. As he navigated the car out of the lot, his reckless thoughts zigged around hairpin turns. At a crosswalk, he stopped to allow passengers getting off a shuttle to stroll in front of him, giving him time to fiddle with the radio. He lassoed a catchy country song, Blake Shelton's "A Guy with a Girl," which galloped around the car's interior, the lyrics manifesting my son's ultimate wish. When Race peeked up from the dashboard, there she was, hustling by him, a few feet away: a woman that serendipity had delivered to his doorstep. Like he'd caught lightning in a broken record. Isn't that how the saying goes?

As stunning as the day they met, Amanda's short blonde hair gleamed under the lackluster parking lot lights. She wore a black jean jacket, which covered the snowy arms that had formed a pillow on his lap four short nights ago. With a red carry-on suitcase in one hand and a small girl's fingers in the other, Amanda scuttled over the uneven pavement—the suitcase's broken wheels and the girl's tiny steps hindering her progress. Wherever Amanda was going, she wanted to get there fast.

"Wait, wait, wait," Race muttered before shifting the car into park, springing out into the road, and yelling, "Hey! It's me!"

Several heads whipped around in response, including Amanda's. When she paused mid-stride, the young child in tow bumped into her legs, while other travelers moved around them, unfazed. Amanda's eyes locked onto my son. Shocked. Delighted. As he jogged toward her, she unleashed a smile that smothered him with imaginary kisses.

Race huffed beside her on the sidewalk. "I… I can't believe I found you," he said.

Amanda replied, "I can't believe I've been found."

He stared at the little girl. "Who's this?"

Amanda crouched down. "Marianne, can you say hi to my friend? He has a funny name, even funnier than Mr. Huggles here." She poked at the purple beanbag dog in Marianne's hand.

The cute girl shook her head, averting her gaze, too shy to look at my boy. Amanda stood and tousled the munchkin's curly blonde hair. Then the magical woman Race thought he'd lost beamed, as if she also hadn't stopped thinking about him since the morning she left him.

"So, is this…" He tackled his tongue before finishing the question.

Amanda glanced down at Marianne. "Yes, this is my daughter," she said. "I'm sorry I didn't tell you about this perfect little part of my life. I swear, I was going to, but you never called, and I figured you… I don't know, had enough of me, or that I overwhelmed you."

"What?" Race couldn't wipe the surprise off his face. "Where did you go?"

"I told you, my sister lives in Chicago," she said. "I went to her place that morning, left Saturday, got here yesterday."

Race's face contorted as he forced a smirk, flummoxed as a kangaroo in a canoe. "How could I call you?" he said. "You never gave me your number."

Amanda paused and pursed her lips. "I wrote it on the notepad on the desk."

Race cocked his head. "You did?"

Amanda exaggerated her nod. "Yes, I *did*. Next time, open your eyes."

A churn of relief wetted Race's heart. "Ugh," he said, the three letters conveying more contrition than three sentences could.

An SUV was stuck behind my boy's abandoned Fiesta, and a chubby man popped his cranium out of the window. "Hey, buddy! This your vehicle?"

"Yeah, sorry," Race yelled.

"Ask the pretty lady on a date already and get this clown car out of the road."

Race lightly touched Amanda's jacket sleeve. "Don't go anywhere." He rushed back into the car and pulled into an empty parking space. When he got back to Amanda and Marianne, he knelt next to the little girl and said, "Know what? You've got your mom's nose."

Marianne scurried behind her mother while my boy stood up, knees cracking like microwave popcorn.

"Yeah," Amanda said, "and we can both smell a forced compliment from a mile away."

After she and Race shared a laugh, Amanda explained to him that she'd met Marianne's grandparents at the airport. The couple had flown with the girl from their home in Nantucket, where Marianne had spent the last month. Amanda put a finger under her daughter's chin, coaxing her to lift her head. "We're going to be spending a lot more time together now. Isn't that right, Annie?"

Marianne hugged her mom. "Mm-hmm," the girl sang, while the duo of fear and love harmonized in her youthful voice.

Amanda added she was planning to rent a car and drive back home to Iowa, but not before she and her daughter found a beach near Boston. As it turned out, Marianne wanted to show her mother how adept she had become at leaping over waves during her stay in Nantucket. "You're a great little swimmer now, aren't you, Annie?"

Race smiled. "She seems brave."

"She is," Amanda said. "More than you know."

Race ran a handful of twittery fingers through his long, coarse hair and shifted from side to side. "Listen," he said, "I'd love to spend a little more time with you. I'm on my way to New Hampshire to see a friend, just for one day. There are great beaches there. How 'bout we go together? I can get a couple of rooms at a nice hotel, maybe one with a pool for Marianne. We'll have fun, but only if you want to."

"I don't know about all that."

Race emptied the reservoir of charm he'd been storing up over the years. "Listen, I'll have you back here in twenty-four hours, no later than seven o'clock," he said. "If we have a blast, which I'm sure we will, I might even offer to drive you all the way back to Iowa myself. That's if I'm feeling generous. Think of the cash you'll save, the laughs we'll have, the incredible conversation I'd grace you with. How can you pass up a deal like that?"

"Wouldn't be the toughest thing I've ever done."

"Come on." He couldn't bear leaving her, or survive her leaving him, not again. "Say you'll go with me." He'd do anything to keep her close.

"Okay, Mr. McIntyre." Amanda's voice tiptoed in the air like a cat on a fence, wary and amused. "You win, but no promises past New Hampshire."

Hitch a Ride

IN THE EARLY evening, the three companions drove up Route 95 in the dark, guided by a sky filled with stars. The gold Fiesta zoomed past hundreds of trees, their fiery fall colors hidden by the night. The road ahead unfurled, on and on, carving through the darkness, while Race and Amanda talked. In the back, Marianne played with Mr. Huggles, both of them safe in the car seat the rental company had installed before they left Logan. After twenty minutes, the highway's lullaby rocked the young girl to sleep.

Race glanced at the child reflected in the rearview mirror and mumbled the words to the song playing on the radio. "Head for the other side, leave it all behind." He envisioned the kids he couldn't have with Jess and wished for a different outcome, but he couldn't figure out what that would look like.

Marianne, with her golden curls and dimples, resembled an angel. Her crimson coat reminded Race of Little Red

Riding Hood, a character from a fairy tale he loved when he was her age. As I recall, back then, my son favored the Big Bad Wolf over Red. Strong and self-reliant, the wolf had journeyed alone, needing no one else. But now, Race couldn't empathize with the wolf. He was no longer someone who trusted few, who relied on nobody, and mistreated women without genuine care or concern. Could his whole life have changed in just one week? Had my little boy grown up?

Amanda interrupted his thoughts. "Any regrets about taking us along on this trip?"

He locked eyes with her. "Not at all," he said. "Best decision I ever made."

She angled herself toward him, her expression growing serious. "You might feel differently if you knew my *real* story."

Race furrowed his brow. "What do you mean?"

Amanda hesitated, as if pulling her answer out of a sleeping lion's mouth. "The reason I was at Logan, you know, picking up Marianne," she said, "is because I'm taking custody of her."

"Custody?" Race blinked. "Who was she with before?"

Amanda leaned in closer before speaking, careful not to wake her daughter. "Two years ago, prior to the divorce, I wasn't in the best condition to take care of Annie, or anyone." Her voiced shuddered. "I had no job, no support group, no good friends. My ex-husband, Chad, he hired a tough lawyer and portrayed me as an unfit mother. He claimed I caused Marianne severe emotional distress; made false accusations of drug use and risky behavior."

Race squinted, head tilted. "How could he lie like that?"

Tears welled up in Amanda's eyes. "They weren't all lies… I did smoke weed now and then," she said, "but it wasn't a habit. I would never give up on my daughter, but the divorce went on forever, and I didn't have the strength or the money to fight anymore."

Her story hit Race hard, the unfairness of it all. "How could the judge not see through that shit? How could anyone keep Marianne from you?"

Amanda nodded, her gaze distant. "I didn't believe Chad was a bad person," she said. "Not at first, not when I met him, and not even during the divorce."

Through the mirror, Race pinned his gaze on the girl in the back seat. How could her father play games with such a fragile soul? "If he wasn't a bad guy," my son said, "he would've let Marianne stay with you."

Amanda sighed, her voice numb. "Chad never wanted me to have any power," she said. "Wanted me below him. But he was a good dad in the beginning. It's just… when he took her away, the universe went dark, and I couldn't find a path through."

That second, Marianne stirred in her sleep and mumbled, "No, no, no… I, I, no, no."

Amanda reached back and stroked her daughter's leg. "Shhhh," she whispered. "It's okay, baby. Shhhh… it's okay. You're okay."

Race's facial muscles relaxed, and his eyes grew wider. "How did you get her back?"

Breathing deep, Amanda shifted in her seat. "Chad's parents, who live in Nantucket, they called me six months ago." She paused, gathering runaway emotions. "They, uh…

they told me they were going to report him to Child Protective Services."

Race's shoulders tensed. "What? Why?"

Amanda wiped a tear from her cheek. "He, he was… beating her," she said, trembling. "They found bruises on her arms and legs, and when they asked Chad about it, he said Marianne was clumsy and kept falling all the time. He said some friends of hers were too rough and that once she bumped into the car door."

Hostility and the urge for revenge coursed through Race. "How could he do that to her?"

Glancing back at her sleeping daughter, Amanda spoke with a hush. "He didn't want anyone staying with him and Marianne," she said, voice quivering. "But my in-laws insisted on visiting for a week. They asked Marianne about the bruises. It didn't take long for her to say that her daddy hurts her."

Silence exploded in the car as Race processed the truth. Clamping the steering wheel, his furrowed brow eased up as he tracked Amanda's body slumping. "Is that why you were crying when I met you?" he said.

"What?"

"On the bus, the day we met, you were crying across the aisle from me. Remember?"

She sighed. "Yes."

"Now I get it," he said. "I'd cry for my kid, too, if I knew what that monster was doing."

Amanda nodded, tears pooling in her eyes. "But I wasn't crying for her." She bowed her head. "I was crying for him."

❧

The minute they entered the coastal town of Portsmouth, New Hampshire, the clock on the old church steeple struck eight. The evening had gotten cool, with a dash of salt in the air and a scant smell of seafood scuttling into the open car windows. With the tourist season over, the charming city was as quiet as a mime in a library.

Waking up from her nap, Marianne wriggled in her seat. When the car stopped at a Residence Inn, glowing from nearby streetlights, a foghorn sounded in the distance. Race noticed a sign on the corner for the Portsmouth docks, located a half mile down the road—where he'd go early tomorrow morning to meet Sam Heatherton, the boat owner who'd ferry him to Star Island. But could he get there and back with no one noticing?

Amanda unbuckled Marianne, who sprang out of her seat like a jack-in-the-box, her energy bubbling over like a shaken can of soda, unrolling like a never-ending spool of thread. Oh, listen to me… I'm like a poet with a million pens, each one scribbling the same line in different shades of ink. Sorry, back to my story… Marianne's eyes sparkled when she asked, "Where's the beach, Mommy? Can we play in the waves?"

Amanda grinned. "Good question, sweetie. I'm sure the beach is close by, but it's too dark and cold to go now. How about you jump over the waves tomorrow, young lady? Because tonight, Mommy wants pizza and ice cream!"

Marianne's high spirits rubbed off on my son, and her excitement livened up the entire state of New Hampshire. The girl hugged her mother and cheered, "Yay!"

After Race and Amanda settled into their rooms, the trio reconvened in the hotel lobby. At the front desk, my son asked a friendly staffer for recommendations on the best pizza and ice cream in town. Outside on the sidewalk, the warm light spilling out of sleepy storefronts bathed the streets in a fleecy amber sheen. While strolling along, clutching Mr. Huggles, Marianne kept a safe distance from Race. He now understood the child's hesitation. My son wanted Marianne to feel comfortable around him—and needed her mother to trust him, too.

"So, beach tomorrow?" Amanda asked, nudging Race as they walked, her curious tone hinting at a follow-up question on deck.

Race paused, a pang of anxiety sticking him in the ribs. "Actually," he said, "I have to see someone in the morning." He braced for her reaction, knowing he'd chosen a path that would change the course of their journey.

Amanda's eyes reflected interest, worry, and patience. "Who are you seeing?"

Without an umbrella in a downpour of nerves, Race cleared his throat and said, "Remember how I told you I was visiting some friends in Boston? Well, I kind of lied."

Amanda's expression shifted. "I knew it," she murmured. "I knew there was something you were hiding when I met you. I knew it... but I didn't want to believe it."

"You didn't tell me the truth either."

"But then I did."

"I wasn't hiding anything," Race said, his voice dropping out. "I just didn't know what I was looking for." He was in too deep, and it was too late to walk back his misstep, like what my daddy used to say about the toothpaste in the tube—what you can or can't do after you squeeze some onto your brush.

"Mommy, there's the pizza place!" Marianne squealed.

Race held open the door for mother and daughter, and they all settled into a cushioned booth. Him on one side, them on the other. Throughout the uncomfortable meal at the snug restaurant, Marianne kept busy with a piping hot triangle of pepperoni pizza, a kiddie-pool-sized cup of lemonade, and a teeny box of crayons, creating a colorful masterpiece on her paper place mat. Meanwhile, the adults avoided the elephant in the booth.

Finally, Amanda made eye contact. "Why did you lie, Race?"

"It's a long story," he said.

"I enjoy a good story."

"Long, not good," Race said before his conscience gave way. Unable to hold back, he unlatched the floodgates and tipped over the beans, relaying the intricate details of his surreal week away from home. He recounted the visit with his maternal grandfather Petrak, his recently discovered Armenian heritage and complex family history, and the truth behind Colin's sorrow-driven parenting methods. Feather-footing around the harsh topic, sparing Marianne's innocent ears, he told Amanda about Sevan, her suicide, her diary. Last, he disclosed that he'd contacted his paternal grandfather, Danny McIntyre, who lived off the coast on Star Island. "I'm going there tomorrow," he said. "Meeting him for the first time."

Amanda glued her gaze onto my son's face, took a breath, and asked, "What else do you hope to learn from him?"

"No idea," he said, shrugging. "But I need to go."

After finishing her artistic creation, Marianne displayed

the drawing. "Look, Mommy," she said with a cherub-like smile. "Do you know what it is?"

Amanda, amused and intrigued, examined the picture. "Of course," she said and paused. "Actually, I have no clue. What is it?"

The little girl turned to Race. "Do *you* want me to tell you?"

My son chuckled, leaning in, playing along. "Nope," he said, "because I already know."

Marianne scrunched up her tiny face. "You do not!"

"I do so."

The girl giggled, offering the place mat to my boy. "Then prove it!"

Welcoming the pint-size challenge, Race accepted the drawing—a fantastical creature with a bushy tail, horned nose, and whiskers—and held it up next to his face. He grinned at the two beautiful souls sitting across from him and said, "It's me!"

Laughter erupted in the petite pizzeria, saturating the space with a doughy warmth and saucy joy. As my son savored the precious minutes, contentment joined him at the table, a comfort unlike any he had experienced before. But in the darkest corner of his mind, a quiet siren hissed a warning that something bad was about to happen. Something with the potential to ruin this peaceful moment, and many more moments to come.

Something About You

FADING LIGHT. MY daughter… the street. Screeching car, shattered glass. Broken, the memories. Windy… the corner! No, don't! Heaven? Peace… with Daddy. Watch me… Please, my baby!

❧

The Portsmouth night was refreshing and crisp. Laughter stocked the evening air as Race made his way back to the Residence Inn with Amanda and Marianne. They skipped and giggled on the sidewalk, bellies full of pizza and ice cream.

"I'm glad I'm six," the little girl cooed, spinning in wobbly circles. "It's the oldest I've been in my whole entire life."

Amanda turned to Race, her voice curious, hopeful. "Hey," she said, "is there room for two more on your trip to Star Island?"

His eyes met hers. "It'd be a nice way to spend the morning," he said, "and Marianne could probably jump a wave or two, if she doesn't mind cold water."

Amanda grimaced. "Boarding a boat would be a big step for me, though. Remember my thing with water?"

"I get it." Race chuckled. "Can't believe I almost got on a plane today."

"Look at us," she said, "two death-defying daredevils."

"Let's meet for breakfast at seven in the lobby tomorrow," he said. "We'll get to the dock at eight."

"Hear that, sweetie? We'll need to set an alarm tonight," Amanda told Marianne, who was now walking between the two daredevils, her little hands in each of theirs.

Then, prying away her fingers, Marianne began leaping like a frog down the sidewalk as she sang, "And I won't forget to bring my bathing suit."

Race laughed while thinking ahead to the next morning, fearing that meeting Danny would be stressful. But Amanda and Marianne would be there to support him, which he hoped might ease his journey into the unknown. As the three of them bounded toward the entrance to the hotel, Race's phone rang. When he glanced at the screen, the contact number stopped his heart: Blue Horizons.

"Sorry, Amanda, I have to take this," he said. "Don't wait up. I'll see you tomorrow."

With a reassuring smile, Amanda nodded. "See you then."

After the automatic sliding doors ushered mother and daughter into the hotel, Race answered the call. "Hello?"

On the other end of the line, Rose's familiar voice greeted him. "Hey, Ritz," she said, her tone gentle as always.

"Sorry to bother you this late. What time is it out East right now?"

"No problem, not quite ten. Everything okay?"

"When are you coming home?"

"A couple of days."

"Well, Miss Holly has had a tough week," Rose said. "It's time I do something for her."

"What kind of something?"

"A letter."

I wasn't present during their conversation, but Race informed me about it later—Rose told him about the agreement she made with me when I first arrived at Blue Horizons. I had written the letter long ago, an earnest story of my affection for Race, my longing for him to understand my truth. My dear Rose paused before reading my words to him, clearing her throat and attempting to speak as I might've spoken, conveying my emotions through her voice. She did her best for me, for my son, for the sake of our bond from that day on.

Dear Race,

I need you to understand how deeply I love you. You are the best thing that ever happened to me, the brightest light in my life. I have cherished every minute we've spent together, every smile, every tear, every win, every loss. There is something important I need to share with you now, though, something very difficult to say. I am not your birth mother, Race. Your father and I made the painful decision to hide this truth long ago, and I apologize for not telling you sooner. We didn't mean to hurt you. I hope with all my heart that this doesn't change your love for me, because it will never change my love for you. You've always been and will always be my beloved son, the one who brought joy back to my life.

You saved me, Race. I needed you, and you saved me.

I am incredibly sorry for keeping this from you for so long. I did it out of love to protect you from unnecessary pain. With time, I might forget, but I hope you'll always hold me close to your heart, just like I hold you in mine. Race, you're an amazing and beautiful person. I'm so proud of you and love you so much. I ask for your forgiveness and want you to know that my love for you is forever.

Always,

Mom

Once Rose finished reading, Race soaked in the retold revelation, peering into a well of emotions but unable to see the bottom. The truth Petrak had recently unloaded about his lineage had flipped my son's life upside down, leaving him confounded in a muddle of misgivings. Now, my letter poured a carton of salt on his already festering wounds.

"Rose, I already know she's not my real mom." Race's voice quaked as his temper flared, heightening by the second. "But how could you not tell me? You've known me for three years!"

"There were days I wanted to share the secret," my loyal friend admitted, "but I made a promise to Miss Holly, and she trusted me."

"You lied to me."

"I kept a vow," she said. "Listen. I understand you're

hurting, but I'm sorry, my word is more important than that."

"I don't mean to take this out on you, Rose."

She paused for what seemed like a lifetime, leaving my son wondering if she'd hung up, then she said, "How did you find out?"

"Let's just say my trip to Boston has been an eye-opener," he said. "I know now that my real mom's name was Sevan Zakarian, and she's dead. I met her father, my grandfather, and he told me everything. Well, maybe not everything."

"I can't imagine how you're feeling," Rose said. "Again, I'm sorry this is happening all at once. I didn't understand what you were going through. I only read the letter to you now because I don't know how much time she has left."

My son had been waiting for that news—not wanting it, just waiting. "Tell me, Rose, has she said anything else?" It was a question he'd asked her many times before.

"No," she whispered through the phone. "She still hasn't spoken since last year, except for repeating her name."

After ending their talk, Race sat on a wooden bench next to a bubbling fountain. Bathing in the gentle light of a nearby streetlamp, he stared into the reflective water below. Slouched with clenched fists, he longed to confide in someone, to release the turmoil building inside him. The question of whom to lean on weighed on his mind. Should he call Glenn or Jess? They'd known him the longest, knew him the best. But things had changed in his relationships with them. Glenn was still his best friend, and Jess had been his wife, but now the two were together and Race noticed they'd become distant. It was clear; they didn't know the real Race McIntyre. No one did but me.

Keeping his angst to himself, for now, he pushed himself up from the bench and staggered into the hotel. Climbing the stairs to the second floor, he paused outside room 210. He hesitated before tapping on the door, unsure if Marianne and Amanda were already asleep. When he got no response, he tapped again, more insistently this time. Still no answer. He stood like a man made of stone, a statue with a human heart.

As he spun away, a voice purred, "Hey, what's going on?" Amanda flipped the latch, propping open the door, and stepped into the dusky hall. A pillow had tousled her short hair, and her gaze conveyed both concern and curiosity. Dressed in gray sweatpants and a worn T-shirt, she appeared more tired and more captivating than ever.

Race composed himself before telling Amanda that he'd received a call from Rose, my caregiver, who had read him a letter from me. The information wasn't exactly breaking news, he admitted, but the growing level of secrecy concerned him. "Everyone kept this from me," he said. "My entire life, they lied."

"They were protecting you," she said.

"I didn't need their protection."

"Shhhh, keep your voice down," Amanda said, taking Race's arm and stepping a few feet away from the cracked door. "For whatever reason, they thought you did. They were doing their best. It's all any of us can do."

"They could've done more."

She rubbed his back. "Maybe."

He shifted his weight, curled his fingers.

She moved her hand down to hold his.

"There's something else I haven't told you," he said,

finding Amanda's eyes. "My mom doesn't talk. I'm not sure if she even knows who I am anymore."

He took a long, calming breath and dropped his head onto her shoulder.

She glided her nails through his long locks. "Hey, this doesn't change how she felt about you, how much she cared. Mothers don't change like that."

In a silent response, Race let his body fall against her slight but strong frame.

Amanda breathed him in. "You know, stuff happens to all of us," she said, prying a barren laugh out of my son. "This thing called fate, it lurks around every corner, shifting all the time. We can't prepare for it, but we still have a choice."

He lifted his chin off her shoulder. "What choice?"

"Either accept our destiny or refuse it." She placed her palm against his cheek.

Race was unwilling to consider his "destiny" and what "choice" he had or didn't have. Still, Amanda's words, and her touch, soothed him. Her breath braided with his, the warmth of her body radiated against his skin, and her scent soaked into his clothing. But as tranquilizing and grounding as her presence was, it couldn't stop him from drifting away. "I don't know what to do," he said.

As a girl, whenever something befuddled me, or I was unsure about which way to go, Daddy always compared the decisions I had to make to jumping into a pool. He'd say that people can leap in lots of ways, but all that matters is *taking* the leap. Once we choose to do it, there's no real danger in jumping. The actual danger is in the tiny moments *before* the jump. Do we stay on the ledge or stay true to ourselves?

Amanda kissed Race's forehead, then his cheek. When they made eye contact, she traced his jawline and guided his lips onto hers. He brought her into him and held her, in a nameless way that he'd never held Jess, his powerful hands pulling Amanda in closer, his arms wrapping around her tighter, offering no escape. Their kiss brought him promise, their embrace brought him hope, and he didn't care what else the future might bring. Under the dim lights of that hallway, on that inexpressible evening, my son was no longer who he'd always been. But whoever he was then, he wasn't alone.

My world appears flipped, as if my eyes are upside down; things aren't what I think they are. I'm not just a sad old woman, unclear about the year or the whereabouts of her dead daughter. No, there's something more to my yearning, something no one else can see. I might misremember names, or mix metaphors, or call an apple a pear, or forget my right from my left. But none of us decides what's real and what's not, and nobody else decides for us. We all live in a maze of illusions, an ever-changing dream, concealing the facts from our eyes. That's what life is.

For instance, I'm here with you, but not really; I'm just a ghost in pajamas. But I haven't vanished yet. I'm only fading, not yet gone. Because each evening, as I prepare for bed, my face still appears in the bathroom mirror, emerging from the steam and fog. Here comes that face again, unreadable as ever. Its patient bones hold steady under the skin, eyes hide the mind's confusion and the heart's pain, lips hint at something amiss within the soul. All the while, the hourglass drains. So, how can I die a good death? What does it matter? The outcome will be the same—I will simply disappear. But if you twisted my leg, I'd say that letting go is the key to unlocking the gate. I wished my son could've heard me say that.

Thousands of miles apart, both Race and I had restless sleeps on the night Amanda kissed him. In Sea Point, the rain outside my window created a terrible racket, upsetting me, a testament to the menacing clouds cloaking my world. The song from my music box and the glossy baseball card in my hand provided solace, advising me not to worry. I had lied to my boy out of love, and I prayed my remorse would someday fade. The chimes tinkling out of the box soothed my brain, and the lyrics rushed back to me… *So many things I would've done, but clouds got in my way.*

Across the country in New Hampshire, in his lonely hotel room bed, Race couldn't switch off Rose's voice in his head—couldn't quiet the thunderclaps of her reading the letter I'd written. He rubbed his temples, failing to eliminate the throbbing behind his eyes. The minutes ticked by, and with every second, he questioned our relationship and the secrets I'd kept. Deep down, however, he couldn't deny the affection I'd always shown him, an affection as genuine as if he were my *actual* son. He understood I had loved him all along, though I'd hidden it beneath layers of unspoken truths. At some point, Race must've passed out, because he told me the nightmare had come back.

The little boy was playing hide-and-seek with his daddy in the forest. The boy hid in a really good hiding spot, but then he grew tired of waiting there. He came out and looked for his daddy. He walked and walked, but he couldn't find him. He yelled for him, but his daddy didn't answer. The trees were all the same. The boy got scared and started crying. Then he heard his daddy's yell. The boy yelled, too. But his daddy's calls got quieter and quieter. The boy tried to follow the fading voices, but he didn't know where they were coming from, and he wasn't sure which path to take. He was all alone in the forest for a long time. He walked and walked some more, but it felt like he was going in circles. He saw gigantic trees and heard strange noises. He was hungry and tired. The sun went down, and it got cold. The boy was terrified. He thought he would never find his way back home. But then he saw a skinny man with a hat and a badge. The man said he would help the boy find his daddy. The man held the boy's hand, and they walked together. The forest got darker and darker.

In Race's recurring night terror, the little boy never finds his daddy.

I slept very little that evening, too. In my simple apartment at Blue Horizons, I sat in my favorite chair, gazing through the window at the quiet night, replaying the blurry events of the day in my mind. The room was lit low, with the grayish glow of a table lamp casting a comforting light. But the modest space had always haunted me with memories of my other life, the one I had longed for. My worn-out recliner had supported me during countless spells of contemplation and solitude. Laughter and tears, shared with Race and Colin as they journeyed through my time here, left stains on the walls. Alone in my room, I had learned the true meaning of love and sacrifice. I had come to terms with the decisions I made and the paths I chose. In this very chair, my yesterdays had mingled with my todays, shaping the person I had become.

Lost in wonderment on that dark night, I reflected on the secrets we all carry, the sacrifices we make for our families. The past, like a well-guarded vault, hides its treasures in plain sight, waiting for the right time to reveal them. Just as Sevan Zakarian made a choice ages ago, motivated by love for her family, I, too, made a tough decision. I gave up my fading dreams to raise a boy I hadn't brought into this world. I had married a person with a formidable history that had the power to stand in the way of our future together. The scars of Colin's loss never faded; they became embroidered on his soul, shaping his decisions and molding my destiny.

Sevan and I would always be bound by a man and a boy who needed and wanted both of us. But each of them could only have one of us. Her decision to leave the world behind had set in motion a chain reaction, giving me a husband and a son. I often ponder the choices others have made, but I never once second-guess my own. In the end, it was love that led me. A love that surpassed bloodlines and secrets, bringing Race into my life. Our fates intertwined back then, as if guided by a song meant for someone else, a song we had sung in perfect harmony.

Until now.

"The Hardest Part"
March 1976

Are we doing the right thing?
Is this love that I feel for you for real?
Are we old enough to understand,
Not all lovers end up in Wonderland?
Should we take a chance?

There are so many questions to answer,
And I'm not sure if I can
Please help me, this is the hardest part of love

I thought it would be so easy
I never knew that love could bring me so
much pain
But if this is what I must do to have you
Well then I tell you, darling, I'd do it all again
Tell me, would you?

There are so many pieces to this puzzle
And I'm not sure they all fit
I can't figure it out. It's the hardest part of love

No man is an island
Everybody needs some help to make it through
Oh, girl, you know it's true, I can't make it alone
without you

:08

Sail Away

THE PASTY MORNING sky colored the quiet dock in a muted gray. Gulls wheeled and cried overhead, their raucous calls slashing through the fog. The spirit of the sea set the scene— the pungency of saltwater, the creaking of weathered wood, and the distant drone of an engine from a freighter parked along the shoreline. A weary ferry, which had shuttled tourists to and from Star Island throughout the summer, lay dormant nearby, its mighty engines at rest.

Race stood at the edge of the bobbing dock and crossed his brawny arms. The rough wooden planks beneath his feet bore the signs of countless expeditions, each scuff and notch telling tales of arrivals and departures. Floating in the harbor, small boats rocked at their moorings, their ropes taut but flexible, bending to the will of the tide.

While waiting for Sam Heatherton to arrive, Amanda and Marianne engaged in an animated game of I spy. They were having such a good go of it, joking around, asking fun questions, easing Race's nerves. With each correct guess, each secret item spied, Marianne's eyes danced with excitement, and Amanda's smile beamed like a beacon. I remember playing that game with my child. Oh, where did the time, and that child, go?

Race's thoughts of Amanda's kiss and his upcoming meeting with Danny rattled my son, building a mountain of suspense about his past and his future. He wondered how this journey to Star Island might shape his tomorrows, and how it might unearth long-buried truths about the hazy days he'd never known. But when he focused, he could see a little hope ahead. The fog that had covered his path for so long had lifted, showing glimpses of his destination.

Suddenly, cutting through the actual fog, a lobster boat appeared, forging through the mist. The old vessel boasted a rugged charm from a lifetime battling the unforgiving sea. The name on the boat's weathered exterior: *Aegaeon's Wish*. My daddy taught mythology and told me all about Aegaeon, a monstrous deity and ally of the Titans in the war against Zeus and the gods of Olympus. Daddy said the name meant "stormy one."

The thirty-foot hull of the boat—painted blue, white, and gray—showed telltale signs of saltwater exposure. The colors were fading, surfaces peeling, and patches of rust had blemished the steel like a rampant bout of psoriasis. As the vessel got closer, Race spied a husky seafarer at the helm, wearing a brown woolen cap and a kelp-green rain jacket. Behind a bushy beard, the man's face showed the marks of a rough life on the ill-tempered ocean.

The lobster boat groaned as it stopped beside the dock, and the bearded man stepped out from inside the wheelhouse. "You Race McIntyre?" His voice was even huskier than he was and louder than the hum of the engine.

Race nodded.

With a gruff scowl, the man identified himself as Sam. Observing his foreign freight he raised his squirrel-tail eyebrows, jutted out his chapped hand, and helped Marianne and Amanda aboard. My son followed, and the three wary voyagers took their seats on a cold bench molded into the sides behind the wheelhouse at the rear of the boat. Sam tossed Marianne a life jacket and watched Amanda slip it over her daughter's adorable blonde head.

When Race told me this story, he likened the mountainous captain to the rugged '70s TV character Grizzly Adams and his bear pal, Ben, rolled into one fuzzy hulk. My son also confessed that he silently prayed to a god he didn't believe in, asking for Sam Heatherton to be the sort of sea monster that wouldn't harm a minnow.

On the deck of *Aegaeon's Wish*, a tangle of ropes and buoys cluttered the surface; nine wooden lobster traps, stacked up in threes, stood at attention, while weathered crates and barrels, used for storing bait or unlucky crustaceans, secured their appointed positions.

"Star Island's in a group of nine called the Isles of Shoals," Sam said, coughing along with the words and handing Amanda a thick, black blanket. "It's a forty-five-minute trip. You and the girl should bundle up."

As they departed Portsmouth, the crew settled in, and their voyage began into a hurting southeast wind. Seven miles away, blurry in the distance, the end of their line awaited. Looming behind the wheel, without looking at his passengers, Sam spoke in a harsh drone about the history, wildlife, and geography of the harbor.

Race's eyes darted across the shoreline, then at Sam's broad back, then squinted ahead toward the vague horizon. "What can you tell us about the islands?"

The boat rocked and cut through the chop, while Sam stood steady as a statue, one meaty hand resting on the metal wheel. "They're split by the border of Maine and New Hampshire," he shouted over the boat's chugging motor. "In Maine, you've got Appledore, Smuttynose, Malaga, Duck, and Cedar. In New Hampshire, there's Star, Lunging, White, and Seavey. Before fishermen and tourists started showing up, Native Americans were out there on the Shoals, fishing and hunting."

Marianne giggled. "I wanna go to Smuttynose!"

Amanda wrapped the blanket tighter around her daughter. "I'll bet it smells yucky there," she said and tapped the tip of Marianne's teensy sniffer.

Sam continued, "In 1614, Captain John Smith discovered the Isles of Shoals, long before the Pilgrims reached Plymouth. Smith's island exploration helped with early mapmaking of the New England coast."

Marianne yelled, "Why are they called the Eyes of Shoes?"

"You were close, honey," Amanda said.

Sam let go of the wheel, whipped around, and grinned under his beard. "The early settlers called it the Isles of Shoals because there were lots of fish around. Their word for *schools* was *shoals*. During mackerel and herring seasons, especially, the water sparkles and shines, like diamonds on a starry night." Then Sam coughed, swiveled, and clutched the wheel.

While the boat churned ahead, Race pictured the brave explorers and settlers who had ventured through these waters centuries ago. He sensed a strong bond with the past, as if he could taste it in the salt on his lips. Far from Portsmouth now, Race leaned forward on the bench, slowly growing more spellbound by the journey and less suspicious of the colossal captain. "What's Star Island like, Sam?"

"Conditions on Star are grim." The man peered over his shoulder at my son and tugged on his wool hat. "Brutal winds from the north and west cut through like demons, carrying the sting of the entire continent."

The chirps of sandpipers flew in the chill, and dubious clouds gorged the sky. The sea shimmered, altering from a playful plum to a violent violet as the wind lashed long streaks on the surface. Sam pointed at the islands in the distance. "You can see Star pretty good from here, since the summer haze is gone."

The engine produced a monotonous thrum, and the breeze ferried along the sweet, threatening sounds of the sea, a cutthroat rhapsody of nature. While Race shivered in response to the cold air's promise of adventure, the hypnotic whitecaps lapped in rhythm, the briny air stung his sinuses, and the ancient stories rang in his ears.

"Those tiny islands have seen it all," Sam said into the wheelhouse's windshield, "from the early days of European exploration up till now. Pirates were all over this area, too, taking shelter in the coves and inlets while they schemed and plotted their next raid."

Marianne's little jaw dropped. "Wow!"

The closer they got to the Isles of Shoals, the more curious Race became of the storytelling captain. My boy plunked his elbows onto his knees and questioned the furry seafarer. "So, how do you know Danny?"

Sam's laugh was loud and deep. "Everyone who makes a living on these waters knows Danny Mac," he said, and the ocean roared in agreement.

Studying Sam's eyes, my son wondered what lurked beneath the surface. "How deep is it out here?"

The hairy hulk stared back at my boy—a sharp and knowing stare. "Deeper than you think." Then, shifting his attention to Marianne, Sam said, "Would you like to help me steer, little lady?"

The girl jumped out of her seat and tugged at her life jacket. "Yes, please!"

The wheelhouse, positioned toward the stern, contained the controls and navigation equipment. The windows of the structure, though streaked with salt and sea spray, still gave the skilled captain a clear view of the surrounding waters. Amid the stink of diesel fuel and dead shellfish, the little girl gripped the wheel and grinned while Sam stood behind her, stroking his beard, attentive as a hammerhead shark.

From a mile away, the islands seemed rough and inhospitable, stacks of granite in the open sea, battered for ages by endless gales and relentless breakers. The rocks outlining the shores—senile boulders bleached by wind and sun—were ancient and weary. To Race, the Shoals appeared daunting and not worth exploring.

At the helm, Marianne's curious eyes lit up, and she turned to Sam. "Which island has the biggest waves?"

"If that's what you're fishing for, then it's your lucky

day." The imposing man chuckled and took the wheel, his narrow eyes crinkling with either warmth or deceit, Race couldn't be sure. "We're headed for a place with the perfect size waves for you."

Marianne scooted back onto the bench between Amanda and Race while *Aegaeon's Wish* angled toward its destiny. In the distance, perched high on a hill, an impressive three-story white building stood sentinel on Star Island. Its wide staircase ascended to a wraparound porch, overlooking the dock. The mighty structure consumed the tiny island, its faded grandeur evoking a hidden history, and Race wondered what terrible tales its timeworn walls had trapped. Squinting, he spied a long string of unoccupied white rocking chairs decorating the porch, moving in the wind as if twenty phantoms were out there enjoying their morning coffee.

"That's the Oceanic Hotel," Sam said as if reading my son's mind. "Last of a dying breed. They don't build things like that anymore."

The island pulled the boat closer, and the low craggy rocks on either side of the dock offered a hostile welcome. Though sparse and dreary, Star transmitted a peculiar charm and discharged an enchanting aura. When Sam cut the engine and the lobster boat coasted toward the dock, Race cast his eyes toward the titanic captain and said, "Thanks. We won't be long."

"I'll be ready when you are," Sam said and threw a look over my son's shoulder. "There's your white whale."

At the highest point of the pier, where the lawn began its climb toward the grand hotel, a crooked old man in a black leather hunting hat stood stiff against a raw ocean gust.

Race nodded and waved.

The stoic figure, his hands tucked into coat pockets, nodded in return.

⁓

You know, I never met my husband's dad. Colin rarely spoke of Danny, and when he did, it was with a guarded reticence that left me wondering about the man—and why he had severed their father-son relationship. What had caused such a rift? Was Danny a man of vices, an abusive ogre, or a neglectful parent? I had pondered these questions, ones of fathers and sons and what comes between them, but I never applied them to Colin and Race. Perhaps I should have.

Colin, to the best of his ability, was a good father to our son, even though he may have had his flaws. His heart was always in the right place, just not with us. I found comfort in the life we had built together, even during tough times, and I believed in the promise of better days ahead. For much of his youth, Race's dreams and determination kept me sane, distracting me from Colin's steady withdrawal and the pain it caused—as well as from a distant past I'd tried to bury. Should he have showered more attention on our boy, and on me? Perhaps. But in those days, my husband's priorities lay elsewhere.

Sometimes I see faces… so real to me. No, wait, where was I?

Oh yes, Star Island…

When Race stepped off the dock, the sadness and loneliness of the place knocked him off-kilter. There were no trees waving hello, no familiar voices wafting on the breeze. Everything was spotless and serene; no dust or noise to be found. Only sky, sea, and rocks surrounded him, but the wildness and desolation were beautiful somehow.

"Welcome to our island," the old man said. "I'm Danny."

The codger wore a heavy brown coat and sturdy boots, and he struck Race as a man who might never remove his black hunting hat. Like a lighthouse keeper who'd become one with his narrow home, the solitary figure blended in with the rugged landscape confining him.

Race offered his hand to Danny. "Decent day for a boat ride," my son said. "Your buddy sure knows his way around a good story."

Danny gripped Race's hand. "Tide will be in soon," the old man said and shoved his hands back into his coat pockets. Then he swerved around to admire the shoreline—every cove and inlet awash with magical waves—their life, light, color, and sparkle.

Other than the arresting Oceanic Hotel and several cottages, the island was a world made of nature. No concerts, lectures, or theaters. No music in the air, besides the occasional whistles of wildlife. No streets, malls, or airports. No postal workers, no nosy neighbors, not even a doorbell on the entire giant rock. Here, life had no interruptions.

"This is an incredible place," Race said and pointed to the grand hotel looming on the hill. "God, that's an impressive building."

"She's why I came here," Danny said. "Got a job as caretaker, going on forty years now. Visitors are only allowed on the island June through September. Otherwise, it's quiet."

Race smiled.

In the old man's worn-out eyes, a trace of youthful energy peeped out, but it seemed the rest of Danny had surrendered to the ceaselessness of his years. His nose and ears had grown while everything else had shrunk. The muscles in his arms and legs had atrophied, and his once strong jawline had succumbed to a weak chin, as if his face hadn't exercised in half a century.

"Yay! Mommy, look!" Marianne, ever ready for an adventure, had spotted a ramshackle playground nearby, complete with rusty swings and monkey bars. She darted toward it, and her mother followed.

Race seized the opportunity to pry Danny open. "It's nice to finally meet you," he admitted, a trace of vulnerability in his voice. "I have lots of questions."

"I thought our paths might cross one day," Danny confessed. "Can't say I hoped you'd find us, though."

Race winced. "Us?"

"I'm an old man," Danny said. "Been here a long time. When I say 'us,' I mean me and my island."

"Understood."

"Follow me," Danny said. "Cottage is up here a bit."

"Hey, guys," Race called toward the playground, "come on!"

As he walked on a dirt path alongside the massive hotel, his three guests in tow, the weathered guide recounted the building's history and its storied past, an ode to the grandeur of bygone days. "She's kept up pretty good."

Along the path, green bayberry bushes sprouted from a short stone wall. Wild roses, having survived the early fall, added a warm blush against the gray rocks. The old wall leaned in all directions, obscured by overgrown grass. Soon, or in a hundred years, no one will remember this low line of stones—the world forgets so much.

With lush vegetation and wildlife flourishing all around, the path curved around a quaint stone chapel on a hill to the left. The weather, overcast yet mild for late October, added to the coded anticipation loitering between the elderly man and my son.

Danny brought them to the doorstep of his storm-beaten cottage tethered to the cliffside, clinging to the edge of the sea. It was a simple, unshowy structure, much like the two-bedroom beach bungalow where Colin and I had honeymooned on Puget Sound. Race stepped inside the place, greeted by the winsome scent of old wooden furniture in the den.

Danny lowered himself into an upholstered easy chair, its cushions worn and flat. "Make yourselves at home," he said.

Race and Amanda took seats on the couch, with Marianne squeezing in between them. Memories and stories littered the cottage floor, omens carved into the walls. The room bent its ears, catching the candid voice of a stranger.

"So," Race said, "why did you invite me here?"

The old man sat up, slow and sloping. "Why did you call?"

"Why hadn't you?" Race leaned forward.

"Why did you give up the game?"

"Why are you on an island in the middle of nowhere?"

"Got my reasons."

Race didn't know what to think of his grandfather, a hermit-like figure who'd been absent from his life for its entirety. Then, in a bitter tone, my boy said, "Did you know your son died?"

"Yeah." Danny sat back in his chair. "An estranged nephew of mine told me he met you at the funeral."

"You mean Billy?" Race's brain now held the clear image of Colin's disheveled cousin. "I didn't know what to make of that guy."

"No one does," Danny said. "He calls me once a year."

"Billy seemed to know more about my dad than he was letting on, like he had some secret he wasn't telling me."

"He had no right," Danny said.

The cottage door swung open. A fireplug of a man, robust and friendly-faced, with a warm demeanor entered first. "Oh, we have company," he declared with an infectious enthusiasm. "Company is great! I love company!"

"Well, hello there." Amanda gave the man a little wave while snatching a glimpse of an older woman standing behind him by the open door.

The short man's aura sparkled with mischief and innocence. "I'm Freddie," he said, pointing at the guests on the couch. "Now, who are you and you and you?"

"My name is Race, and this is Amanda and her daughter, Marianne." My boy directed his stare at Freddie, who had the merriest gleam in his almond-shaped eyes. It was as if God had constructed the stocky man's heart out of rainbows and chocolate.

"Everybody," Danny said, "this is Freddie, as you already know." He then gestured toward the woman by the door. "And that young lady, well, younger than me at least, is Nara. She's sort of our helper around here, keeps me and Freddie in line."

Nara offered a slight grin. "Very nice to meet you all."

As Race regarded Freddie and Nara more closely, an unmistakable tension descended on the room, failing to go unnoticed. Freddie had a short neck, a small head and ears, and slanted eyes with heavy lids—the clear traits of a genetic condition. He exuded an authentic warmth and appeared to be in his late thirties. His face, round and flat, bore laugh lines from frequent smiles and chuckles. His hair, showing tints of gray, was thick and wavy. With his solid build, he projected a sturdiness. "I give great hugs," Freddie said. "But not for newcomers."

Across the room, Nara stood slim and silent. With her short salt-and-pepper hair and hunched posture, Race figured she was at least sixty. The depth and intensity of her ebony eyes caught his attention, while her gaze held a fire, a wildness like the untamed ocean, a force of nature itself.

"I'm going to make a big bowl of cereal," Freddie exclaimed. "It's going to be Lucky Charms if anyone else wants some."

Marianne's eyes glimmered with delight as she tugged at Amanda's sleeve. "Mommy," the little girl whispered, "can I have some, too?"

"Of course, if it's okay with our host," Amanda said with a warm smile.

Danny grinned and nodded.

"Oh, yes!" Freddie shouted, and his laughter resonated throughout the room as he escorted Marianne into the kitchen.

Danny looked at Nara, uncertainty behind his wrinkled eyes. "Once they finish eating, maybe we can go outside," he suggested. "We should show our guests the island while they're here. Who knows if they'll be back?"

"Yes," Nara agreed. "I'll go help with the cereal."

As his grandfather fidgeted in the worn-out chair, Race sensed a familiar disconnect. Like the skill Colin had perfected in parenthood, Danny spoke volumes without uttering a word. An undeniable air of detachment surrounded the reunited strangers, creating an unbreakable barrier between them and the world. In that instant, without knowing why, my boy yearned for a bond with Danny, the type of genuine connection he never had with his dad.

I was luckier than Race; my father and I shared a special relationship. When I was little, I asked Daddy about the meaning of life, and he said, "All you need to know, Holly, is the meaning of *your* life." He'd explain that each person is on a unique journey, and the real question isn't just about what's out there—it's about what's inside you. He told me that all the wise religious people and brilliant thinkers are like guides, but the real answers lie within our hearts. The true lesson, he said, is that life's mysteries hide in the questions we ask ourselves, and that the Creator is most interested in the unique path of each person.

Oh, and Daddy once told me this story about an old woman, the Mother of Fate, who weaves the world. He said she's the one who waits at the end of each life's journey. She sits at the entrance of a cave, this place between day and night, between our world and something else—something ancient and hidden. When someone passes, she sees them approach and remembers the thread of their life's story from the very start. She helped weave that thread at the beginning, and now she wonders what that soul did with it. Did they find the story that was meant to unfold? How did they handle the twists and turns of fate that brought them trouble and darkness? At the entrance to her cave, the old woman draws the pattern of their soul's journey in the dust. But she only shows half of it—the other half comes from the life they lived. When we die, Daddy said, the riches and fame we've gathered don't matter. What matters is the life we lived, the love we gave, and whether we found and followed our inner purpose. He told me the real question at the end isn't about obeying rules or avoiding vices. It's about whether we lived our true story and if we matched the design the Mother of Fate gave us. If we did, we move on to the realm of the ancestors; if not, we return to the daylight world and try again. It's just another myth my daddy loved so much, a story about what might happen after we're gone, meant to remind us that each life has a purpose, and even when everything feels like it's falling apart, we should look inside ourselves to find our true thread.

Someone

WITH A LOUD clatter of dishes, Freddie and Marianne sprung from the kitchen, their voices ratcheting up a few octaves with sugar-induced excitement. "We're ready!" Freddie called out.

Marianne chimed in, "Yep, we're ready!" Her eyes lit up as she pinwheeled around. "Can we go see the waves now, Mommy?"

Amanda placed her hands on her hips. "What's the magic word?"

"Please!" Marianne and Freddie sang in unison.

Amanda laughed and shared a sweet glance with Race. "I did promise, you know," she said in a playful voice. "It's chilly outside, but she's got her bathing suit on under her clothes. Maybe I'll just let her dip her toes in."

While admiring the simple vow between a mother and her daughter, Race's mind wandered to the complex history Amanda and Marianne had and their effort to build a new relationship. He reflected on Chad, the man who had betrayed them, leaving them to confront a tough world on their own.

I can relate, trust me. Life's obstacles pound against us, like waves against the shore. But with someone we trust beside us, those breakers become easier to endure. They may not disappear, but together, we discover the courage to stand tall, to weather the storm, and to come out stronger on the other side. Same as how the ocean's waves shape the coastline, our challenges shape us, molding us into who we need to be—for ourselves, and for each other.

Nara finished washing the dishes and came out of the kitchen, then she faced Amanda. "Well, I'll show you a bit of the island now and take you to the water."

Danny cocked his head. "Smells like rain."

Marianne's enthusiasm bubbled over once more. "Yay!"

A stern stare covered Nara's face, as Amanda clarified, "My little girl loves the water, no matter its form."

Freddie, radiating enthusiasm, leaped into the middle of the den. "But Marianne, you need to be careful, okay?" He delivered his words with genuine concern. "The ocean doesn't always play nice."

In his easy chair, Danny nodded in agreement. "That's right, Freddie," he said in a voice defined by decades of practicality. "We know some folks who learned that lesson the hard way, don't we?"

As everyone hurried to get their coats, Danny grabbed Race's arm. "We'll all meet up at the gazebo," the old man said, his baritone packed with purpose. "I need your help with something. Stay here for a minute, will you, son?"

The others bounded outside and down a dirt path

toward the rocky beach as the gathering rain clouds intensi-fied. While the voices and laughter faded into the distance, Danny and Race remained standing on the doorstep, their gazes fixed on the world around them. After sitting down on a step, Danny rubbed his knees with weary fingers and groaned, "Jesus, never get old."

Race took a seat next to his grandfather and wondered what other nuggets of caution rumbled around in the old man's noggin. "So what do you need help with?"

"Just thought we'd try this again," Danny said. "Maybe get off on a better foot this time."

"Yeah." My son grinned. "So, do I call you Grandpa, Grandad, or Gramps?"

"Danny will do." The man pointed toward the faraway group walking toward the water. "So, what do you think of Freddie?"

Race composed himself before responding. "Seems like a good guy," he said as the constant crush of the sea eroded the edges of his consciousness, blurring the sharp outlines in his mind like charcoal sketches.

Danny glowed. "Gotta say, Freddie finds happiness in the small stuff." The old man stared into his grandson's emer-ald eyes. "He's strong in ways not everyone understands, a bright spot of joy in a world that forgets what being genuine is all about."

Race nodded. "How did you two end up here?"

Danny let out a warm chuckle. "Freddie and I have been together near half my life," he said. "See, when your father took you to Oregon, he left behind more than just bad memories."

Race narrowed his eyes. "Huh?"

Shouts of delight and laughter resonated from a distance, and Danny frowned at the commotion. "Come on," he said. "Let's head to the gazebo, make sure things are shipshape."

While walking on the dusty path behind the hotel, Race couldn't stop thinking about what Danny had said. Besides a dead wife and all his loved ones, what else had Colin McIntyre left behind in Watertown when he relocated to Sea Point, the farthest place from home he could find? Upon reaching a paltry cemetery overgrown with weeds, my son's train of thought derailed when he eyed a dozen deteriorating headstones. "Who were these people?"

"The Caswell clan," Danny said, happy enough to converse about a different family. "They arrived in the early 1700s, with the Shoals community already a century old. Seasonal fishermen would commute from Europe, but the Caswells built homes on this rock, survived the dangerous fishing trade and brutal winters. Patriots cleared Shoalers off these islands during the Revolutionary War, but the Caswells came back to Star, got rich by some standards, and became royalty here. Not much of a kingdom, though, reeking of stale fish and covered in run-down huts. Women did most of the labor and grew old before their time. When the men weren't fishing, they were drinking rum or lounging on the rocks." Then a wide grin stretched across Danny's face. "They say there were only two types of Shoalers back then: the chain-smoking, hard-drinking, fish-smelling, tobacco-spitting, foul-mouthed heathen type… and their husbands."

Race tried to smile. "What about your wife?"

As they approached the gazebo, a striking wooden structure high on a hill with a commanding view of jagged rocks and the boundless sea, Danny shared a long-lost story.

"Your grandmother wasn't always hateful," he said, his voice shouldering cumbersome memories. "But at some point, after our eldest, Liam, was killed in that godforsaken war, Orla stopped seeing the good in the world."

Race nodded, absorbing Danny's account. "So you left your family and moved here?"

"Got to Star about a year after splitting with Orla," Danny said. "Didn't want to come, but we all got reasons for doing stuff."

"And then you met Freddie?"

Danny's eyes fell upon a dead leaf hanging on the twig of a scrawny tree beside the gazebo. He reached out and plucked it from the branch, then let the withered thing fall. "No, Freddie wasn't here when I arrived on the island," the old man said. "*He* is what your father left behind in Watertown."

"I don't get it."

"Guess there's no other way to say this." Danny fixed his gaze on Race. "Freddie, well, he's your brother."

My son's mind whizzed as he considered the puzzle piece presented before him, while a cannonball sank to the bottom of his gut. "That makes no sense." He took a step back, walloped by the one-two punch of dismay and disbelief. "Petrak never told me anything about a brother," he said, voice trembling. "So, we're twins?"

"No," Danny said, biting his thin lower lip. "Freddie's two years younger."

Race needed to pry the truth from his grandfather. "I don't know what you're trying to do here, or if this is some kind of joke." My son's voice quivered. "But you need to explain."

"It's not a joke."

"What do you know?"

"All of it."

"Tell me, then," Race said, failing in his attempt to stay calm. "Tell me about my mother's death."

"It was hard on everyone," the old man said, "and Colin didn't handle it well. He was devastated, but it wasn't his fault."

"What happened, Danny?" Race was yelling now.

"You have every reason to be angry."

"Goddamn right I do!"

Danny lowered his head, his demeanor weighed down by the altercation. "Christ, I'm sorry," he said, his voice colored with repentance. "This was a mistake. I shouldn't have invited you here and sprung this on you."

Race, his heart blasting out of his chest, closed the distance between them, his face now mere inches from the old man's. "Tell me," my son demanded. "Right here, right fucking now!"

When Race's baseball career ended, he returned to Sea Point, just thirty-one years old with his entire future in front of him. His homecoming brought me so much joy, and I hoped he'd stay for good, believing he and Jess could build a beautiful life together. However, their dreams soon took a nosedive.

For five long years, they tried to get pregnant, but I wasn't sure they had the same reasons for making the effort. Throughout Race's thirteen years competing in the minor leagues, baseball had taken him around the world, and his unfaithfulness during that time had fractured their relationship. The trust they thought they had was gone, and the life he led was not the kind that gave a woman peace of mind. While their vows might've sustained them, Jess yearned for a family, and Race couldn't provide that for her, or what she needed most from him: his true self. Their love story unraveled on a rainy Monday morning, during an otherwise dry spring, when Jess told him she was walking away for good. Race blurted out his final plea minutes before she slammed the door in his face: "You can't leave me," he cried. "My world is a disaster!"

"Yeah, because you always rationalize stupidity."

"It's not my fault."

"You keep saying that."

"I keep meaning it."

"You know what, my bad," she said. "You're right, it's not all your fault. You're only half of the problem. You *and* your world are equally responsible for the disaster."

When Jess requested a divorce, Race bowed without argument. He didn't ask for another chance, didn't suggest counseling or propose a romantic getaway. Back then, he believed he'd be fine without her and that she'd be better off without him. But life humbles us, especially when we find ourselves alone, facing an uncertain road ahead.

Following Race and Jess's breakup, I began experiencing memory lapses. It started with trivial things like forgetting words, misplacing car keys and my cell phone, but then it escalated. Colin, my dear husband, remained oblivious to my struggles. His work consumed him, demanding that he stay for long hours at the park, sequestered in his office or wandering the forest. He offered private tours on the trails, but his derring-do was a far cry from the adventurous spirit of Meriwether Lewis and William Clark. He was just a man who'd lost his way after Sevan's actions almost forty years earlier. At home, Colin retreated to the basement, his cave, spending his days playing the guitar and losing himself in his record collection.

They say you receive the love you give…

When I started forgetting my friends' birthdays or the directions to the grocery store, heaps of frustration piled up inside me. In a blink, it was like I'd gone from a poised crooner to a petrified newbie with incurable stage fright. Almost overnight, I needed folks to speak a little slower on the telephone for any chance of a coherent conversation. More often, my words stayed on the tip of my tongue, and when they came out wrong, it would surprise me more than anyone else.

I didn't share my struggles with Race or Colin because I didn't want to burden my son, and I had little faith in my husband's support during that difficult time. Race would take care of me if he had to, but something told me Colin suspected I was faking my problems. What he couldn't see was my disorientation and my pain. I hadn't meant to irritate him, and I knew he was tired of hearing me repeat things three times in a row. I just prayed he'd be patient.

But then, I grew old all at once, without aging a bit, and my doctor suggested testing to pinpoint my condition. The impact of his diagnosis enslaved me like a dense fog, blotting out what lay ahead. My knowledge of the impending threat left me feeling isolated, just like Race on Star Island when Danny revealed Freddie was his brother.

When the clouds cracked and a light drizzle began to

fall that morning, the sky darkened, creating a peculiar midmorning twilight. It was only ten thirty, yet the surroundings outside resembled dusk, as if day had already given up and surrendered to night. While Danny stayed silent in the gazebo, head down, my son waited him out, defiant and vigilant, like an angler refusing to let a stubborn tuna off the hook.

"I'm not moving till you give me answers," Race said.

Danny broke his silence. "You deserve to know the truth."

"But you don't have the balls to tell me, do you?" Once again, my son's understanding of his world shook, and his mind roiled like the furious sea.

A bleak mist corralled the wooden structure as Danny hunched over on a bench beneath the sheltering eaves. He avoided the falling droplets, but he couldn't evade the intense scrutiny in his grandson's grimace. "Life as a lobsterman wasn't easy," the old man said, diverting from the line of questioning. "Took skill and patience. Setting traps just right, knowing where and when to drop them." He raised his gaze to Race. "But what I loved most was the peace of the ocean, the solitude of the waves, the salty air. It was a tough job, but it was honest work, and that meant something."

"Might be the only thing honest about you."

Danny stared hard into my son's eyes. "You know, people and lobsters aren't so different, pinching and clawing their way through life, jockeying for position, crawling all over one another, all soft under tough shells."

"What about my mother?"

"I loved Sevan like a daughter," Danny said, his gravelly voice laced with nostalgia. "I was over the moon for her and

Colin when they tied the knot, even though they were still in their teens. And when you were born, well goddamn, I assumed everything was gonna be perfect."

"Why wasn't it?"

Danny said that his wife, Orla, had disapproved of Colin's marriage because of her deep-seated prejudices and racism. The tension led to their eventual separation, but Danny's love for his two surviving sons never regressed. He vacated his family's home but remained close by, moving into a modest apartment. He tried to see Colin and Kyle as often as possible, yet he confessed he was most at ease on the water. "My biggest regret was not seeing you more after you were born."

For Race, in that hush of time, Colin's absence loomed larger than ever. My husband's silent presence was a concrete slab my son still carried, but our boy mourned the man's death less than the love he withheld—and Race still yearned for that love, though he'd never admit it.

Danny continued, "When I wasn't lobstering, I was fishing the Charles, in a smaller boat I kept at a marina near our house in Watertown. Being on that river gave me some comfort, like being wrapped in a blanket. It was quiet out there, just the birds chirping and the boat moving, everything else fading away, leaving me alone with the water."

More laughter reverberated off the rocks by the beach. "Come on, Marianne," Freddie yelled. "You're such a slowpoke!"

Race glanced over Danny's shoulder. At the bottom of a rolling hill, Amanda and Nara watched from the sand as Marianne and Freddie stepped from rock to rock in the light rain, giggling and hurling stones at the rolling waves. Standing far from the water, Amanda observed her daughter. "Not too far, Annie!"

Race admired Amanda's cautious, yet freeing, motherly approach. She didn't project her own fear of the ocean onto her daughter; instead, she encouraged Marianne's youthful bravery, allowing her to explore the world with wonder. It was a striking difference from his own impaired upbringing.

Refocusing, Race glared at Danny. "What about Sevan's death?"

Danny covered his face with his hands, fingers clenching as he spoke, as though he were pulling the truth from his bowels. "I was out on the Charles that afternoon."

An earsplitting silence enveloped the men, broken only by the steady rain on the gazebo's rooftop and the distant rumbles of thunder. The world seemed to hold its tongue, waiting for the untold story to unravel.

Down by the shoreline, Nara's voice rang out. "Come back to the beach, you two!"

"The rocks are too slippery now," Amanda added as the rain picked up.

With a wary sigh, Danny said, "No one else was on the water that day. The Sox and Yanks were playing for the pennant. The entire city was watching that game."

Race gave a nod; that classic matchup in 1978 remains etched in the minds of baseball fans everywhere. The Yankees' miraculous comeback from a fourteen-game deficit in August had forced this dramatic showdown, the key moment coming when an unlikely hero—whom Boston fans still call Bucky "F-ing" Dent—smacked a late-game home run to give the Yankees the lead.

Danny paused, his scowl fixed on a distant memory. "I

was alone on the river." His voice was steady but splattered with sorrow. "Exactly how I liked it, no one around but the lily pads. The bass weren't biting though, and I called it a day, started heading back to the marina, toward the bridge. It wasn't quite dusk when I saw her up there on the ledge…" His words trailed off, vanishing into the ether, and the silence that followed sounded like death.

Like my son there on Star Island, I never did like the silence very much, that godawful void, inching closer in the dark, ready to swallow my thoughts. The feeling that I'm fading away into nothing is the scariest part. That's why I love to sing, filling up the quiet spaces with stories and memories, keeping my wilting recollections alive a little longer.

Surrender to Me

MY GIRL! HER smile… laughter. Slipping away. Gone? Hold her, tell her… love her. Memories, haunting, dancing, taunting. Clutch, hold… tighter, lost. She's gone! Why are you gone?

A clap of thunder shattered the island's serenity.

Sitting stiff next to Danny, Race wrestled with unearthed secrets, a wild animal on the loose under his skin. The growing tension dangled in the air as an impending cloudburst brewed on the horizon. "You were there when she jumped?" my son said, more an accusation than a question.

"I should've called her name," Danny said, chin low. "Should've said something."

Before Race processed the revelation, a bone-chilling scream broke the calm. "No! Freddie! No!"

My son's head snapped around. Down on the beach,

Amanda, Marianne, and Nara huddled together, their faces contorted in sheer horror, their voices a chorus of desperation. "Help!" they cried, their outstretched arms reaching toward the treacherous waters.

Freddie thrashed in the waves, struggling against the undertow, the merciless sea swallowing him whole. Race's veins surged, each beat of his heart resonating with a new-found connection. He tore out of the gazebo and dashed onto the fifty-yard path leading to the beach.

"Race!" yelled Amanda. "Hurry!"

With each wild stride down the muddy hill, Race's thoughts picked up speed. Brotherly concern fired through him, extinguishing all other notions and ideas. Needlelike thorns in the thigh-high thicket scratched at his clothing. His sneakers pounded the uneven ground, thumping along with his pulse.

Marianne's screams cut through the rain. "Mommy! Get Freddie!"

Amanda stayed still as a shell on the beach, while Race's mind convulsed. He couldn't bear the idea of losing Freddie, not now. With each passing second, the strings of uncovered secrets constricted my son, squeezing him tighter and tighter. The image of his brother drowning was an anvil dropping in his soul.

Amanda cried, "Race, please!"

My boy ran faster, his breathing erratic, frantic. He ripped off his jacket, shoes, and soaked shirt, exposing a muscular body marked by the scars of his playing days. He bounded over the slippery rocks and dove into the depths below.

You know the minute in all our lives when everything

changes forever? I can't quite pinpoint the instance when it happened to me, but I know it did. It happens to everyone, like fate has its own plans. Even if you try to cling to who you were before, you can't. It's scribbled in the stars. Sometimes you just know when it's happening, and I know when it happened to my son.

The Atlantic turned hostile, cold currents yanking at Race's limbs, each tug leaving him more disoriented. The salt's sharp sting blurred his vision, the cloudy sea denying any view of Freddie. As Race searched and struggled, deeper and deeper, the water began to glow and an enchanting figure shimmered into view, a woman in a swishing gown taking shape, emerging from the shadows. Her flowing hair caressed her face, framing piercing eyes that seemed to house the ocean's secrets. Was she a mirage conjured by delirium? That's what I deduced when Race shared the story with me.

My son assured me this was no illusion, however, and as suddenly as the figure appeared, she was gone, leaving Race alone in the impenetrable darkness. His heart hammered in frenetic, fitful beats, and he prayed his lungs wouldn't burst. When panic overtook him, he wanted to give up. But then, once again, the unknown woman appeared from the depths. This time, she cradled a large object in her arms and presented it to Race, as if offering a sacred gift. During the transfer, my son's fingers brushed against the woman's arm, a fleeting touch charged with inexplicable energy. Through the murkiness, their eyes locked, and an unspoken promise passed between them, a bond formed in the space of a heartbeat.

With a mystical smile, the enchantress receded into the abyss, leaving Race clutching Freddie's limp body in his arms. My son kicked and flailed under the crush of water, while the weight of his brother, the truth, and the mysteries of the island dragged the two men down. Sinking, lower and lower. Until, in the chilling silence of the ocean, their story unraveled.

Memory's a puzzle, isn't it? Pieces scattered across the floor of your mind, some lost in the dark corners, others gleaming in the light. You try to fit them together, but some won't cooperate. Stubborn fragments and segments, bits and parts, refusing to slot into place. So you force them, bend them until they comply, hoping to reconstruct the picture of a life slipping away piece by piece.

Somehow, I don't believe you. Hollyann, how does this yarn go again? Why don't I trust what you say? These stories are always tangled up in knots...

Twenty yards from shore, Race rocketed up through the surface, gasping for air, holding Freddie's head above water. During the struggle, the wicked thunderstorm churning over Star Island drenched everything beneath its domain. As sheets of rain crashed down, Race swam with all his power to save the younger brother he'd only recently discovered. But, perhaps, my boy was also swimming to save his own soul, each desperate stroke at war against the forces of nature.

When a jagged bolt of lightning split the heavens, the entire world lit up, converting the gloomy morning into a fireworks display. The sky's quick glow revealed worried faces on the beach, and Race spotted Amanda through the downpour, her short blonde hair pasted to her forehead, horror alive in her eyes. Beside her, young Marianne clutched her mom's wet dress with jittery hands. Mother and daughter had been a picture of happiness minutes earlier, laughing with Nara and Freddie, playing and dancing. But their joy had turned to terror when Freddie slipped on the rocks and fell into the roaring sea.

As Race pushed himself up in waist-deep water, his muscles wailed in protest. Using all his strength, he hauled Freddie's slack body, two-hundred pounds of dead weight, out of the grasp of the merciless ocean. He staggered to shore and laid his waterlogged brother onto the sand, where his body remained still. Racing against time, my boy pressed down with both hands on Freddie's chest, over and over, his voiced edged in panic. "Freddie! Come on, breathe!"

When another crackling bolt of lightning streaked through the atmosphere, Marianne screamed and held on tighter to her mother. Nara shivered, shaky hands covering her mouth, eyes harboring the kind of fear reserved for the worst disasters. The ensuing thunder muffled the welcome sound of ragged huffs as Freddie coughed, expelled water from his lungs, and drew in the shuddering breaths of life.

Then a cry broke through. "My son! My son!"

Whipping around, Race locked eyes with Nara. Her relieved face, wet with rain and tears, released a flow of memories upon him, the stark revelation in her cry crushing him like a tidal wave. He didn't want to believe it, not at first, that Nara, the stranger Danny had called his "helper," was, in fact, Sevan. His mother, she was alive.

A rush of hate and love shot through Race's veins. He recalled the woman's deep dark eyes from his earliest memories—before she vanished, leaving a gaping hole in his youthful heart. But the memories shattered, affection and joy and loss strewn about like the shards of a broken mirror. Alongside those recollections was me—the woman he'd grown up thinking was his actual mom. Throughout his life, I had been a steady source of comfort and warmth, his one and only bellwether.

Knowing that I wasn't his birth mother had threatened to destabilize everything Race believed in. Now, the thin threads holding his life together were fraying, and a twinge of guilt snuck into his soul, for the resentment he held toward Nara, now believed to be his *real* mother, Sevan. How could he reconcile this when I'd been nothing but a beacon of devotion for him? Her abandonment and reappearance pitted him between two moms who he loved in different ways. How could he balance his reconnection with Sevan and his loyalty for me?

I remember Race describing that disturbing morning of enlightenment on the island. Oh, the sorriness that settled in my joints as he spoke. "When I looked into Nara's eyes," he had said, "it was like dreaming a forgotten dream. There was pain and confusion, but also recognition." As he relayed his tale, my spirit ached for him.

Yet, as Race fought through an inner tempest, finding his footing between two mothers, I grappled with a storm of my own. There was a weight, a pressing suspicion that my cherished memories—of his first day at school, his giggles, his sobs, that beautiful smile—might soon slip through my fingers. Will I ever forget Race's confession, that he had recognized Nara, as Sevan, from when he was a baby? Will the pain of protecting our entwined past subside? While he disentangled his two worlds, I held on with all my strength to the precious memories of the son who had become *my* world. Because now, he and I were losing both of us.

Being abandoned is a peculiar thing. You never get over it, no matter your age. It lingers on. Imagine the hurt, the blame, the longing. If you were an orphan, even in adulthood, you'd never stop questing for a home, or for a parent, would you?

:05

Don't Look Back

SEVAN ZAKARIAN WAS not herself on October 2, 1978, the day she turned twenty, when a decisive plan took root in her mind. In the backyard of their Watertown home, her father chased after and laughed with seventeen month-old Race, while Sevan sat at her small desk in the upstairs bedroom—with a pen in her delicate hand and a piece of yellow paper staring her in the face.

Her husband, Colin, was at his mother's house that afternoon, caught up in a nerve-racking baseball game between the hometown Red Sox and their archrivals, the New York Yankees. Once upon a time, Sevan had enjoyed a multitude of passions, including the very sport that captivated Colin's attention. Those days of youthful exuberance, however, had dissolved into distant memories.

For the duration of her young life, the death knell of her grandmother's prophecy had ensnared her soul. The unrelenting weight of collective trauma, etched into the

Armenian people's history, had stomped her spirit. The ruthless claws of guilt grabbed her by the throat. Why should she survive when so many others had died?

With gritted teeth, Sevan inscribed a heartfelt letter to her son and sealed it within an envelope, tucking it away in the drawer of her desk. After taking off her jeans and sweatshirt, she changed into her most elegant possession—a flowing azure gown, reminiscent of the ocean's deep, boundless hues. She slipped into a pair of wool socks and the knee-high suede boots Colin had gifted her for Mother's Day. In the mirror on the wall, she saw a face that wasn't her own.

Downstairs, her mother, Yeva, rooted on the Red Sox with several neighbors gathered in the living room, their claps and cries reverberating through the floorboards. In a united effort, the city of Boston had rallied together on that breezy afternoon, cheering on their team against the Yanks in a sudden-death playoff game. It was one silly game, a child's game, but the most important event in all of New England. Strange how baseball, a timeless escape from reality, brings us together. In the havoc of life, the field becomes a sanctuary where dreams soar, and worries vanish. Finding happiness in the little things helps us stay hopeful and strong, I suppose, even in the darkest times. People always say life is like a game, with the same stakes, consequences, and struggles. But that's not how I view it—life is more than a game; our experiences are too complex to minimize our existence.

Sevan marched across the hall to her grandmother's room and retrieved a faded red scarf from the lowermost drawer of her pine dresser. Peering through the window at the somber, cloudy afternoon, the young mother grinned at a pigeon gliding above Porter Street. Off in the distance, a lone plane embarked from Logan Airport. On this strange day, an alien lightness cocooned Sevan, as if an unseen hindrance had dissipated, melting beneath the magnitude of her simple yet willful plan. She draped a warm brown sweater over her shoulders, wrapped the red scarf around her neck, then tiptoed downstairs. She pocketed the car keys from the kitchen table and slipped out the front door.

Amid the strains of her father's singsong voice and the infectious laughter of her son chiming from the backyard, Sevan crawled into her car. When she turned the key, her favorite band's new single, "Don't Look Back," began on the radio. Images of Colin and Race and her parents and grandmother blurred inside her brain. She blinked twice and those thoughts disappeared, far away and left behind.

A brief drive led her to the North Beacon Street Bridge that straddled the Charles River, close to the McIntyre residence, where she parked her vehicle along the roadside. Long after the final triumphant notes of Boston's song had rung out, Sevan killed the car engine, feeling a wave of emptiness, despondence. Through the lasting echoes of the awe-inspiring guitar solo, her intention remained unaffected, and she walked onto the concrete bridge.

Sevan strolled halfway across and hopped onto a narrow ledge, just two feet tall, one foot wide. Her body bending at the waist, she gazed at the dark water below. In the embrace of an overcast sky, she tied the red scarf around her suede boots. One knot. Then two. Her long, blue dress billowed in the breeze as she stood tall, closed her eyes, lifted her chin, and faced the clouds. She extended her arms out to the sides then raised them, palms facing upward, as if she was lifting the air itself. She breathed in and whispered, "I invoke thee, Nar, thou goddess of the wind and storm."

Under darkening skies, Sevan Zakarian remained determined—the embodiment of a silent prophecy waiting to be realized. But she didn't *want* to die; she only wanted the pain to stop, the suffering to disappear. She couldn't do it anymore, life the way it was. She needed help, someone else to take over. Balancing on the bridge, suspended between heaven and the depths, her decision lingered in the atmosphere, like a held breath.

Sometimes, the most significant moments in our lives have nothing to do with us. The day Sevan stood poised on that bridge above the Charles River, my destiny took a drastic turn.

Back then, in early October 1978, as a thirty-year-old single mother with a young daughter, I was living in the Pacific Northwest, resuscitating my dying dream of becoming a singer. Have I mentioned my daughter? Oh, everyone loved her. Anyway, that's neither there nor here. On that fall day in '78, I should've been soaking in stardom in New York or Los Angeles. That's where people like me go to find fame. But a few years earlier, something told me to go to Oregon.

Like mine, Danny McIntyre's life changed direction that October afternoon. As he steered his boat along the Charles, fifty yards from the North Beacon Street Bridge, his heart skipped two beats when he spotted a figure teetering on the ledge. Panic rushed through him when he saw it was Sevan, his son's wife. Yes, it was her. Wasn't it?

Danny sat still, his eyes locked on the spectacle unfolding before him. The woman, whoever she was, stood on the bridge, her silhouette against the stormy sky, wearing a lovely dress of azure silk that clashed with the ominous clouds overhead. The dress, elegant and flowing, clung to her form, accentuating her graceful figure while it danced with the wind. As his boat glided closer, Danny didn't speak, didn't call out, didn't know why not.

Time slowed to a crawl as the woman, her facial features etched with anguish, leaned forward and toppled off the bridge. The dress swirled around her like a final, desperate plea, and at that sickening instant—one that lasted forever—Danny was certain it was Sevan. Her hair, a dark cascade, twisting in the breeze, whipped around her face. Her outstretched arms reaching for the heavens, fingers splayed in surrender. And then, the inevitable, brutal impact with the water.

Danny winced as Sevan hit the unforgiving surface, the dress tangled around her like a shroud, the water swallowing her. He gunned the throttle on his little boat, speeding through the serene river under the somber sky. His temples throbbed, and every thump punctuated his mission: saving his daughter-in-law before time ran out.

Approaching the spot of her fall, Danny scanned the area and saw only Sevan's brown sweater floating away. But then, a swatch of her delicate blue dress materialized beside his boat, caught in the river's clutches. Without a thought, he leaned over the edge, plunged his trembling hand into the water and gripped the thin fabric. Straining against the deceptive current, he pulled at the material until it yielded Sevan's wilted form, her boots bound with a burning red scarf.

He hoisted her onto the boat, her sodden clothing impeding the effort. Suddenly, Sevan's eyes became frenzied, reflecting a hurricane of intensity that Danny couldn't decode. She began thrashing and screaming, "No, no, no!"

Danny wrapped his arms around her. "It's all right, you're okay," he said, panting, scouring the riverbank for help. "Don't worry now, it's okay." When she calmed, he untied the scarf around her ankles.

The signs of Sevan's affliction had been present for a while, including her paranoia, vacant stares, and disjointed conversations. The doctors had confirmed her postpartum depression but also diagnosed her with another condition, "schizophrenia," a word that barked like mad in her mind. Just like Cerberus, the three-headed watchdog of the Underworld, making sure souls stay put and the living stay out, Sevan guarded the gates of her psyche, contending with villainous grumbles and schemes. This constant vigilance mirrored Cerberus's duty, as she strived to maintain order amid internal bedlam.

After Danny saved her, Sevan faced him on the boat, her voice no louder than a sigh. "Please, hide me. Keep me safe."

Danny nodded, his heart crumbling. Seeing the desperation in Sevan's eyes, the fragility that needed protection, he brought her to his compact apartment two miles away, above a taco bar in Allston, far from prying eyes and scathing rumors. He figured she'd stay for a couple of days, until she built up her strength and recovered. But after one week, as the police's search for the missing woman intensified, her courage weakened, and Danny couldn't find it in him to act against her wishes.

Ten days later, an anonymous caller reported spotting a woman matching Sevan's description walking toward the bridge on North Beacon Street the day she went missing. Soon after, divers found a brown sweater, which her family confirmed was hers. Hiding out with her father-in-law, Sevan was scared and unstable, far from healed. It was then, during those tenuous days, that she began calling herself by another name: Nara.

Though still alive, by erasing her identity, Sevan had essentially ended her life. Weeks turned into a month, and that nondescript apartment became Nara's haven. Danny had barely seen his ex-wife or sons since summer, and the authorities hadn't called about his daughter-in-law's apparent suicide. With a new name and renewed purpose, the wounds within Nara's core mended, albeit slowly. Yet, the fear of going back to Colin and her young son, Race, gnawed at her. The idea of facing them, thus allowing them to witness her troubled state and exposing them to her dark inner world, was a prospect she couldn't entertain. In time, her remembrance of the man and boy faded, even as her love for them remained. However, each day, Danny pleaded with her to reconsider her stance, to seek professional help. But Nara refused, asking to stay for "just a while longer."

Then, one day in mid-November, as she and Danny shared another simple and silent meal at home, Nara opened up, revealing a truth that had been growing like a storm cloud. "I can never go back to them," she said. "I'm carrying a part of my pain within me, a piece of the chaos. I can't let them see this."

Danny's heart hurt for her, for the agony her words couldn't express. "Reach out to your parents, to your husband," he begged once again. "At least tell them you're not dead. They love you and they need to know you're okay."

Nara shook her head, tears glistening in her eyes. "I don't want to be okay in… in that way anymore. I need to find a new kind of okay, a new kind of life."

And so, they made an impossible decision: They would disappear together. The day after Thanksgiving, after fifty-two days of isolation, two ghosts moved to Star Island off the coast of New Hampshire, a place on the edge of the world. An old friend set Danny up with a job maintaining the Oceanic Hotel, offering him and his "helper" an unadorned cottage to stay in. There, Nara found peace in the seclusion, as her growing belly symbolized a fresh start and a chance to overcome a troubled past.

It was on that harsh island that Nara gave birth to a baby boy, a child whom Danny named Freddie—after Fred Lynn, another of Colin's baseball heroes. Born with Down syndrome, Freddie reflected the beauty and uniqueness that life could hold. As the new mother embraced her perfect son, she discovered solace, his coo a balm to her harrowed heart, his innocence a beam of light. She found a sanctuary in his presence, where love reigned once again, and her anxieties found their quiet release.

Time did what time does; it moved slow and fast at once, while the three outcasts became a family, bound not only by blood but by the trials they'd faced together. It was in this secluded corner of the universe, where no one questioned her background, that Nara left Sevan in the past. She cut off her hair and all ties to the dark days behind her. The trauma she'd been born with still smoldered, however, and the nightmares continued for some time, but the tranquil rhythm of the island's waves helped cure her wounded soul.

Years passed, and as Freddie grew older, Nara watched over him with conviction and tenderness, with the kind of love Sevan hadn't given to Race. The world beyond their island held many challenges, and she was determined to shield Freddie from the pain she once knew.

While witnessing the woman and boy thrive, Danny became a surrogate father to her and a devoted grandfather to him. The old man aged with pride, having seen the scars of Nara's journey, the mania she had battled, and the strength she had discovered within herself. On early mornings, in quiet moments spent on the rocks, Danny McIntyre convinced himself that their disappearance wasn't about running away. No, it was about healing and rebuilding, crafting a new future together. It was rewriting a story that darkness had marred and bringing it into the light. It was singing a new song.

Petrak and Yeva Zakarian never found their daughter. Colin McIntyre never found his wife. Sevan's absence remained a mystery, becoming part of Watertown lore, the curious tale of a woman who had evaporated into the unknown. One day, while paying me a visit, Colin admitted he blamed himself for what happened to Sevan. He could've been a better husband to her; he'd sensed her slipping away for over a year and regretted not trying harder to pull her back. She still loved him when she left, maybe, he was almost positive, but he was powerless against unseen forces, ones that told her their love didn't matter, not more than the sacrifice she needed to make. After the town presumed her dead, everyone told him the suicide was unavoidable, that she had been unstable, that it wasn't his fault. It was all true, and he didn't believe a word of it.

When Colin lost Sevan, he lost sight of any landmark that might've led him some place happier, and he was certain he'd love no one like that again. He had written a song for his wife two weeks before she jumped, tucked it into her purse just days before she went missing. But even then, he knew she was already gone. He'd seen her disappear with his own eyes, those magical green eyes of his. Yes, he watched Sevan vanish right in front of him the minute their son was born.

"Let the Feeling Stay"
September 1978

As you lie asleep beside me, I can feel your rest-
less heart
You've been dying to release me, but you don't know
where to start
It's not easy being me, but I've done the best I can
I've poured my soul into your life, my love, but am
no less a man

You feel you have to go, I understand, though I
cannot accept
The string of broken dreams and promises we so
carelessly kept
Now your choice is made, the love is gone, there's
nothing I can do
But wait, before you walk into the dark, I ask one
thing of you…

*Don't take the feeling away, although you have
to leave
You know, I never asked for much. Oh, please just
do this for me
Don't take the feeling away. Girl, can't you see?
It may not matter to you, but it means the world
to me*

*Looking back on all the endless nights you spent
here in my arms
I see how easily I fell for you, your innocence,
your charms
If you only knew how much I cared, oh god, how
hard I tried
You would understand why, when you left, I held
my heart and cried*

*I still love you now, as I did then. My feelings will
not fade
My only chance to love again rests on a vow that
you once made
Remember on the day our child was born, when
words were hard to say
The tears fell from your eyes and promised they
would let the feeling stay*

You Gave Up on Love

THE DRIVING RAIN on Star Island had ceased, giving way to a glittering mist that covered the beach like a gentle blessing. Freddie gasped for breath, lying on the wet sand, while Amanda and Marianne huddled around him. Race, shocked by Nara's cry for her "son," staggered away from his younger brother and approached the woman, whoever she was—the cryptic figure who had entered, or returned to, his life.

Race's thoughts erupted like a waterspout, a maelstrom whirling within. Could his mother, presumed dead for forty years, be alive? The possibility destroyed everything he had held on to, immersing him with sorrow. She had vanished, leaving everyone she abandoned to struggle with the pain of her absence, a betrayal that Race couldn't wrap his head around. Only Freddie's brush with death had caused her to slip up and reveal the truth.

Nara rushed toward Freddie and cried, "My God!"

Race stepped into her path, anger flaring. "It's you?"

"You're okay, Freddie!" She pushed Race aside and hugged her soaking son. "Yes, you're okay. I'm here."

Race clutched the back of his neck. "Are you… Sevan?"

"I am Nara."

"No, you're not." He moved a step closer to her. "You're my mother. Why did you leave me? You ruined my life. Why?"

Nara's face transformed, revealing a collection of woes. "Sevan didn't mean to." Her voice warbled like a killdeer's cry in the wind.

"But *you* did!"

Danny, having witnessed the altercation from a distance, staggered down from the rocks and onto the sand. "That's enough, Race. Yelling won't settle this."

"It's *your* fault, too!" Race's fervor was white-hot. "You knew all about this, and you never said a thing."

"It's more complicated than that," Danny said, measuring his words.

Race's temper remained unquenched. "No, no," he said. "This is all very simple."

The noises of the beach devoured the argument. Waves created a raucous chorus as they lapped at the shoreline. Frantic seagulls wheeled through the overcast sky. The scent of salt and seaweed stirred in the brackish air. In that moment, Race didn't know down from up, back from front. The tape in his brain rewound to minutes earlier, and he envisioned the ethereal woman who had emerged in the water, rescuing Freddie from peril. Her dress. Her hair. Her touch. I once told my boy, after his father skipped his very first Little League game, that events of the past never happen twice, that history doesn't repeat itself—it just rhymes. Now, I live in that lie, forage for it, wallow in it.

Was that alluring apparition, that siren of the sea, a heroic savior or a figment of Race's fears and longings? Was the ancient legend of Tsovinar, the pagan goddess, real? Was anything true in his world?

Race snatched up his rain-soaked shirt and shoes, his sneer fixed upon Nara. "Who are you?" he yelled and pointed, stomping toward her, now an arm's length away. "How could you do this to me?"

She tried to touch his shoulder, but he recoiled.

A breeze swept across the beach, and the gulls circling above continued their plaintive cries. Danny stepped between the two combatants, intercepting Race's steely gaze. "Son, there's an explanation for all of this," the old man said, his voice painted with understanding.

The young man, however, had reached his breaking point. He couldn't endure any more explanations or revelations that would further shatter the life he had known. "I don't care what you have to say," he said. "I don't want anything to do with either of you."

Amanda hastened to Race's side and grabbed his arm, her eyes imploring him to reconsider. "Race, please, hear them out."

Race pulled away, his mind spinning. "I'm leaving," he said, glaring at Amanda. "You can come with me, or you can stay."

With that, my son ascended the hill, his footsteps firm and quick. He passed the small graveyard and disappeared beyond the wildflowers. Amanda called for Marianne to follow, and they trailed behind him.

Sometimes, I think about that cemetery on Star Island, the lost souls who died on that desolate slab of turf, so far from the rest of civilization. Their bodies buried on a sliver of land floating in a vast ocean. It must've been such an isolated life for them there. And now, when I think of their lonely graves, a stalking sadness murders me. I hope eternity isn't such a barren place for them—as I hope it won't be for me, for any of us. Is there a heaven? A hell?

Halfway up the hill, Amanda cast a final glance back toward the beach. "I'm sorry," she called, her voice stretching through the mist.

Danny stared at the mother and daughter, his eyes reflecting a keen sadness. "Me, too." The words tumbled off his tongue and crashed to the ground, the ponderous stones of gloom.

On her knees beside Freddie, Nara held her face in her hands while the wind whimpered a ballad about being lost at sea.

Songs and memories, twin threads weaving through the quilt of our lives, sew themselves into our existence. They're the melodies of our survival, each note representing a year, an occasion, a heartbeat. They take us back in time, letting us relive those special instances like they're happening right now.

I'll never forget the first song I ever wrote, a silly but honest tribute to my father. I was ten years old, and my tiny fingers struggled to find their way across the piano keys as I composed a rudimentary sequence of notes. The innocent lyrics flowed from my pen, capturing the spirit of the man who had donned funny glasses and walked me to church every Sunday. With each word, I celebrated his quiet snoring during afternoon naps and the extent of his love for my mother.

"Part of My Heart"

Daddy wore glasses, oh so round. He carried me to church, high off the ground
His spectacles twinkled, funny and bright. Guiding my way, like stars in the night

He'd snuggle and nap, snore soft and low. In dreams, to a world only he would know
I'd giggle and watch, as he sighed and sighed. In the warmth of his love, I'd always hide

With Mommy he'd dance, their love in flight. Two hearts entwined, in calm candlelight
He whispered of hope and sweet lullabies. Under his wing, I'd always rise

Now, Daddy's not here, but his love's still near. In each memory, I hold him dear
Through songs and years, he lives, you see. A part of my heart, he'll forever be

From that day forward, songs became the diary of my life, preserving the moments and the people I held closest. In every verse and chorus, I found remnants of my past, a cherished rhythm that brought me back to days of innocence, wonder, and boundless love. That sentimental song for my father, though, was my only original. I never wrote another one, just covered other singers' songs. Their words may not have been my own, but I made them mine.

Since I was ten, since the day I wrote that silly tune for my dad, I longed to be a performer. But more than that, I wanted someone, anyone, to compose a melody for me—with as much love as I poured into that song for my father. When I met Colin, I thought we might make amazing music together. With his words and my voice, we could set the world on fire. I thought a lot of things back then. In the end, my husband never penned a ballad for me, but he gave me something better. He gave me a son.

On the island, Race waited halfway down the weathered dock with his arms crossed, focusing on Amanda and Marianne as they approached. It wasn't quite noon. Behind the frazzled mother and daughter, the grand Oceanic Hotel cast a monstrous shadow.

From his boat, Sam Heatherton bellowed, "Ready to leave so soon?"

Race swiveled and faced the lobsterman. "More than ready."

Sam tucked a stray wisp of hair under his hat, his beard a rowdy tangle, his expression blending certitude with skepticism. "You sure you wanna go?"

A threatened piping plover made a racket somewhere in the distance, and the icy breakers, like an enduring drumbeat, pounded out their rough cadence against the shoreline. A thick spray coated Race's arms as he caught a fleeting whiff of fall, reminding him that the seasons keep changing and no one can stop them. With his tendons tightening, he gawked at the choppy sea, longing to flee from the island's dark secrets. The mist in front of him was a transparent iron veil, a flittering wall of isolation, while the billions of tiny droplets, like restless spirits, seemed to mourn the mysteries haunting Star.

Amanda's arrival on the dock ushered in a fresh wave of

turmoil. With her shaken daughter by her side, she implored Race to reconsider his decision. "Go back to Nara," she said, "please."

"You're out of your mind."

"Stop running away."

"Oh, that's brilliant." He laughed and pointed a finger in her face. "You're telling *me* to stop running? Wow, priceless."

"I'm telling you to give her another chance."

Race threw up his hands and imploded. How could Amanda stand against him now? How could she not care about his agony? "You don't get it," he shouted. "That woman doesn't deserve another chance. She abandoned me once, and now she pops up out of nowhere like it's all okay? She hid from me for years! My whole life! She's not allowed to skip back into my world and play the loving mother card, like you did."

"What?"

"Yeah, sorry, but moms who give up on their kids don't get to come back and slide right in where they left off."

"I did *not* give up on my child!"

"I didn't mean it that way."

Colliding like opposing currents, the disputers created a calamity that crashed down upon them. Then Amanda took a breath, steadied herself, and shifted the course of my son's struggle. "Race, I'm not telling you to absolve that poor woman," she said. "I'm asking you to free yourself." Her words formed a spotlight, illuminating a path toward reconciliation. "When I found out what Chad did to Marianne, I didn't *have* to forgive him. Lord knows, he didn't deserve it. But I had to forgive myself for believing his lies, for doubting my worth as a mother. Forgiveness, Race, is a gift you give yourself, a way to go forward. So, listen to me, and listen to her."

As Marianne latched on to Amanda's leg, a subtle change occurred in Race, like the turning of a tide. He reconsidered his decision to flee, and it tore him apart while stitching him together at the same time. He had no intention of being like Sevan or Colin, leaving when things got tough. No wish to abandon people, physically or emotionally. No desire to run away. Not anymore.

It's interesting, now that I think about it. I've always imagined that the troubles in our past follow us like shadows, haunting our every step. Yet, slinking away from them only feeds their power, allowing them to loom larger in our minds. It's in facing our demons, in acknowledging the pain, that we find the first glimmers of healing. It begins with acceptance, with the brave act of staring our trauma in the eye and saying, "I see you." If we confront our past, we can pave the way for a brighter future, one where our wounds may still ache, but they no longer hold us captive.

The island's sounds enveloped Race and Amanda—the lapping of waves, the gentle rustle of leaves, the creaking of playground swings, and the persistent bleats of hungry seabirds. Amid those noises, a cry resonated from the Oceanic Hotel. "Race, please don't go!"

He spun and saw her, Nara or Sevan, standing on the long porch, a distant figure protected by the white wooden railing. A solitary presence, she somehow looked different to my boy now. There was a softness to her, a vulnerability in her stance. She was an apology of a woman reaching for redemption.

On the rickety dock, Amanda and Race stood inches

away from each other. "Don't get on the boat," Amanda said, her voice overflowing with conviction, her eyes holding buckets of mercy. "Go back to her, just for a while."

"And say what?"

"Nothing, just listen." Her request sailed into the misty air, each syllable a delicate note in a simple song. "No matter how you feel about her right now, she's your mother," Amanda said. "She needs you to hear her truth. You may not think so, but you owe her that much."

In that charged snippet of time, Amanda's words transcended mere dialogue—they resonated with the vibrations of history, knotted family ties, and the possibility of understanding. For my boy, her plea provided a shot at reconciliation, a brittle bridge suspended amid the mist, connecting the fractured fragments of one man's story.

Race stood at a precipice, torn between escaping the island's painful secrets and facing the perplexing woman on the hotel porch—his mother, a stranger. His gaze returned to Amanda, searching her eyes for guidance. "Okay," he said, "I won't be long."

The woman he adored offered an unguarded smile. "We'll be right here, waiting."

Their parting kiss signaled they could make things right, understand each other better, and have a sunnier future. Embraced by the ocean breeze, Race saw the chance for a permanent bond, not only for tomorrow, but for all the days after. Still, he couldn't help but wonder if that trust was strong enough to withstand the challenges ahead, or if the tide would wash it all away like grains of sand.

:03

Life, Love & Hope

*My God! Come back, my daughter, so young. Her name is…
what? Memories, again… the wind, her hat, the corner. Her
hand! The car! Careful… come back. Please, tell me her name!*

Want to know what I believe? The Earth will shift, the light
will change, the sea will grind down rock. The water will
rise, the night will fall, and our children will cling to us.
But the moment we stop holding each other, the moment
we distrust one another, the sea will engulf us, and the light
will go out. Life has taken me so far from shore. But holding each other? Trusting each other? I still believe in those
things. Even if my husband never bothered.

I remember the day Colin drove me to Blue Horizons.
Rain was pouring down, and the roads were slippery. The
storm outside mirroring the one within my soul, I held fast
to the bits of my fading memories.

When we pulled into the facility's parking lot, I was nauseous, a toxic mass in my stomach. Colin probably knew I was ill at ease, and he might've comforted me with kind words, assuring me I belonged in memory care. But the situation made little sense to me—I was a rudderless ship pushed out to sea, lonely and abandoned.

Why are you doing this to me? I must've asked, wishing I were back home, where things were somewhat more familiar. I had so many questions: *Why did he bring me here? What have I done wrong?* I worried that my dear Race wouldn't be able to find me, wouldn't know where I had gone or why I left him.

At first, Blue Horizons was spooky and gave me the willies. The halls extended on and on, and the lights above flickered as though they were nervous, like they'd seen too much anguish, too many suffering residents die on their watch. The stinging stink of ammonia rubbed elbows with the stench of despair, and it was so quiet you could hear your own breath echo. The nurses gossiped behind their hands, and everyone walked like they were in a never-ending dream, unsure if they'd ever wake up. The walls screamed at night, as if being tortured by memories that wouldn't let go.

After Colin settled me into my room, a kind lady named Rose introduced herself. She had a pleasant smile, and she made me comfortable, but I still longed for the world I'd lost. Colin stayed with me all that day and into the night, washed me and brushed my hair. He serenaded me with my favorite songs and confessed secrets he had kept hidden for years. He opened up about his childhood in Watertown, and even talked about love and admitted that he was sorry for not making me as happy as I deserved. Why did he wait so long to tell me?

My daddy used to say there are only two reasons for being sad: hoping and not knowing. When Colin left me alone at Blue Horizons, the most terrible ache stabbed my heart. I guess it was for both reasons I just mentioned. In the beginning, my husband visited often, but as time went on, his visits became more sporadic, like faint thrums of an offbeat song. Then the visits stopped altogether, and I didn't know why. He left me adrift, and now the only thing I lament after everything that's happened is that he never wrote me a song. Silly, isn't it? All I ever wanted from Colin was validation that he loved me as deeply as he loved that sad girl who craved revenge against herself.

I feel sorry for Sevan, truly I do. Impossible for me to think of that poor woman now without thinking of her suicide attempt, as if her death had preceded her life. The fog of my memory looms heavier now, smothering my recollections. Unlike the wistful mist on Star Island, which dissipated, offering a clear view of Race and Nara on the porch of the Oceanic Hotel, high on the hill, overlooking the endless, unforgiving Atlantic.

The midmorning wind danced out of rhythm, and distant waves splashed against the rocky shore. High above the island, a mottled gray willet glided in slow motion, capturing subtle hints of sunlight within the folds of its snowy feathers. Like a guardian angel, the bird soared under the cottony clouds, its wings tilting with an eerie perfection and grace. Meanwhile, the old building creaked and groaned like a wayfaring ghost ship lurching on the sea.

Rough hands gripping the damp wooden railing, my son stared out at Amanda and Marianne snuggled on Sam Heatherton's lobster boat, warm woolen blankets wrapped around them. Race's wet clothes stuck to his body, chilling him to the core. Clueless about what to say or how to bridge the divide, he didn't even peek at Nara. He knew nothing about who she was or why she did what she'd done, but he had traveled forever to reach this point. Now, after the truth had eluded him for so long, he wanted to know, deserved to know, and he wouldn't leave until his mother came clean.

"This grand hotel has fifty rooms," Nara said, "all of them very different." She turned her back to the ocean and leaned against the rail, admiring her close-up view of the weathered structure as if setting her eyes upon it for the first time. "I've gotten to know our island pretty well, but I'm just now beginning to appreciate this hotel for more than its separate spaces. I finally see how the combination of its rooms forms a complete structure."

Race couldn't have cared less about the Oceanic Hotel.

"Walk with me." Nara glanced at him, then toward the sea, lost memories shimmering in her eyes. She stepped down from the porch and started along a worn pathway with our son beside her. Far ahead of them, on the crest of the hill, Star's chapel stood like a stone beacon calling wayward sailors home.

While walking on the path, Race spotted a tiny scarlet pimpernel growing near the edge of the dirt. Looking like something more than a flower, it had a humanlike quality. With soothsaying awareness, its bitsy red petals had closed, protecting its golden heart from an upcoming storm, though the threat of rain had ended.

"The pimpernel flourish all over the island," Nara said, reading his mind. "Takes root in every nook and crevice where it finds any trace of nourishment."

Without really caring, Race wondered how the flower knew when to protect itself and what it needed to grow. He turned to Nara and asked, "Where are we going?"

Nara pointed at the chapel before pausing and picking up a smooth black stone along the path, a rock that fit perfectly in her small hand. She felt its weight, smiled, and said, "Yes, this will do."

"You're a rock collector?"

Nara continued walking, running her fingers over the stone as if summoning its supernatural powers. "Not in the classic sense," she said. "Sometimes, when I feel lost, I pick up a stone to anchor myself."

"Lost?"

While ascending the hill, side by side with Race, Nara asked, "Did Danny tell you about the Pirate-Bride Ghost of the Shoals?"

Our son shook his head. "Danny didn't tell me much."

"Well, legend says Blackbeard buried a great treasure on one of these islands, leaving behind his wife, Martha, to guard it till he returned. People claim to have seen her, glaring out at the sea on foggy evenings, draped in a white cloak, waiting, whispering into the wind."

"What does she say?"

"'He will come again.'" Nara stole a glance at Race.

"I don't believe in ghosts," he said.

"Me neither," she sighed. "Though I believe some souls have a connection to places, held by promises or hope, like how I'm tied to this island. Same as Blackbeard's bride, I've been waiting for the fog to clear, wondering if you'd find your way back to us." She dropped her chin. "But unlike that poor ghost, for a long time, I wasn't sure I wanted to be found."

Oh, I can relate to Nara. In the dreaded quiet, there's a tug-of-war inside all of us, isn't there? Sometimes we want to be discovered, to have someone see us, hear us, and know we're here. But we worry about what that might mean, about feeling exposed. Other times, we'd rather stay hidden, keep to ourselves where it's safe. But then we feel so alone, like nobody cares or even notices. It's hard to know what I really want these days.

It's like harboring a secret that's been pressing on you for years. On one hand, there's this longing to open up, to share who you are and what you've been through. But there's also the worry that if you let that secret out, it'll change everything, maybe even push others away. It's a tough place to be, pinned between wanting to share your truth and the fear of what might happen if you do. And sometimes, that fear can hold you back, leaving you trapped in your own silence.

Our son never forgets a thing. He got that from the old me.

That was a blessing and, um, the thing… a big problem that follows you around like a black cloud. That stubborn boy remembers everything, like who did and said what, when such and such happened, why this thing worked, why that thing didn't, and how he failed at everything and why. Without the ability to leave his memories behind, Race's past always weighs on his *right now*. I've always marveled at how he can get through a half hour like that, let alone an entire day. Living is far more tolerable for those who can't remember.

Now, I should confess…

I'm afraid I haven't been entirely forthcoming. The account I've provided so far may be mostly true, but there could be some discrepancies. Honestly, I'm uncertain if I've intentionally spun any lies or if I've simply forgotten the facts. In any case, I wish to express my apologies and commit to conveying the truth regarding the rest of Race's journey. You deserve that much from me—from each one of us.

Back on Star Island, within the cramped confines of the quaint chapel on the hill, the smack of aged cedar and musty hymnals stuffed the tiny space. The aroma brought an earthliness to the room, highlighted by a sprinkle of salt whisked in by the sea. Minutes earlier, the sun had fought its way through the clouds. Now, like sheeny stadium lighting, radiant rays streamed in through a stained-glass window above the altar, casting a kaleidoscope of colors onto the pews below. Coming in from outside, the honeyed hum of the wind played a stark, serene concerto for the two tentative souls sitting beside each other.

"Settlers constructed the first church on Star using timber from Spanish shipwrecks," Nara said, picking at her nails. "After a few fires, someone got smart and rebuilt it with stone."

Race glanced around, taking in the place's simplicity. There were seven rows of rustic pews, split in half by a worn purple carpet leading up to the pulpit. Plus, an army of candles sat on a table in the back with flickering flames throwing shadows onto the walls. When our son adjusted his position in his seat, the old wooden bench creaked underneath him. Despite the tranquility, an unsettling tension remained in the air. "This whole place, it's so quiet." Race's voice reverberated in the silence.

"That's why we called you to the island, so we could finally meet and talk, without distractions." Nara's focus fell onto her clasped hands pressing into her lap. The pain of decades apart from our boy, and the regrets that came with it, cried out her name. "I've spent many days in this chapel," she said, "trying to find peace with our past, with who we are."

Race paused and drew in a long breath. "Why didn't anyone tell me about you? Why did they all let me believe my mother was dead?"

Nara swallowed hard. "After the incident in Watertown… the grief, the hurt, it was too much to take, for all involved, especially Colin. It seemed easier if everyone moved on, thinking we were no longer here."

"So you just escaped, leaving the rest of us to figure it out?"

"Not selfishly," she said. "No, we hoped an escape might be a *gift*, a way to spare those we loved from our torment. We thought what happened was a curse, for us, for others, for you, a shadow that would cover your life in darkness. Leaving you was the only way to let the light back in."

As he listened to Nara's explanation, Race saw parallels between her saga and his own life. He realized that he, too, had been running—from his past, from his pain, from the darkness that haunted him. But now, in this moment, he was tired of the endless chase, of hiding in the shadows. It was time to emerge from the night, to embrace the truth, and to face the light, no matter how blinding it might be.

He pulled his father's worn-out notebook from his backpack and placed a gentle palm on the cracked leather covering. "After Dad passed away, I found this," he said, a touch above a whisper. "They're songs he wrote for you, every page filled with longing and guilt. You have no idea how much he loved you."

"He didn't love me. No, not me." Tears glistened in Nara's eyes. "Those songs were for someone else."

"They were for *you*," Race said, tapping a finger on the title *Seven Songs*, written on a strip of white duct tape on the cover. "It says so right here."

"No," Nara said, "the songs were for Sevan, and she made a choice, one that affected many people." The woman's voice climbed as high as the chapel's crossbeams before she calmed herself. "Sevan may have left the world behind, but she left a piece of her heart as well. That piece belonged to Colin, to you, to all those she loved. I am Nara, not your mother."

"Changing your name doesn't change who you are." He gazed directly ahead, ignoring a blinding downpour of confusion. "You know, my dad never cared about me, ever. I grew up thinking that. But after reading these songs, I see that losing you crushed him." Our son turned to Nara. "Now, I think every time he looked at me, he must have seen you."

"I'm so sorry, I don't know what to tell you," she said, a sob lodged in her throat. "Colin was a good man, and if he was distant, it was the grief consuming him."

"What about Freddie? How could I have a brother and not even know?"

The woman's body loosened, and her voice became hazy as she gathered wayward memories. "Freddie," she said, "has always been this island's sunshine. His laughter sweeps through every corner of our home. His eyes, they see wonder in everything, from the crashing waves to the tiniest seashell. He views the world differently than others do, but in lots of ways, it's a purer, more genuine perspective. Danny and I, we've learned so much from him as we've carved out our simple lives here, fishing, exploring, following our routines. Most of all, Freddie loves to watch the sunset every evening, says it's like the world giving us a hug. It's been a quiet existence for the three of us on Star—isolated, but full of warmth."

"Freddie's a lucky guy," Race said.

"We're all lucky."

"Not all of us."

"Race, I didn't mean…"

"Why did you leave me? I'm your son, too." He searched her face for answers. "I needed you, too. You should've come back, you should've taken me back."

"I didn't, I couldn't…"

"Why?"

"There was just…"

"Tell the truth!"

"Race, please…"

"Why didn't you come back for me?"

"Because you're not mine!" As soon as it left her mouth, the woman's words crumbled into a cry, a desperate plea for understanding.

"What?"

"I want… I… I need you to listen to me," Nara said, choking on the words. "Sevan lost herself after you were born, didn't know who she was, lived with voices in her head and a constant dread. Please understand, she knew peace only when her dread slept, but it awakened, always, and repossessed her. It was everywhere." Nara wiped her eyes, inhaled slowly, and locked in on Race. "Long ago, after we settled here, after Freddie was born, a therapist from Portsmouth diagnosed us with a condition called dissociative identity disorder, known as DID. It's a complex disorder that manifests itself in different ways in different people. That's part of the reason we didn't come back."

"Diagnosed *us*?"

"Yes… Sevan was the original host of our body, but she's just a part of a system," Nara said. "When she was very young, she couldn't develop into just one personality because of what happened to her. To help her cope, to survive, the rest of us emerged in her mind. We've kept her safe from terrible things, and for a while she assumed she was only one person."

Race wrung his hands, pulling hard on his long fingers. "If all of this is true, where's Sevan now?"

"She's hiding inside, we could say. Her panic attacks, the sadness, her trauma, all of it was unbearable." Nara turned away from him. "Her life was like a dream of a dream, like she was watching herself in a horror movie."

"Can I talk to her? Can you tell her to come back?"

"I wish it was that easy." Nara's eyes swelled, pooling with tears. "We never wanted things to turn out this way. After we… after the bridge, Sevan left us, and I came to the front. Since that day, I've been the host. We thought the switch would be best for everyone, if one of the others could take care of you and give you a better life."

"The others?" His voice tightened. "Who?"

"In our system," Nara said, "we have seven alternative personalities, or alters. There are five women and two men, each with separate lives, histories, behaviors, and memories. But we all exist inside this one body, like many rooms under one roof. For instance, one of us is fun and flighty. That's Daisy. She makes us feel good about ourselves. One is strong and quiet; his name is Nathan. He stores our guilt and pain. One is intelligent and independent, Imani, our problem solver. Another is our caretaker, a wise man called Jeb, our gatekeeper who protects us. The last of us is, well, she likes to sing and make up stories. She's motherly and very, very forgetful. She came to our rescue, thankfully, after the incident on the bridge. Her name is Hollyann."

"So, *you* aren't my actual mother?"

"Not exactly," Nara said. "Sevan gave birth to you with this body, but Hollyann offered to raise you, mostly. There were times, however, when Jeb and I helped, depending on what we all needed."

"I don't get it. My father was a single dad and raised me on his own." Race wiped a tear off his cheek. "You and I just met, and I don't know anyone named Jeb or Hollyann."

Nara shifted in her seat and stared into him, as if picturing the contents of his trembling heart. "That may be your reality, Race, but we choose to remember our past differently." Then she closed her eyes and dropped her head. "We *need* to remember it differently. But doing that now is difficult."

"What are you saying?"

"I'm saying… that through psychoanalysis and hypnotherapy, our seven personalities are in the process of merging into a singular identity." Nara gazed up at him, her voice splintering. "Some of us alters share memories now, and as a result, our experiences within our individual existences have become jumbled. We've confused certain recollections, or we've lost them altogether. Some of Sevan's memories may have become Hollyann's, just as some of my memories may have tangled with the others. In our scattered minds, though, we've always been with you. It's a lot to absorb, we know. But please believe, if you can, that Sevan and Hollyann, all of us… *we* are all *me*… and we all love you."

Race stood up, and the old pew creaked. "I don't know what to believe," he said.

Nara watched him, as if hoping for a glimpse of understanding, a sign of forgiveness in his evasive emerald eyes. He smiled a flat smile, and she attempted one of her own. Our son held out his hand, and she took it, standing to face him. She tilted her head upward, and their eyes linked, the occasion steeped in a mutual desire to recover a lost need.

In those extended seconds, Nara's explanation of our disorder, my role in Race's upbringing, and Sevan's complicated life—her childhood trauma, depression, hiding, and decades of silence—tore at our son's insides. Resentment, dejection, and longing roiled within him, battling for dominance. Unsure of what to do or think, he wavered between extending grace and hanging on to the pain. The entire cosmos fell into a hush as Race made a choice.

What would I have done if I were in his skin? Hard to say. When faced with the truth and mixed feelings, making decisions becomes a daunting task. As a mother, reminiscing about the crucial choices I've made fills me with both nostalgia and strife. I remember those times now, looking back. I wanted nothing more than to ensure my child's happiness and well-being, yet the weight of not always knowing the right path was heavy. Each decision felt like a tightrope walk between love and uncertainty. Trying to take the emotion out of those choices seemed logical, but it was wrenching because that emotion was at the core of why I cared. In the end, though, it doesn't matter what I think.

Buoyed by the honesty saturating the sanctuary, Race pulled Nara into his arms, creating a human bridge across the chasm of time, reconciling their past and charting a course toward healing. Her frail body warm against his, Nara hung on like she might never let go.

"I've got you," Race said.

"Now we're not alone," she whispered. "None of us are alone."

When they separated, she dried her eyes and gazed at the ceiling, breathing in as if inhaling the first sniff of rain after a long drought. In that quiet moment, Race slipped his father's long-cherished possession, *Seven Songs*, into a wooden holder on the pew in front of him and tucked the book away among the musty hymnals.

:02

Peace of Mind

AFTER FORTY-ONE YEARS, our son was calm. Not content or happy, but calm. It was like a giant hand had stopped a clock in his head. There was a day when I had wanted such a tranquil life, too. But now, as I drift away, that goal seems pathetic and silly, an over-inflated nothing.

Though I'm not quite calm, I can see a little further ahead, and this isn't the end yet. What Colin and I had will never exist again. But these memories and my powerful love for Race will remain. Now something new is coming, something unavoidable.

It was late November, I'm almost positive, and Race had been back home for a month after his life-altering trip to New England. Inside the familiar walls of his childhood home in Sea Point, he hustled about, unpacking cardboard boxes that held the remaining remembrances of his father's life. Inside the family room, the well-worn furniture and ambient lighting provided a fitting backdrop for the heartfelt chore.

A stew of scents clogged the room: the boldness of antique oak, the ripeness of old mystery novels, and the waxiness of candles that Colin would light in his cave on darker-than-usual evenings. The faraway, high-pitched peeps of a solitary wandering tattler added a touch of coastal comfort, while the rain's soothing patter against the windows served as a reminder of Sea Point's unchanging climate.

As Race sifted through Colin's keepsakes and belongings, he mumbled to himself, torn between sentimentality and practicality. Which items should he retain as mementos of his dad and which ones should he discard? The strain of his decisions pressed upon him, causing a bead of sweat to form on his forehead.

Some boxes contained our son's old baseball equipment and uniforms, and the familiar scent of leather gloves and weathered jerseys transported Race back in time. The recollections from his youth, spent on the ball field, flooded his muddled brain—the camaraderie, the competition, the joy, his father's absence in the bleachers.

While rummaging through the past, Race stumbled upon a shoebox wrapped in electrical tape and struggled to remember if he'd seen it before. When he peeled off the tape, he discovered old letters and cards addressed to him from his grandparents, Petrak and Yeva Zakarian. All those years, his father had kept the box hidden, denying Race all correspondence, any chance at connection. But look at it this way: Colin could've thrown the box away if he wanted to. I'd like to believe my husband hoped his boy would find those letters someday.

A bell rang, chasing away Race's thoughts. He rushed through the living room, flung open the door, and found

Glenn and Jess waiting on the steps. She held a blueberry pie, while he cradled a potted houseplant.

"Welcome to Chez McIntyre," Race said with a chuckle. "Twenty bucks says I finish the pie before I water that fern."

"I'll take a piece of that action," Jess said.

Glenn smirked. "Just give me a piece of the pie."

Warm air followed the three friends into the kitchen, where they convened around a small island in the center. "Hey, G-Dog, congrats on knocking your mayoral campaign out of the park," Race said. "You were never much of a power hitter. Feels good, right?"

"Sure does," Glenn said, exchanging a glance with Jess. "But we've got bigger news."

Race took the fern from his buddy and said, "You got impeached already?"

Her eyes shining, Jess blurted, "We're pregnant!"

"And we set a wedding date," Glenn said, pecking his fiancée on the cheek and hacking into the pie with a butter knife.

Our son gulped before his face lit up, advertising his excitement for Jess. She had always dreamed of being a mom, and now her dream was coming true. But then the light in his face dimmed.

She grabbed Race's arm. "Tell me that dopey look means what I think it means."

"It does," he said. "I mean, no, yeah, that's great."

Glenn waved a fork at his buddy. "How do you feel about being the godfather?"

Race pulled away from Jess and drummed his enormous hands on the countertop. "We need to celebrate." He started toward the basement door. "I think there's still champagne in the downstairs fridge from my dad's Employee of the Year awards."

After descending the stairs, Race found himself encircled by the remaining relics of his father's life—the broken guitar, boxes of vinyl records, and the stereo system with imposing hip-high speakers. The sight stirred something in his soul.

The last conversation our son had with his dad—well, more an argument than a conversation—happened the day before Colin died. Race was at the house when he heard strumming coming from "the cave." When our son went downstairs with a plastic bag stuffed with dirty laundry, he stared at his father seated in a corner, but the old man didn't look up, too busy plucking his guitar. Race had needed a ride to and from work later that week because his bike was getting fixed. So, he asked Colin if he could give him a lift, but my husband didn't hear him. Our son asked again, still no answer. Then, in an outburst of rage that had been brewing for decades, Race ripped open the bag and dumped clothes all over the cement floor. He cursed at his father, said all kinds of terrible things, blamed him for not being around and not caring, accused him of not loving him. In typical form, Colin didn't react or respond, hardly moved a muscle, and so Race did what Race always did—he ended things, then and there. He yanked the guitar out of Colin's hands and cracked the neck in half across his knee. Then he dropped the broken instrument at his father's feet, told him to "go to hell," and stormed out.

Now, at the scene of the crime once again, Race longed for another day with his dad. If his wish came true, he'd share his discoveries about his heritage, about Amanda, and about Sevan. But after the way Colin had treated him, did the old man deserve to know any of that?

"Hey," Jess said, smiling at the foot of the stairs. "Drinking alone again?"

Race tried to laugh. "Nope, just *thinking* alone again," he said, moving toward the refrigerator. "You know I'm happy for you, right?"

"Yeah, I do." Jess dropped her head and shuffled next to him. "It's funny, you know, when you were in Boston, I had a horrible feeling you weren't coming back. Part of me wanted you to stay out there and make a new life, but the biggest part of me wanted you back here with us. I don't know why, you're just… you know what I'm saying?"

"I'm sorry," he said, water gathering in his eyes. "For everything."

"You don't need to apologize." She embraced him, rose onto her tiptoes, and planted a kiss on his cheek.

"What was that for?"

"I never blamed you," Jess said, sniffling and gazing up at him. "We just didn't make sense, not together." She backed away while holding his hands. "You know, I think sometimes people confuse blame with accountability."

"*People* as in you and me?"

"Blaming each other creates more problems," she said, "but being accountable means taking responsibility and trying to make things better." She set his hands free. "I admit, I messed up lots of times with us."

Race laughed. "Yeah, you did."

"Okay, quit gloating." She slapped his beefy arm. "I'm serious, you Neanderthal. If we want things to change now, we both need to own up to our mistakes, like we couldn't before. Let's try to understand each other, forgive, and move the fuck forward."

When she hugged him again, Race's spirit brimmed with gratitude for all the good times they'd had. Was Jessica thankful, too? Who's to say? Regardless, he hoped that she'd carry the memories they'd created together with her, the good and the bad, even as their lives split off in different directions.

He grabbed two bottles of champagne from the fridge and handed one to Jess. "Cheers," he said as they clinked the necks together. "To moving the fuck forward."

"I'll drink to that," she said, patting her belly. "But I'll need to wait five months."

After returning to Sea Point, the "new Race" split from the "old Race" and merged into a greater whole. But even before he got back home, the transformation had started. It was the weather's doing, I believe. On Star Island, while rescuing Freddie from the ocean during that punishing storm, Race had turned into someone different, letting the rain baptize him and evolving into a better man. He shed his ego and accepted help based on belief alone. Now, he was who, and where, he needed to be.

The day after he patched things up with Jess, or maybe two weeks later, inside the Lewis and Clark Middle School gymnasium, Race sneered at a group of peppy young ladies—the members of his basketball team. As the sweaty stench of another hard-fought loss consumed the court, Coach McIntyre prepared to address his troops, but they'd already scattered around the gym. Some chatting with boys, some scrolling on their phones, two or three giggling at the concession table while buying candy. Such was our son's new life, begging for the attention of twelve-year-old girls, like capturing a cluster of caffeinated cats.

"Hey, bring it in!" As the team huddled around him, Race crouched down and glanced upward at their tired faces. "All right, I know things didn't go the way we hoped, but listen up for once. Winning and losing, they're both part of the game, like peanut butter and jelly on a sandwich. Sometimes you're the peanut butter, sometimes you're the jelly, but either way, you're still part of something tasty."

"Excuse me, Coach," the shortest girl said, stepping forward and tapping Race on the shoulder, "I'm allergic to peanuts."

Race's frown broke into a smirk. "Oh, my bad, Scarlett," he said. "I hope my analogy doesn't give you a rash."

Scarlett giggled and covered her mouth with her hands.

"So, yeah," the coach continued, "that other team crushed us by forty points, but I don't want to hear any whining." He scanned the circle with a pointed finger. "Because being a good sport? That's like the crust on that sandwich, holding everything together. Now, I know it stinks to get beat, but remember, even Michael Jordan lost some games."

"Who?"

Race rolled his eyes. "Anyway, the key is to learn from losing, keep practicing, and come back stronger each game. Here's the thing: Winning isn't everything. But if you put in your best effort and never give up, you'll always be champs in my book. So chins up, knuckleheads, we'll get 'em next time."

"I have an idea that might work," the tallest girl said, raising her hand high. "I think we should shoot more shots."

"You know, Clara, that's not a bad strategy," Race said. "You miss one hundred percent of the shots you don't take, right?" He stood up from his crouch, knees cracking into place. "Unfortunately for us, we also miss one hundred percent of the shots we *do* take."

"Oh, and also, Coach," Clara said, holding in a snicker, "my mom thinks you're cute."

While the team erupted in muffled laughter, Race's gaze wandered to the bleachers, where Clara's mother beamed and waved. "Okay, hands in," he said as ten arms jutted into the circle like spokes on a wheel. "Scarlett, shout it out."

The short girl inhaled and yelled, "One… two… three…"

"Chameleons!" The group's collective shout reverberated through the gym.

As the players ran off to gather their things, Clara's mom came down from the bleachers, careful in her black skirt, white blouse, and heels. She stood in front of Race and tipped her head, her wavy, lemony hair falling over her shoulders. "Great game, Mr. McIntyre."

He smiled his irresistible smile. "We're still working out the kinks, Becca."

"So, how do middle school coaches decompress after tough losses?"

He eyed the woman up and down, then up again, marveling at how different she looked from when they first met thirty years earlier, as pimply preteens, on that same wood floor. "Since when did our gym install a dress code?"

"Where you headed?"

"Home," he said.

"Still getting around on your bike these days? We can give you a ride if you'd like."

"I'm good," he said, "but thanks."

"Hmm." She grinned and angled toward the exit. After three steps, she stopped and whirled around, ran her tongue over her teeth and cocked an eyebrow. "I don't know what it is exactly, but you've changed."

He left the gym and strutted into the parking lot, stopping next to a bicycle locked to a metal post. The familiar hubbub of downtown Sea Point—the screeching gulls, the muddy puddles on the asphalt, and the glow of neon signs from local shops—did their best to grab his attention. He squinted into the distance, peeking at the Pointbreak Bridge, but the fog rising from the river clouded his view. He made his way, steady and slow, to the back of the lot and hopped into his pickup truck.

As Race drove, his eyes steered toward a plastic box on the passenger's seat, an ancient symbol of his grudge with Colin. He made a left onto Marine Drive, heading west, a thick mist coating his windshield and worn-out wipers adding to his frustration. Then, he traveled back in time, reliving his days as an accomplished minor leaguer. The constant criticism he'd endured over those tortuous thirteen years for not reaching his potential had left him battered. Now, in his imagination, as he stepped to the plate again at Fenway Park, in the most significant moment of his life, fear paralyzed him. Even in that make-believe situation, he still couldn't muster the courage to swing the bat. *What's wrong with me?* He pounded his fist on the dashboard and rolled down the windows. As the freezing air attacked him, he tried to gag the voices in his head, the ones haunting him since he left Star Island.

With his long hair fluttering over his eyes, he sucked in a blast of salty wind riffling in from the Pacific. He pumped the brakes when he passed the entrance to the Pointbreak Bridge and remembered the old cannery where Colin used to work. The voices inside screamed, urging him to stick to their initial plan. In a snap decision, Race made a U-turn and hit the gas, speeding onto the on-ramp leading to the bridge. As he raced through the entrance and started across, the steel trusses above flew past, while the wind howled in his ears.

A mile farther, on the highest point of the bridge, two hundred feet above the black water, Race's mind tangled itself into knots. Sevan's tortured, twisted sense of self and thoughts of her suicide attempt consumed him. Discovering Nara's alternate identities and Danny's involvement in their hidden family history weighed on him. Caught between the clash of the past and present, he wrestled with reality. *Why should I exist?*

He veered onto the shoulder, slammed on the brakes, and stepped onto the bridge. Trucks and cars zoomed by like growling meteors as he gripped the cold steel railing with both hands, leaned over, and peered into the water. Sunlight rippled on the surface, resembling wavy fingers strumming a guitar. Unsteady, his body swaying in the wind, Race turned toward a large, rectangular metal sign clasped to the rail: *Desperate? There is hope. Make the call. We can help you cross this bridge.* He scowled at the crisis intervention phone number, yanked open the passenger door and stared at the plastic box labeled *Special* silently mocking him on the seat.

When he removed the top cover, his father's collection of Boston albums glared back, each record sleeve tattling tales of abandonment and loneliness. Scoffing and sneering, our son contemplated hurling the box, and his own self, into the rushing river below, hoping to wash away the ghosts of his past.

Now, I understand about indecision, but I also know that throwing away those vinyl reminders, no matter how haunted, would never erase the pain in Race's soul. He fastened the lid back onto the box, climbed into the truck, and took off. Fast. Faster.

While the horizon in front of him glistened—a striking shade of blue—he glanced into the rearview mirror, and everything behind him faded into nothing. However, he realized it was all still there, like how a person walking away from you shrinks and vanishes. You know she hasn't disappeared off the face of the Earth, or from herself, just from your sight. As Race drove, he remembered what Becca had said to him earlier at the school gym, that he'd "changed."

Yes, I'd agree with that pretty lady, though our son hadn't moved completely away from who he believed he was. Fortunately for him though, that long journey ahead would require no bus tickets, and it would take as long as it would take. His continuing on this other *trip*, by definition, meant he'd surely fall on his face again. But I only hoped he'd find a way, over and over, to stand up after each tumble. Hoped he'd get back into the batter's box after every strikeout. Unlike baseball, you see, there were no rules to this new game, and he couldn't lose if he played with an open heart.

My Destination

I'm sorry for the gaps in my story, for the redundancies and pieces that don't quite fit. For the little white lies. The truth is, I've been fighting the facts all along.

Sad to say, the clock has ticked by faster than I'd like, and I'm afraid I have little time left. But I've got more stories to tell, songs to sing, memories to share, and as long as I'm still here and capable of feeling, I'll be bound to the *act* of remembering—if not to the remembering itself. But don't forget: when I'm losing the way, I'm here inside, right here inside.

You know what Daddy used to tell me? He'd say, "Some people are made for living and some are made for loving. But the point, little Holly, is to live."

On a warm summer's day in 2023, Race and Amanda stood on the expansive shores of Lake Sevan, nestled in the heart of Armenia. The landscape before them was a stunning vista of natural beauty, as far as the eye could see. Extending toward the horizon, the undisturbed waters of the lake mirrored the vibrant blue sky. The subtle fragrance of forget-me-nots frolicked in the air, as their delicate petals flittered in the gentle breeze. Overhead, passing geese honked joyous melodies, adding their voices to nature's serene symphony.

Nearly five years had passed since the couple's initial meeting, and the world had undergone profound transformations. Race had made a drastic switch, getting his long hair cut short, whereas Amanda took the opposite approach, allowing her short hair to grow longer. She had opened up a salon in Sea Point, while Race now taught history and coached basketball at the middle school. The Red Sox were languishing in last place in the American League East, and Race was the best player on a dominant men's softball team called the Oregon Bears. Despite his ongoing knee and back pain, the Bears deemed him indispensable, and he had played a crucial role in their most notable achievement: a loss in the 2021 semifinals of an international tournament in Las Vegas. During that week in Sin City, by a stroke of luck, or a twist of fate, Race encountered the daughter of the catcher whose career he'd ruined in Venezuela. The young woman, Izzy Dominguez, had become a magazine reporter, and Race welcomed the chance to ask for her forgiveness. His honest apology went a long way with Izzy, but the regret in his bones didn't budge.

In April of that year, the United States had changed their approach as well, deviating from a safe stance and seizing an opportunity to make things right. After over a century of neutrality, our country acknowledged the atrocities inflicted upon the Armenian people, officially labeling the mass killing and forced relocation of nearly one million Armenians in 1915 as "genocide." Change, no matter how insignificant or monumental, takes time. Whether switching hairstyles or shifting the views of an entire nation, the mission requires mindfulness and perseverance.

Lake Sevan stood before the two foreigners like a looking glass, reflecting the memories of their life together thus far, on their first wedding anniversary. It held the history of their past and promise for their future. But for Race, he equated the placid water to the present day, a fleeting instance of calm and clarity on his journey. Like the lake, he was at ease in the stillness of his surroundings, content with what was gone forever and looking forward to what lay ahead.

Amanda gazed out across the Jewel of Armenia. "I could stay at this lake forever." She leaned into him, nudging his shoulder with hers.

"Wish we could have extended our vacation," Race said. "Maybe if we ever have kids, we can come back again. You know, to show 'em their old man's homeland."

"I'm still not sure I want children," Amanda said. "If we had finished our game of five questions the day we met, you'd be certain of that."

"You'll change your mind if you seriously consider my incredible potential and, uh, overall fatherliness." Race smirked, wondering if he'd just invented a new word. "Come on, admit it, you've never met anyone like me."

"I've met a thousand men like you." Amanda laughed, moving behind him and throwing her arms around his broad chest. "You're lucky I'm letting you stick around."

Race hoped they'd make babies someday. Worrying

about someone else, really worrying, for the first time, was the greatest thing that had ever happened to him, and he wanted more of it. "If we're not having kids," he said, "then what's our next adventure?"

"How about a trip to Singapore? We could visit your Uncle Kyle?"

"That'd be surreal." Race grinned and stared across the lake, though he couldn't quite see the other side. "We could finally meet in person; I still have so many questions for him about my parents," he added, lamenting that Kyle wasn't able to come back for his father Danny's funeral.

"But Kyle barely knew Sevan," Amanda said, her husband's disappointment parading before her eyes. "He couldn't give you all the answers you're looking for. You know that, right?"

"Yeah, not sure I'll ever stop searching, though." Race took a smooth black stone from his backpack and placed it into the shallow water along the shore. "Here you go, Mom, wherever you are. Hope you and the Zakarian family have found some peace."

Amanda smiled. "She's home now."

When Race looked into the lake that vivid afternoon, he saw his heritage. His face was a living testament to his origins—the place where Asia, Africa, and Europe collide, and where all religions began. In his reflection, he didn't see the same ugliness or terror his great-grandmother, Akabe, had seen. He saw the birth of languages, geometry, astrology, medicine, and chemistry. He saw the dawn of papermaking, textiles, currency, music, wine, gems, and spices. He saw the conception of architecture, poetry, art, algebra, trigonometry, physics, democracy, and philosophy. But above all else, when Race stared into the clear water of Lake Sevan, he saw an Armenian, strong and proud.

He and his wife got into their rental car and headed toward Yerevan, the capital city where they'd spend one last night before flying home to Oregon the next day. While on the road, Amanda reached into her travel bag and retrieved a book titled *Seven Souls: Living with Dissociative Identity Disorder*. "I can't believe Nara finally published her memoir," she said. "Imagine how difficult it must've been for her to write this."

Race nodded, his firm hands clutching the steering wheel. "They say the keys to writing a memoir are authenticity and introspection. From what we know about Nara, she's got what it takes to tell an honest and thoughtful story."

Amanda flipped to the first page of the book and read aloud the opening paragraph:

Inside the mind's maze, there are countless chambers, each with fragments of a separate reality. My name is Nara, and within these pages, I invite you to wander alongside me through the corridors of my life. Going beyond the struggles of one individual, this tale shows the capacity of the human spirit to persevere during times of turmoil. My goal is to uncover the intricacies of living with dissociative identity disorder (DID) by exploring my identities, intending to offer healing through sharing my story.

Race tightened his grip on the wheel, his narrowed green eyes glued to the road. "She told me the book would've never happened without the help of her therapist," he said.

"That woman, Rose Uki, wrote all the scientific passages in the memoir."

"Apparently," Amanda said, "Rose is one of the most respected clinical psychologists in the world." She turned to a passage in the middle of the book.

Not all individuals with DID have a desire to engage with their traumatic experiences. If the person with DID agrees and achieves safety and stability, the next phase involves recalling their life history, often experienced as PTSD flashbacks. Hence, this stage also entails ongoing efforts to address the care and steadying of symptoms related to both DID and PTSD. In the third and final phase, symptoms may reduce significantly, and the individual's alternate personalities may merge, resulting in a complete blending of their characteristics. This frees up energy for a focus on living better in the present.

"It's heartbreaking," Amanda said before reading silently for a minute, her mouth open wide. "It says here that the root of Sevan's childhood trauma, which Rose discovered through hypnosis, was when her first-grade music teacher sexually abused her. Every week, he'd coax her into a hallway bathroom, claiming to help her wash her hands. He'd run the water full blast, so no one could hear her sobbing. After eight months, the school's janitor figured out what was happening and reported the teacher to the administration. My god, what a monster." She continued reading aloud:

Through hypnotherapy, we created a safe space for Nara and her alter identities to communicate and comprehend the trauma that Sevan endured as a child. Together, we delved into the depths of her psyche, uncovering layers of memories and emotions that she had buried deep within. With patience, compassion, and trust, we forged a path toward healing, fostering integration and understanding among her alters. It was a collaborative effort, guided by empathy and a shared commitment to Nara's well-being. Through our work together, Nara found the courage to confront the past and embrace the journey toward wholeness.

Amanda read another page. "Listen to this. Rose says that under hypnosis, Sevan came out front and spoke of her trauma, but she only verbalized the abuse by saying it happened to another little girl named Marianne."

An alter of someone with dissociative identity disorder may also have a separate alter of their own. In the complex internal world of DID, these "nested alters" can serve a unique role. Sevan was a primary personality within Nara's system, while Marianne was another of Sevan's alters. Marianne emerged as a protective mechanism, acting as a buffer between Sevan and the traumatic experiences she endured in grade school. This dissociative process allowed Sevan to distance herself from the pain and distress connected with her trauma, preserving her sense of identity and coping with the overwhelming emotions. As a result, Marianne became a significant figure within Sevan's internal world, carrying the burden of her memories while shielding Sevan from their full impact.

"Jesus." Amanda pressed the book against her chest. "You know what? I really hope that during one of our trips to New Hampshire, Sevan will come out and talk to us. I just want to tell her how sorry I am for everything she went through."

"For a long time," Race said, "without even knowing it, I searched for her, trying to fill a void I didn't understand." He turned to his wife. "It doesn't matter if we never meet face-to-face with her, or if you and I only get to speak to Nara. I'll always know Sevan is my mom, and she'll always be a part of me."

The last paragraph of Nara's book hit Race and Amanda the hardest.

Our scars do not define us. Rather, they are a testament to our strength, our resilience, and our capacity for love. With each day lived, I trace the contours of my existence, navigating the hallways of memory and identity. Deep in my soul, Sevan's whispered secrets echo, her pain embroidered into the fabric of my being. Yet, amid the shadows of the past, there is a flicker of light—a lantern of love that pierces through the darkness. It's a love that knows no bounds, a love that transcends the confines of our own minds. And so, I, Nara, embrace each part of myself, knowing that together, we are whole.

While driving along the outskirts of Hrazdan, thirty miles northeast of Yerevan, Race turned a sharp corner, where a colossal silver statue, sixty-feet tall, rose out of a reservoir beside the road. "Look," my boy said, "it's what we've waited for."

Amanda touched his elbow. "You ready?"

"Yes," he said, slowing down to better appreciate the ethereal embodiment of Tsovinar, the pagan goddess of water, sea, and rain.

They got out of the car and followed a sparkling stream that wound its way to the rim of the reservoir. Shielding their eyes from the setting sun, they squinted to get a clearer view of the spectacle. The goddess's eyes were closed, giving the impression of grave contemplation. Her long hair defied gravity, suspended in midair, flowing upward as if reaching for the heavens.

"She's beautiful."

With her arms raised high, Tsovinar seemed to summon lightning and thunder, looking ready to invoke a vexing storm or save a struggling soul. The gleaming sculpture held dominion over the immense body of water that surrounded her, her sphinxlike presence both subservient and commanding—the perfect marriage of benevolence and power.

"This is it," Amanda said, "what we came here for."

Race reflected on the legend that had woven itself into their journey. "It's also where our story began," he said. "Regardless of our belief in her, she's part of the reason we're together."

They recounted the myths behind the statue, the ancient goddess tied to water, fertility, and the cycles of life and death. They spoke of Tsovinar's towering likeness, symbolizing the link between humanity and the natural world. And they talked about how legends provide glimpses into the boundless realm of imagination, offering a way to confront the mysteries of the universe.

"I'll never forget today," Race said.

"Only two days matter," Amanda replied with a knowing glance, "the day we're born and the day we find out why."

As the sunlight faded and the night crept in, Race stood beside the reservoir, enjoying the peacefulness, not wanting the light *or* the dark to win this competition. For him, the moment of contact between them was enough, the two becoming one, only to part again and prepare for another reunion. The lilting lines of the hills spoke to him, and before the sun set off to sleep, the steady hand of evening calmed his previously troubled heart. "My whole life, I've pushed people away," he said. "Until you."

"Before and after," Amanda said. "Everything is before and after."

The couple faced the magnificent statue of Tsovinar, and a serenity caressed them. Her ethereal presence reminding them that, despite life's challenges and uncertainties, they could always find timeless beauty in the world.

"Ready to go?"

"Yes."

With the sun slipping away, Race took Amanda's hand, and they followed the sparkling stream to the car. Their fingers and futures braided, they'd confront whatever came next together, guided by the mercy and strength of the goddess who watched over them.

Life, like memory, is rarely straightforward. As I've recalled Race's journey, I realize that the lines between reality and imagination can blur in ways that surprise even me. Perhaps it's not about the people he encountered along the way, whether he actually met each part of our system, but about the truths those moments revealed—truths about love, loss, and the yearning for connection. We all carry pieces of each other within us, and sometimes, those fragments help us understand who we are and who we might become. In the end, maybe the true journey is not just about what is real, but about what it means to be human and the stories we create to heal ourselves.

Our assumptions dominate us, and the most compelling arguments or speeches won't alter our opinions. The only thing that can change our minds is a good story, especially one that speaks to the kinship of the spirit. Isn't that what this is?

Thirty is a funny number. You can accomplish grand feats in thirty years and watch a whole TV show in thirty minutes. You can judge a song in thirty seconds—decide if you love it or hate it—and if you turn your back on the person you adore most for that cruel span of time, she could simply vanish. But half a minute doesn't last forever, trust me. While counting down from thirty during the initial stages of hypnosis, your whole life rolls through your consciousness like a movie, scenes from your past flitting and flashing, one after another. Above all else, *thirty* goes by in a snap when it's the number of days you have left to live. Now, for yours truly, those days are dwindling, disappearing much faster than I thought they would.

Race doesn't visit me anymore. For ages, he would stop by every weekend and share so much. But that was then. No matter, there's no guarantee I'd recognize him now anyway. Besides, he found what he was after and doesn't need me. Then again, he never really needed me. I provided what was necessary for Sevan's sake, telling my tale to absolve her of the guilt she felt for abandoning her family. I accomplished what the system asked of me, fulfilled my role; the boy grew up, became a man, and is safe.

Resting in Race. That's how I think about him, where he is at this stage. Staying still, while coming and going. Like a quiet sanctuary where a candle burns bright, even when the wind blows relentlessly. Where he's only himself, not trying to be a superstar athlete or an irresistible hunk. Life is different for Race now, more settled, more peaceful. Of course, a storm will catch him by surprise every so often, and he gets scared sometimes. In all that mess, though, there's beauty and perfection in the way things are.

He has his downs and ups, fears and doubts. But it's not all about him any longer. Now, when he looks out at the world, he hurts because he feels what others feel. He's even adopted a dog, a greyhound named Edgar. He mostly sees things in white and black, bad and good, but it's not that clear-cut. He's discovered nuance. Here and there, he'll wish for a better job or a nicer car, but he understands that everyone's playing the same game, and we're all waiting for our chance to swing the bat. As I reminisce about his journey, and my own, I see the richness of our experiences, the depths of our souls. I find solace in knowing that he'll carry on without me, an example of what it means to live with grace.

Nowadays, sometimes, an interesting young fellow stops by to see me in my apartment. He's tall and very good-looking, with moonlit emerald eyes and a mesmerizing smile. Usually, he brings a pleasant woman along with him. I enjoy their company, on the whole, although I don't always like it when they're here. They frighten me when they talk about things I don't understand. Why must they torment me like that?

After those visits, if I'm sad or upset, I sing my favorite songs. Often, I tell myself the stories I've heard, or the ones I made up, replay them in my brain, to keep a connection with the people I love. Those folks have told me such interesting things during our time together. With Rose's help, I've gained access to lots of information and memories, merging with the minds of the others. Now, in our system of seven alters, I know what everyone's thinking. Almost like we're the same person.

Have I mentioned my father? He taught literature, Greek classics. Remember the myth of Sisyphus, the man ordered by the gods to push his rock uphill, over and over, forever and ever? Well, that man is like me, and I'm like him. I tell my stories and sing my songs when my head is clear and above the clouds—before my rock tumbles down from the peak of the hill, and I follow that rolling boulder. For a brief time, I'm happy, free, aware, and the world is glorious. However, when I'm at the base of the hill again, surrounded by darkness and fading memories, I accept my fate and begin pushing the rock up once more. That's when my stories and ballads end, and the music stops. It's a terrible thing, this hill I climb.

My time here is nearly done. My songs are fading out, drifting away into the unknown. There's so much I don't remember, but this is certain: I'm dying, knowing that I'm dying. I'm living my death, curious and content. But I won't be gone for all eternity; I'll just lie dormant in the darkness—though I'll view my slumber as a kind of death. Because it's in death that we reunite with those who've gone before us.

Soon, I'll be with my daughter again, and I'll be a mother once more. I'll lie to myself, like I've lied to Sevan all these years, if that's the requirement to be free. If it means seeing my little girl, I'll fake my own death. If it helps me cope with the memory of letting go of her hand at that busy intersection. If it allows me to forgive myself for losing her. Yes, certainly, for that I will gladly lie and die. But what will it matter if I cheat death? We deceive ourselves all the time, every single one of us, for various reasons. How would this be any different? You couldn't really call it lying, anyway. It'd just be a story I tell, and stories are how we survive.

The other alters will go on without me, living their quiet lives together—as one now—with Freddie in Portsmouth. Nara has been out front for years. She's calm and responsible, like Jeb used to be, and she makes excellent decisions for our entire system. Nara and Jeb had always been there for Sevan, long before that day on the bridge, her saviors deep inside. These days, sometimes Daisy will want to pop out front for a bit of excitement. Or Imani will feel the need to show up when we can't figure out an impossible problem. Nathan, though, is content staying in the shadows, having isolated himself from the rest of us from the beginning. He'll wait in hiding, quiet and patient, keeping our pain and shame from hurting us. Before, he only appeared when we needed him. And we don't need him anymore.

No one in our system has heard from Sevan, not since Race returned to Sea Point. That's the last time I spoke with her, and she was thrilled to know that our son was okay, happy that he had found his heritage and himself. Happier than she'd been in quite some time. Sevan didn't want or need to know the whole truth about Race, and she doesn't have to come out anymore either. We know she's somewhere safe inside. Part of me is afraid of leaving the system, of dying, of sleeping, of going away. What if Sevan needs me again someday? Like she needed me all those decades ago.

Before he went away, after many years of writing, my husband finished the lyrics to a song he'd been working on for eons. He jotted down the verses on the last page of an enormous book of songs he had written, and guess what? The first thing he did after he wrote the last word was visit me, sit down with his old guitar, and sing that song. It's a sad but sweet ballad, a gorgeous ode to a cherished woman in his life, all about letting go of your greatest love, then finding that person again. Oh, I adore that song, even though he didn't dedicate it to me. But sometimes, when I get lonely, or when the room gets too quiet, I sing those closing verses to myself.

> *"The Story"*
> *(cont'd...)*
>
> *Now the boy and the girl withstood troubles*
> *and pain*
> *Like a rock withstands nature's rough hands*
> *But their love couldn't last without wearing away*
> *As a rock must, in time, turn to sand*
>
> *"I need time," the girl said as she sat holding hands*
> *With the boy by a sparkling stream*

"I need time by myself to discover the wonders
of life
That I haven't yet seen."

"I'll discover them with you," the boy
answered fast,
Not wanting to hear what she'd said
"You've come with me this far. Now I must
go alone,"
She replied as she lowered her head

"I will love you forever." He choked on his tears,
And her eyes told him she felt the same
They trusted each other, the boy and the girl,
And knew neither of them was to blame

"You'll find me again. I promise you will."
The girl smiled so that she wouldn't cry
And the boy held her closer than ever before,
Then he gently kissed her goodbye

Now in some other time, in a faraway place,
Two lovers hold hands by a stream
Just a boy and a girl who, because of their love,
Found strength to have hope in a dream

"My name is Sevan…"

"Yes, we're finished counting down, Sevan. It's safe to come out."

"My name is Nara…"

"It's okay, dear, you can rest."

"My name is Hollyann…"

"You sleep now, my friend."

"My name is…"

*You'll never know how strong your heart is
until you learn how to forgive who broke it.*

— Anonymous

Acknowledgments

I am endlessly thankful for my family and friends from Massachusetts and New Jersey, whose unwavering support and encouragement sustained me throughout the completion of this novel. To my incredible wife, Jackie, and our children, Caleb and Lucy, your unconditional love is the foundation of my life.

Special thanks to my sisters, Cheryl and Linda, for their backing and belief in my creative pursuits. Your constant reassurance means the world to me.

I owe a debt of gratitude to my mentors, authors Will Allison and Dan Barry, whose skill and kindness directed me as I embarked on my writing journey. Your wisdom and expertise continue to inspire me every day.

To my editors, Jennie Cohen and Nicole Fegan, thank you for your invaluable advice and guidance in shaping this manuscript.

To my beta readers, Cindy D'Altorio Sherman and Andrea Soulellis Erickson, your feedback and constructive criticism were essential in making this book the best it could be.

I am deeply appreciative for my sensitivity reader Dayna Day, whose careful consideration and insights ensured the authenticity and acuity of the narrative.

Many thanks to my readers, who have played the ultimate role in making my writing career a reality. Your trust and enthusiasm mean more to me than words can express. Like I always say, it's people like you who keep people like me going.

Lastly, I want to honor the memory of my late mother-in-law, Hilda Cortina Rowe. Her strength, humor, and the stories she shared are cherished by all who knew and loved her.

Questions and Topics for Discussion

1. What does belonging mean to you? Discuss Race's path toward finding his heritage and how it shapes his sense of belonging, particularly in his quest to connect with his family's past.

2. Examine the legend of Tsovinar and its significance in the novel. How does mythology and magical realism contribute to the narrative's study of survival, belief, and healing?

3. How do you define love in its various forms? Explore Race's relationships with Amanda, Jess, and Khloe. How do these experiences challenge his understanding of love, especially as he navigates through loss and new connections?

4. Discuss Hollyann as an unreliable narrator. How does her perspective shape the reader's understanding of Race's journey, Sevan's DID system, and the broader themes of memory and truth in the novel?

5. Is healing a linear process? Consider Race's trials and the setbacks he faces, such as his ongoing struggles with abandonment, regret, and family secrets, and how this mirrors the nature of healing in our own lives.

6. How do trauma and resilience intersect in your experiences? Reflect on Sevan's trauma stemming from the Armenian Genocide and the resilience she shows as she battles with her identity and mental health.

7. What impact do secrets have on relationships? Analyze the secrets surrounding Race's birth and family history, and how they shape his relationships with others, particularly with Colin and Nara.

8. In what ways do you cope with grief? Discuss Hollyann's and Sevan's unique experiences with grief, particularly how Hollyann copes with memory loss while remembering her son Race.

9. Can we truly know another person? Explore the complexities of Sevan's identity and her system of alters, considering how this challenges Race's understanding of his mother and what it means to truly know someone.

10. What role does forgiveness play in your personal growth? Reflect on Race's road toward forgiveness as he learns to forgive his father and himself. How does forgiveness help us move forward in life?

11. How do stories shape our understanding of reality? Discuss Hollyann's storytelling and its impact on Race's perception of his life, especially as she recounts memories that may not align with reality.

12. How does the theme of identity play out in the story? Explore Race's struggle with his past, particularly the revelations about his heritage and Sevan's alters.

13. What does it mean to find one's purpose? Discuss Race's desperate quest to discover the muse behind Colin's

songs and how this reflects our broader search for purpose in life.

14. How do family dynamics shape who we become? Analyze the relationships within Race's family, especially with his father and mother, and how these dynamics influence his development and choices.

15. What does it mean to embrace vulnerability? Consider how Race learns to accept help from others, especially from Amanda, and confront his own vulnerabilities as the story unfolds.

16. How can heritage influence identity? Discuss how Race's exploration of his Armenian roots impacts his sense of self and understanding of his family's tragic legacy. How do you relate to your family's history?

17. What role does memory play in shaping our identities? Reflect on Hollyann's struggles with memory loss and how the fragmented memories she shares define her perception of herself and her relationship with Race.

18. How do chance encounters affect our lives? Explore the strangers Race meets on his journey—such as Amanda, Sonia, and Petrak—and consider the role these encounters play in his self-discovery.

19. What does it mean to reconcile with the past? Discuss the importance of addressing unresolved issues as Race navigates the complexities of his relationship with Colin, his baseball career, and the truths he uncovers about Sevan.

20. How can art and music help us heal? Analyze the role of music and storytelling in Race's adventure, particularly

through the songbook and its significance in connecting with his father's legacy.

21. What are the implications of survivor's guilt in the story? Reflect on how Sevan's experiences with the Armenian Genocide influence her identity, her relationship with Race, and the burdens of guilt that flow through generations.

22. Discuss the theme of personal growth and transformation. How does Race evolve as a character from the beginning to the end of the novel? How does his worldview change?